THE GOOD ANGEL
OF DEATH

Also by Andrey Kurkov

Death and the Penguin
The Case of the General's Thumb
Penguin Lost
A Matter of Death and Life
The President's Last Love

Andrey Kurkov

The Good Angel of Death

Translated from the Russian by
Andrew Bromfield

Harvill Secker
LONDON

Published by Harvill Secker 2009

2 4 6 8 10 9 7 5 3 1

Copyright © Andrey Kurkov 1999
Copyright © 2000 Diogenes Verlag AG Zürich

English translation copyright © Andrew Bromfield 2009

Andrey Kurkov has asserted his right under the Copyright,
Designs and Patents Act 1988 to be identified as the author of this work

First published with the title *Dobryj Angel Smerti* in 2000

First published in Great Britain in 2009 by
HARVILL SECKER
Random House, 20 Vauxhall Bridge Road
London SW1V 2SA

www.randomhouse.co.uk

Addresses for companies within The Random House Group Limited can be found at:
www.randomhouse.co.uk/offices.htm

The Random House Group Limited Reg. No. 954009

A CIP catalogue record for this book is available from the British Library

ISBN 9781846551178

The Random House Group Limited supports The Forest Stewardship Council (FSC),
the leading international forest certification organisation. All our titles that are
printed on Greenpeace approved FSC certified paper carry the FSC logo.
Our paper procurement policy can be found at:
www.rbooks.co.uk/environment

Typeset by SX Composing DTP, Rayleigh, Essex
Printed and bound in Great Britain by
CPI Mackays, Chatham ME5 8TD

THE GOOD ANGEL
OF DEATH

1

Early in the spring of 1997 I sold my two-room flat on the edge of town and bought myself a single-room flat right in the centre of Kiev, beside St Sophia's Cathedral. The old couple selling it were leaving for Israel, and as well as the flat they also tried to sell me loads of useless junk in it, such as the home-made wire coat stand in the hallway. Grigory Markovich, the man of the house, kept repeating over and over again: 'I know what everything's worth! I won't overcharge you!' I rejected most of the bric-a-brac out of hand but I did fancy a shelf full of books: that was how it was being sold, to avoid having to take the shelf down off the wall and carry the books to the second-hand bookshop – after all, why go to all that bother? I don't know what proportion of the five dollars I paid was for the books, and how much was for the shelf, but in any case, I gave the books no more than a cursory glance, and the only one that really caught my interest was an academic edition of Leo Tolstoy's *War and Peace* – a large-format volume that must have been published back in the fifties. I've always liked books like that, not necessarily for their contents, but for that sturdy, respectable look they have.

On 12 March the moment arrived for the handing over of the keys. I arrived there in the early evening to find a minibus from the 'Wither' travel agency standing outside the front entrance to the block, and the old couple loading their things into it with the considerate assistance of two of the agency's representatives.

'Right then, Kolya Sotnikov,' I said to myself, when I was finally left alone in my newly purchased flat, 'this shambles is all yours now!'

I looked around one more time at all the cracks, contemplating the repairs that were needed. Then I went over to the bookshelf, took down the large-format volume that had stuck in my memory and opened it. Between the covers there was a surprise waiting for me – a secret compartment had been cut out in the middle of the pages, exactly the same way I'd seen it done in all those spy movies, only here there wasn't any gold or a gun. Instead, the neatly carved recess was occupied by another book, published at a later date – *The Kobza Player* by Taras Shevchenko.

Surprised, I lifted the book out and opened it, expecting to find something else unusual between *its* covers. But this time the book proved to be genuine, it hadn't been transformed into a casket. I leafed through a few pages and was just about to reassemble this literary matryoshka doll and put it back on the shelf, so that I could astonish my guests with it at some time in the future, when my eye was caught by the notes written with a sharp pencil in the margins of *The Kobza Player*. Holding the book open in my hands, I went across to the lamp and read a few of the tidy lines of writing.

'*T.G. defined patriotism as love for woman and hatred of military service, especially of mindless drilling.*'

'Could these comments perhaps have been made by some teacher of literature with dissident tendencies?' I wondered, recalling my own experience as a teacher.

After teacher training college, I had spent the three mandatory years as a history teacher in a rural school, but in all that time I had never succeeded in instilling into those wholesome, ruddy-cheeked offspring of milkmaids and tractor drivers either the slightest interest in history or any desire whatever to unravel the numerous historical riddles and mysteries I had gleaned out of heaps of books analysed with a pencil in my hand.

It was impossible even to imagine Grigory Markovich as the author of these notes. He was a retired army man, and very proud of the fact. One day I had found him packing his medals: they were all laid out on the table and he was wrapping each one in a separate handkerchief – he had a lot of handkerchiefs; in fact, there seemed to be far more of them than medals.

He showed me one of his awards and declared proudly: 'I took Prague!'

'But did Prague notice?' I wondered at that moment, scarcely able to repress a smile as I looked at this skinny, little old man who was still so spry at the age of ninety.

The dirty kitchen was also in need of repair. Its old owners had to be scrubbed out of it – somehow people's possessions, even the very walls, take on the age of their owners, and if you don't want to feel suddenly older yourself, you have to change the finishes and the colours, freshen everything up a bit. Who knows, perhaps timely repairs prolong the life of the occupants, as well as the flat?

I put the kettle on the sooty old gas stove and began leafing through the book again, thinking about those strange inscriptions. On one page I came across a remarkable idea very much in keeping with my own way of thinking: *'The patriotism of a hungry man is an attempt to take a crust of bread away from a member of some minor nationality; the patriotism of a satisfied man is a magnanimous attitude that evokes respect.'*

I felt a real desire to understand what kind of person had written these annotations in *The Kobza Player*, I really wanted to find concrete evidence of the period when it had all been written. My job at the time, as a nightwatchman working on a humane schedule – every third night – didn't require me to make any use of my brain, and my brain was feeling bored. Then suddenly here was this mysterious 'present', far better than any brain-teaser or crossword!

I turned page after page, the way people skim through a book to decide whether they should not just read it, but study it with a notebook and pencil. And another idea caught my eye: *'The absolute patriot recognises neither the national majority nor the national minority. His love for woman is stronger than his love for the motherland, because a woman who reciprocates his feelings is herself a symbol of the motherland, and the ideal of the absolute patriot. Protecting a woman who reciprocates one's feelings of love is the highest manifestation of patriotism.'*

In another place, under one of the poems, there was a straightforward diary entry: *'16 April 1964. Met Lvovich in the beer parlour opposite the pawnshop. Told him about the manuscript I'd written. He wanted to read it, but he can take a hike. After that provocative incident in the cinema, even his hand looks too clammy to shake. And then there's that habit he has of looking over his shoulder all the time.'*

I sat up until midnight, then reassembled the matryoshka book and put it back on the shelf.

2

The next day I went to see a sculptor I knew who could name almost everyone who'd lived in Kiev over the last thirty years.

'A beer parlour opposite a pawnshop?' he said. 'Of course, that's where the "Russian Tea" cafe is now. No, sorry, it's not "Russian" any longer. It's either just "Tea", or . . . Everything there's different now, and all the people are different . . .'

'But did you know anyone called Lvovich back then?'

The sculptor paused in thought.

His two-storey studio was full of blocks of undressed stone, maquettes and small sculptures, and there were huge numbers of photographs stuck on the walls instead of wallpaper. He got up from his low dining-cum-coffee table and went across to the photos.

'There are lots of faces here from that beer parlour, but I don't remember . . . Lvovich . . . Lvovich . . . I don't think he was one of the regulars in our set. A lot of "extras" used to come in, but even if they showed up fairly often, they still didn't get to be one of the in-crowd. Maybe he was one of those? I'll try to remember again, but not today. It has to be very wet weather, or a thunderstorm – then I remember everything very well . . .'

'I'll give you a call to remind you next time there's a thunder-storm,' I promised on my way out.

The repairs in my new flat proceeded slowly and, I must say, in pretty half-arsed fashion. The friends who'd promised to help me paint the place suddenly disappeared, leaving me on my own to face the walls and all those tins of matt white paint. I was afraid to start painting alone, so I got on with all sorts of little jobs, like scraping patches of old paint off the pipes in the bathroom and other such nonsense.

Then suddenly the sculptor phoned.

'You know, he died yesterday, that Lvovich of yours – if it was him, of course. An old friend of mine called and asked me to help out with the funeral – there's no one to carry the coffin. You could come with me, if you like?'

This suggestion was both unexpected and puzzling.

'But I didn't know him,' I blurted out.

'But you were trying to find him, weren't you? I don't think I knew him, either,' said the sculptor. 'In fact, I couldn't even remember Alik, the guy who called me. But he assures me we used to get together in that beer parlour . . .'

Going to meet a dead man for whom I had questions that had never been asked seemed, to put it mildly, rather stupid. But I agreed.

We buried him at Berkovtsy. Or rather, we didn't just bury him, we laid him to rest with his relatives, who had already settled in there for the rest of eternity. His yellow, shrunken face meant nothing to me. And the sculptor leaned down to my ear beside the grave and whispered: 'I just don't remember him.' But Alik, who had organised the funeral, reminded the sculptor of several episodes from the distant past, and the sculptor nodded. Then they reeled off a couple of names in my presence.

I plucked up courage and asked Alik about the man with a keen interest in Taras Shevchenko's literary heritage and questions of patriotism. I explained that he had been a friend of the deceased Lvovich.

Alik scratched himself behind one ear. He said nothing for a while and then shrugged. 'Later,' he said at last. 'Are you going to the wake?'

I nodded.

3

It soon emerged that the sculptor had organised for the wake to take place in his studio. There were about seven men sitting round the dining-cum-coffee table. The sculptor was really enjoying himself frying beef liver on an electric cooker standing in the corner. The others were already drinking vodka, without waiting for the hors d'oeuvres. They drank in silence, without any toasts, not even a sigh.

When the first serving of liver appeared on the table they brightened up a bit. The sculptor tossed some forks on to the table and put down some bread. The meal acquired a more lively character after that and for the first time someone started talking about the deceased, but then immediately switched his attention to the living and concluded his almost incoherent speech with the thought that things used to be better in the old days.

'Yes,' someone else agreed.

The wake went off just as a wake should, and everybody went home drunk. Not a single bad word was said about the deceased. In fact, after that first time, no one even mentioned him again. When we got up from the table to stretch our legs, one of the guests recognised his young self in one of the old photos.

'Oh!' he exclaimed, sticking out his lips with an air of puzzlement, as if he were annoyed with the person he'd been thirty years earlier.

I went over to him and asked him about the man who'd been so keen on Shevchenko and questions of patriotism.

'Ah, yes,' he said. 'Lots of people took an interest in that kind of thing back then.'

'And did anyone write manuscripts about it?'

'Yes, they wrote, of course they did. Samizdat! But what good was all that? You know, he who never struggled, never lost.' Then he carried on and on about something or other until he suddenly said: 'But there were a few hoaxers, I remember one of them – Klim – used to pretend he was writing something philosophical. Everyone asked him to let them read it, but all he ever did was take out the manuscript, flick it under your nose and then put it back in his briefcase. He was just sitting in his kitchen at home and writing out Pushkin's poems in prose, you known, not in columns, but continuous lines . . .'

'And where is he now?' I asked, thinking he could very well be the author of the commentaries on *The Kobza Player*.

'Klim? God only knows. I saw him once in the garden square beside the university. You know, where they get together to play chess for money. Two years ago. But I haven't come across him since then.'

Every society or club is exclusive in its own way. Beekeepers get together and talk about things that only they understand. And they probably think a long time about whether or not to let anybody join their club. Chess players are no exception to the rule. The ones who play beside the university know each other, but they're very stand-offish with everyone else. And they only play with outsiders for money.

I made several rounds of the small groups of people playing chess and draughts that had huddled on the benches in the small public garden. Nobody took any notice of me. Every little group was frozen, immobile, watching the action on the board at its centre. They weren't watching the players, whose presence seemed to be no more than an annoying necessity. You couldn't tell who was supporting whom, or if anybody was supporting anybody at all. The situation on the board was contemplated in mysterious silence, and the board itself was the hero of the action.

Klim ought to have been sixty-something by now, a description that fitted most members of this informal chess and draughts club. And since they played in silence, it wasn't even possible to overhear anybody's name by chance. I simply attached myself to one small group and began waiting patiently for events to develop, trying to insinuate myself into the trust of these fanatics of the chequered board by my sheer physical presence.

Suddenly I found myself plunged into a strange, inexplicable trance and for a while I evidently must have actually become part of that living, breathing chess-and-draughts organism.

I spent about an hour in this condition, until the game came to an end, and then, together with all the other figures enslaved by the trance of the chessboard, I breathed out my torpor with a sharp breath, straightened my back and realised that an hour of collective standing had brought me closer in spirit to these people. I was a poor chess player, and could hardly have given even the most elementary commentary on the game that had just finished, but the others could, and I proved to be a grateful listener. At first, it's true, two old men almost came to blows as they argued over a supposedly wrong move by a bishop. My abstention from their argument had a positive effect, and they enlisted me as their audience, rehearsing the main moves of the game from memory.

'But who was playing?' I asked at the end, feeling that now I had the right to ask a question.

'Filya and Misha,' answered the one who was taller and more stooped. 'They're new, haven't been here long.'

I asked if Klim still played.

'Oh, Klim!' said the other old man with a gesture straight from Odessa, lifting an immense, invisible watermelon in his arms. 'Klim plays, but when he plays nonsense like that' – he nodded towards the bench that was now empty – 'doesn't happen.'

Five minutes later I knew that Klim lived in a communal apartment on Shota Rustaveli Street, he sometimes came to the garden square on Fridays, he didn't drink any more because of the pain in his liver, and he'd stopped breeding aquarium fish, so nobody knew what he lived on nowadays.

I left, feeling that I was already a member of this club. Now all I had to do was learn to play a half-decent game of chess or draughts. But there wasn't much chance of that. I would have begrudged the time, and in any case I didn't like slow games in general.

On Friday morning I leafed through *The Kobza Player* again, revelling in the comments in pencil.

'The softness of one's native earth in no way differs from the softness of foreign earth, since all earth has been the primary foundation of mankind and it could not have been distributed between nations according to the quality of those nations.'

What amazed me was not so much the clarity of the formulation as the very subject matter of the thought, as if the man who wrote it had only taken Taras Shevchenko's feelings and rhythms as a starting point, in order to say something about a particular sore point of his own. But then, why was he so concerned about this in those halcyon years of the 1960s? He was not a nationalist, otherwise the notes would have been in Ukrainian. There was no Russian chauvinism here either, since, in addition to the writer's own thoughts, there was also respect, sympathy and perhaps even love for Shevchenko. At one point I thought that his ideas might be close to the ideas of Lenin – especially concerning the complete absence of any nations and nationalities in the future. But I immediately imagined what Lenin would have said about the idea that a beloved woman is your homeland. No, I didn't think the Great Lisper would have agreed with that assertion, no matter how beautiful Krupskaya might have been in her young days.

But time was passing and so I set the book aside – without, however, forgetting about it – and began getting ready to go to the small garden by the university and continue my search for the author of these comments. My intuition told me that Klim would be there today. It was more than just intuition. Outside my window the sun was shining and the birds were singing. It would have been stupid to stay at home in weather like that, especially if your home was a room in a communal apartment on Shota Rustaveli Street, with its noisy trams.

And I did find him in the garden square. First of all I sought out the two old men who already knew me. They pointed to one of the benches, where the chess championship of the university garden square was being contested. It was not difficult to tell which of the players was Klim, since the other was no more than forty years old.

I waited for the end of the game, which was being followed closely by at least twenty members of the 'club', and then approached Klim. The hard-won victory had obviously brought him a feeling of satisfaction, and although as soon as the game was over all the fans immediately scattered to other benches where there were games taking place, without even bothering to congratulate him, the victor himself was jubilant – the sunken eyes above the high cheekbones of his thin face were positively glowing with youthful ardour.

'You really showed him!' I told Klim instead of saying hello.

'Yes, I played pretty well,' he agreed. 'But Vitek can play a bit too – only I wore him down!'

Afraid of disgracing myself if I got any more deeply involved in chess talk, I went straight to the point.

'Do you remember Lvovich?' I asked Klim, who was still smiling happily.

The smile froze on his face.

'Of course I remember him . . .' he said, peering at me through narrowed eyes. 'Why, are you a relative of his?'

'No.'

'But you look a bit like him . . .'

'I think that, purely by chance, I have come into possession of one of your manuscripts . . .' I said.

'You don't say!' old Klim exclaimed in surprise. 'Which one's that?'

'Well, not exactly a manuscript, it's some annotations to Shevchenko's *Kobza Player* . . . very interesting, as a matter of fact.'

The old man touched his carelessly shaved chin and looked at me intently again.

'Annotations?' he repeated. 'That's not mine . . . I wrote different annotations . . . And did you happen to come by this *Kobza Player* too?'

'Yes, the comments are in its margins . . .'

'What kind of book is it? Ordinary? What kind of format?' the old man asked cautiously.

'Not exactly ordinary . . . Like a matryoshka doll. Enclosed in a volume of Tolstoy.'

The old man nodded and smiled, looking down at the asphalt under his feet.

'Well, fancy that, it's shown up at last,' he said in a quiet voice. Then he raised his head and gave me a look that wasn't intent any longer, but somehow calm and relaxed.

'If you've got the money for a bottle of dry white, why don't you come round to my place?'

I had the money, and so after a brief detour along the route 'garden square – delicatessen – Shota Rustaveli Street', we found ourselves in a spacious room with a high ceiling weighed down by heavy moulding and cut across by zigzag cracks. There were two cupboards in the room – a bookcase and a wardrobe – both old, solid pieces from the fifties. A small table, more appropriate for the tiny kitchen of some microscopic flat, looked like a stunted dwarf in this room.

The old man handed me a little knife.

'Open the dry!' he said and went out into the corridor. He came back with two glasses.

'As a decent man, will you invite me back to your place?' he suddenly asked with a smile.

'Of course,' I promised.

'Then I'll show you something!' The old man walked over to the bookcase and opened the door.

'Here.' He pulled a massive volume off the bottom shelf.

4

I took hold of the book – it was an academic edition of *The Kobza Player*. My hands delighted in the pleasant roughness of the calico binding – there are some objects and substances which it is a positive physical pleasure to touch.

'Go on, open it. Open it!' said the old man. I opened it and found myself looking at another matryoshka book. Lying in a hollow cut into *The Kobza Player* was a plainer volume, although it was published during the same period: *The Idiot* by Dostoevsky. I looked up enquiringly at Klim. He was smiling, but not at me, more likely at his own past, which had suddenly been stirred up – by my appearance.

A vague hunch suddenly made me remove the book by Dostoevsky from its cosy secret lair and leaf through its pages. I was correct – I caught glimpses of comments in pencil in the margins of *The Idiot*, only the handwriting here was a bit larger.

'Did you write this?' I asked Klim.

'Yes, I did,' he said, sitting down at the small rectangular table.

'And *The Kobza Player*?' I reached out one hand to the bottle and started pouring the Riesling into the glasses, at the same time arranging my thoughts into some kind of logical order.

'*The Kobza Player*? No, it was someone else who wrote about *The Kobza Player*...' the old man said slowly, picking up his glass.

'Lvovich?' I asked, trying to encourage him to remember.

'Why Lvovich? Lvovich chose *Dead Souls*.'

'Listen,' I said, feeling my head drowning in a thick fog of confusion, 'did you have some kind of literary club, then?'

'Not literary, philosophical,' the old man corrected me. 'And it still exists . . . At least, while I'm alive it does. I'm a one-man club all on my own!'

'But then, who did write the comments on *The Kobza Player*?' I asked.

'Slava Gershovich . . . may he rest in peace.'

'What, is he dead?'

'He was killed . . . They killed him with electricity.' The old man lowered his head dolefully. 'He was a great guy. A brilliant mind.

Long before all these Kashpirovskys and psychics he knew all about that stuff . . . That's why they killed him . . .'

The fog started swirling around my head again.

'What has *The Kobza Player* got to do with psychics?' I said, totally bewildered at this stage.

'What kind of question's that?' The old man looked at me as if I were an idiot. 'And just what do you think high literature is? Nothing but letters and metaphors? It's an instrument for transmitting spiritual electricity, a sort of conductor! Feel like charging yourself up with deep, dismal energy? Then open one of Dostoevsky's books. Feel like purging yourself and spending a while in a lucid, enlightened state? Then pick up Turgenev's prose . . . These idiots like Kashpirovsky have turned it all into curing haemorrhoids on the television. But mark my words, St Iorgen's day will soon be over, and literature will be left once again as the only conductor for any kind of bioenergy.'

'Well then, what kind of energy does *The Kobza Player* transmit?' I asked.

'That's something you ought to have asked Gershovich . . . But, I tell you, there's more serious business involved there, with that *Kobza Player*, and Shevchenko too . . . That's really serious business . . . Well, they killed him because of that . . .'

'Because of what?'

The old man finished his wine. He stroked his flabby, stubbly chin again.

'Because Gershovich had figured out where something very important for the Ukrainian people was hidden . . . But you'll never understand it from that. And don't you go thinking that I've turned senile – if Gershovich were still alive, he'd explain it all to you in five minutes!'

15

'And are there any of this Gershovich's manuscripts left?' I asked hopefully.

'Manuscripts? There was one manuscript, and there was a letter in it . . .' said the old man, nodding in time to his own words. 'Lvovich and I put the manuscript under his head in the coffin . . .'

'And you didn't read it?'

'No. He asked us not to. He told us lots of things, he told us everything he thought about. And we saw that letter. The letter mentioned it, that buried . . . A letter written by Shevchenko himself, from Mangyshlak . . . Maybe it was because of the letter that they killed him! After all, that night, it was in '67, when they killed him, someone broke into this flat. They stole a crystal vase, turned everything upside down . . . But they didn't find the folder! He hid it at Grisha's place – that's my sister's husband. It was afterwards that we took it from Grisha's place and put it under his head in the coffin.'

'From Grigory Markovich's place?'

'That's right!' Old Klim's eyes suddenly flared up brightly. 'So you're Grigory Markovich's relative?'

'I'm not anybody's relative! I'm just curious.'

'Well, young man, being just curious can prove very costly.'

I turned a deaf ear to the old man's final comment. The fog enveloping my thoughts had cleared a little. This first link discovered between the deceased Gershovich and Grigory Markovich, who had gone to Israel, had titillated my curiosity even further.

'Maybe I could sell you this book?' the old man suddenly said with a mysterious kind of intonation. 'I've already sold the fish tanks, there's almost nothing left here now . . .' He looked around.

'The book?' I said, 'Why, are you going away?'

16

'Yes, on foot though . . . Not right now, of course . . . In a while. You remember how Tolstoy died?'

I nodded.

'I love him . . .' said the old man. 'I've read him over and over again, I wanted to learn how to live from him . . . Well, at least I'll learn how to die from him. He had a wonderful death . . . Don't you think so? I'll set out from here on foot to Konotop. Not in order ever to get there . . . You know what I mean?'

I drank a second glass of dry white, but the wine was too weak to help me lay out these fragments of the past and glue them all together, like some ancient amphora. Of course, I realised that all these men for whom Klim now acted as a kind of extraordinary spokesman were lunatics, crazy 1960s types, seekers of meaning in literature and philosophy in life. As a member of a different generation, I found it hard to talk with him. We used the same words, but he clearly endowed those words with more meaning than I did. I think the wine was the only thing we both understood in the same way. Wine from the same bottle couldn't be different in two glasses.

The old man took a map of Ukraine out of the bookcase and pointed out a thick pencil line running along the railway track that was shown on it. 'This is where I'm going to walk,' he said, running his finger all the way along the line, stopping every time he reached a railway station.

I eventually reached a point at which I felt the old man had overburdened my brain. I made a note of his telephone number and promised to treat him to wine in my new flat sometime in the next few days.

'But don't you want to buy the book?' he asked again at the very end when I'd already reached the door on my way out.

17

'Well, how much do you want?' I asked.

'A hundred hryvnas!' he declared proudly, with an expression that suggested he had deliberately named an unacceptable price, not in order to sell that high, but to indicate that the item was priceless.

'I don't have that much on me,' I said, and heard something like a sigh of relief in reply.

5

Two days later old Klim came to visit me. We drank two bottles of dry wine, and while we were drinking them the conversation never faltered. What I heard from the old man enflamed my somewhat inebriated imagination. The late Slava Gershovich had apparently discovered some secret – either philosophical, or more material in nature – as a result of which he had been killed by a home-made electrical shock device. As far as I could understand, the secret that had led him to such an unusual death was revealed either in full or in part in the letter that Shevchenko wrote from Mangyshlak, which had come into Gershovich's possession in some manner unknown and had then been buried, together with his own manuscript and body, in the cemetery at Pushche-Voditsa.

The first thought I had was bound to be rather ungodly – I wanted to extract the manuscript and the letter from the grave in order to confirm the existence of the secret in which old Klim believed so solemnly. The word 'exhumation' occurs quite frequently in criminal literature. But it refers only to the removal from a grave of the body that is buried there. My idea of exhuming the manuscript and the letter seemed somehow less sordid and repulsive although, knowing as I did that the manuscript and letter were lying under Gershovich's head, I found it hard to imagine how I could lift that head without coming into contact with the very essence of death, with that very substance that could not be called anything but dead.

On Monday – the day everyone hates – I set off for Pushche-Voditsa on the tram.

As I had expected, the cemetery was deserted. A light wind was swaying the long ship-mast pines that grew between the graves. The creaking of this forest created an odd impression – as if I were wandering through a long-abandoned city overrun by nature, among invisible ruins covered over with earth.

At first I simply strolled about, looking closely at the neat lettering on the monuments. But then the time came when I had to plunge into the narrow tracks between the low little fences.

This cemetery was located on a hill and its natural boundary on one side was a steep slope down to a forest lake. I methodically checked through the names on the monuments and the headstones until I found the familiar surname at the very edge of the cemetery, right beside the slope. It was carelessly engraved on an iron tablet attached to a welded iron cross that was painted silver. The poverty of the grave surprised me at first, but when I sat down on a bench and listened to a cuckoo counting off the remainder of someone or other's life, I naturally arrived at the thought that a man who had been concerned with philosophy all his life couldn't possibly be interested in marble monuments. Perhaps he might not even have wanted a cross. But the cross had probably been put there by his friends. Relatives are usually more particular about their dead – we can't have our dear departed put to shame, why, some

Bosonozhenko or other has an entire monument with bronze letters, what's wrong with our . . .

After sitting there for about fifteen minutes with thoughts like that for company, I looked at the grave with different eyes – seeing it as a safe that had to be opened somehow. And I realised that every kind of work has its own specialists. And I also realised what kind of specialists I needed – not gravediggers, of course; they were very expensive and they might turn me in – after all, the business I had in mind could hardly be called legal. What I had to find was a couple of vagrants who hadn't been completely destroyed by drink, and two spades. The digging would have to be done at night too, and there was a certain mystical allure about that. But I regarded the forthcoming job without any fright or alarm – I was driven by the passionate desire to discover a secret and I was prepared to take risks, while at the same time I felt that basically there wasn't really any risk. If no one nowadays gave a damn for the living, why would anyone be bothered about some dead man being taken out for a few minutes simply in order to adjust his head and put something softer than a manuscript under it?

On Wednesday night I was back at the cemetery, this time in genial company that also inspired a certain degree of apprehension. I had found two vagrants at the railway station and promised each of them enough for two bottles of vodka when the job was done. And now here they were walking round the little grave with their spades, either squaring up to the job or seeking inspiration.

'So what is it you want to find in there?' one of them kept asking. His name was Zhora, a stocky man with a bluish face, and every time he looked at me he gave a tense, ugly smile.

'I told you, there are some documents under his head . . .'

Zhora cleared his throat and stuck his spade in first. At the other side, his friend Senya, a short but skinny man of about forty, immediately grabbed the handle of his own spade.

They threw the earth out on to the little path running between Gershovich's grave and the low fence of the next one, which was better cared for. The heap of earth grew. The low, dark blue sky radiated warmth, and every now and then birds called abruptly and tunelessly.

Despite several breaks for a smoke, the taciturn diggers worked on feebly and without enthusiasm. Finally Zhora's spade struck wood and they livened up. They cleaned off the lid of the coffin.

'Are we going to lift it up or rummage in it like that?' Zhora asked me.

'Can you get the lid off without lifting it out?' I asked them, for some reason assuming that vagrants knew more than me about opening graves.

Zhora looked down expertly into the pit that they had dug.

'We can pull it off here. Even if it gets a bit broken, what the hell does he care anyway?'

Zhora and Senya prised off the lid of the shallowly buried coffin with their spades and hoisted it up. Bright as the moonlight was, even with the support of myriad stars it could not light up the inside of the open coffin lying in the excavated grave. I could see a dark, amorphous mass in it. I leaned down, expecting to make out at least the general contours of a body, but in vain. And the smell rising up from below was sweet, as if it was permeated with cinnamon.

'Well?' Zhora asked. 'Are you going to climb in?'

I realised he was talking to me and I turned round. 'Why me? We had a deal . . .' I said indignantly.

Suddenly something heavy came down hard on my head, covering me with a net of some dark, impervious material, as if I were a butterfly. Then immediately, as if the butterfly hunter had abruptly jerked his net backwards, I lost my balance, swayed and crashed down on to the warm night earth, hearing cautious whispering voices fading into the distance.

6

When I came round it was already getting light. The early birds were calling to each other in ringing voices; it was like a morning roll call. I got up off the ground slowly and hesitantly. I looked around: one spade was stuck into the ground, the other was just lying there – that was obviously the one I'd been hit with. My pockets had been rifled and naturally all the money – not very much, thank God – was gone. There was a dead man lying on his side in the coffin in the opened grave. His head – totally black – was also lying on its side, and beside it there was a package with a cardboard folder protruding from it.

I thought about my helpers of the night before and couldn't help smiling.

I imagined how they had worked themselves up, expecting to find some genuine treasure – gold or something of the sort – and then, following the plot line familiar since childhood, they had tried get rid of the superfluous third man and split everything two ways. They'd tried so hard, and all the treasure they'd got was the money I'd promised them anyway.

When I was completely awake, I climbed down into the grave. Gershovich seemed to be lying on his side especially so that I would

22

have somewhere to set my foot. I took hold of the package with the folder and put it up on the edge of the grave. Then I clambered out myself. I took the lid of the coffin, set the narrower end at Gershovich's feet and dropped it. The lid snagged on a piece of root that hadn't been trimmed back properly and hung there above the head end. I took a spade and with a couple of blows forced the lid down into its proper place. And then I spent another half-hour burying the coffin, smoothing out the grave and sticking the welded iron cross painted with silver paint back in its place.

When I was finished, I picked up the package with the folder and once again noticed that strange, sweetish smell of cinnamon – now it seemed as if all my clothes were permeated with it, and the package exuded the same smell too.

The sun was beginning to warm things up. I gave the cross a glance farewell. I had to be going – someone might turn up here soon. I wondered what time it was.

I automatically pulled back my shirt cuff and looked at my watch. It was a little after five. 'Why didn't they take the watch?' I thought with a sad smile at my helpers. 'Or has life really only taught them to clean out pockets?'

I walked to the stop at the end of the tramline. Somewhere in the distance the first tram was probably already running along the forest section of the track between Kuryonovka and Pushche-Voditsa, clanging like a huge alarm clock. Coming to take me home. To distract me from the caked blood on the back of my head and the sweet smell that seemed to have eaten right into my clothes.

A smell that had a calming effect and also evoked a light, even frivolous smile, regardless of the nature of my thoughts.

When I got home the clock on the wall in the kitchen said five to seven.

23

Halting in front of the mirror in the hallway, I noticed that my clothes were in need of a good wash, and I myself looked very much like a vagrant who had spent the night on a heap of clay. I quickly changed into my dressing gown and put my clothes to soak in a large basin. Then I decided to soak myself in the bath. I filled it up with hot water and dived in, spilling water over the edge on to the floor. The heat of the water worked its way through to my bones and I started feeling a pleasant ache in my collarbones, like in a sauna. My body gradually began feeling more lively and so did my head, ridding itself of the quiet buzzing that had been reminding me of the blow from the spade and lining my thoughts up in a row one by one, so that each of them could be contemplated calmly, without any haste.

The nocturnal incident had already receded into the past. And up ahead, waiting on the kitchen table for the newly washed, fresh me in just half an hour from now, was the folder, for the sake of which the whole risky adventure had been undertaken. But any adventure seemed appropriate to me in those dangerous and dynamic changing times.

After rubbing myself down with a big, fluffy towel, I noticed to my surprise that the sweetish odour I had first noticed at the Pushche-Voditsa cemetery was still there. I leaned down over the basin with my dirty clothes but the basin gave off a smell of washing powder, while the scent of cinnamon was 'floating' somewhere higher, at the level of my shoulders and face.

'OK,' I thought. 'It's not the worst smell in the world, and there's no smell that doesn't fade in time.'

I sat down at the kitchen table and opened the folder. It contained a stack of paper covered in small handwriting that was already familiar to me. But in the state I was in, I didn't feel like straining to

24

make out this superfine script – I wanted to find the letter that Klim had mentioned. I picked up the stack of paper and fanned it out to leaf through the sheets. And an envelope twice the usual letter size really did fall out. It flew out and fell straight on to the floor. In the envelope I found a small, worn piece of paper that looked rather like a page from an exercise book with barely visible lines of writing in ink that had turned lilac with age.

I read it through quickly, and even before I had fully grasped what I had read, I had the feeling that I was in contact with something genuinely interesting and mysterious. The sheet of paper was titled 'Report', but in fact it was an ordinary piece of informing against a colleague. A certain Captain Paleev informed a Major Antipov that 'when Private Shevchenko leaves the Novopetrovsk Fortress, he often sits behind a dune on the sand and, contrary to the prohibition, writes things, and yesterday he buried something in this sand about three sazhens from the old well in the direction of the sea'.

Outside the window bright sunlight was already streaming down on to the earth. The morning was catching fire, effacing the boundary between spring and summer. I set aside the informer's letter that was written in January 1851 and drank my tea, wondering what Taras Shevchenko could have buried there, in faraway Mangyshlak. He didn't have any money, and if he did, why would he bury it in the sand? No, he wasn't the kind of man to go hiding his kopeks from others. I recalled my distant schooldays and the story of the 'free' book in which the soldier Shevchenko wrote down his poems, always carrying it with him in his boot. Maybe that was what he had buried, to keep it away from the curious eyes of informers like this Captain Paleev?

'Perhaps I could find it there, in the sand,' I thought, and immediately imagined what a joyful clamour there would be in

Ukraine over that. 'And perhaps they'd pay me a couple of hundred thousand dollars or give me a state pension for life? After all, it's an important historical relic!'

But then the value of this unknown item buried in the sands of Mangyshlak was rather uncertain; it was probably of interest only to a museum. A few scholars would write doctoral dissertations, and that would probably be all that came of it.

I pulled over the stack of paper that Gershovich had covered in writing and leafed through it again, and suddenly my eye caught a glimpse of a sheet with a drawing that was clearly topographical. I picked it out and inspected the hand-drawn map, and then immediately lost interest in it, since written underneath it in Gershovich's own handwriting was this:

'Copied from the materials of the "Shevchenko Expedition" at an exhibition in the Literary Museum Archive.'

I sighed and looked out of the window. The rising tide of bright yellow sunlight was almost lapping at my kitchen table. I yawned and rubbed my eyelids that seemed to be stuck together – the invigorating effect of the bath hadn't lasted long. My body was demanding sleep.

Early in the evening, when I had recovered, I sat down at the kitchen table again. First I satisfied my hunger with a piece of healthy sausage, then I took Gershovich's manuscript and ran through its lines of writing with a fresh eye.

And once again my nose was struck by the sweetish smell of cinnamon. I raised a sheet of paper to my face and sniffed it. Then I automatically sniffed the hand that was holding the sheet and realised that my hand was giving out a much stronger smell than the paper.

Unwilling to make the mental effort to discover the reason for the appearance of this smell, I turned my attention back to the lines of Gershovich's manuscript.

The first few pages seemed to me to be a repetition or rehash of the same ideas that he had expressed in pencil in the margins of *The Kobza Player*, but then, on the seventh page, his thoughts moved off into a different sphere.

'The national wealth is born inside a chosen individual, condemning him to wander in a tormented search for the way to apply this wealth, since as a chosen one, he may be loved by his nation and respected by it, but clearly not understood, or at least not understood correctly, which only increases his inner tribulation, and the suffering that results from the impossibility of applying the riches granted to him from on high can result in insanity or perplexing and tragic twists of fate, capable of leading him to regions far away from his homeland (woman).'

This was followed by a description of the route of Grigory Skovoroda's travels round Ukraine. But on the next page Gershovich returned to Shevchenko's tragic fate. And here I immediately noticed a similarity to the thoughts concerning the denunciation by Captain Paleev that I had already read.

'The spot (by a well) chosen by T.G. Shevchenko to bury the unknown object indicates a clear desire either to come back himself and recover what he had hidden or to make it easy for someone else to find the place from its description.

'This spot must still exist, it is at least two kilometres away from the sea. As for the object itself, it is most probably a manuscript or a notebook – both of these survive well in sand in hot dry conditions. Perhaps in this notebook he expressed those thoughts and feelings that his contemporaries were not yet capable of understanding. And so it is unlikely that they were

expressed in poetry (the form most accessible to people of that time).'

After reading this page, I recalled a recent announcement about the manuscript of Einstein's theory of relativity being put up for auction in New York – the asking price had been four million dollars, but the buyer had paid only three million.

'Interesting,' I thought. 'I wonder how much they would pay for an unknown manuscript by Shevchenko at an auction somewhere in Canada? That's where the richest and most sentimental Ukrainians live, and one of them could easily shed tears of tender emotion as he laid out a couple of million dollars, even if they are Canadian.'

After a smile at the liveliness of my own imagination, which had conjured up this touching scene from the life of the Canadian diaspora, I started thinking how since Soviet times the idea of buried treasure had changed in the minds of the new generation. In the eighties, in their teenage years everyone read Stevenson's novels, but at the same time they read works by the classic writers of Soviet literature in which boy treasure hunters didn't find gold and diamonds buried in a pot buried in the ground, but instead discovered somebody's Communist Party card and a Second World War medal. And they immediately stood to attention like good Young Pioneers and saluted those who had fallen fighting for the righteous cause. That was probably where the late Gershovich's ideas had come from too. This was the source of that desire to seek non-material values, symbolic treasures and spiritual treasure troves. But what if what was still lying there under the sand was simply an old gold coin or two? What if he had hidden them there so that they wouldn't be taken from him by some drunken officer reduced to the beastly depths of complete moral degradation by life on the margins of the empire? Eh? And then all these thoughts that Gershovich had written down would amount to nothing more than a way of playing hide-and-seek with the reality in which he lived. Another game, just like the one with matryoshka-doll books that he or Lvovich or Klim had invented.

'OK,' I thought, 'this is all very interesting, but as the old alcoholic who was my neighbour at my previous flat says, "Have a good time, but don't forget to take all the bottles back!" So I'll calmly finish reading this manuscript and just maybe I'll be spiritually enriched, but I still have to earn the money for my healthy sausage . . .'

I hid the manuscript away in the folder, once again putting my nose to the hand that smelled of cinnamon, and went to get dressed. Every third night was like a period of active combat – I guarded a storeroom of Finnish baby food that belonged to the Corsair Charitable Foundation.

7

After taking over from Vanya, a student from the college of physical education, I sat down at the old office desk with its full set of night-watchman's gear: an electric kettle, a small portable television, a rubber truncheon, a telephone and gas cylinder. As you can see, the means for providing protection and defending yourself were minimal, and they didn't exactly encourage any desire to give my last drop of blood in protecting the material property entrusted to me. But the wages here were paid on time and in full, and the place seemed fairly safe: the baby food – which was in any case out of date according to the markings on the cardboard boxes – was hardly likely to attract the interest of any of today's would-be expropriators.

A large rat ambled lazily past the boxes and the table. I watched it go with a quizzical glance. Then I switched on the television and took the kettle to the sink that was just three steps away – the ritual of 'getting into' the job was beginning.Usually, after tea and a couple of films, I would arrange four chairs in a row along the wall and would sleep peacefully until the morning, when a knock at the door would wake me and I'd open the door to admit Grishchenko, the chairman of the Corsair Charitable Foundation, with his battered old attaché case. Grishchenko was about fifty years old and he looked like a classical accountant – a bit on the fat side, round-faced, balding. He didn't seem to know how to smile, but the expression on his face – eternally perplexed – was enough to raise a smile on anyone else's.

After casting a quick glance round the spacious semi-basement premises stacked with cardboard boxes bearing blue square paper stickers with a picture of a happy baby, he usually nodded to me. That meant I was free to go. And I would go away for three days and two nights until my next shift.

But that night I was not destined to get a good night's sleep at my workplace. First the phone rang in the middle of some action movie or other. I picked up the receiver, but all I heard was someone breathing hoarsely. It didn't sound like a joke, so I enquired patiently: 'Hello?'

'Close the door!' Grishchenko's abnormally hoarse voice said. 'Block it with something . . .'

'It is closed!' I said, glancing round at the heavy metal door locked with two bolts.

Grishchenko put the phone down without even saying goodbye. I did the same and carried on watching the small black-and-white screen on which some hoodlums had just riddled a good guy with bullets from a machine gun and spots of black blood had appeared on his white shirt.

After watching the film to the end, I remembered the recent phone call and inspected the storeroom thoroughly. There were no windows here, and so the door was the only point through which uninvited guests could break in.

But it was a warehouse door from Soviet times, when the country had at least a tonne of thick iron plate for every member of the population. To break in from the outside you would have to use a tank. The tinplate pipe of a ventilation system stretched across the ceiling and disappeared into the wall. It was a thick pipe, and sometimes rats ran through it, using it as a way into other rooms. One rat set off enough dull rumbling to make the air shake. The cardboard boxes piled on top of each other in several rows propped this pipe up from below, so it was not hard for the rats to clamber up the cardboard and in through the gaps in the ventilation system.

But at that moment it was quiet in the storeroom, and the only rat I had seen that evening had virtually tiptoed across the floor, moving silently and quietly.

I clicked the switch to change channels and found myself halfway through a martial arts movie. I started staring at the screen and realised that one and a half films would be enough before I went to sleep.

The phone rang again.

'Hello?' said a woman's voice. 'Can I speak to Victor Ivanovich?'

'You have the wrong number,' I replied calmly, without taking my eyes off the fight on the screen.

'Well, who can I speak to?' the woman asked gaily.

'Is that some kind of joke?'

'Listen, you!' a harsh man's voice suddenly said in the earpiece. 'I don't give a damn what your name is . . . If you want to stay alive, open your door and scram, quick. Got that?'

I instinctively put the receiver down and immediately switched off the television.

The silence allowed me to gather my thoughts. I realised there had been a reason for Grishchenko's call. There was something going on there, outside the storeroom. But as long as I was inside, I had nothing to be afraid of.

Even so, I was frightened. It actually seemed rather odd that just the night before I had been hit over the head with a spade, and what had I been doing? Digging up a grave, even if I was using someone else's hands to do it. And I hadn't been afraid. But now this was a quite different matter. Here I was sitting in a room like a fortress, but I *was* afraid.

I shrugged and listened a while. It was quiet.

A minute later the phone rang again, I picked it up and put it straight back down. It started again. This time I raised the receiver to my ear.

'Kolya! Is that you?' Grishchenko wheezed hoarsely.

'Sure . . . What's going on?'

'Don't open up for anyone! They're scum! I'll come round in the morning! Goodbye!'

And he hung up.

I laid the receiver on the desk, thinking that I'd had enough telephone chatter for one night.

While I was dozing on the chairs lined up against the wall, someone knocked on the door. Loudly and aggressively.

I lay on my back without moving, feeling tense. Just lay there waiting for silence. It came after about twenty minutes. But I was restless all night.

8

Shortly after eight o'clock, feeling shattered after a sleepless night and all the shocks to my nerves, I made some tea and switched on the television. I performed all my actions very cautiously and quietly, at the same listening for activity from the street outside. Of course, not much sound penetrated into the baby-food depot. I could hear cars driving past. Then one of them drove up and fell silent somewhere close by – as far as I knew, there was another storeroom on the other side of the wall, but I didn't know what was on the upper floors of the building.

I drank tea and waited for nine o'clock – the time when Grishchenko usually came. Nine o'clock soon arrived. An advertisement for toothpaste appeared on the television and I turned it off, as if that could speed up the passage of time.

But Grishchenko didn't come. I looked at the pieces of paper weighted down against the top of the desk by a sheet of plexiglas – business cards, some kind of waybill. There was also a list of the phone numbers of all the nightwatchmen, including me, and at the bottom was Grishchenko's own number. I phoned him, but no one answered at the other end.

At ten o'clock I began feeling uncomfortable. I walked round the storeroom a few times, glancing at those cardboard boxes. I started thinking about the commotion during the night that had left me with a slight headache. Why would anyone break in here? Surely not for out-of-date baby food?

I went up to one incomplete pile and put the top box down on the floor.

After overcoming my qualms, I tore off the sticky tape with which it was sealed along the joint and glanced inside. The box was full of tin cans with blue labels showing some foreign infant smiling light-heartedly and rather stupidly. I picked one of them up and shook it. I heard some heavy mass shifting up and down like flour – the can was not full, but there was nothing particularly surprising about that.

I carried the can back to the desk and plugged the electric kettle in again. Glancing at the label, I realised that the can contained infant milk formula. I felt a sudden desire to drink coffee with milk. I had instant coffee, and I had dried milk.

I opened the can, tipped some yellowish-white powder out of it into my cup, added a spoonful of 'Nescafe' and then poured in the boiling water.

After I took a few sips I immediately started feeling better, my tiredness disappeared and my mood improved. I'd never tasted coffee with milk like this before, and I immediately had the criminal idea of taking home several cans of the infant formula. It might be out of date for children, but it was just right for coffee.

After that cup of coffee I lay back down on the row of chairs, no longer thinking about the events of the night, or about Grishchenko, who had still not shown up. I felt a strange sensation come over me, as if I were flying, and in a couple of minutes I was soaring through a boundless space full of bright colours and fantastic shapes. Meteorites went rushing by, some yellow, some red; comets swirled past, leaving convoluted, fiery tails fading in their wake. My body obeyed my thoughts with ease – I only had to think that I needed to turn right in order to avoid a collision with some flying object and my body was already turning right. It was the first time I had ever experienced the unity of soul and body so distinctly, and my body itself felt weightless, it was no burden, it was light and easy to control. It didn't require any effort, it didn't require any work by the muscles. I was flying, and I didn't even look back at the earth that I had left far below. By this time it must already have been lost to view among dozens of other small heavenly bodies.

9

My flight lasted for at least two full days. And when I 'landed' and found myself in my original position, lying on my back on the row of chairs set against the wall, the first thing I wanted to do was scream out loud. Apart from a feeling of savage hunger, my entire body was racked with pain, filled with a stiffness that was transmitted directly from my bones and joints to my thoughts and emotions. With a struggle, I raised my hand to my face and looked at my watch. It said half past one. And the first question that came into my mind was: Which 'half past one' is that? Night-time or daytime? To find out, I had to get up, open the door and look outside – to see if it was light yet. However, this extremely simple decision proved difficult to put into effect. I managed to sit up on one of the chairs, but that triggered such a searing wave of pain in my waist that I immediately lay back down in my original position. About five minutes later, I repeated the attempt, and with an effort of will like I'd never made before, I remained in the sitting position, despite the pain. I began slowly moving my arms, performing micro-exercises, tensing the muscles and stretching the joints. I finally got to my feet about an hour and a half later. I stood there for a while, feeling slightly dizzy. I took my first steps – towards the office desk. Eventually I sat down on that desk, staring stupidly at the phone with its receiver off the hook and lying beside the electric kettle. Looking at the phone awoke the memory of that sleepless night. I also remembered that soothing cup of coffee with 'milk', and my gaze shifted to the can of 'infant formula'.

'Yes,' I thought, 'it's more like rocket fuel than dried milk.'

After sitting there for while, I went across to the metal door and listened. Outside it there was silence. 'So,' I thought, 'that means it's night . . . Now what am I going to do?'

Should I sit here until morning? Or try to slip out straight away? Yes, and why hadn't anyone come here for the last two days? After all, Grishchenko had the keys! But then even with the keys he wouldn't have been able to get in – the door was locked from the inside with two bolts. Only I could have opened them, but in a certain sense, I hadn't been there to do it. Maybe he had come and knocked, tried to phone . . .

Anxiety began invading my thoughts. Being inside that storeroom made me feel like someone who had been buried alive in a crypt. But, of course, I could leave this tomb. I just needed to be lucky enough to get out of the place without being noticed and forget everything, as if my flight through space had never happened. But my flight had happened. I could remember it in the most minute detail, and if I had been an artist I could have drawn some of the meteorites and comets I had encountered in the void.

There was a small mirror hanging on the wall above the sink and I went across to it to rinse my eyes and take a look at myself. My face reminded me of newsreel footage from Auschwitz. Perhaps that was an exaggeration, but I had never seen such huge greyish-blue circles under my eyes before or my nose looking so sharp, like a dead man's.

I washed my face with cold water and went back to the desk. With some squeamishness I ate the healthy sausage sandwich that I had brought with me. The bread had turned as tough as wood, and the sausage was as far from being fresh as I was from feeling satisfied.

I switched on the electric kettle and looked at the jar of instant coffee again, and then – automatically – at the 'infant formula'.

'No,' I thought, 'we'll leave the coffee alone for a while – one more flight like that and I'll die of physical exhaustion.'

I brewed myself some tea. I looked at my watch – it was five to four. And it was quiet. Not even the rats were giving any sign of their presence.

After finishing my tea, I put three cans of the 'dried milk' into my bag. Why did I take them with me? Perhaps I wanted to shoot off into orbit again sometime. Then I went across to the door, listened again and, when I didn't hear anything, cautiously drew back the heavy iron bolts. After that I paused, then I opened the door a little and the fresh night air came rushing in through the narrow gap – it was pleasantly cool, like a gin and tonic with ice.

'Right, I'm off!' I said to encourage myself, opening the door wider and slipping through the gap. Then I closed the door just as quietly, took out a key and turned it in the lock. The heavy lock grated softly. I put the key away in my trouser pocket, hunched over and set off on tiptoe along the wall of the building. When I had almost reached the corner, someone suddenly switched on a car's headlights and the beam of light struck me on the back. I jerked forward as fast as I could, flung myself round the corner and started to run, without bothering to head left or right into the darkness. I heard a motor start up, and at one point I even thought the sound of it was overtaking me, but when I finally stopped, panting hard, everything was quiet.

'I got away!' I thought delightedly, but I couldn't manage a smile.

Not only had I got away, I had brought a bag with three cans of dried milk in it. I hadn't dropped it, despite the horror inspired by the real or imaginary pursuit.

And once again, when I got back to my new flat by the light of early dawn, I started the day by washing my clothes and taking a bath.

After soaking myself thoroughly and finally restoring my wits, I felt the pangs of profound hunger even more keenly and I didn't even bother to dress before I left the bathroom. I just rubbed myself down with the towel and went straight to the kitchen. In the fridge I found a tail end of healthy sausage, a can of sprats and a well-chilled piece of black bread. As my stomach was gradually filled with food, I began feeling the cold. It wasn't really cold in the flat, but my body was evidently adjusting to the temperature of the earth's atmosphere after two days in orbit.

Before I drank the tea I threw on my dressing gown. In the dressing gown even the tea tasted sweeter. The sensation of comfort somehow enlivened me and I was already glancing in the direction of the windowsill, where Gershovich's manuscript was lying in its grey-green folder. I looked at it differently now, after my unexpected adventures. But my interest in the thoughts and ideas of the deceased amateur philosopher had not faded. If anything, quite the opposite.

I leafed through the manuscript, but I didn't have the strength to struggle with the small handwriting. And then I remembered that my black bag with the three cans of dried milk was lying in the corridor of the flat. I brought the cans into the kitchen and put them in the tiny locker. After all, whatever they had inside them, it was certainly very edible!

Then I went to bed, obeying the summons of my body, which was tired after all the flying.

The next day came, fresh and sunny. And to my delight, I woke early, at about seven. I brewed some coffee.

'Well now,' I thought, 'no job any more. And whatever it was that happened there, I'm not interested. It's not worth risking my life.'

I raised the little cup of coffee to my lips with an aesthetic gesture. I held it balanced there to catch the aroma of arabica, but my nostrils were assailed by the stubborn smell of cinnamon, which returned me to a state of perplexity. Yet again the smell of my hand had overpowered the smell of coffee.

I shook my head. I took a gulp of coffee. Its taste was the real thing, rich.

'Life is for living!' I thought (optimistic thoughts are usually quite stupidly banal). I was never going to be a teacher of history. That was such a thankless job! I would have to look for another job as a watchman. I was in good health – after eight years of swimming and three years of fencing. That made some kind of impression on employers. If only I could find work one night in three again. So that there would be time left for solving philosophical riddles. Life ought to provide pleasure – unto each according to his needs.

Outside the window the spring sun was shining and I could hear booming fragments of phrases from a megaphone – there was yet another rally taking place on St Sophia's Square.

I felt like going out for a walk. I left the house and walked past the people involved in the rally, who had red-and-black UNA-UNSO flags flapping above their heads. A man with a long grey moustache that drooped almost below his chin was standing on a truck, exhorting them to do something or other. I didn't want to listen to him – the shifting moods of large masses of people don't really interest me very much. Politics is only the building material of contemporary history, something like cement. Once you get stuck in it, you're finished! They'll trample you down in it and then dig you up again – and you'll wind up as an exhibit in some godforsaken provincial history museum.

I walked between the truck and the crowd, whose attention was completely focused on the orator. As I passed by I noticed several irritated glances in my direction. Probably because I was just walking by, showing no interest in joining in their great vigil. But though I feel sympathy for all who suffer and value any sense of purpose in people, just as long as they don't hang themselves or kill anyone else, sympathy was as far as my feelings for such people went. To offer them more than sympathy would be dangerous for me. I loved myself and my freedom, and in my relations with women I preferred passion to love – passion was more powerful, it was not subject to any rules, and it disappeared just as suddenly as it appeared.

The orator with the megaphone carried on yelling behind me for a long time, but by the time I reached Opera Prospect, I had forgotten about him. I walked down on to Kreshschatik Street. Took a stroll. Dropped into a cafe.

Topped up the caffeine in my blood.

10

After sitting at the table in the cafe for fifteen minutes, I continued my aimless stroll. Of their own accord, my feet led me to the garden square by the university. It was obviously not a 'club day'. There were only two old men on one bench, playing draughts without any spectators.

When I stopped to look down at them, I noticed that a strange couple also stopped about five metres behind me – a thin-faced young guy with a black moustache and an equally thin-faced woman with black hair. The guy was smoking a pipe. For an instant our glances met and I caught a glimpse of tension and hostility in his narrowed eyes.

'Maybe I just imagined it?' I thought, wondering what I could have done to upset them.

I turned back towards the two men playing draughts and gazed obtusely at the board, forgetting about the couple. When I looked round five minutes later, they were no longer there.

Soon I set off back home – the stroll had refreshed me and improved my mood.

As I walked along Vladimirskaya Street, people from the rally that had just finished came towards me. It was like running into drift ice, but there weren't very many of them, so I manoeuvred my body carefully and avoided any unnecessary contact.

As I was approaching the doorway of my building I caught something suspicious out of the corner of my eye. Looking round, I saw the same dark-haired couple again on the other side of the street. They had clearly been watching me, but when I glanced back, they turned away sharply.

Puzzled, I walked in through the doorway.

At home I sat down in an armchair and started thinking. Peace of mind gradually came to me.

Most likely it was just a chance coincidence – things like that happen to me, walking round town and bumping into a man with an unforgettable face three or four times. No doubt he takes me for someone else, and I myself start trying to guess why he's following me. The important thing was that this couple didn't look like bandits, or drug dealers, so they couldn't have anything to do with what had happened at the 'baby food' storeroom.

11

That night I was woken by the phone ringing. 'Do you hear me, arsehole?' the unpleasantly hoarse man's voice said, irrupting into my sleepy head. 'You were asked to leave, but no one asked you to lock the door behind you! Now you owe us ten grand for the extra hassle. Someone will be coming to you for the greenbacks in exactly one week. If you can't get them together, that's your problem. We'll take your flat instead.'

'Who is this?' I instinctively blurted out.

'You mean you haven't got it yet?' the voice asked indignantly. 'If I tell you who this is, you'll owe us twenty grand instead of ten, you lousy jerk!'

The line went dead, but I was still holding the receiver up to my ear.

Sleep had fled, and a depressing, sordid sense of reality was gradually seeping into the place it had occupied.

And just why did I close the door? Maybe I wouldn't have had to run for it if that lock hadn't clicked . . .

A wave of despondency flooded over me. The night was ruined, and I really wanted to believe that it was only the night. Although the ten grand that someone wanted from me for the closed door didn't sound much like a joke.

I got up, doddered around the room that was lit by nothing but the dull glow of the night sky coming in through the window and making the darkness amenable to the eye.

Once again the night was a sheer waste of time – I would never get back to sleep now.

I took down the matryoshka book and went into the kitchen, put some coffee on and sat down at the table. I took *The Kobza Player* out of Tolstoy and with my eyes still screwed up as I got used to the unshaded light bulb dangling on its wire from the kitchen ceiling like a hanged man, I opened the book that had unexpectedly brought something bright and mysterious into my life, something that took me away from dingy everyday reality.

It would probably have been more interesting to read Gershovich's manuscript, but I was afraid of the intense concentration of his thought. Here, in the margins of *The Kobza Player*, every annotation written in that fine handwriting was like a separate picture, beautifully composed and framed, so that it was possible to contemplate this picture and think about it, without suffering any thought fatigue.

'All his life a man struggles with his supposedly natural role of "being strong", he sometimes wastes his entire life on deliberately developing this characteristic, while subconsciously always seeking

43

the protection that only a woman can give him. He devotes every demonstration of his natural male quality to the search for this protection. In politics this natural process is exploited precisely to inculcate patriotism: every monument erected to the homeland portrays a woman, and often in a militant pose. A woman as the defender of the weak, that is, of men.'

The bitter taste of the coffee settled on my tongue, and I wanted to keep that taste until the morning – it cheered me and distracted me from the smell of cinnamon that seemed to be hovering in the air everywhere, no matter where I went in the flat.

I leafed through a few more pages.

'A man easily transfers his love for himself and his own life to love for a woman in the attempt to make her an integral part of his life.'

This thought struck me as a little banal. But since I realised that all these annotations had not been meant to be published, I didn't accuse the deceased thinker of admiring his own ideas so excessively that he lost sight of their quality. After all, this was a discovery he had made for himself, and if there was nothing new in it to me, that was only because I had already realised it intuitively anyway.

I sat there, leafing through *The Kobza Player* and reading Gershovich's notes. But at this stage I was reading inattentively, without remembering or appreciating his thoughts. I was waiting for the night to be over. For the approach of dawn to start scattering the darkness that curtained the window.

12

Next morning, when I remembered the night-time phone call, I started feeling really anxious.

The cold light of day seemed to introduce a sense of reality into the threats made over the phone. Ten thousand dollars was such a large amount of money that even earning it, let alone giving it away, was an absolutely fantastic idea to me. But the threat to take away my flat instead of the money threw me into a cold sweat. After I'd sold a two-room flat in the suburbs to buy a one-room flat in the centre, now someone wanted to make me homeless! I realised that I had ruined all plans of these unknown visitors who were so keen to get into the 'baby food' storeroom. But then, that was why I'd been hired as a watchman . . . Only they couldn't give a damn about that, of course. I didn't even know if they had managed to get in or not.

'No,' I decided quite firmly, 'not a single step backwards. I don't have that kind of money, and I won't let them have the flat!' I had five hundred dollars in the emergency fund – what I ought to do was install a metal-plated door. They were hardly likely to try cutting through it with an arc welder. And if they did try, I would have time to call the police . . . The idea of relying on the police made me smile. But I had to hope that someone would protect me. The police could certainly offer more real protection than the new constitution, but they couldn't provide me with round-the-clock protection.

By eleven I had already phoned a firm that manufactured and installed armoured doors. A representative came round to see me, took measurements and offered me a choice of locks. We signed a computer printout of a contract on the spot, and then I only had to survive another two days without protection. And the door proved cheaper than I was expecting – only three hundred bucks.

Once I had signed the contract, I felt more confident. I noticed the fresh sunlight outside the window and I heard the sparrows chirping. Life was going on, and I had to go on with it, taking as much as possible from it and giving as little as possible back, so that what was left would last longer.

13

The two days went by, and my flat was transformed into a fortress. When the heavy armoured door had been installed and I had said goodbye to the two craftsmen, the feeling of freedom struck me like a thunderbolt. For the time being, the security of my flat was left in my own hands. And I set off, securely protected, to take a stroll along the street.

It was about two o'clock. The sun hanging above St Sophia's Cathedral looked as if it was about to fall. The spot at which the innocent patriarch Vladimir lay beneath the asphalt was empty, and I walked hurriedly past his unwanted grave, past the secret headquarters of the state border guard, where every now and then a bald little man who looked like a boletus mushroom would appear out of the door with a mobile phone in his hand and conduct telephone negotiations that were no doubt top secret out in the street in front of the building. But he wasn't there right now.

I met only the odd person walking by, no crowds organised into any kind of rally or demonstration.

As I walked along, I pondered the unjustified sense of freedom that my new metal door had given me. Suddenly a 'number 9' Lada pulled up beside me. The tinted glass of the side window slid down and I saw a man of about forty-five wearing a blue T-shirt.

'Tell me, how do I get to Bessarabka?' he asked.

I explained and then watched the car drive away.

The registration number on the number 9 was from Odessa.

When the car disappeared from sight, my feeling of freedom and security disappeared with it. And a good thing too, I must say. I started peering around cautiously and immediately spotted the familiar dark-haired couple. The man with the moustache was watching me, and his girlfriend was examining a magazine through the glass of a newspaper kiosk.

'Another chance coincidence?' I thought. 'Or do they live somewhere close by?'

I walked round the Golden Gates and went back home.

That evening the phone rang again.

'How are the greenbacks coming along?' the familiar voice asked me.

'They're not,' I replied.

'Look here, arsehole, we're not going to leave the meter running for you – times have changed. I warned you: if you don't come up with the ten grand, we'll relocate you to the "Missing Persons" noticeboard.'

After saying 'I get it' I didn't expect any reply and I hung up.

My mood was suddenly dismal.

What good was that door, if I could feel secure only when I locked myself inside?

'No,' I thought, 'I need to clear off to somewhere else for a while. Close the flat and get away. Sooner or later they'll forget about me anyway.'

And although those were not times that really encouraged tourism, I started thinking seriously about leaving the city that I loved. I had to go, and I had to go quickly. And the direction I would go in seemed to choose itself – the Cossack coast of the Caspian Sea, to the Mangyshlak Peninsula, where the Novopetrovsk Fortress once used to stand.

Getting my things together took my mind off the unpleasant feelings that had come flooding in after the phone call.

I stuffed Gershovich's manuscript into my Chinese rucksack, together with the three cans of infant milk formula and two cans of something else that I found in the kitchen cupboard. I put my clothes in on top.

Then I sat down in the kitchen with a cup of tea. Outside the window it was already dark, and the darkness reassured me. Maybe my nameless enemies were sleeping? Now was just the right moment to slip out of the building and dissolve into the darkness.

And so I did. And I greeted the dawn on board the Kiev–Astrakhan train, in a half-empty carriage with a conductor with a crumpled, red face, who was vainly trying to get the coal to burn in his hot-water boiler.

14

At about noon the train stopped on the border. First the dreary Ukrainian customs officers walked through the carriage. One of them cast a glance at me and asked with a note of hope in his voice: 'Taking anything out, are we?'

I shook my head.

'All right, show me your luggage,' he demanded. I lifted up my bunk and showed him my lean rucksack. I could tell from the customs officer's face that he felt like spitting at the sight, but he restrained himself.

Then the Russian customs men arrived. Two of them walked into the carriage.

'What are we bringing in?' one of them asked.

'Just myself,' I joked.

The second customs man narrowed his eyes and sniffed.

'Are you carrying cinnamon for sale?' he asked.

'No.'

They didn't believe me, and I had to show them my rucksack too. But at that point they took the dignified approach and didn't ask to look inside it.

The train started panting and hammering on the rails again. The same landscapes flitted by outside the window, only now they were Russian. The water in the boiler finally came to the boil, and the conductor brought me a glass of tea with that special 'railway' sugar that's almost impossible to dissolve.

As I drank that tea, lulled by the senseless motion of the landscape outside the window, I thought that I had left behind in Kiev two closed metal doors and one opened grave. No more, no less.

15

The salty smell of the sea overpowered even the usual smell of a railway station. The sun shining down on Astrakhan was an albino, as if it had been heated to an incandescent white. But I didn't feel the heat – perhaps because of the breeze that was blowing from the sea.

Moving rather sluggishly, I walked away from the station without knowing where I was going, simply gazing around, taking a look at the unfamiliar town. There was almost no one about, and those people that my eyes did light on looked like vagrants, or followers of the teachings of Ivanov: a fat man with bare feet wearing tracksuit bottoms came walking towards me, thrusting out his immodest belly as proof of his normal past. And he walked straight by.

I noticed an immoderate number of Russian flags hanging on the buildings. The pleasant sound of banners flapping in the breeze accompanied me everywhere I went, inspiring an unaccountable, smug pride, although it was quite obvious that I was an outsider here, a foreigner, an incidental visitor with a rather unusual goal in mind.

'Ah yes!' I remembered. 'It's Saturday today. But just because it's the weekend is that good enough reason for decorating the town so patriotically?'

Speculating in this way, I ambled along the street. I passed a sign that told me I was on Togliatti Street. Somewhere above my head a window opened noisily. I automatically looked up and saw an elderly woman sweep her sleepy glance along the street like a broom, after which she hid herself away again, leaving the window open. The town was waking up. Ahead of me a banner appeared, hanging above the deserted street.

The Kulibin Joint Stock Company – General Sponsor of Day of the City.

'Well, now,' I realised, 'I've arrived on a holiday. Maybe there'll be something for me in this celebration of theirs?'

The town, however, was still at rest, although on my watch the hands had met to show ten to ten.

Fifteen minutes later I saw a queue of people running into the door of a bakery. When I approached them an expression of concern flickered across the faces of those in the queue, and I understood the reason for it almost immediately – from deep inside the shop, a stentorian woman's voice announced that there were no baguettes left. Before my eyes the crooked line of intent people fell apart and its contents went dashing off in two opposite directions. A couple of minutes later, the bakery and the street behind me were deserted and dead.

'Well, OK,' I told my hungry self, 'on holidays they usually have stalls of different food, so I'm sure to get something to eat before I find a ferry or a ship.'

Half an hour later, without knowing how, I arrived back at the railway station, although I didn't think I'd made any turns anywhere – the town was obviously round, like a small version of the globe. But now the station was a hive of activity – perhaps some other trains had arrived, or perhaps people had already started waking up. This time I walked away from the station along a different, equally wide street. And after I had taken only ten steps, I saw a citizen of Astrakhan walking towards me clutching a prodigious sandwich. It was a baguette cut in half lengthwise and plastered thickly with black caviar. He was holding this super-sandwich in both hands and taking obvious pleasure in nibbling on it as he walked along.

I already knew there was a lot of fish in Astrakhan, and so I took this scene as a case of patriotic affectation. But ten minutes later, when I met several other citizens with identical sandwiches – including an old woman dressed in rags and wearing a 'Victory over Germany' medal on her chest – I started thinking more deeply on the matter. Now it all looked less like affectation and more like some kind of charitable event. That conclusion didn't do anything to satisfy my hunger, though; in fact, it even provoked a certain feeling of envy for the deprived – they, at least, had been remembered and fed caviar on the Day of the City!

As I continued my semi-aimless wandering, I observed that practically everyone I encountered along the way was holding similar huge sandwiches. And not all of them looked as if they were deprived, there were some perfectly respectable-looking individuals.

I then came out into a square where there were Russian flags fluttering even above the trading kiosks. In front of the kiosks stood citizens queuing holding flat empty sandwiches – long baguettes cut in half lengthwise. After stopping and observing for a while, I understood the way in which the Day of the City was being celebrated. The citizens thrust their baguettes in through the little kiosk windows and received them back covered with caviar. And nobody demanded to see the citizens' documents, so if I could find myself a baguette, then I would also receive this same Astrakhan aristocrat's lunch.

If I could find one. But after striding athletically round the nearby streets, I realised that I was too late – all the bakeries were closed, and outside the door of one of them an old woman who was walking by informed me compassionately that the town had run out of bread the day before.

Feeling desperate, I walked up to a kiosk where I had just seen the queue dissolve.

'You wouldn't have a baguette, would you?' I asked.

'Are you crazy?' the young salesman said.

'A bit of black bread, then? I'm really hungry,' I confessed, trying to play on his pity. 'I'm just off the train . . .'

The young guy sighed.

'Give me your hand,' he said.

Not really understanding what was going on, I held my hand in through his little window, expecting him to put a free Snickers bar or something of the sort into it. But the young guy leaned down for a couple of seconds and then I felt something sticky oozing across my palm.

'You can eat it like that!' he told me.

I pulled my hand back out of the window. My palm was covered with a centimetre-thick layer of black caviar.

I thanked my generous provider and walked away from the kiosk, still not really knowing how I was going to eat it.

'Come again!' the young guy shouted behind me. I walked along the street, carefully balancing my open hand spread with caviar. Every now and then I raised it to my mouth and licked off the tasty, salty little grains. Now the holiday atmosphere in the town felt real to me too. I no longer envied those who had stocked up on baguettes in good time – I was doing all right too. I asked a passer-by how to get to the port. He gestured like a man sowing grain. I realised that the port here was immense and set off in the general direction of his gesture, licking at my palm sandwich.

Early in the evening, having licked all the caviar off my hand and walked round several huge port jetties without finding a single passenger ship, on the point of exhaustion I sat down beside a monument to Kirov in a park. It was still light. I realised that if I communicated on a deeper level with the local population, I would find what I wanted. But I really didn't feel like communicating with anyone – I already had experience of chance encounters and their consequences. If it had been an ordinary day, I would have bought a map of the town in a newspaper kiosk and found everything for myself. But all the kiosks were closed, apart from those that provided caviar. And I sat there alone, resting on that massive, green park bench with its cast-iron side pieces.

After resting for about half an hour, I walked out of the park and back on to one of the town's streets. Looking this way and that, I spotted a cafe that was open. Hanging above its door was a broad wooden signboard that had been repainted many times. When I got closer, I realised the sign had been repainted because of frequent changes of name. The cafe was now called 'The Sailor'. The dim light bulbs glowing inside had been painted red and yellow. They stuck straight out of sockets screwed to the low ceiling, without any shades. Standing on the counter was an entire battery of vodka bottles – Frontline, Pugachev, Teardrop, Caspian Wave . . . There was definitely a choice of brands on offer here, but I didn't feel like having vodka.

'What do you want?' the woman behind the counter asked me in a voice hoarse from smoking.

'Do you have wine?'

'Port for a thousand a glass.'

I took a glass of the pink port and parted with a crumpled Russian thousand-rouble note. I sat down at an unsteady plastic table and leaned my rucksack against the wall.

I took a sip from the glass. I didn't taste anything, but I did feel the wave of warmth that ran through my tired body.

An old granny came running into the cafe.

'Nyurka, lend me three thousand,' she shouted. The woman at the counter gave the granny the money, and she ran back out again just as quickly.

I sipped away at the port, and when I got halfway down the glass, I could feel that I was getting drunk. I needed a bite of something to go with it, but alcoholic sloth had already spread through my body. I mechanically raised the hand that had been covered in caviar to my mouth and licked the palm. The taste of caviar seemed to have eaten into my skin, and I carried on, enjoying licking the invisible grains off my palm and washing them down with port. Until I fell asleep there, sitting with my head lowered on to the rickety table, which made it steadier.

I was woken by a fear that filtered through into my sober, but still sleepy consciousness. I lifted my head up off the table – it was dark in the cafe, although the light of morning was coming in through the solitary barred window. My head felt heavy after the wine, but that didn't really hinder my thinking. I looked around and walked over to the door – it was locked from the outside. Naturally, I was alone in the cafe. The vodka bottles were still standing there on the shadowy counter. I found the switch beside the door and turned on the light. Behind the counter I saw an electric kettle and a jar of instant coffee. I looked into the back room, found a washbasin and washed my face. I made myself a coffee, poured a couple of drops of milk into it and sat back down at my table. My head had cleared now and the freshness was gradually returning to my body. I was hungry, it's true, but when you drink coffee, thoughts of food recede into the background. My watch said half past eight.

At nine the lock on the door grated and sunlight came streaming into the cafe.

'Ah, you're awake!' the owner's smoke-roughened voice exclaimed. 'How come one glass put you out like that, eh?'

I shrugged.

'I noticed,' she continued, already behind the counter now and putting on a white blouse over her blue T-shirt, 'he only has one glass, and he arrived looking sober, and he's out like a light. And he has a rucksack too. Well, I thought, if I drag him outside and lean him against the wall, when he wakes up he won't have any rucksack, or any clothes either . . . So I decided to leave you here, my little Kiev darling . . .'

'How do you know I'm from Kiev?' I asked in surprise.

She unlocked a drawer under the counter and put my passport down on top of it.

'You don't think I'd leave someone in my property without checking, do you? Here!'

I got up, took my passport and automatically felt the pocket where my passport and wallet had both been.

'What're you doing that for, darling?' she laughed. 'I didn't go looking for anything else of yours, and if I did, I'd have been looking a bit lower down, only you won't find that on a drunk . . . I see you know your way round the kitchen . . . Kolya . . . Do you want another coffee? Or something for a hangover?'

'I wouldn't mind some breakfast . . .' I said, emboldened by her familiarity.

'Coming up. Will you eat an omelette?'

Fifteen minutes later I was greedily eating the omelette and she was sitting beside me at the table, pressing it down with her pointed elbows and watching me closely, like a mother or a police investigator. Her kindness persuaded me to be open with her, and I said I wanted to get across to Mangyshlak. Of course, I didn't say why. I just said I'd like to touch the sand that Shevchenko had walked on.

'Don't times change!' she sighed. 'They used to visit the places Lenin had been, or Brezhnev, but now every republic has its own idol.'

'Why do you call him an idol?' I protested. 'He was a perfectly normal man. In Petersburg he used to steal geese and roast them with his friends.'

'You don't say!' she exclaimed. 'Like Panikovsky!'

After she'd fed me, she served a rapid-transit customer, who came running in to down his morning shot of a hundred grams of vodka and immediately went dashing on his way again.

'You can't get straight to Mangyshlak from here,' she said when she came back to my table. 'If you like, I'll find out the best way to go.'

'Please do!' I said.

'OK. You work here behind the counter for a while,' she said briskly. 'All the vodka's a thousand for a hundred grams, the wine's a thousand a glass. And I'll be back in an hour . . . Oh yes, give me your passport!'

I held out my passport to her.

'And another thing,' she added. 'Have you got anything to pay with?'

'I have a bit . . .'

Left alone in the cafe, I stood behind the counter and looked out through the open door, which revealed a vertical rectangle of street lit by bright sunshine and traversed by occasional passers-by.

A man about fifty years old came in, unshaven and wearing a vest.

'Is Nyurka here?' he asked.

'She'll be here in an hour.'

He nodded and went out without drinking anything.

Then two serious-looking women, also in their fifties, but tastefully dressed, came in.

They took a hundred grams of vodka each, drank it immediately without sitting down and left.

Eventually Nyurka came back. By that time I was so well used to the cafe, I felt as if I could quite easily move in and settle down. But did I want to? No, I wanted to go to Mangyshlak, even though I didn't know what was waiting for me there. Perhaps that was why I wanted to get there so badly. And anyway, was there anything at all waiting for me? If not for that stupid business at the baby-food storeroom, I wouldn't have gone anywhere just now. It was simply point A, from which I had to run to point B. A fine ambition. There's nothing like a threat to your life to make travel seem appealing.

'Well then, darling, in a couple of days there's a fish-processing ship going through the canal to the Caspian. If you like, I can try to make arrangements with them.'

'But where's it sailing to?'

'It's a floating factory, not a tourist ship. It'll anchor in the Caspian, then go to Guriev or somewhere else to unload the canned fish.'

'But how will I get to Mangyshlak?'

'A lot of ships dock there . . . I have a friend who works on board, Dasha. She'll help you . . .'

I was pleased with the outcome of this chance encounter. Even Nyurka's smoke-roughened voice sounded agreeable and considerate to my ears. Until the fish processor left I stayed in her cafe, helping her and sometimes taking her place. And I slept there too, giving her my passport and remaining locked in overnight. But three days later, in the morning, Nyurka led me to the port and handed me over to her friend Dasha, a round-faced woman of about thirty-five who looked from a distance like a brightly coloured can of condensed milk.

16

The unwieldy, multi-deck rectangular block of the fish-processing plant cast off from its mooring at noon. I was standing on the third-level deck, and it seemed to me as if it wasn't the floating factory that had left, but the town itself that had pushed off from us and gone floating away into the distance. On that day the sun was particularly vicious – it seemed to be hanging low and broiling as hard as it could. The metalwork of the massive, clumsy vessel was so sizzling hot you could have fried an egg on it. Only a Volga breeze could have dispersed the sweltering atmosphere surrounding the processing plant, but the air was motionless. The plant didn't sail like a ship, it crept imperceptibly across the smooth water, moving so slowly that even the surface of the Volga was unaffected, remaining alarmingly still.

'Hey, kitten! What are you standing here for? Let's go to the cabin!' Dasha called to me.

I went back to the cabin, which I hadn't had time to examine so far – I'd just dropped in my rucksack and left. It was a twin-berth cabin, with a little square window that was curtained off with a piece of lettuce-green material. In the corner beside the oval door there was a washbasin, with a rubbish bin standing underneath it. Under the window there was a low table with an alarm clock and a heavy ashtray of moulded glass. There were two narrow beds set along the walls of the cabin, like in a compartment on a train. They were both neatly made up, with their pillows standing Napoleon-style, one corner pointing skywards.

'That one's yours,' Dasha told me, pointing to the bed on the right. 'You can sit in here during the day, and in the evening – when everyone's drunk – wander around the decks. Only don't get lost!

'Will it take long?' I asked.

'That depends on where you're going,' Dasha said reasonably enough. 'You need to get to that place . . . Young Communist, don't you?'

'What young communist?'

'You know, Young Communist Bay?'

'Why do I want to go there?'

'Nyurka said you want to get to Mangyshlak, right? Well, that's the closest point, after Guriev we'll go there, and then back in the opposite direction, to Mumra . . .'

I started thinking. Young Communist Bay? The name didn't have a very Cossack ring to it, and apart from that, I didn't know how I was going to get out of the place afterwards. What was there? A port? A town? A fishing village?

'Dasha, what's there, is the factory going to dock there?'

'What for? No, we'll take the fish off the trawlers, hang about for a day or two and move on.'

'But how will I get off?'

'We'll arrange that with some ship,' Dasha promised confidently. 'OK, you stay here. If you want, there's vodka in the locker under the table and water in the tap. There's some canned food in the locker too, in case you get hungry. I've got to go to an urgent meeting.'

60

The heavy oval door smoothly opened and closed. I was left alone.

I sat down on my bed, stretched one hand out to the window, moved aside the improvised lettuce-green curtain and glanced out at freedom. Two metres away from the window I could see the grey-painted wall of the hull, beyond which the invisible shoreline was slipping past.

A strip of light blue sky baked by the sun – that was the only view from this window of the famous scenery of the Volga.

I lay down on the bed and listened to the silence. The silence proved to be rather loud – deep humming noises and various other sounds appeared to infiltrate the cabin from every side. But there were no abrupt tones, and so all this noise seemed peaceful and natural, like the sound of nature. It made a good background for thinking.

I remembered the town of Astrakhan. I remembered it with gratitude. I raised my right hand to my nose, sniffed the palm and smiled at the persistent smell of caviar. It didn't annoy me, quite the opposite in fact – I seemed to have been given yet another proof of the variety of life and its smells. And I remembered Kiev, and the Pushche-Voditsa cemetery, and the folder with the manuscript in it that I had extracted from the grave. I didn't want to remember anything else about Kiev after that, and I sniffed at my right palm again. I was amused that a smell could switch over my memories and thoughts. I smiled at the recent past with a lazy, rather drowsy smile. And I dozed off.

17

That evening when she got back from work, Dasha let me out 'for a walk'. In order not to get lost – I had a genuine fear of that – I strolled around on my own level. I walked out on to the deck and in twenty minutes or so of walking without hurrying or stopping and looking about, I had gone all the way round the huge bulk of the floating fish-processing plant. On each side in the distance the banks of the river with their sparse sprinkling of green slipped back towards Astrakhan. The sun, now red, was suspended on my right, and I could see it retreating in the face of the powerful tide of evening coolness in the air. The air smelled of the river and the breeze ruffled my hair. The fresh dampness of the evening was exhilarating. And I was clearly not the only one to be exhilarated. Inside the fish-processing plant life was seething. From deep in its entrails voices, laughter and shouts leaked out to the deck through the long iron corridors and the curtained windows of the cabins. And as the sun sank under the weight of evening, gradually turning crimson and growing weaker, the voices and the noises sounded louder and louder, until I was absolutely certain that any moment now they would erupt out on to the deck and spill overboard, and somewhere far off, on one of the banks, a fisherman sitting by his campfire would turn his head to watch the distant behemoth floating past with its dozens of square windows glowing and its multitudinous voices spreading out across the evening Volga.

It got dark more quickly than I had expected. Somehow I suddenly found myself surrounded by darkness and the darkness was immediately emphasised by the light falling from the window of someone's cabin. And then someone stopped nearby – two figures, two glowing cigarettes, fading alternately like glow worms.

I listened, expecting to learn who they were from their voices. But they didn't say anything.

They were silent for five minutes. Suddenly one twinkling cigarette went flying overboard like a falling star, and a woman's voice murmured: 'Serve the arsehole right!' A second voice, also a woman's but clearer, said: 'Aha!' and both figures began moving away from me, leaving behind a small light fading away on the handrail of the side. I walked over to it and flicked the glowing butt overboard with my finger. I looked in the direction they had gone. The oval iron door connecting the general corridor with the deck creaked.

I decided to stand there for a bit. I remembered the number of the cabin, and while I was on my own level, I wasn't afraid of getting lost any more.

Twenty minutes later I went back to the cabin. Dasha was sitting on her bed in a cotton-print dressing gown. Standing on the table were an open bottle of vodka, two water glasses and a large cup of cold water.

'Had a good walk?' she asked.

'Yes.'

'Will you have a drink?'

'Just a small one . . .'

She poured about fifty grams into each of the glasses.

'A lousy day today,' she complained as she handed me a glass.

I took the glass and sat down at the head of my own bed, close to the table.

I looked at Dasha – no matter what clothes she put on, the remarkable roundedness of her body seemed to bulge its way out of them. She was somehow round from top to bottom, and only the uplift of her large breasts disrupted the impression that she was smooth and round from all sides.

'What are you staring at?' Dasha said with a smile. 'Haven't you ever seen a beautiful woman before? Drink up!'

We clinked glasses and drank. Dasha picked up the cup of water and took a swallow to wash the vodka down. Then she handed me the cup and I took a swallow too.

'Hungry?' Dasha asked. I nodded.

She leaned down, clicked open the door of the locker under the table and took out a can of fish.

'These are ours,' she said with a hint of pride. 'In oil. She deftly cut open the tin with a small craftwork knife, the kind cobblers usually work with. Then she took two forks out of the locker and handed one to me.

We ate loudly and with pleasure, emptying the can in a couple of minutes. Then she asked: 'More?'

I nodded, and history was repeated. After the second can a feeling of peaceful contentment filled my soul. We drank another fifty grams each.

'Today was a lousy day . . .' she said slowly, after putting the cup of water down on the table. 'First the conveyor system wouldn't start, then there was a short circuit in the autoclave shop, then that arsehole Mazai – the industrial safety engineer – was drunk from early in the morning and kept pawing everyone . . . Couldn't do it like any normal human being, out on deck in the evening, oh no – right there in the workshop. And what's he got for you to paw, when it's just hanging there like a dead man? Eh? What's he got to paw? Yuck.'

I listened to Dasha, and although the vodka had relaxed me a bit, what she said put me slightly on my guard, as if I had suddenly found myself facing a lioness ready to pounce. But three minutes later, I realised my apprehensions had been groundless. Dasha had moved on from Mazai to the way Caspian sardines are packed in a barrel, and now she was talking excitedly about the flavour of lightly salted fish.

'I'll take you there at night, when everyone's drunk. We'll take it out of the temporary store and eat it right there by the barrel – I tell you, it's sheer heaven! You'll never forget it! Will you have another drink?'

I nodded. Dasha poured the rest of the vodka into the glasses.

'We won't have any more today,' she said, putting the empty bottle away under the table. 'The economicly challenged should be economical. I can't stand going round the cabins in the morning the way they do here, trying to cadge a hundred grams . . . What's your own should be your own!'

We drank. She took another gulp from the cup, then went over to the washbasin, got more cold water and came back to the table.

'Don't get any ideas, I'm not a drinker, it's just to keep my strength up and help fight the empty time . . .There's nothing to do here. Float along, work, drink. But when we get home or we moor somewhere – then you can have a bit of culture in your life. Buy a book, watch a movie . . . Do you read books?'

'Yes.'

'That's a good thing, reading books . . .' Dasha nodded and fell silent, pondering.

'Only that's not enough,' she added about two minutes later when she emerged from her deliberations and gazed into my eyes.

Her eyes were brown.

Someone knocked on the window of the cabin.

'What?' Dasha shouted.

'Can I come in?' a rather gruff woman's voice asked. 'For a talk . . .'

'No, you can't, Katya. We can do all the talking we like tomorrow in the workshop!'

There was the sound of footsteps that seemed too heavy for a woman receding from the window.

'She wanted to have a talk!' said Dasha, jerking her chin indignantly in the direction of the window. 'When she took Vaska from me, she didn't want to talk then. But as soon as he tells her where to get off, then it's "Can I come in?" If you want to sleep, don't mind me, you can get undressed and lie down. I will myself, in about five minutes . . . I'll just go out first for a cigarette . . .'

She got up off the bed.

Left alone, I quickly took off my jeans and T-shirt and climbed in under the light blanket. 'I wonder,' I thought. 'What would Shevchenko have done if he found himself in my situation? How would he have behaved with this Dasha? Would his doleful love for women have extended even to her, this strong young woman with her coarse, motherly kindness? She certainly has something of a "homeland" about her – it doesn't matter which one. Yes indeed, the comparison seems a perfectly natural one – a country of a woman. Self-sufficient, determined, independent . . .'

Some man walked by outside the window, swearing quietly. When his hollow footsteps faded away, my thoughts had already turned in a different direction. I was thinking about the future, the near future that I was always heading towards. 'Wouldn't it be great,' I thought, 'if only I, a Russian, could find these notes by the Kobza player? What a contribution to the promotion of friendship between two fraternal peoples!' And with that thought I fell asleep.

18

All the next day we floated down the Volga–Caspian Canal, which I at first had taken for the Volga. But Dasha enlightened me.

'Wait till we get out into the Caspian, kitten – it won't be so calm then,' she said in the morning as she glanced out of the window, through which the only thing that could possibly look calm was the bright blue sky, since there was nothing else to see.

Then she went off to her factory workshop and didn't come back until almost six in the evening. And I stayed in the cabin, either sitting and thinking or dozing. Basically building up my strength. In the evening I wandered round the perimeter of my level, scrutinising the inhabitants of the fish-processing plant as they walked by in groups or one at a time. Just normal people, except that their eyes were red and some of them seemed to be really blazing. I realised that living and working in the same place was fraught with the danger of psychological deviance. I even remembered that they had explained something to us at school about the difficulties of one-man and two-man space flights – to make it clear that, sadly, wanting to be a cosmonaut and being one in reality had nothing at all in common. But it would clearly be quite wrong to compare the difficulties of life on a floating fish-processing plant and those faced by cosmonauts. There were a lot of people here of different sexes and different ages. And they found ways of passing the time to match their own level of development and power of imagination. And the very fact that their glances didn't even linger on me indicated that they were not suffering from loneliness or a lack of new faces.

I leaned my chest against the wall of the deck and looked at the grey bank floating past in the distance.

The swollen, reddish sun was hanging in the sky on the other side of the vessel, so the approach of evening was especially noticeable here. The water down below was silver. The same calm filled the air and my soul. And having clattered their shoes across the ringing iron of the deck, the people had gone off to the various places where they intended to drink or simply talk.

After filling myself up with the freshness of the damp evening air, I went back to the cabin. We ate canned fish again and drank vodka slowly, washing it down with water. And once again Dasha spoke matter-of-factly about the events of the working day.

'Tomorrow we're setting the freezer belt and the canning line going,' she said in a firm voice. 'There's fish in the freezer for four days' work, just enough to last until we start taking in fresh fish – we'll empty the freezer. Run off about ten tonnes' worth of cans . . . pity there's only mackerel and herring in the freezer . . . If a sturgeon ever gets caught, whoever spots it, grabs it. And I'm not on the belt, I'll be on quality control this time . . . Listen, what are you going to Mangyshlak for? Not some kind of opium courier are you?'

'No,' I said, shaking my head. 'I want to take a look at Shevchenko's fort . . . and wander round the places he went to . . .'

'And what's he to you?' Dasha asked.

'Well, a poet, a champion of the national idea . . .'

'Like Zhirinovsky?'

'No, he was calm and quiet. He wrote poems about women . . . with compassion . . .'

'Did he feel sorry for women then?'

'He did,' I confirmed.

'That's interesting,' Dasha said sincerely. She thought about it. 'I don't really read poems. I've read a few books about Angelique and Gorky's *Mother*. I like Gorky more, but Angelique's more amusing.

I don't remember who wrote it . . . but even when I was a kid I didn't really like poems. Only when Robert Rozhdestvensky read on TV – I listened then. But he only used to read on 8 March . . .'

She yawned, covering her mouth with her hand.

'I'm feeling pretty sleepy,' she said in a tired voice. Then, taking no notice of me, she took off her cotton dressing gown with the faded flowers, leaving herself in nothing but beige-coloured pants or shorts and a cotton bra, also with a flower pattern.

She climbed in under the blanket.

'Turn out the light!' she told me. 'And finish the vodka, if you can. It's not good to leave tears in the bottle . . .'

There really was a little bit of vodka left on the bottom of the bottle, and I poured it into my glass. Then I turned out the light and, with my glass in my hand, walked along the internal corridor to the outer edge of the deck. I leaned against the deck rail and watched the water shifting between a green patina and shimmering silver.

There were big, bright stars in the sky. Three of them, hanging low down, and above them all the other small stars, as countless as a swarm of midges in the night clustered round the only lamp lighting up the road.

Behind my back the window of someone's cabin was lit up, and there was a loud, jolly conversation going on inside. Glasses clinked and events from the past were recalled – ordinary things that happen to everyone many times in their lives. But here, against the background of merriment and the vodka, it was natural to listen to them with thoughtful respect, and even I stood there, stock-still, for about fifteen minutes. As I listened, I smiled. It was like some evening in a village. A glass with the final drops of vodka in my hand. Stars in the sky. A window behind my back and voices talking behind the window.

I finished off the vodka. After I got back to the cabin, I gradually fell asleep to the sound of Dasha's gentle but persistent snoring.

19

The next evening the fish-processing plant sailed out into the Caspian Sea. The early stars were glimmering gently and unobtrusively in a sky that was still bright. The workers of the floating giant were strolling around its outer deck. I was standing at the side and looking at the water – Dasha had told me that as soon as we entered the Caspian, the water would turn green.

A group of women walked by, laughing, and the smell of fresh fish was left hanging in the air around me. But thirty seconds later, the clear, salty breeze had driven it away.

The processing plant was swaying on the low waves, and that was a new sensation for me. Earlier I had found it hard even to imagine that any waves could be strong enough to set this massive hulk swaying, but now I understood that the Caspian Sea could do anything: refresh you, feed you or drown you . . .

'Hey, kitten, be careful, don't go catching cold!' I heard Dasha's voice say behind me.

'It's not all that cold,' I replied without looking round.

'The winds here on the Caspian are treacherous – they blow straight through you,' Dasha said knowingly. 'Let's go back into the cabin.'

I woke up in the morning with a thick head. The processing plant was still swaying – no doubt that was the reason for my restless night and the difficulty I had in waking up. Dasha was already in her workshop. There was a can of 'Caspian Herring' on the table, with the familiar short knife and a pickled cucumber.

'Considerate,' I thought, looking at the breakfast that had been left for me.

I ate and then got washed. I looked out past the curtain – the sky had a leaden shimmer. The weather seemed to have changed for the worse.

How much longer would I have to keep sailing with them? It wasn't as if the journey was actually unpleasant, but I was starting to tire of its sheer monotony: always the same canned food, the same sea. Only the sky actually changed colour, but otherwise everything was always the same.

Somewhere in the corridor a muffled but incredibly loud mechanical voice started speaking. I bounded over to the door, opened it and listened.

'Medical assistant report immediately to workshop 3!' the loudspeaker repeated.

The voice summoned the medical assistant to workshop 3 another three times, and then everything went quiet again.

Twenty minutes later Dasha suddenly arrived back at the cabin. She was dressed in overalls that had once been white and she had a green headscarf over her head. Her face was red and her eyes were sparkling.

'A short day!' she said with a little smile, pulling off the headscarf and letting her chestnut hair tumble down on to her shoulders. They've stopped the belt . . .'

'What's up?' I asked.

'An emergency. The girls forced that drunk Mazai into a corner and sliced the top of his prick off. While the others held him down,

71

Mashka tossed the knob into the batching bin, so it went to get canned with the fish . . . What an uproar there was!' Dasha laughed. 'Him dashing around the place, stopping the belt and opening the cans – looking for his knob in the herring . . .'

'Well, did he find it?'

'How could he? Five hundred cans had come off the line – you couldn't open them all, and if he did find it, what would he do, sew it back on? Eh?'

I shrugged. 'The doctors can sew anything back on now, except a head,' I said.

'And where will you find any doctors here? We've got one medical assistant, Kolya, he used to be a vet, then he retrained to deal with people. He just came, poured some antiseptic over Mazai's stump and bandaged it up – so much for sewing anything back! Someone will buy that can! Ha, they'll think they've got a cod's liver!'

I was unable to share Dasha's merriment. I even felt rather sad.

'And who is it that goes digging up graves in the middle of the night?' my own mind sneered spitefully in response to my change of mood. 'Ah, but graves are a different matter altogether,' I objected. 'Anyone lying in a grave is already dead, they couldn't care less if the grave is dug up or not. Perhaps they might even be glad to see someone taking an interest in them even after they're dead . . .'

Completely unembarrassed by my presence, Dasha changed into a pink sarafan, and washed her hands and face. Then she sat down on her bed, still with that smile on her round face.

'There's going to be a gale tonight, so we can't drink today,' she said. 'Are you hungry?'

I thought about it. And meanwhile she leaned down under the table and took out two cans of Caspian Herring.

I must have pulled some kind of face at the sight of those cans.

72

Dasha giggled and said: 'Don't worry. This is an old lot, the girls didn't throw anything in here . . .'

We dined, but I didn't really enjoy the food.

'I'll go and have a smoke,' said Dasha. She stood up and went out of the cabin, taking the empty cans with her.

The gale struck at about eight o'clock. It blew up suddenly and powerfully. Dasha was already lying in her bed, but I was standing at the side, clinging on tight to the rail. I watched the bituminous black water rear up to a height of several metres. The waves didn't strike against the side, as I expected, instead they tried to toss the floating fish-processing plant up out of the water.

At first this happened lightly and gently, but after a little while the swell picked up momentum and began lifting the plant and tossing it around like a little toy boat. In my fright I almost tumbled overboard and I retreated, locking the heavy iron door with its side clamps behind me. I went back to the cabin.

Dasha seemed to be asleep, although I couldn't hear her usual snoring. In any case, she wasn't making any sound, just lying there with her face to the wall. The cabin staggered and I staggered with it, trying to keep my balance. I quickly got undressed and lay down under the blanket, but almost immediately a blow from the storm threw me out on to the floor. I grabbed hold of the iron leg of the table, got up and lay back down on the bed. But five minutes later another blow threw me on to the floor again.

'Come here, kitten!' I heard Dasha's voice say gently. 'You're too light. You haven't got enough weight to keep you on the bed!'

That was when I realised why most of the women working in the processing plant were so large and rotund. I took my blanket and moved across to Dasha's bed, and although it was cramped in there, that side of the cabin proved to be 'less dangerous during artillery

73

bombardments', as they used to write on the streets of Leningrad during the seige.

And Dasha put her heavy arm round me, tenderly restraining my light body and so protecting it against the fearsome Caspian storm.

I woke up thoroughly impregnated with Dasha's warmth and the smell of fish that was exuded, for some reason, by her armpits. Dasha was sleeping sweetly, and I didn't want to wake her, so I lay there without moving. And to escape from the smell of fish, I stuck my left hand under my nose. Enveloped in the scent of cinnamon, I felt free of all irritation.

20

The storm abated by noon the next day. Its place was taken by the military monotony of endless low waves moving in unison. These waves were weak, and even en masse they were unable to set the processing plant swaying. It proceeded confidently about its industrial business, firmly on course to celebrate the achievement of ever-new production targets, which must have provided a pleasant contrast to the background conveyor-line monotony of its life. Its double existence continued to astonish me. Even though it was a clear and obvious fact, the very concept of a floating or wandering factory seemed absolutely fantastic to me. And even my personal presence on board still did not prove to me the reality of my surroundings and what was happening in them. Although, you might say, what was really so very surprising about it? The factory ship goes sailing on, the captain chooses his course, the factory director takes care of production, and the two of them together feed the country with canned fish. But no, it still doesn't sound real . . .

I took a can of Caspian Herring out of the locker under the table, opened it, inspected the contents to make sure they included no foreign bodies and then had lunch.

Dasha was in the workshop. I still didn't know where her workshop was, above this deck or below it. But it wasn't that important. I didn't work there.

After lunch I stood at the side, watching the junction between sea and sky. Every now and then the dots of ships appeared on the hazy, quivering line of the horizon, and that made the sea seem small and cramped to me. I wasn't afraid of this sea – surely it would be hard to get lost in it . . . But then, who could tell, better not try . . .

A couple of days later Dasha announced that the following night there would be a schooner that would drop me off at Mangyshlak. I was absolutely delighted by the news and began waiting impatiently.

What I remember most vividly about the night-time transfer to a fishing schooner are the strange metallic noises. The schooner came right up alongside, and sacks full of something metal were tossed down on to it from the lowest perimeter deck. At first I thought the sacks contained cans of fish, but when they started tossing down canned fish, not in sacks, but in cardboard boxes tied round with string, I immediately realised I was wrong.

Meanwhile, the nocturnal loading operation continued. I stood beside the stocky Vanya, whom Dasha had charged with putting me on the schooner. He kept a careful eye on what was going on, every now and then exchanging shouts with two fishermen on the schooner. Finally he yelled: 'That's it. All debts are paid. And you can take this lad ashore!' So saying, he slapped me on the shoulder, which made me start. A man down below nodded. Vanya threw my blue-and-yellow rucksack down on to the schooner. The rucksack clattered heavily against the deck – Dasha had filled it generously with cans of fish as a farewell gift, and now it probably weighed fifteen or twenty kilograms.

'All right, now jump!' said Vanya, looking at me. It was three metres down to the schooner, and it was swaying slightly with the waves. I felt a little afraid.

'Come on, come on, stop playing the coward,' Vanya urged me. I clambered over the side wall and froze again, suspended above the schooner's deck.

'Come on, they'll catch you!'

I jumped, and two fishermen really did catch me, cushioning my landing.

'Marat, start the engine,' one of them said to the other, and the two men disappeared incredibly quickly on that small schooner, leaving me alone surrounded by the sacks, the boxes and the nets with their big white floats, which had been stashed to starboard.

The schooner shuddered and began moving away from the towering side of the floating fish-processing plant.

Down below, close to the water, it was cool. I sat down on a sack and immediately jumped back up, because I'd impaled myself on something sharp. When I felt the sacks with my hands, I was stupefied – there could be no doubt that they contained guns, either rifles or sub-machine guns . . .

'Would you believe it!' I thought, shifting over on to a box of canned fish. 'A fine fishing schooner, and a fine catch . . .'

'Hey, brother, come over here!' shouted a figure that peered out from the side of the wheelhouse.

I took my rucksack and went over to the wheelhouse. The entrance to the cabin below deck was there too.

'Stepan,' said the man who had called me, holding out his hand. 'And that's Marat over there at the wheel.'

'Kolya,' I said, introducing myself.

'Do you want a drink?' asked Stepan.

'No, thank you.'

'Well, if you do, let me know. We don't drink ourselves, but there's always something for guests . . . You wouldn't happen to be a poppy runner, would you, Kolya?'

It was the second time I'd heard that question.

'No,' I said. I didn't know what the phrase meant, but I could guess.

'That's a shame,' Stepan drawled, 'or we could have put a bit of work your way . . . OK then, go and have a lie-down . . . We'll put you off in the morning . . . It's all the same to you where, isn't it? As long as it's well away from where anyone lives? Is that right?'

I nodded.

I suddenly started feeling sleepy. Those small waves were lulling me. I went down into the cabin and lay on the nearest bed. A patch of colour flashed before my eyes, and then there was absolute darkness – I was already sleeping, my ears filled with the growling of the industrious little diesel engine hidden somewhere below the floor of the cabin.

In the middle of the night, through my shallow sleep, I heard voices talking and metal clanking. Then there was a blow and I automatically huddled down into the bed, pushing my right hand out. But then everything went calm and the diesel engine started growling soothingly again.

In the morning they woke me up. I went out on deck, and the first thing that struck me was the absence of the sacks containing the guns.

The cardboard boxes of canned fish were still standing there, though, neatly lined up along the port side.

'That's your coastline!' Stepan said to me. I looked at the desolate and jagged shore. There was nothing inviting about it. I was paralysed by a sudden feeling of desperation or embarrassment. I said nothing, gazing straight ahead. The deck swayed under my feet and the yellow, indifferent shoreline swayed a hundred metres away from us.

'Marat will steer us in now, it's deep enough here for us to get in close. Have you got any water?'

'Water?' I asked, surfacing from my stupor.

'Drinking water.'

'No.'

'What are you thinking of?' Stepan said, shaking his head in amazement. 'OK, we'll give you a bottle.'

What he called a bottle was a five-litre plastic canister. He brought it up out of the cabin and put it beside my rucksack.

'This is a desert,' he said, slightly annoyed. 'You won't find any taps or beer cellars here!'

I nodded to let him know that I realised my own stupidity. I must say, just at that moment I felt very keenly aware of this stupidity, thanks to which I now found myself God knows where, with the intention of being even further away from all roads and people in twenty minutes. My lips felt nervously dry. I mechanically picked up the five-litre canister, screwed off the top and took a swig of water.

I felt ill at ease. But the shoreline was approaching implacably. It was only forty or thirty metres away now. A rocky plateau, undercut at its base by the waves that had also licked it smooth, rose up about two metres above the water. At irregular intervals the upper line of the plateau was broken, and at those points the waves licked at the rocks that had tumbled down and which it was possible to scramble up, like a stairway.

The moment arrived when the schooner jolted and Stepan turned his neck in the direction of the cabin and shouted: 'Marat, throttle back!'

The shore was just three metres away.

'Let's throw your things over, so they don't get wet,' said Stepan, walking over to the rucksack.

Swinging the rucksack between us, we tossed it ashore, and then the canister of water thudded down beside it.

'Jump!' Stepan said to me, nodding towards the shore. 'The sun will soon heat things up a bit – you'll dry out in five minutes!'

I said goodbye to him and Marat, thanked them, then pushed off with my feet from the side of the boat and plumped down into the turbid water of the Caspian in my jeans and T-shirt.

'Hey,' Stepan called to me when I had clambered out, with my clothes heavy and waterlogged, on to a narrow little bank that ran into a shallow grotto washed by the waves. 'If you need anything shipped across, we can always do it! Find us! The schooner *Old Comrade*.'

The diesel engine started growling quietly again and the schooner slowly drifted to the left, gradually increasing the distance between itself and the bank. I watched it go and read the name on its side. I waved, although they weren't watching me any more.

The further the *Old Comrade* moved away, the more keenly I felt my isolation. And then, when the final trace of my 'comrade' had dissolved into the fidgeting waves of the Caspian, I experienced an unexpected tranquillity, a feeling akin to acceptance of the inevitable. I carried my things up on to that unusual rocky elevation, which turned out to be covered with warm sand, and looked around.

I sat down on the sand beside the rucksack and the canister. The sun was shining above me and a light breeze that carried the smell of the Caspian was drying my hair. I didn't feel like going anywhere.

I didn't have a compass and I knew absolutely nothing about the desert. I did have water and cans of fish, but one thing was no substitute for the other. I had to focus my mind on making a decision, but I realised there was no logic that would tell me which direction to walk in. I ought to have asked Marat or Stepan, but I simply hadn't thought of it.

'OK, for the time being I'll walk along the shore,' I decided. 'Maybe I'll come out somewhere. But first I need to dry off . . .'

I lay down on the warm sand and turned on to my side. But it still felt uncomfortable in wet clothes. I got up and stripped naked, leaving only my watch on my wrist. I spread my clothes out on the sand and lay down beside them, feeling like the proud owner of some massive nudist beach.

21

I was woken by the heat. Thoughts that seemed to have been melted were wandering about sluggishly in my head, overheated by the sun. It was like sunstroke. I reached out for the T-shirt and covered my head with it. My clothes had completely dried out. I shook my jeans and the sand ran off them lightly. But it was hard to imagine that I was going to put my jeans on in that kind of heat. I looked at the sun – it was hanging almost at the centre of the sky.

Glancing at my watch I saw water under the glass, and under the water the hands had stuck at nine in the morning – the time of my landing on this coast.

'Well,' I thought, 'now I'm getting close to Robinson Crusoe conditions.'

Covered by the T-shirt, my head gradually cooled down and my thoughts once again assumed a readable form and regular rhythm. I put all my clothes in the rucksack and left on a pair of pants in case I met anyone unexpectedly. Although it was hard to imagine who I could possibly embarrass here. I looked around resolutely, hoisted the heavy rucksack on to my back, picked up the canister of water with my right hand and set off almost along the edge of the rocky plateau that held back the sand from creeping into the Caspian. I set out after the schooner *Old Comrade* that had sailed beyond the horizon long ago.

The shoreline that followed the plateau was jagged and irregular. I quickly realised that it sometimes made sense to cut the corners that the plateau thrust out into the waters of the Caspian. Economising my strength on these corners, I walked for at least a kilometre before I felt pain in my shoulders and fatigue in my feet, which were not used to walking across hot loose sand.

To make a halt under the scorching sun was not a very rational idea and when I came across a projection of the plateau into the sea, I climbed down on to the wet shore and sat in a cave hollowed out by the waves. The sudden cold there raised goosebumps on my skin – the drop in temperature was incredible. There was a smell of dampness and the sea. The sun could not reach this little spot of the shoreline.

I took off the rucksack and sighed as I looked at the red stripes left on my shoulders by its straps.

Feeling hungry, I took out a can of Caspian Herring, opened it with a knife and then poked about in the lumps of fish with the knife and, not having discovered anything extraneous, transferred the lumps of fish to my mouth with my fingers and followed it with its own juice, the 'added oil', as it said on the can. I washed the food down with warm water from the canister – there was an aftertaste of plastic left on my tongue. To cool the canister down a bit, I lowered it into the water at the very edge of the shore, between two rocks that had fallen off the rim of the plateau at some point in time.

My body gradually grew accustomed to the coolness, the goose-bumps disappeared and little by little my spirits began to revive.

I was sitting on a cool rock. Looking at the sea, at the slanting lines of the waves calmly and monotonously polishing the shore.

'Life is beautiful . . .' I thought, although I thought it with a certain sad irony. I didn't know whether I was mocking myself or the thought was some kind of inner mirage caused by the heat of the sun. But if a mirage could arise internally, in the form of a thought, on the very first day in the desert – that really was sad.

What I felt wasn't really sadness, though. I felt calm, and I didn't want to move or to leave this cool secluded little spot. I didn't want anything. Except simply to sit there and watch the bright sea glittering in the sun from which I had managed to hide so well.

I don't know how long I spent sitting by the sea, resting and delighting in the absence of heat. My watch refused to work, no matter how much I shook it. The inside of the glass was covered with condensation, through which it was hard to make out the two stuck hands.

Something told me that it wasn't so hot now even in the sun. The line of the horizon seemed to have moved closer and to be quivering more. Evening must be coming on.

I took the canister out of the water, put on the rucksack and clambered back up on to the sand. It was true – the sun was already sinking. The sandy horizon was tinged slightly red. And the air itself was no longer so dry and prickly hot.

I continued on my way and now I found it much easier to walk than in the recent heat. This discovery roused a memory of some book in which travellers also walked through a desert, and they walked only in the evening and at night.

'Right then,' I thought. 'Forward with a song.'

22

I fell asleep late at night, in the dark, above which the stars were shining to each other. The sand had cooled a little, but retained the warmth of the sun. The air also warmed me, like a blanket that I couldn't take off. I covered my head with the T-shirt.

I was woken by a sensation of alien movement close to my face. Jerking the T-shirt away, I saw a small scorpion and pulled back sharply, screwing up my eyes against the morning sun. The scorpion lazily turned round on the spot and unhurriedly buried itself in the sand.

This morning encounter with the local animal world had woken me up better than any cold water, but it was still a good idea to have a wash. I walked towards the sea, found a little gap, went down on to the shore and splashed my face with several handfuls of the cool, dirty-green Caspian.

Remembering my discovery of the previous day, I decided to use the time before it got too hot for travelling and to ensconce myself in some little shoreline grotto when the sun's heat became more fierce.

Without taking breakfast, I hoisted the rucksack on to my shoulders – it seemed even heavier than the day before. I picked up the canister and was just about to set off when I noticed some tracks in the sand. It was hard to tell what kind of tracks they were, since the sand hadn't retained any precise lines or forms. But these tracks ran around the spot where I had spent the night. Looking at the tracks that I myself had just left in the sand, I found the same thing. As I followed my own tracks to the sea I saw that a similar line of tracks ran parallel, about two or three metres away, down to the sea at the next cleft.

Mystified, I listened to the silence surrounding me, but it was crystalline, absolutely quiet.

I shrugged and set off, still thinking about those tracks.

The sun was climbing higher and already beginning to scorch me, even reaching my head through the T-shirt. I managed to go a couple of kilometres, no further.

Realising that it wasn't worth the risk of playing games with the desert sun, I went down to the sea and sat on a rock beside the water. Again the abrupt descent into shade sent a cold shudder across my skin, but the coolness felt like a pleasant, refreshing wave on my body.

I ate breakfast and drank some water from the canister. I bathed in the sea – for some reason this idea hadn't occurred to me the day before, but today I revelled in splashing about in the cool water. And I dried out in a few minutes when I went up to the plateau. Once I was dry, I went back down to the rock and sat on it, keeping an eye on the horizon and waiting for the evening.

The distant, quivering horizon inclined me to reflection, and in the state I was in just then, I found it easy to accept everything that was happening to me and no longer felt angry either with myself, for having ended up in such a lifeless area in pursuit of a crazy adventure, or with the dead man Gershovich whom I had disturbed and who had prompted me to travel in this direction. But then, he wasn't the reason why I had come here. It was the threat from bandits I didn't even know, whose plans I had disrupted, that had really launched me into my journey. And it had launched me abruptly, leaving me no time to make any preparations.

For a moment I suddenly felt sad when I thought that bandits have good memories. When I went back to Kiev – if I went back – they would show up again. And I hadn't paid for the flat, or my telephone calls . . .

I gazed with spellbound eyes at the quivering line of the horizon. I saw a little ship in the distance and it sailed straight along that line for several minutes, then disappeared as it moved away beyond it.

When the midday heat had abated and there already seemed to be more warmth rising up from the sand than coming down from the sun, I climbed back up on to the plateau and walked on.

I walked for a long time. For hours. And I would have walked for longer, if I hadn't suddenly spotted a piece of tarpaulin, faded by the sun, sticking up out of the sand. Simple curiosity made me tug on it. The sand wouldn't let it go, and that whetted my appetite even further. I took off the rucksack, cleaned the sand off the piece of tarpaulin with my hands and tugged again. The tarpaulin yielded slightly, but literally only ten or fifteen centimetres. I raked more sand away with my hands, trying to free the coarse material. When

85

another twenty centimetres or so of tarpaulin slid out from under the sand, I could see that I was looking at a tent. It took me at least an hour to free it completely from its sandy captivity. I got incredibly tired and started feeling hot again – more from the physical effort than from the sun hanging in the sky. The sweat ran off me rapidly, dropping on to the sand and immediately disappearing, discolouring the sand with its vital moisture for only a brief instant. I sat down by the tent and got my breath back. Despite feeling tired, I was very pleased with my find – it was as if I had found a house! Now I could hide from the rain, and the sun . . . Although, if it had started to rain just then, I wouldn't have wanted to hide from it.

Leaving my trophy on the sand, I went down to the sea to bathe. When I got back, I shook the sand out of the inside of the tent and thought about the possibility of using it that night, especially as my body was demanding rest.

I got a bit tangled up in the ropes, but finally managed to sort them out and flatten the tent on the sand. Then I found the entrance, took hold of the opposite end and shook the tent. Something rustled inside it. I shook it again and saw that there was almost no sand tipping out, so I put my hand inside, feeling slightly afraid of coming across another little scorpion. But I was lucky. There were no representatives of the local fauna in the tent, but I did drag out a yellowed newspaper. Imagine my surprise when I picked it up and read the name: the *Evening Kiev*. My jaw dropped and stayed stuck in that position for several minutes, I was so astounded to see an edition of the *Evening Kiev* for 15 April 1974.

When I had recovered my wits somewhat and put my hand back into the tarpaulin tent, I pulled out a box of matches and a Smena camera. There was nothing else inside.

The owner of the tent had most likely been a solitary traveller. To judge from the newspaper, he must have set out from Kiev on 15 April in the distant year of 1974. That was all I knew about him. And he himself must have dissolved into the sand. I automatically glanced around nervously at the sand, afraid of spotting traces of a mummy desiccated by the sun.

Turning my attention back to the Smena camera, I took it out of its case and inspected it. There seemed to be an almost completely used film inside – the little window showing how many shots had been taken said '34'. Two frames left.

My tiredness was augmented by a certain feeling of fear. I remembered the tracks around the spot where I had spent the night.

I started thinking.

'Maybe it's border guards?' was the first thought. 'After all, this isn't the USSR any more, it's Kazakhstan!'

'What is there to be afraid of?' was the second thought to come up. 'They walked round you, but they didn't touch you, they didn't wake you and they didn't ask to see your documents!'

'You've got it backwards,' I said to these thoughts. 'According to you, I ought to be glad that there's some other life around here and it's showing a lively interest in me. But I'm already tired of interest being taken in me . . . I'd be happier if no one even knew I existed . . .'

Although I was tired, this vague fear forced me to collect up my things, put the camera in the rucksack, pick up the canister and the tent and walk on for a kilometre before settling down for the night.

I didn't sleep soundly, but I was comfortable, because I laid the tent I had found on the sand.

Occasionally I would wake up suddenly and listen. But the silence reassured me, and I dived back into a shallow sleep until the next internal alarm signal.

23

Next morning I walked several more kilometres along the edge of the waterside plateau. The shoreline was moving away to the left. I was feeling irritated by the monotonous trembling of the horizons surrounding me – the horizon of the sea and the horizon of the desert, which was blurred by a warm haze, as if at that point land was being smelted into sky, or vice versa.

I no longer looked for ships on the sea or eagerly examined the distant expanse of desert. I simply walked forward, not completely certain that I had chosen the right direction.

There was no more than two litres of water left in the canister, although it seemed to me that I was using it more than sparingly, not to mention the fact that I was washing myself in the sea. But the pleasant weight of it glugging in the canister gave me confidence that I was safe here in the desert. And the weight in the rucksack gave me confidence that I would not go hungry, even if the diet was monotonous.

The tent was hanging partway out of the rucksack, but I had already calculated that if I ate another five or six cans of fish, it would fit in completely.

All in all, my progress along the shore of the Caspian felt both spontaneous and planned at the same time. And in addition a certain faith, or even confidence in my luck – good luck, of course – also cheered my mind and my body.

After all, the one-man tent I had found was an example of a stroke of good luck. Who could say what else I might find?

And so I walked on until the heat became unbearable. Beginning to feel in my lungs the parching force of the air heated to incandescence by the sun, I made a halt in my journey and went down on to the shore.

I found a comfortable rock, spread the tent on it and settled in, like a seasoned traveller.

I automatically glanced at my watch, but it didn't show the time. The frozen hands merely reminded me of my arrival on this desert coastline, they reminded me of the recent past.

I cooled my lunch – a can of Caspian Herring – in the waters of the Caspian, and I lowered the plastic canister into the water too. After waiting for half an hour, I ate and then lay down on the same rock, revelling in the damp Caspian coolness.

I fell into a doze in the shade, listening to the quiet splashing of the waves. Through my doze I felt the gusts of the Caspian breeze on my face and in my mind I tried to prolong their touch, as if they were a woman's fingers – gentle, light, caressing.

Time passed imperceptibly, urging the sun on towards evening, towards sunset. And while still in my doze, I sensed the approaching evening, although it was still a long way off – the sea breeze simply became bolder and the surface of the Caspian gleamed less brightly than a few hours earlier in the sun that I could not see from my grotto.

I had to continue with my journey. I clambered up on to the plateau and moved on.

When the sun was already turning crimson, hanging just above the sea, I saw ahead of me the outlines of low mountains or hills. I felt a sudden thrill somewhere inside.

Although I was tired, I quickened my step, as if I intended to reach the hills that very evening. But my sudden spurt was almost entirely psychological. My body could not sustain it. My shoulders started to ache, and the increased pace made my legs start to feel heavy.

And so very soon I stopped, realising that today's march was over and it was time for another halt.

I could hear noise from the direction of the sea – the waves had risen higher than usual. The cool salty breeze carried their smell up on to the plateau. I thought that in addition to the noise of the sea I could also hear the whisper of creeping sand.

Carefully, I looked down at my feet and I really did see some kind of movement but because I was tired and the sun had been so bright just lately, my eyes were unable to focus more sharply on the state of the sand. I squatted down on my haunches and looked at my feet again, and at that short distance I saw tiny little sand dunes piling up beside my feet. It didn't seem to be anything to do with the wind, it was simply that every step I took set the sand shifting and tumbling into the hollows of my tracks.

But the wind was growing stronger – there was a storm gathering at sea. Not knowing what I should be more afraid of – the storm itself, or the wind that was raising it – I decided to move further inland and settle down there for the night. I walked about eighty metres and found a small hollow in the sand, like some giant's footprint that had been filled in. I saw that the wind was flying over this spot without touching the sand. It seemed to me that the wind was also getting colder with every gust and so I settled down for the night by simply climbing into the tent as if it was a sleeping bag. I pulled all my things inside the tarpaulin as well and lay on my back with only my head sticking out. I looked at the sky, but I couldn't see the stars. I couldn't see anything at all. Where the blue sky had been so recently, there was nothing left.

The wind moaned constantly, sometimes suddenly speeding up and changing its sound to a hissing whistle. I felt alarmed. The wind brought the sounds of the sea on its gusts, and every gust made me feel afraid and I thought I could feel the sand under my improvised sleeping bag starting to sway and shift about. My body was remembering the storm I had lived through on the floating fish-processing plant. I turned over on to my stomach and crept deeper into the tarpaulin shelter of the tent. The rucksack was lying on my left and the canister of water on my right.

I didn't know that tarpaulin had the property of absorbing sound. As soon as I moved down inside the tent, the sound of the wind almost disappeared and the darkness and warmth reassured my body. I put my arm across the rucksack lying beside me. My hand found a smooth, soft spot, and stayed there. I even dozed off. But I didn't doze for long – after only twenty minutes the wind, stronger now, whistled above me and tossed a handful of sand on to the tarpaulin. I shuddered. And again I felt afraid. I realised how this tent had come to be buried under a heap of sand. But I still didn't know what had happened to its former owner. Maybe he just thought 'To hell with it all!' when he got tired of fighting against the sand. Just dropped everything and walked away. Maybe some fishermen spotted him from the sea and picked him up.

But the wind, which couldn't have cared less for my deliberations, flapped its invisible sail again and the blow sent a new wave of sand showering on to the tent. I stuck my head out of the tarpaulin and then clambered all the way out and looked around.

It wasn't really that dark. I shook the upper layer of tarpaulin and tossed the sand off it. Actually there was barely any sand there, it's just that when you're lying down, trying hard with all your body to sense what's going on, any sound and any movement is amplified as it passes through you.

Seeing that the wind was noisy but not really dangerous, I calmed down a bit and climbed back into the tent.

I was drawn back into a doze. I put my arm round the rucksack and fell asleep to the rhythmless sound of the wind.

About two hours later I was woken by some kind of weight. There was something lying on my back, above the tarpaulin that covered me. I was petrified, and lay there without moving as sleep deserted me. Then I moved a little and heard a kind of hissing sound.

I slowly turned over on to my back and felt the weight that had been pressing me down growing lighter. I raised myself up on my elbows with a bolder movement, without climbing out of the tarpaulin, and the weight slithered off me. I realised that the wind had almost buried me in sand. I got out, shook down the top sheet of the tent and climbed back in again.

I didn't feel like sleeping now. I listened to the wind and beat on the tarpaulin from below to throw off the invisible sand. And I couldn't think about anything any more. I was on duty, protecting my life and my journey against the dangers that the Caspian wind carried into the desert.

But the wind increased in strength. My back began to hurt – either from the uncomfortable position or the constant squirming about. My hands began hurting too. Without even noticing it, I had worn myself out. The thought came to me that the effort I had made in struggling with this flying sand had been excessive. That I could toss the sand off the tarpaulin simply by turning from one side on to the other every half-hour. And I stopped moving completely, to allow my exhausted body some rest.

I lay there, listening to the wind. I tried to guess what time it was, but that soon made me tired again – this time mentally.

Then, suddenly, either the situation or my own condition reminded me of the flight into invisible space that I had made in the baby-food storeroom where I was working as a nightwatchman. I recalled the amazing sensations of flight that the 'out-of-date dried milk' had given me when I added it to instant coffee. A sensation of flying, granted me in exchange for the fear I was feeling at the time. The exchange was clearly unequal, but to my advantage. I gutted my rucksack and found a can of the powder, then opened it.

I stuck two fingers in and licked the powder off them, then turned over on to my other side, towards the canister of water, and took several sips. At first it seemed as if these two components really had combined in my mouth to produce warm milk. But after about thirty seconds my tongue felt an unexpected sweetness, and then the sweetness flowed downwards, spreading throughout my whole body. I started losing weight, and this unexpected lightness carried my body beyond my control. I couldn't move an arm or a leg, although I could still feel them. I tried to regain at least some physical contact with my limbs, without attempting to make any movements. I simply tried feeling my hands and then my feet by turns. I thought I managed it with my right hand. I even seemed to feel the tips of my fingers from the inside. But just then my weight became negative and I started rising up above the ground. I was lighter than air, soaring up higher and higher, without knowing where the tarpaulin tent that was covering me had got to. I was borne along on the Caspian wind, whose strength and smell I knew so well, it was lifting me higher and higher. I saw grains of sand flying along beside me, but they were heavier than me, and as soon as a gust of wind eased off, they went tumbling downwards, as if some invisible supports had been knocked away from under them. But I went on flying along, and I went on rising higher. And the point came when I realised that I had risen higher than the wind. Now my ascent was smooth and vertical. I could already see the stars coming closer, which meant I had pierced the black shroud in

93

which the sky had draped itself for the period of the storm. There were some bizarre celestial insects bustling around me, sometimes catching me with a sharp foot or a feeler. But I didn't feel any fear – somehow I was sure that they were perfectly harmless and friendly. One of these insects rose with me for a while, right in front of my face, examining me with frank curiosity. It reminded me a bit of a crayfish, only instead of claws it had a multitude of long spider-legs. I felt like shaking one of them and tried to reach out my hand.

Although my hand did not obey me the insect, clearly sensing my intention, took fright and disappeared into the dense blue mass of the sky that was drawing me into itself.

24

Time stretched out like a piece of chewing gum. Then it retracted back into a single lump and changed shape, while still remaining frozen. I toyed with it, like a playful cosmonaut with a drop of water in free fall. My flight turned into a glide, my arms and legs obeying me now, and I used them to continue my smooth movement, feeling more like a slow bird than a man.

I was floating in a dense blueness that allowed my eyes to see only for ten or fifteen metres ahead. I kept gazing around, noticing strange creatures and objects appearing in my field of vision. They floated past me unhurriedly and disappeared back into that tender, alluring dense blueness, as if they were concealing sweet secrets or the gates of heaven from my eyes.

At one point I noticed a man with a large bald spot and a grey moustache drifting past me, dressed in old-fashioned clothes – a long shirt belted round with a piece of rope. He had a blissful smile on his face and his eyes seemed to be smiling too, but the expression was fixed and motionless, like the lens of a film camera. He ran this gaze over me and I felt a wave of warmth, as if the fire screen of a village stove had just been opened in front of my face. After he disappeared into the dense blueness, the warmth remained there inside me and seemed to be living a life of its own. It enveloped me in its gentle embrace, and when I thought with a vague discontent that any moment now I would start feeling too hot, the invisible warmth released its grip on me slightly, moved away to an invisible distance and warmed me from there, gently and just a little insistently.

Someone else soon went flying past, waving from inside the diaphanous sphere. He flew past slowly, and I had time to see that the sphere was not homogeneous and whirling around inside it, together with the man, there were some small, round objects. 'A planet-man,' I thought, and immediately felt a twinge of pain in my chest. An image of the planet Earth, softly muffled in the same kind of sphere, appeared before my eyes. Through the semi-transparent blueness I could see the familiar outlines of continents and seas, and I suddenly realised the Earth had surfaced out of my imagination, materialised as a small, soft, round globe and begun moving away from me, with its outer sphere fluttering. I wanted to catch up with it, and I started swimming forward with the crawl stroke, as if I were in water. As if it had spotted my pursuit, the Earth speeded up and at the same time started moving downwards. I carried on swimming after it. I picked up so much speed that the warmth I had been given went flying off me, and then my speed increased again, but at the same time I started feeling cold. And the Earth started feeling cold too – I saw the way its sphere thickened and the forms familiar from my geography lessons disappeared in its turbid whiteness, so that what was flying along ahead of me now was simply a sphere of milky whiteness. But I knew that it was the Earth, and so I continued to pursue it until I ran into an invisible barrier.

When I ran into it, I felt a pain in my neck. My throat suddenly felt dry and itchy, then it became hard to breathe, there wasn't enough air. I opened my mouth and stretched my lips so wide that it hurt, but it didn't help. My vision blurred. My arms and legs went limp, and someone grabbed me by the legs and started dragging me back. 'Back to where?' I wondered as I lost consciousness.

25

Jamshed, a short, lean Kazakh with eyes that were always smiling, lived in a nomad tent, or yurt, with his two daughters, Gulya and Natasha. Gulya was staggeringly beautiful, with long legs and an incredibly clear complexion, which was especially noticeable when she was standing beside Natasha, whose face had been cruelly affected by smallpox. They were both a head taller than their father.

I was slowly recovering, lying on a heap of rags in the yurt and squinting at the bright sunlight coming in through a triangle where a flap of material had been folded back.

It was the second day I had been there, still feeling the woodenness in my muscles and joints.

But this was the second day of consciousness. I didn't know yet how long I had been lying there before that. The owners of the yurt took care of me, but without speaking, as if they were afraid that it was dangerous for me to talk. I must say that I myself was by no means certain that I could speak. My tongue lay in my mouth like a heavy, immovable stone and its bitter, sour immobility occasionally made me feel sick. I wanted really badly to rinse my mouth out with some kind of mouthwash.

Gulya came in wearing a long green shirt-dress and white trousers. She had a large cup in her hand. She leaned down over me and set the cup to my lips. I opened my mouth and a bitter, milky liquid poured into it – not exactly what I felt like just at the moment. But I drank it, especially since my lips had dried out, and the touch of the cool earthenware of the cup proved more pleasant than the drink itself. Still without saying a word, Gulya moved away from me, rummaged in a cardboard box standing on the floor of the yurt and went out.

I lay there alone for about half an hour, hearing the Kazakh language being spoken loudly and beautifully outside the yurt – Jamshed was arguing about something with his daughters. Then it went quiet.

I fell asleep.

I was woken by a sensation of coolness. Surprised, I opened my eyes and immediately looked at the yurt entrance. It was still light outside, but no longer sunny. I could hear the crackling of a campfire; glimmers of light flickered just beyond the open flap. I raised myself up on my elbows. My body was heavy, but it was already beginning to obey me again. My arms, at least, were back completely and I leaned on them, to lift myself up, then lowered my feet on to the carpet and froze. I sat like that for about ten minutes and then stood up, staggering on legs that were not fully under control, and walked to the exit.

I looked out.

Jamshed was sitting by the fire, with a heap of dry feather grass and some kind of brushwood on his left. His daughters were sitting facing him, with their backs to me, and there were two camels standing about ten metres behind them close to the tent. The camels were standing quite still, so that at first they seemed like a single camel with multiple humps, blocking off part of the evening horizon and the sky. But one of them suddenly shook its head and my vision was immediately replaced by reality. Then the other camel took a step backwards and lowered its muzzle to the sand.

'Ah! Come over!' Jamshed called to me. 'If not for Khatema, you would have been done for.'

'Who's Khatema?' I asked, looking round at the girls, whose names I already knew. Jamshed nodded towards the camels.

'Khatema noticed a piece of tarpaulin and went over and started pulling it . . . We shouted and shouted for her, then went over and saw too. So we got you out . . . Not everyone is that lucky . . .'

'Thank you,' I said and cast a glance at the camels, to one of which I owed my life.

'Where were you going?' Jamshed asked.

'Fort Shevchenko.'

'But why on foot?'

I shrugged.

'A traveller?'

I sighed. 'I make a lousy traveller,' I said with feeling after a long pause.

'Why?' Jamshed objected. 'You got here, so already you're a traveller. But why alone, with no woman?'

'I don't have a woman . . .'

Jamshed pondered on that, then turned and looked at his camels.

'But why you want Fort Shevchenko?' he asked, looking at me again.

The fire crackled, rapidly consuming more and more of the sprigs of uprooted brushwood that Jamshed fed to it without looking. And his daughters sat there quietly without moving, as if they weren't listening to the conversation.

'I've come from Kiev,' I began slowly, trying to answer without deceiving them, but also without revealing the purpose of my journey completely. 'I wanted to take a look at the places where Shevchenko served . . .'

'You Ukrainian?' Jamshed asked in surprise.

'No, Russian. But I've lived in Kiev all my life.'

Jamshed nodded. 'It would be good for you to meet Akyrbai,' he said, nodding his head thoughtfully. 'Akyrbai knows a lot about *akin* Shevchenko. He was friends with his kinfolk.'

'With what kinfolk?' I asked in amazement.

'With his Kazakh kinfolk . . . With his great-great-great-grandson, until he got lost in Karatau. There's nowhere to get lost there, but he went and disappeared . . .'

'But he didn't have any sons or grandsons,' I said rather sharply.

'Well, he couldn't marry, of course. Soldiers weren't allowed to. But a Kazakh woman, a shepherd's daughter, had a son by him . . . The line continued after that, and all the men in it were good *akins*. And the last one, who disappeared in Karatau, was a fine *akin* too. A very good *akin*, he was . . . back in Soviet times he could retell any article from *Pravda* in verse as he read it. What an *akin* he was! I've never heard another one like him, before or since!'

Meanwhile, Jamshed's daughters went on sitting there as

motionless and silent as sphinxes, and that made me feel awkward. Even the camels moved, snorting and making other sounds, but there wasn't a single sigh or a breath from Gulya and Natasha. And I suddenly wanted very much to hear a woman's voice. Especially since I had heard them talking to their father while I was lying in the yurt.

'Jamshed,' I asked, casting aside my reserve, 'why don't they say anything?' I nodded at the girls.

'The men are talking,' Jamshed explained calmly.

Then he smiled, as if he had guessed what I wanted. He said something to his daughters in Kazakh. Natasha went into the yurt and came back with some kind of musical instrument that looked like a mandolin. And she started singing, plucking at the strings with her fingers.

She sang in Kazakh. Her pretty voice was enchanting, melodic as though designed to encourage you to sing along. But although the melody was not complicated, I didn't even try to hum. And I suddenly noticed that while Natasha sang, Gulya was watching me intently and very frankly. I felt myself melt under the gaze of her eyes, which seemed to glow in the brand-new night that was lit only by the campfire and the deep blue sky. Frightened, I turned my eyes to Jamshed and saw the fixed smile in his eyes, only now that smile seemed to have come to life. But Natasha's song went on and on, and I had the idea that their attentive gazes were connected in some way with the words of this song that I couldn't understand.

And surprisingly enough, I was quite right.

'This is a song about a traveller who is saved by a she-camel and brought to a house where two girls live,' Jamshed told me when it was quiet again.

I was stunned. At first I didn't know what to say. But then I asked:

'And what happens afterwards to this traveller in the song?'

'The girls' father tells him to choose one of the girls in order to continue his journey with her. One of the daughters is beautiful, the other is not. One will never love him, the other will love him and remember him forever. But he chooses the one who will not love him and leaves with her . . .'

'And then?'

'She did not finish the song,' Jamshed said with a sigh. I turned my eyes to Natasha. She was sitting there in silence, having put her instrument down on the sand beside her. I looked at Gulya and met her intent gaze again. And I immediately turned my eyes away, still perturbed by the words of the song.

'Do you have any water?' I asked in order to distract myself from my thoughts. Jamshed looked at Gulya. She went into the yurt and came back with a large cup in her hand. She held out the cup to me. I took a gulp – it was something like kefir again.

'Don't you drink pure water?'

'We do,' Jamshed replied. 'When there's nothing else . . .'

I stopped talking and finished the kefir. Then put the cup down on the sand.

I looked at Natasha. 'Excuse me, but do you know how the words of that song go on?' I asked her.

She looked at her father in fright, as if she expected him to help her.

'You know, she was making it up as she went along . . . She is an *akin* too, but you must not tell anyone. Women are not supposed to be *akins*. If they find out, no one will take her as a wife . . .and she did not finish it because every complete story ends badly . . . A good *akin* never finishes even a well-known song with a bad ending . . .'

My mouth had gone dry again, and I asked for another drink. Gulya went into the yurt again and refilled my cup.

'Which of my daughters do you like?' Jamshed suddenly asked.

I gaped at him, stunned. But he used his eyes to direct my gaze in the direction of the girls.

'Gulya,' I confessed.

He nodded with an air as if he had known beforehand what my answer would be. It wasn't really that hard to guess, although a little later I did think how good it would be if Gulya had Natasha's voice . . .

26

When I woke up in the morning, Gulya was sitting on my rucksack on the carpet in the yurt and looking at me. The canister was standing beside her, full of water.

I realised that I had been 'packed' for the road. I remembered the strange conversation of the night before and Natasha's unfinished song.

I looked around for Jamshed, but he wasn't in the yurt. He was sitting on the sand. The sun was not yet hot and he was thinking about something, gazing wistfully at the sand. I walked over to him.

'Good morning.'

'Hello,' he replied, looking up.

'Jamshed,' I said, addressing him in a gentle, polite voice, 'where do I go from here? Which is the best way to get to Fort Shevchenko?'

'Gulya knows the way,' he replied.

'Are you letting her go with me?' I asked in amazement, still unable to believe what was happening.

'Listen,' said Jamshed, looking me in the eye, 'you were saved by my she-camel, and now you have to do as I wish . . . you chose Gulya yourself . . .'

'Yes, but . . . does she want to go?'

'When a father travels with two daughters, they think bad things about him. It means that no one wants to take them for wives.'

'Yes, but you don't know me!' I went on, still not entirely grasping the situation, although even to me it seemed stupid to continue the conversation, especially since I really did find Gulya attractive.

'My she-camel saved you,' Jamshed repeated wearily. 'You smell of cinnamon, that means you are a good man, filled with a spirit that will survive you and preserve the memory of you in another . . .'

I said nothing more, standing there between the yurt and Jamshed. What was there to argue about? Why on earth would I try to persuade the old man not to let his beautiful daughter go with me?

I simply nodded. And went back into the yurt.

Gulya was doing something with my bed of rags, turning layers over and folding them, as if she were changing bedclothes.

When she heard my breathing, she looked round and smiled at me timidly. She was wearing white trousers again, this time peeping out from under a long blue shirt-dress with a short standing collar.

'Well, shall we go?' I asked, thinking that I hadn't even heard her voice yet.

'Yes,' she answered. 'We just have to wait for Natasha – she went to get some cheese.'

'Where from?' I asked, thinking that there couldn't be a market or a grocery store anywhere close.

'Marat is camped nearby, my father's nephew. He has lots of goats – he makes cheese . . . Do you want some tea?'

I nodded. Then I realised that apart from their kefir I hadn't eaten anything for the last few days, but I still didn't have any appetite. But my lips were feeling dry.

Gulya went out of the yurt and came back with a small bowl of unsweetened tea.

I sat on the carpet, trying to fold my legs in the same way as Jamshed did when he sat down. I managed to get down, but as I did my knees cracked so loudly that Gulya looked away. I somehow felt guilty, without understanding where the feeling had come from.

I sat there, slowly drinking green tea, using it to pass the time. Eventually Natasha came back. After exchanging a few words in Kazakh with her father, she walked into the yurt, holding a small linen sack in her hands. She handed it to Gulya with just a faint nod, saying nothing. Gulya took hold of the bag, took out several small white balls, chose the smallest one and popped it into her mouth. I could see her rolling it about on her tongue, as if she was examining its taste intently. A light smile of satisfaction appeared on her beautiful face. She rolled the ball against her teeth with her tongue, then took it in her fingers and held it out to me. I put the ball of cheese in my mouth.

After the green tea, the salty-bitter taste of the cheese, with a slightly acid bite, filled my mouth. It was a pleasantly cool sensation. And the air I breathed in seemed to be enriched with this taste, transporting it into my lungs, so that the pleasing coolness filtered inside me, bringing with it a kind of physical tranquillity.

Tranquillity of the body, not the soul. But my soul was also at peace. I wasn't thinking about what Jamshed had said any more. Life was simpler than words: the wait for the cheese had been replaced by the taste of the cheese. The taste of the cheese had been transferred to my breath. My breath, imbued with this taste, had brought me a pleasurable sensation of tranquil certainty. The wait for the journey was just about to be replaced by the journey.

Half an hour later Jamshed helped me to throw the rucksack and canister of water, tied together, across the back of the she-camel Khatema. We also threw up a double bundle of Gulya's things.

'Go as far as the hills,' Jamshed said, 'and then let Khatema go. She will come back here.'

I didn't know how to say goodbye to Jamshed. If he had been Russian, I would simply have given him a hug. But if he had been Russian, he wouldn't have let his daughter go with me. And if he had let her go, I would have had to call him 'Dad' and have a drink with him for the road.

While I was thinking, Jamshed himself came up to me, put a white pointed felt cap on my head and held out his hand.

'Pleasant journey,' he said. 'If you're going to beat her' – he nodded in Gulya's direction – 'don't beat her on the face!'

I nodded automatically, although after a while, walking beside the she-camel, these final words of Jamshed's seemed a bit harsh to me.

But before I thought about that, I felt a desire to repay him somehow for his gift. I pulled the tarpaulin tent out of the rucksack and presented it to him.

We walked towards the hills that could be seen in the distance. The sun was already heating up the sand.

The yurt had been left behind.

Walking on my left was the she-camel, carrying our baggage. Walking on my right was Gulya.

'Your father told me you know the way,' I said, simply in order to start talking to her.

'I do,' she replied. 'We used to walk there, but we never went as far as the fort. There was no need . . .'

The sun was scorching and if not for Jamshed's present of the felt cap, my brains would have been boiling in my head already. But even so, I didn't know how to continue the conversation. I didn't say anything. And Gulya didn't say anything either. We walked on like that, side by side. I kept looking at her, admiring her profile – vivacious, proud and feminine all at the same time.

'Maybe this evening, when we make a halt, we'll get talking,' I thought hopefully.

27

We stopped for a halt when the sun had just turned white, as if it had been cooled by the cold wind that had suddenly blown up. It was still hanging high, but in the sunset half of the sky. There was a long way to go to the hills. They didn't seem to have come any closer, although we had been moving towards them for eight hours or even longer, only stopping once to take a rest and feed Khatema.

'Gulya, is the sea a long way from here?' I asked, recalling the soothing coolness of the Caspian shoreline.

'Yes, a long way,' Gulya replied, looking at me with her brown eyes.

I started thinking, wondering how we had ended up so far from the Caspian.

'Do you like the sea?' I asked Gulya, who was taking her bundle off the camel.

'No,' she replied. 'It's cold.'

I shrugged. Then I helped her lower the double bundle on to the sand. She took out a striped linen bed mat, then another one. She laid one on top of the other.

When the sun was lying on the distant sands and its cooled fire had seeped down and away, like water, it became chilly in the desert. The air was instantly colder than the sand. We lay side by side on one mat, covered up to our chests with the other. We looked at the sky. Every now and then the she-camel, tied to the strap of my rucksack with a short rein, sighed huskily.

'Gulya,' I said, 'doesn't it seem funny to you that the two of us are here together?'

'No,' Gulya replied, so decisively that I lost my train of thought and now I just wanted to talk to her about anything at all. I wanted to learn something about her, so that the distance between our eyes and our thoughts would be reduced. I wanted to understand her and I wanted her to understand me.

'She already understands you anyway' – the thought came to me unexpectedly.

I started musing again, looking up at the sky and trying to find the reflection of her eyes, which were also looking up to where the seeds of the stars were sprouting on the blue inverted ground of the sky. They were emerging rapidly and chaotically, as if they had been scattered by a sower in love who was not thinking at all about what he was doing. And there was a satellite creeping between them like some lazy heavenly tractor. Its movement caught my eye and, squinting sideways at Gulya, I thought that she was watching that satellite now too – a person's gaze always searches for movement. A person's gaze is a curious investigator and loves to follow what is going on.

As the celestial field sprouted above us, we both watched this everyday miracle. I didn't even want to talk any more – our shared observation seemed to bring us close without any words.

As the sand cooled, the sky moved lower and the stars became clearer.

I wanted to hear Gulya's voice again and turned towards her. But she was already sleeping, with her eyes closed. Her gentle, regular breathing warmed the silence of the night and I listened it to it with secret delight, as if it were something forbidden, and therefore even more greatly desired.

The satellite-tractor dipped behind some celestial hillside and was hidden from view, leaving the stars behind. I was falling asleep to the delicate music of Gulya's breathing. The still air seemed to be listening to her breathing as well. And in that silence I felt something creeping across the thick striped material covering my legs.

I froze, listening to the movement with my skin, until I saw either a scorpion or a lizard on my chest, posing beautifully with its fantastical profile thrust up into the sky.

'Don't move,' I told myself. And so I didn't, and neither did this nocturnal denizen of the desert until I fell asleep.

28

The she-camel's snort woke me so abruptly that after I opened my eyes I lay there for several minutes, waiting for my body to wake up. The sun was barely on the rise, which meant I hadn't slept for long. Finally I turned my head to look at Gulya, but she wasn't there beside me.

I was overcome by a sudden, obscure fear when I felt an alien weight on the striped cover on my chest. I looked and saw a chameleon wearing the same stripes sitting there with his head held high, entirely motionless except for his round little eyes, which seemed to move together with their slightly protruding sockets. Catching my gaze on his, he froze likewise.

Khatema snorted and sniffed again. I looked round at her – the she-camel was clearly uneasy about something. She was stepping from one foot to another and looking towards me.

Then she took a step back, dragging my rucksack, to which her rein was tied, after her over the sand.

I had to get up. I tried to shake the chameleon off gently, but he had taken such a firm grip on the striped bed mat that he was almost part of it.

Remembering that chameleons are not aggressive, but rather the opposite, I climbed out from under the mat, got up and looked around. Gulya's disappearance had frightened me. If she had simply gone somewhere, then why hadn't she told me, and if . . . ? At that point a chilly shiver ran across my skin and I didn't even try to complete the thought. There was a dry, unpleasant feeling in my mouth. I walked over to the canister of water and took a gulp.

When I looked around again, I was delighted to see Gulya about two hundred metres away. She was carrying an armful of dry brushwood.

'Good morning,' she said with a smile. She struck a match and the fire, built in the shape of a little tent, began crackling.

'Good morning,' I answered.

Gulya took an iron tripod and a cooking pot out of her bundle, set this travelling contraption over the fire and poured water into the pot. All her movements were graceful and precise. I watched her admiringly, but at the same time I felt an almost parental desire to admonish her, for educational purposes.

'Gulya,' I said, trying to speak as gently as possible, 'please, don't do that again. I was worried . . .'

Gulya turned to look at me. Her beautiful face expressed surprise, which was replaced a moment later by a half-smile.

'You don't need to worry about me,' she said. 'I grew up here . . . I'm the one who should worry about you . . .'

'Why?' It was my turn to be surprised now.

'Because you are mine and I have to take care of you . . .'

'I am yours and you are mine?' I asked her, pronouncing the words slowly and too distinctly, listening carefully as I spoke, afraid of hearing a note of platitude or banality – and even more afraid of hearing them in her reply to this strange question.

'No,' Gulya said calmly. 'You are mine . . .'

'And you?' I asked again, getting confused in her logic.

'And I am beside you . . . It was our she-camel Khatema, who saved you.'

'That means I belong to all three of you, and not just to you,' I said with a nod, recalling my last conversation with Jamshed. The meaning of the old man's words was beginning to seem a bit clearer.

'Do not be offended,' Gulya said, smiling and looking into my face with her brown eyes. 'You are mine. You chose me, didn't you?'

'Because I liked you,' I said, but my voice sounded sad.

'But it is good when a present chooses its future owner,' said Gulya, glancing into the pot of water hanging above the crackling fire.

I didn't say anything. Her final words had floored me completely. So I was the one who was the present!

I sat on the mat with my eyes fixed on the chameleon who was still frozen on it, apparently pretending to be stuffed.

Gulya brought me a bowl of green tea and offered me several small balls of cheese on her palm. I took one, put it in my mouth and began rolling it around with my tongue, spreading the salty taste out across the roof of my mouth.

Gulya sat down beside me. She looked at me and then, following the direction of my gaze, saw the chameleon.

'How lovely!' she exclaimed, leaning forward slightly. I thought I saw the chameleon twitch in fright at the sound of her words and look at her.

I gradually calmed down as I came to terms with what she had said. Perhaps there really was nothing bad or even odd about a present choosing who it wants to belong to . . . For thousands of years, at least, women, who had often been presents, had not had the choice.

The sun was rising higher. We sat beside each other on the striped bed mat and identical bedspread. We drank tea, rolled little balls of cheese around in our mouths, and watched the chameleon, who looked at each of us in turn.

'I got a bad fright,' I eventually confessed to Gulya. 'The camel starting snorting and dragging the rucksack away. I jumped up and you weren't there.'

'Khatema started snorting?' Gulya asked in surprise. She got up. Leaving her tea bowl on the mat, she walked over to the she-camel, stroked her and looked at the track of the rucksack that had been dragged a couple of paces. Then she followed the line of the track further in the opposite direction. She walked about thirty metres and stopped.

'Kolya!' she called to me from there. 'Come here!' I walked over to her and saw the indentations of tracks on the sand. It was a single pair of tracks. Someone had reached this spot, then stopped, crouched down and stood up again, dawdled on the spot and gone away again.

I immediately recalled the tracks I had seen around myself that morning on the Caspian shoreline. Should I tell Gulya about that? Or would she be frightened?

'It's not a Kazakh,' Gulya said calmly.

'How do you know?' I asked in surprise.

'Kazakhs don't run on sand, and someone ran away from here.' We walked back to the camel without speaking. We gathered our things together. Only the bedspread with the chameleon clinging to it was left on the sand. I didn't know what to do with him.

'He wants us to take him with us,' said Gulya.

I sighed. I didn't feel like picking him up, although I knew that chameleons don't bite.

'They say chameleons bring good luck to nomads . . .' Gulya said pensively.

She crouched down in front of him and stroked him and he took a jerky step and turned his ugly little face, so unlike his motionless nocturnal profile, towards her.

'That's why he likes to roam about at night,' I thought. 'You should always roam at the time when you look most handsome.'

Gulya folded up the bedspread, and the chameleon stood on the sand beside her, watching her movements.

'Now we'll find a place for you,' Gulya told him. After all the luggage was stowed on the camel, she picked up the chameleon and set him on my blue-and-yellow rucksack. The chameleon gripped the yellow part of the rucksack with his claws and turned yellow, then he moved to the blue part and just as quickly turned blue. He froze there in anticipation of the journey.

I put on my pointed felt hat – the present from Jamshed to the present to his daughter – and we set off. We walked slightly ahead of Khatema, and Gulya held the camel's rein in her hands. She looked like the mistress of the spreading sands around us, and also of our little caravan and of the hills that were still visible in the distance, but were simply not coming any closer.

29

The next night I slept lightly but sweetly. I dreamed that Gulya and I were lying beside each other so that I was enveloped in her warmth, and every now and then I held my breath in order to hear the beating of her heart through her skin. I woke suddenly and easily when I felt a movement on my chest. I opened my eyes and saw a familiar sight – the chameleon was sitting on top of the striped bedspread that covered me, with his handsome profile uplifted towards the sky. He seemed to be on guard, his motionless stance was akin to revolutionary vigilance.

'Why has he latched on to us?' I wondered, raising my head to get a better look at him in the blue gloom of the night. 'Has he taken such a great liking to us, or is he simply lonely in the desert? Well, OK, if he brings good luck it would be stupid to drive him away.'

The chameleon's appearance had focused my thoughts on him, and I started thinking we ought to give him name, since he had joined us. I began running through names in my mind, but human names and dogs' names didn't suit him. I had to find some kind of human prototype. But as the chameleon-like political leaders lined up inside my head, I began feeling embarrassed for the poor reptile: why should I want to name him in honour of people unworthy of either love or trust? And so, in order to make amends, I decided to name him in honour of my grandad – Petrovich. The patronymic without a given name sounded far more respectable and at the same time more homely than a name without a patronymic.

'Well then, Petrovich,' I whispered to him, 'how do you like Gulya?'

Petrovich didn't answer. He continued his motionless posing, without even shifting his ball-and-socket eyes.

I sighed and looked at Gulya, sleeping peacefully on her side, with her face turned towards me.

'That's a good sign,' I thought. 'Last night she slept on her back . . .'

I moved closer to Gulya, trying not to disturb her sleep. I moved in to the distance of her breath and glanced into her beautiful face. I looked at it for a long time, until my eyes, completely accommodated to the blue gloom, forgot that it was night.

Displeased by my movement, Petrovich moved across on to Gulya and froze on her thigh, apparently believing that this was the highest point of the desert, from which he could maintain his watch.

And then I fell into a sweet sleep so sound that in the morning I couldn't remember anything I had dreamed about during the night.

30

The white hills were gradually drawing closer. We had been walking for four days already and I had told her in more detail about the reasons that had obliged me to make my present journey and about its goal. And thanks to that we had got to know each other. She listened attentively, but she didn't ask any questions – on the contrary, she demonstrated a mystifying, lofty kind of respect for what I said. But I wanted so much for her to ask about something, to take a personal interest in some details of my story. I thought that would be a fairly good sign that she was interested in me. But she kept silent and listened, without filling in the pauses that arose, and I saw this as simply the traditional respect for a man when he is speaking, rather than anything more. Even so, walking along and telling her about my life was so enjoyable and amusing that at one point I suddenly noticed I was exaggerating a little bit, adding tragic details to certain events and elements of pathos or humour to others. But I could see from her eyes that she found it interesting to listen to me, and I carried on. Not until my mouth was completely dried out from talking did I fall silent and reach out my hands for the canister of water dangling from the camel's side.

We stopped. I drank.

The sun was already high in the sky and, without knowing what time it was, I instinctively estimated the length of the dotted line of its remaining journey to sunset. It turned out that the lamp of heaven's working day was due to end in about five hours.

'Are we going to climb the mountains, then?' I asked Gulya when we set off again.

'No,' she replied. 'We'll go as far as Besmanchak, then we'll let Khatema go back, and walk round the hills on the sand.'

I nodded. Naturally, the idea that soon I would have to carry all my luggage on my own shoulders was not a very cheerful one. We spent the night on some kind of salt crust instead of sand. The cracked, white ground looked as if it had been sprinkled with crystalline powder and felt hard after walking on the sand. This surface had risen from under the sand and abutted the gently ascending hills, acting as a kind of foundation for them, forming a narrow strip – about a hundred or a hundred and fifty metres wide – that stretched along the foot of the hills, trying to follow the line of their curves. But nature's geometry was rather poor, and so in some places the strip of salt crust disappeared altogether, allowing the sand to reach right up to the very base of the hills.

As we settled down for the night, we spread out some additional throws from Gulya's double bundle on the salt crust, and then put the two little pillows that smelled of camel and the striped mats or covers on top of them.

It was cool under the hills, and when the sun had finally seeped all the way down behind the horizon, the chill seemed to pierce right through me. Somehow it just happened that, as we lay down to sleep, we found ourselves closer to each other than ever before and I put my arm round Gulya. She was lying on her side with her face towards me, but her eyes were already closed.

Perhaps she was already asleep and she simply didn't feel my hand, or perhaps she was pretending. I lay like that for a long time, probably about half an hour. I lay with my eyes open, admiring her, and at one point I moved my lips close to hers and froze like that, feeling her warmth and her breath on the skin of my face. I didn't kiss her that night. I don't know why. I wanted to kiss her terribly, I wanted a lot more than that. But can a present kiss its owner without first asking permission? What nonsense! Those ideas had got stuck in my head! It made just as much sense to think that Jamshed had given her to me. After all, I had chosen her! If not for that conversation, that was what I would have believed. But a peculiar mixture of tradition and democratic feeling had introduced such confusion into the situation that I couldn't even think about it without getting annoyed.

I suspended my face in front of hers again but then, still not having kissed her lips, I lowered my head on to the pillow and gazed at the sky, with the satellite-tractor creeping across it once again, intent on its own business. Then I felt the chameleon Petrovich climb up on to my chest and thrust his profile into the starry sky once again.

'Everything's fine,' I told myself. 'The nightwatch is at its post. I can go to sleep . . .'

31

The following day we reached Besmanchak. This was the name of a beautiful spot at which two shallow spurs of the hills formed a regular triangular gorge, open on one side. At the centre of the triangle of salt crust there was an old grave – a slab of stone that had either sunk deep into the ground or had been set into it sometime. Rising up out of one side of the slab was a narrow stone column the height of a man, with a green kerchief tied around its top. I had never seen any graves like it before, and my curiosity encouraged me to go closer. I made out Arabic cursive script on the narrow column.

Gulya came up to me from behind.

'A wandering dervish is buried here,' she said. 'He was killed by Kirghiz nomads.'

'Why?'

'The daughter of one of them fell in love with the dervish and said she would stay with him until he died. Her father killed the dervish and took her home. Then he came back with his brothers and they buried him here.'

'But why didn't he let her go with him?' I asked, thinking that this story bore a distant resemblance to my own.

'A dervish cannot have a home and so he is not supposed to have a wife,' Gulya replied.

'Well, thank God I'm not a dervish,' I thought. 'After all, I do have a home in Kiev.'

Right there beside the dervish's grave, we took the luggage off the camel, sat down to rest on a striped bed mat and had something to eat. Then Gulya gathered up an armful of the dry stalks and branches of plants that had attempted unsuccessfully to survive on the salt crust in this place, started a fire and set the tripod with the cooking pot over it. Soon we were drinking green tea, holding it in our mouths and rinsing salty balls of cheese about in it.

Having told Gulya practically everything about my life during our journey together, I was feeling more comfortable with her now, despite the fact that I knew almost nothing about her own life. The peace and quiet of this place encouraged conversation.

'Gulya,' I asked, 'have you always lived in the yurt with your father?'

'No, not always . . . I went to Alma-Ata to study, for six years . . .'

'And where did you study?'

'I graduated from medical college,' she said, lowering her eyes modestly.

'And then you came straight back to your father?'

'Yes,' she said with a nod. 'If I had married there, I would have stayed . . .'

'But why didn't you marry?' I asked.

Gulya shrugged. 'There were a lot of boys there with rich parents, who wouldn't have let them marry me . . . But I didn't want to anyway . . . Have you ever been married?'

'No,' I answered. 'I lived with one woman for two years – she was from another city. Then she wanted to bring her mother to live us, and I realised it was time to put an end to our cohabitation . . . It was a small apartment, and our relationship was already on the wane, so the arrival of her mother was unlikely to add any romance to it. Then I decided to live on my own, and I found I liked it. And I've already told you what came after that.'

Gulya nodded.

'Do you like me?' I asked her. We looked into each other's eyes.

'Yes,' she said in a quiet voice.

I felt good. The warm, slightly salty air caressed my face. Sitting there facing me was a beautiful woman who had just admitted that she was attracted to me. What more did I want? Nothing really, apart from to search for something that Taras Shevchenko had buried in the sand. And to be honest, even searching for something buried in the sand by Taras Shevchenko seemed a rather pointless, petty waste of time, not much like the goal of a great adventure. I didn't even know what he had buried there, or if he had really buried anything at all. Perhaps it was just the usual sort of false denunciation, made simply to stir up trouble for a detested Little Russian. It felt absurd even to think about Shevchenko at that moment, but then I immediately recalled the deceased Gershovich's notes about how Shevchenko adored woman more than anything else in the world.

I got up and sat down beside Gulya. I turned to face her and looked into her brown eyes.

'May I kiss you?' I asked awkwardly.

'A husband should not ask his wife's permission . . .' These words killed my feelings of exalted romance once again. But even so I took them as a simple 'yes' and leaned down towards her face, and our lips touched. What I feared most of all at that moment was that her lips would be still and passive, but fortunately I was wrong to have been afraid.

We kissed for several minutes. The kiss was sweet and salty. Its saltiness came either from the little balls of cheese that we had just been rolling about in our mouths until they dissolved, or from the very air surrounding us. I embraced Gulya and pressed her against myself. My hands felt her warmth. I kissed her neck, with my nose nuzzling in the silk of her hair.

The saltiness of her skin tasted sweet now, words became meaningless, leaving untouched those feelings and sensations that every man longs for and tries to cling to for as long as possible once he has found them.

32

The she-camel Khatema walked away from us slowly, stopping every now and then to look back.

'Will she go back on her own?' I asked.

'Yes,' said Gulya. 'It's time for us to go too.'

I packed the things, hoisted the rucksack on to my shoulders and picked up the canister of water. Then I glanced at the double bundle.

The bundle looked heavier than the rucksack to me, and I stepped towards it to check.

'I'll take it,' said Gulya, getting there before me.

She effortlessly slung the bundle's connecting belt across her shoulder and looked at me expectantly.

We walked along the strip of salt crust skirting the elevations of the hills, leaving Besmanchak and the grave of the murdered dervish behind us.

In this place the sun was not as hot as in the desert, although it seemed to hang at the centre of the sky, as if it was deliberately trying to maintain an equal distance from all horizons on every side. I thought how, when you look at the horizon, whatever direction, you never perceive it as the boundary line of a circle, although in simple logic it cannot be anything else. 'Evidently the Earth itself is not sufficiently round,' I decided and left it at that.

We walked beside each other. I kept glancing at Gulya, but she walked along without speaking, also absorbed in thoughts about something or other. And I didn't want to disturb her. After all, it was far more agreeable to make conversation in the evening, sitting on the bed mat, when I could not just talk, but also embrace her and kiss her again.

This time I wasn't going to ask permission, in order not to feel stupid. My complicated status seemed to have been defined, the i's had apparently all been dotted and the t's had all been crossed, and that allowed me to feel a bit more confident. It didn't matter whether a husband had been given as a gift, been chosen or had chosen for himself, he was still the head of the family, and at least the equal of his other half.

As evening approached we slowed down. The coolness descending from the sky mellowed the fatigue of the journey and the inertial effect on our fading energy allowed us to walk on for at least a kilometre before we halted in the small 'v' of a pseudo-ravine, like a miniaturised copy of the ravine with the dervish's grave. Shrugging off the rucksack and setting the already half-empty canister at my feet, I suddenly felt more cheerful again. Or perhaps it was simply that I had straightened up my shoulders once they were free of the weight of the rucksack.

Gulya also set down her double bundle, and immediately pulled out the bed mats. I watched her and caught myself not simply watching, but already admiring her with a feeling of either quiet boastfulness or pride: 'Look, if I have a wife like that, I can't be all that bad myself!'

And there was no one else around, apart from the chameleon Petrovich, frozen on the highest hump of a bundle that hadn't been emptied out yet.

That evening we ate the last can of Caspian Herring for supper.

Under the bewildered gaze of Gulya's brown eyes, I carefully inspected the contents of the open can and only then set it between us. The can was rapidly emptied, and after washing down our modest supper with water, we both began gathering the dry stalks of some plant or other and light, tumbled clumps of feather grass, camel's thorn and saltwort. Then we started a fire and began waiting for the water in the pot to come to the boil.

While the water was heating, the sun sank lower and lower, becoming darker and cosier. Then, as the steam rose from two tea bowls, I tried to make out its colour, for some reason thinking at that moment that the steam rising from green tea ought to be green too. Then a ball of cheese, rolled around my mouth, filled my mood with tart saltiness, and once again I was energised by thoughts and desires, this time as I watched Gulya slowly and gracefully lifting her tea bowl to her mouth. She was wearing a purple shirt-dress with her white trousers. 'When did she manage to get changed?' I thought, remembering that earlier in the day she had been wearing a lettuce-green shirt-dress with patterns that I had seen somewhere before on carpets.

The evening sheltered us in darkness and when we finished our tea we started settling down for the night.

The fire had extinguished itself and the final sparks were running along the smouldering stalks. Total silence fell, and as I covered myself with the striped bedcover, I cast a glance at our chameleon – he was still sitting on the bundle.

That night I was bolder and after several kisses I hugged Gulya against me energetically. I kissed her neck, untied her hair and immediately felt helpless in the face of her oriental clothing, which she did not remove for the night.

'Do you want me to get undressed?' she suddenly asked me in a half-whisper.

'Yes,' I answered, also in a half-whisper.

'Then I will have to rinse myself with water . . .' Gulya said, gazing at me in tender enquiry.

'All right,' I said.

'Then we will have no drinking water tomorrow.'

'Never mind.'

She got up and moved away a few steps. She undressed slowly – I followed her gentle, unhurried movements, which expressed her entire character. In the darkness, to which my eyes had already grown accustomed, Gulya stood there naked between the stars and the cracked salt crust, like a vision from the *Arabian Nights*.

She stood there without moving for a while, either listening to the silence or breathing in the air of that night with her body that had been liberated from clothes. Then she leaned down and picked up the canister of water. She unscrewed the lid, lifted the canister above her head and began gradually tilting it. I couldn't see the stream of water, but I heard it murmuring as it fell on to her shoulders and ran down over her body. She turned, and the full profile of her body made me think, ironically, of the beauties who pose for the various men's magazines. The water kept on babbling and flowing, and I envied it as it ran across her body, momentarily halting on the pointed nipples of her beautiful breasts before it fell, streaming down her smooth back, across her thighs, along her legs.

And a few minutes later, I already felt that the water and the entire world must envy me. I dried Gulya's tender skin, cool and moist, with my own body, I warmed her body with kisses, feeling the burning heat of my lips. The two of us warmed up together, and the palms of her hands, pressed into my back, felt very hot, but that heat was not enough for me, and we carried on heating each other until we reached that boiling point of passion beyond which there lies only death. Then we cooled down, listening to each other's breathing, seeing the desert dawn our through half-closed eyes. The morning that descended with the cool breeze from the hills into the small, irregular triangle of our shallow gorge felt like the earliest morning in the whole of my life. I wanted to prolong it, delay it, slow it down. And while the sun was clumsily scrambling up over the line of the horizon that was hidden from us by the uplift of the hills, that morning lasted, it endured almost for eternity, frozen motionless, like the hands of my watch. And I was glad of it.

33

Despite our sleepless night, we found it quite easy to rise and set out on our way. Although my dry lips were begging for water, I said nothing. I carried the unusually light plastic canister in one hand and Gulya walked beside me. Although she had the strap of the double bundle across her right shoulder, she walked lightly, as if the law of terrestrial gravity didn't apply to her. Our little chameleon sat on her left shoulder. Now he was pretending to be an extension of her emerald-green shirt-dress.

The sun was rising higher. I wanted green tea. I wanted to hear Gulya's voice, but my mouth was so dry, it felt as if any word I spoke could leave bloody scratches on my tongue or my gums.

At one point I noticed Gulya glancing sideways at me in a playful manner. I turned to look at her as we walked on. Our glances and our smiles met.

'There will be a well soon,' said Gulya, as if she had read my thoughts.

'And what if there isn't?'

'I'm used to it, but it will be hard for you.'

I nodded and immediately felt ashamed of my question. The blaze of desire should not depend on the presence or absence of a well. And thank God that the evening before I had not enquired about the nearest one.

The slopes of the hills that we were walking round grew steeper and steeper. Occasionally I raised my head and looked at these white ribbed monoliths tempered by the sun and the winds. What were they here for? What purpose did they serve? If nature was the basis of life, then these huge rocks had nothing to do with nature. Perhaps they were like immense weights, balancing some cordillera or other on the far side of the world. What did the existence of these huge rocks mean? Or was it pointless to seek for any meaning?

We walked without stopping for about six hours, until we saw the well, surrounded by a crudely built circle of large stones. When we reached it, I noticed that the salt crust round the well was somehow sleek and smooth, there were no cracks in it. But the well itself was unexpectedly shallow – no more than half a metre deep. And there wasn't much water in it – when I immersed my hand vertically, it went in only as far as my wrist until the tips of my fingers hit the slippery clay bottom. Lying there in the water was a large one-litre mug.

We filled up the canister. Then we got washed, sluicing each other down from the mug.

After that I was alarmed to notice that there was no water left in the well. I looked up in bewilderment at Gulya and saw a condescending smile on her face.

'It will fill up again while we brew the tea,' she said with a nod at the well.

There was enough material in this place to get a fire going. Soon we were drinking green tea.

We talked and I began feeling sleepy. Gulya noticed this and took one of the bed mats out of her bundle. I lay down on it and fell asleep instantly. When I woke up it was already late evening. The white tops of the hills were illuminated by the sun that was invisible from here below, but the light was climbing higher and higher as the sun slowly disappeared. After pausing on the very peak of the hill closest to us, it retreated higher still, dissolving into the sky.

I looked around and saw Gulya sitting on the stone rim of the well. And then I saw her shirt-dresses spread out on the stone slope of the monolith: red, lettuce green, emerald green, blue and another two, in colours that were hard to make out in the advancing darkness. While I was sleeping, Gulya had washed her clothes.

I ran my hands over my jeans and looked at my T-shirt. I started thinking.

'Not sleeping any more?' Gulya asked, turning towards me.

'No,' I replied.

'Tonight the sky will be very beautiful.'

'How do you know?'

'The sunset was very intense,' Gulya explained. I was no longer tired, and although night was advancing, my body felt rested and full of energy.

'All right, we'll watch the sky,' I said, and Gulya laughed briefly in reply.

'What is it?' I asked.

'Oh, nothing . . .'

I got up and walked over to her.

'I'm so happy today . . .' Gulya said, looking up at me when I stopped in front of her. 'I want to be this happy always . . .'

I leaned down to her face and kissed her lips. Words seemed inappropriate, and so I said nothing.

'Look, look!' Gulya whispered abruptly, pointing upwards.

I followed the direction of her gesture and saw a comet with a fiery tail.

The comet drifted sluggishly towards the horizon, but disappeared from view before ever reaching it.

That night I stretched out my arms and the warm sand that my hands touched felt soft and downy.

34

The dream that came to me just before morning left my body feeling invigorated, as if it had only now become mature enough for real life.

I rose from the mat with remarkable ease. Looking about, I saw the same beautiful coloured patches of Gulya's clothing laid out on the rising incline of the monolith. Gulya herself was not around, but her absence seemed natural, like part of the ritual of the morning, which started two hours earlier for her.

In about fifteen minutes, she would appear, carrying an airy, voluminous bundle of desert brushwood, on which our morning tea would be made. I wouldn't have been surprised if she'd returned with a hunting gun in one hand and a dead deer or young saiga in the other. Although, of course, that vision transformed me into a member of the third sex, a weak child in need of protection and care from both men and women.

My energy naturally sought an outlet and I set my feet apart at the width of my shoulders (following an instinctive response acquired long ago from the morning exercises on the radio) and started swinging my arms about. Then for a long time I did squats, leaning in different directions. And all with only a single goal in mind – to make myself feel at least a little bit tired. But it was no good. I seemed to have more energy after every swing of my arms. I stopped exercising and looked around again. And I saw Gulya, who had just emerged from behind one of the ridges that sloped down into the ground.

She was carrying brushwood. She was wearing her lettuce-green shirt-dress. She was walking slowly.

That light, airy clump of dry twigs and stalks looked like the frame for the bottom sphere of a snowman. And in the background the overlapping stone tongues of the rocky outcrops, retreating behind each other until they disappeared, looked like the ingenious stage setting for this clearly ancient epic poem. An epic performance in which everything remains immutable: the mountains and the sky and the sand and the beautiful Kazakh woman in the bright clothes. And only the traveller towards whom she is walking is in any way impermanent, or inconstant, like the electricity supply in the country. Beauty is immutable and eternal.

It is only those who fight for it, to possess it, who die, disappear and are lost in the sands. My own presence in this production rendered it somewhat modernistic. I had not the fight to possess beauty. I had not fought at all. I had been saved by the she-camel Khatema and then been given as a present, without my permission. I had been given to the beautiful Gulya, as if from now on I would be a prize ornament.

I thought to myself that I liked all this – this eternal epic – very much. I even wanted it to be really eternal. I wanted the world in which we presently found ourselves, on the way to a goal that was probably more imaginary than real, to remain my world, beautiful, austere and in some ways cruel. I didn't want this world to release me.

The brushwood with the pot hanging over it blazed up from the match. Gulya rolled up her dry shirt-dresses and put them into the bundle. The sun rose over the mountains. The little chameleon Petrovich climbed on to the bundle and froze with his neck extended towards the sky.

After drinking tea and rolling a couple of salty cheese balls around on our tongues, we set off further along the winding track that followed the crooked line of stone tongues running down into the ground.

We walked for a long time, only once making a halt to drink our fill from the canister of water.

The sun was already sinking, but there was still no end to the mountain spurs.

And again the night was spent in a narrow ravine between two tongues of rock. The night was quiet and starry. But when morning came it was not good. While I was still asleep my arms started aching, as if they were constrained at the wrists. And when I woke up I realised that my hands really were tied behind my back. And I was lying on my stomach with my nose stuck into Gulya's small pillow embroidered with diamond shapes. I turned my head, not yet feeling fear. I was only surprised and puzzled.

Shifting on to my side, I gathered myself and sat up with an effort, like a wobbly toy – my legs were tied together too. I looked around. Gulya was not there again, but I could see a lot of human tracks in the sand around the mat.

'Could Gulya have tied me up, then?' – the crazy thought flashed through my mind. 'She just got fed up of me and decided to leave, and to stop me chasing her, she tied –'

Before I could finish the thought, I heard the sound of two voices, a man and a woman.

They were unclear at first, but as they move closer, it became possible to make out the words and, to my amazement, I heard pure Ukrainian speech . . .

'Why didn't you catch her, you fool, eh?' asked the woman.

'And what about you? Well? Why didn't you run after her? I have to do everything!' the man replied.

The couple emerged so suddenly from behind a nearby spur that I started. I gave a chesty, frightened gasp that was almost a groan – I recognised those faces. But before I realised where I had seen them before, they stopped two or three metres away and looked at me in a hostile, thoughtful way, as if at that very moment they were deciding my fate.

That pause lasted for several minutes. Then the young guy with the dark complexion and the pointy nose leaned down over me – I thought he was going to peck me, because it was his nose that reached out towards me, but all he did was sniff.

'Hey!' he said, turning towards his girlfriend. 'His body smells of cinnamon, and one hand smells of caviar. He must have touched Russian capitalism with that hand!'

His dark-haired companion laughed.

'What do you want from me?' I asked, trying to slacken the stiff rope restraining my wrists behind my back.

'Oh, nothing, don't get all hot and bothered,' the guy laughed. 'We'll have a talk, maybe we'll come up with something that's good for the homeland . . .'

131

Now I clearly remembered the moments in the past when we had not exactly run into, but noticed each other. Or rather, now I understood that they had been following me. They were the couple who had turned up on St Sophia's Square during the rally and later on when I was getting closer to home. But how had they turned up here, in the Kazakh desert? Was it their tracks that had accompanied my journey since the moment I disembarked from the schooner *Old Comrade* on to the Caspian shore?

'You might at least introduce yourselves!' I said to them, trying to sound as relaxed as possible.

'Why bother with introductions?' the guy said with a shrug. 'I'm Petro, that's Galya. That's all the introduction you need . . .'

'Have you been following me all the way from Kiev?' I asked, trying to understand what was happening and what their plans were.

'No way . . .' said Petro. 'We knew where you were going. So we came out to meet you. That's the way it is . . .'

'But what did you tie me up for?'

'If you weren't tied, we couldn't talk calmly . . . But like this we can talk in a civilised fashion. If only your Kazakh girl hadn't run off, the four of us could have talked.'

'So what is it you want to talk about?'

'What about? About you, you Russian trickster. You found out about something like this and didn't tell anyone about it . . . You decided to grab it all for yourself . . . You wanted to take something sacred to our people! You should be killed just for that!' said Petro, unexpectedly raising his voice.

'Quiet, quiet,' said Galya, trying to calm him down. 'There'll be a landslide!' and she glanced up at the mountains.

'I haven't hidden anything from anyone,' I said. 'On the contrary, I wanted to bring everything home, to Kiev . . .'

132

'Stop playing the fool,' said Petro, calm now. 'You'd have taken it wherever they paid you the most.'

35

The heat of the day was beginning to make me tired. I was sitting on the bed with my hands and feet tied. Nearby, Galya was tinkering with our tripod and cooking pot beside the fire, and Petro had gone off somewhere. I thought it would be stupid not to take advantage of the man's absence and looked closely at this dark-complexioned woman.

'Excuse me,' I said. 'My arms are numb . . . Couldn't you untie my hands for just five minutes?'

'First your arms, and then your legs will swell up . . . What am I supposed to do, go chasing after you? No . . .' And she turned back to the cooking pot, in which there was something already boiling. 'You'll feel better once I feed you,' she added, no longer looking at me.

Apparently it wasn't so simple getting a conversation started with this Galya.

'And where's Petro?' I asked a few minutes later.

'Petro? He'll be here in a minute. He'll collect our things and come back . . .'

I fell over on to my side – balancing on the fifth point of the body had already become painful. My eyes were beginning to close – either fatigue or the enforced immobility was making me feel sleepy. And I would probably have fallen asleep if my nose had not suddenly caught a familiar smell.

I opened my eyes and saw the cooking pot on the bed mat. It was full of boiled buckwheat. Galya was sitting beside it, holding an aluminium canteen spoon in her hand and looking at my face.

'Let me feed you,' she said. 'Only sit up, you can't eat like that.'

I obediently jerked myself up into a sitting position. A spoonful of buckwheat immediately appeared in front of my face.

'Open your mouth,' Galya ordered. The buckwheat was too hot.

'Let it cool down,' I said.

'You fool! Petro will come any moment and tell me not to give you any.'

That lunch was like torture. I sucked air into my mouth, hoping that it would cool the buckwheat down at least a bit before I swallowed it. But the air was warm and salty. Finally I couldn't eat any more, and to avoid pointless explanations I simply fell on to my other side with my back towards Galya.

'What are you doing?' she asked in surprise. 'What, you don't like it? Well, please yourself!'

My mouth was burning. I rolled the mucous membrane that had been scalded off into little balls with my tongue and spat it out on to the bed mat. The pain eased a little after that and I fell asleep.

Petro's voice woke me when he came back. I lay there without moving and pretended to be asleep while I listened to their conversation.

'What did you bring so much food for?' Petro asked indignantly. 'Is there famine here? Has he eaten?'

'Of course. I gave him some buckwheat . . . Don't be angry, he's as meek as a calf . . .'

'And if I tied you up, would you start kicking out? Eh? . . . I've

134

brought the spade . . .The spades here are so small, they're like toys for children.'

'And what's there to dig for here? Eat, eat, you must be hungry . . .'

'Why isn't it salted?'

'And who gave the bag of salt to those Kazakh kids? Me?'

'All right, all right. Calm down! Has he found out anything?'

'No.'

'It's bad that the girl got away.'

This quiet family discussion of theirs, in which I didn't hear any particular hatred for myself, or any explicit or covert threat, prompted me to try talking to them. I sighed loudly, as if I was waking up, squirmed about and then turned on to my other side, facing them. They looked at me without saying anything.

'Look, he's awake,' said Petro.

'Good evening!' I said.

Petro laughed and stroked his moustache. 'And what makes you so cheerful?'

'Cheerful? I'm not cheerful.'

'Why aren't you shouting or swearing?' he went on.

I shrugged.

Petro took out a pipe and lit it from the fire.

'There's something wrong with him,' he said, turning to Galya and breathing out tobacco smoke. 'He's been caught and tied up, and he says "good evening". That's not normal.'

'And maybe he *is* a normal person,' Galya said, taking my side. 'He doesn't want any fussing and fighting, he wants to live in peace . . .'

'Sure, until we untie him. Then what?'

'Listen,' I said, already tired of hearing about myself in the third

135

person. 'Tell me what you want from me and we'll sort things out . . .'

Petro and Galya seemed taken aback by such a concrete suggestion coming from me. They exchanged glances.

'Well, if we're being specific,' Petro eventually said. 'I've brought the spade, you're going to dig while we supervise . . . You know where to dig?'

' "Three sazhens away from an old well," ' I recited monotonously, recalling the old 'report'.

'And where's the well?'

' "Outside the wall of the fort." '

'There hasn't been any well there for a long time,' said Petro, peering hard straight into my eyes. 'You know, I won't let you go until you find what Shevchenko buried!'

'You could at least untie my hands for an hour!' I said slowly, realising that there was no point in pursuing a conversation on 'concrete' matters just at the moment.

'I'm not going to untie you, no chance,' said Petro. 'If you work out how to find the place, then I'll untie you and put the spade in your hands, like Lenin on a working Saturday.'

I lay on my side again. My swollen hands and feet were hurting – it was as if they weren't part of my body, but some kind of ballast attached to me that prevented me from moving or feeling free.

Darkness was descending from the sky. The fire was crackling behind my back. Petro and his Galya were whispering about something beside the fire. I was feeling lousy. Gulya wasn't there. Somehow everything connected with her seemed like a dream now, and all the horror of the present day was simply a return to reality. The reality of Kiev had caught up with me, found me and bound me hand and foot. And this was only a part of the reality that could catch up with me. Not the best part, and not the worst, simply one part. And so I lay there on the bed mat that was warmed from below by the sand. My wrists hurt, restrained by the ropes, my entire body ached. There was nothing I could do but grit my teeth and lie there, waiting for the moment when my tormented body would go to sleep and I would drift off with it. Where was my Gulya now? Where had she run off to? I just hoped that she was all right.

That night I woke up beneath the lofty stars. I heard Petro and Galya breathing together, lying on their bed mat about three metres away from me, on the other side of the extinct fire with the tripod standing over it. The peaceful night encouraged my thoughts to flow calmly.

Lying to the right of them were my rucksack and Gulya's double bundle. Neither Petro nor Galya had touched them, which now seemed very strange to me. All they'd taken was the canister of water, which was lying by the dead campfire. I looked at my things and Gulya's. Surely it wasn't the respect for property inscribed in the new constitution of the Ukraine that had prevented my captors from taking an interest in the contents of the rucksack and the bundle? Gershovich's manuscript was in there, and Captain Paleev's denunciation, which essentially defined the goal of my flight-cum-voyage. It was odd that they hadn't even asked what we had in there . . . On the one hand, I was reassured by their behaving like that – in fact, from the very beginning there had been something amateurish and unprofessional about their aggression, something that allowed me not to take them seriously as a threat to my life. They seemed to be playing at aggression. I remembered everything I had heard about UNA-UNSO in Kiev. I remembered the harsh and aggressive slogans, the manifestos, the election campaign programmes. And, through some obscure association, the Lesi Kurbas theatre surfaced in my memory from out of the distant past. Yes, there was something theatrical about their aggressive attitude.

Reassured by these reflections, I fell asleep again.

I slept soundly, but I was disturbed by mysterious sounds, either sobs or cries. Then I had a dream of Gulya with the beautiful clear skin of her face and her brown eyes looking into my eyes. In the dream we seemed to be talking with our eyes, and then I stroked her hair, so soft and silky. And I caught her breath, salty-sweet, in my mouth and made it my breath. I wanted us to breathe the same air, for us to share everything and for it to be ours alone.

I was woken by the touch of her hot lips on my forehead.

My hands were free, but my wrists, chafed and tormented by the rope, itched as if they had been bitten all over by mosquitoes.

'Shhh, it's me,' Gulya said in a warm, breathy whisper, leaning down over my face. 'Wait, I'll cut the rope on your feet.'

Her head floated away from my face. And I lay on my back without moving, waiting for her to lean over me again.

'All done,' she whispered, sitting down beside me on the mat.

'What about them?' I asked, also in a whisper.

'I've tied them up.'

'Then why are we whispering?'

'Because it's night. They might want to sleep a bit more . . .'

I nodded and tried to lift myself up on my elbows. But Gulya stopped me.

'It's too soon,' she whispered. 'Let's lie down until dawn. I want to sleep too.'

36

In the morning we fed the bound Galya and Petro tea 'by hand'. They didn't look too good – naturally enough – interrupted sleep is not good for anyone.

'You won't get away with this!' Petro said, heaving a sigh. Then he stopped talking and didn't say anything for about half an hour.

'Listen,' I said, 'you were following us for a while, I saw your tracks several times after I came ashore. Why didn't you make a move before now?'

'What tracks?' Petro asked with genuine surprise. 'As if we had nothing better to do than follow you around. We found you here, alone, without that Kazakh girl.'

'She has a name, by the way – it's Gulya,' I said severely. 'She's my wife.'

I read astonishment in Galya's tired face. She started looking at Gulya in a different way, as if she had just discovered something she had failed to notice before.

Petro also squinted at Gulya, but his dark face with the moustache remained morose.

'Give me my pipe,' he said.

I found his pipe and then, under his instruction, I packed it with tobacco, stuck it under his moustache and gave him a light.

'So what are we going to do then?' he asked, releasing a puff of tobacco smoke.

'I don't know,' I confessed. 'I wasn't counting on meeting you. Untying you would be dangerous – you'll tie us up, and we've already been through that . . . Let's wait and see if something comes to mind. Maybe we'll leave you here and just carry on –'

'What, have you lost your marbles?' said Petro, his eyes flashing. 'How can you leave us here? Untie us, or you'll pay for it.'

'Well now,' I said, spreading my hands, delighted to find that my wrists had recovered from the rope. In this place, in the very possibility of its existence, I felt that my freedom had returned to me. 'You see, you're already threatening me, and what will happen later, if I untie you?' I asked rather acidly.

'Calm down, Petro,' Galya suddenly said. 'We have to be reasonable. Perhaps you could untie our feet and then we can go together?' she said to me.

I shrugged. 'I need to think about it. First, let's clarify what everybody's up to. I can start with myself. Basically, I wanted to find what Taras Shevchenko buried and take it to Kiev in order to, so to speak . . . win fame – and money – in my native Ukraine . . . or perhaps just fame . . . And you, respected people, what are your objectives?'

'Then our objectives are the same, only we're doing it for our homeland, we don't want money or fame,' said Petro. 'The important thing is for everything that belongs to the Ukraine to go back there . . . especially things as sacred as this.'

'Well then, if our objectives are the same, all we have to do is conduct negotiations on how to achieve them . . .' I looked expectantly into Petro's eyes. 'And if we can agree, we can go on together. Only how did you find out that I was planning to come here?'

'A comrade of ours, a captain in the SBU, told us all about you.'

'You have friends in the SBU?' I asked in surprise.

'There are decent people everywhere,' Petro replied and turned away.

I looked round at Gulya – she was absorbed in thoughts of her own. Then she turned to look at Galya, who had also lowered her eyes and was contemplating something: I thought she had a poetic, melancholy air, whereas my Kazakh wife's face had an expression of serious concentration.

'Untie my hands,' Galya suddenly piped up. 'I'll cook you some buckwheat. Petro has to eat, he has an ulcer.'

I turned towards Gulya and we exchanged glances.

'I'll cook the buckwheat,' Gulya said in a stern voice. 'Where is it?'

Galya nodded towards a bag beside the fire.

The sun was already roasting hot. I was hungry too, and the thought of boiled buckwheat distracted me from exalted international matters.

We fed Galya and Petro with a spoon, and after that we sat down, got comfortable and ate ourselves. We brewed tea and again we both worked 'for two mouths', alternately sipping ourselves and holding up the tea bowls to the prisoners' lips. Gulya took out some cheese balls and fed them to Petro and Galya.

The food and the sun made us feel quite tired, we'd lost that vigorous morning feeling and were probably ready to fall asleep, but Gulya resolutely got to her feet.

She straightened out her bright lettuce-green shirt-dress.

'We have to go,' she said.

The prisoners' faces looked tired.

'Well, shall I untie their feet?' I asked Gulya.

She thought about it.

In the silence I thought I could hear the quiet whispering movement of the sand – the voice of the desert. I surveyed the edge of the sand, where it licked at the rocky shore of the mountains like a dry sea.

There was no movement to be seen, but I already knew that the slow progress of the sand was as invisible and impalpable as the movement of the air.

'Listen,' I heard Petro say, 'maybe we can reach an agreement . . . for the time being. Only without any of those Russian tricks!'

I turned round and heaved a sigh. It seemed bizarre to me that I wasn't setting the conditions on which he would be untied, but he was setting them for me.

'Well, how about it?' he asked after a minute's pause.

'You know what,' I said, heaving another sigh. 'Let's arrange things like this: I untie you, but on condition that not only will there be no Russian tricks, there won't be any Ukrainian ones either!'

Petro worked his lips, as if he were taking a very important decision.

'OK,' he said eventually with a sigh. 'Untie us!'

I glanced at Gulya again. She nodded.

37

We walked no more than ten kilometres before the evening. In silence. Each of us carried our own luggage – Gulya and I had much more than the others, but neither Petro nor Galya offered to help. Petro was carrying a spade over his shoulder, and in his left hand he had a shopping bag with long straps, which he could also throw over his shoulder if he wished.

When the heat abated, we stopped and put everything down together.

'I'll go to get kindling,' said Gulya.

When Gulya had gone about fifty metres, Galya cast a questioning glance at Petro and went after her.

Petro and I were left alone. Neither of us spoke. I felt no desire to start a conversation with him, and he apparently shared my lack of interest.

Petro lit his pipe.

'Is it still a long way?' he suddenly asked.

'I don't know. Where did you come from?'

'From Fort Shevchenko.'

'And how far is that?'

'About two days.'

'Well, the spot is right beside Fort Shevchenko,' I said. ' "Three sazhens from an old well in the direction of the sea." '

'That's nonsense. There isn't any old well there . . .'

'Well, there used to be. We'll have to look for it.'

'Then you'll do the looking.'

I looked Petro in the eye. 'I shouldn't have untied him,' I thought. 'This joint venture is not going to end well.'

Soon Galya and Gulya came back, each bringing an armful of the meagre desert brushwood. They lit a fire and set the tripod with the cooking pot over it.

The women worked away without speaking, but they worked together, which surprised me greatly. I also spotted a couple of sidelong glances that Petro cast at his girlfriend.

We ate buckwheat again for supper. In silence. We drank tea. It was already getting dark, but something made us reluctant to sleep. Either we were too wide awake or we were afraid of waking in the night to find ourselves tied up and playing the role of prisoners again. We sat there in silence until Galya suddenly started singing a Ukrainian song.

In that desert place her voice sounded strange and foreign, but beautiful. She sang about a Cossack who went off to war against the Turks and was killed and about the black-haired beauty whose husband never returned to her.

Not long after the Ukrainian song, Gulya took me completely by surprise and started to sing in a very pleasant voice. She sang in the Kazakh language and the melody and her voice were both in the subtlest possible harmony with the sand and the mountains. I remembered her sister Natasha's song. Of course, Natasha's voice was brighter and stronger, but Gulya's voice had a hypnotic emotional power. I sat absolutely still, listening without understanding the words. She sang for a long time, and when she stopped, the quality of the silence seemed to have changed, it had become whiter and purer.

'What were you singing about?' Galya asked.

'It's a song about two nomads who met one day in the desert. One had a son in his family, and the other had a daughter, and they fell in love at first sight. Each set of parents tied up their own child and set off in a different direction. And when the camels had carried them far away from each other, the father said to his bound son: "When I was as you are now, I also fell in love with the daughter of a nomad whom we met by chance travelling across the desert. And my father did the same thing to me. I suffered for a long time, but in the end I forgot my grief. And then my father found me a bride, and she and I were happy. And if it had been otherwise, we would not have had you for a child, but someone else." And the girl's mother told her daughter exactly the same story about herself, and about how she had suffered for many years and finally married according to her father's choice. And there was just one thing that the father of the boy who fell in love and the mother of the girl who fell in love failed to notice: they didn't recognise each other – for they were the ones who had met in the same way in the desert so many years before, and their parents had bound them and carried them away, just as they had done to their children.'

These two songs not only brought the evening closer, they seemed to dispel our mutual suspicions. We unhurriedly laid out our bed mats and settled down for the night not far away from each other in yet another hollow between two rocky projecting tongues of the Aktau.

Before I fell asleep, I thought for a long time about various ways of overcoming international barriers and mistrust. The atmosphere that the two songs had created no longer seemed magical to me. I could see that the situation was as old as the world itself, that it is the women of warring nations who bring peace and tranquillity into the world with their singing, and this is not surprising, but quite natural. This is the universal, ancient means for pacifying conflicts between nations at every level. Of course, other means do exist. When the Ukrainian Miklukho-Maklai landed on the shore of Papua and found himself facing an agitated crowd of armed natives, he demonstratively lay down to sleep right there on the sand. We shall never know what the Papuans thought about him at that moment. It is hard to imagine Miklukho-Maklai landing on the beach and suddenly breaking into the Ukrainian song 'Unhitch the Horses, Lads' for the Papuans. In that case, for everything to end peacefully, he would have needed a simultaneous interpreter. 'Yes,' I thought, 'songs are good for settling conflicts between nations, but not between races.'

I lay there, tired, with my arm round Gulya, who was already asleep, and looked up at the stars. Petro's snoring seemed to me like a peaceful melody, setting the mood for good dreams. I lay there and pondered in time to this snoring until I fell asleep.

38

My sleep was leaden and its conclusion was repulsive and sickening. I was woken by pain in my arms and legs. My hands were tied behind my back again, and my wrists were aching where my skin was twisted by the rope, which restrained them far more tightly than the previous time. 'Yes,' I thought, 'that's what you get for believing in songs.' I rolled over on to my side and for a while I couldn't understand a thing. There in front of me, also bound and lying in the same position, were Gulya, and Petro, and Galya. I was so astounded by this sight that I forgot about my own bonds for a while. We were awake but in a state of shock, and none of us said anything as we mentally digested what had happened. All kinds of guesses flashed through my mind, most of them best suited to movies about Red Indians in America. I couldn't see anyone else around who could be the owner of the ropes restraining us. And the silence was beginning to give me the jitters, making me afraid of the unknown.

I forced my thoughts to slow down. I tried to analyse things calmly. If the Ukrainians had been tied up as well as me, perhaps it was Kazakhs who were responsible?

But then, they had tied Gulya up too. Perhaps they had tied us during the night and not got a good look at her. And they would come back soon, and then, if they were Kazakhs, Gulya would find a way to talk to them. Perhaps she wouldn't have to sing.

The silence was suddenly broken by loud footsteps from behind the nearest tongue of stone. It sounded as if someone was deliberately stamping as he walked in order to make us feel afraid. Petro heard the steps too and turned his head in their direction.

The man who emerged from behind the tongue of stone was not an Afghani mujahedin or a Kazakh, but a strapping Slav in an Adidas tracksuit. He looked about fifty years old.

His well-tended moustache and the gleam of his smoothly shaved cheeks didn't really fit in with the wild beauty of the desert or even with our own rather wild appearance.

'Mafia!' I thought, but then almost immediately I felt a sense of bewilderment. Who were we? What had we done to deserve the honour of being ambushed and bound in the night? Nobody would pay a ransom, at least not for me, and almost certainly not for Galya and Petro either. That left Gulya, but although it seemed to me that she at least was worth taking captive without any prospects of a ransom, wouldn't it have been simpler just to kidnap her while we were sleeping, if they were so crafty?

The Adidas man with the moustache stopped, looking down at Petro with a spiteful glance that bored right through him.

'Well then?' he asked in a surprisingly velvety voice, leaning down until his face was just above Petro's head. 'It wasn't enough for you to organise rallies and arrange other disgraceful incidents all over Kiev, you had to come to Kazakhstan as well! Just you wait – when we get back home, I'll teach you a lesson! We have an entire video about you already!'

'Phooh!' said Petro and spat off to the side. 'Just look who's come visiting! Mr Colonel . . . what's your name and patronymic?'

147

'You mean you don't know?'

'I know, but Rooski over there,' said Petro, with a nod in my direction, 'might not have seen you before.'

'My name is Vitold Yukhimovich Taranenko, Colonel of the SBU,' the Adidas man declared, glancing in my direction with no particular interest. The person he was interested in was obviously lying on the mat in front of him with his hands and feet tied. 'And who are your chums here?' he asked, half squatting down and leaning even closer to Petro.

'They're no more my friends than you are, Mr Colonel.'

'A pity,' Taranenko drawled. 'And I was hoping you would make friends! You made friends with Captain Semyonov! Politics is all well and good, but human relationships are quite a different matter! Right, Galya?' He turned to look at the black-haired Ukrainian woman.

She turned her head away without saying anything. Although until then she had been watching the colonel attentively.

'Well, OK,' the colonel chuckled, then got up and came over to me. 'Right then, Nikolai Ivanovich Sotnikov, I'm pleased to meet you.'

'I'm sorry, I can't shake hands,' I said, trying to be impertinent.

'You can do that later,' he said, leaning down and peering into my face. 'How excellent that we've all met up today like this,' Colonel Taranenko said in a sing-song voice as he unwrapped a stick of chewing gum.

He popped the gum into his mouth, chewed it and continued in a quite different, serious voice.

'Well now, whether you like it or not, we're all one big happy family now. Although first of all we'll have to learn to trust each other. We have a single assignment . . . that is, you have an objective, and I have an assignment. But in the given situation it comes to the same thing.'

He went back behind the tongue of rock and re-emerged carrying a tightly packed canvas rucksack. He set it beside our things, opened it and took out a small folding chair. He unfolded the chair and sat down.

My neck started to hurt – in order to see the colonel I had to lie in a twisted position. And there he was, sitting on his little chair in laid-back style with his legs stretched.

'Well now, let me you inform you in more specific terms about the present situation,' he began. 'First of all, you have to understand that the financial difficulties of the country have inevitably affected the SBU. We now have to get by with less manpower and rely more on outside help. But, as you no doubt understand, no one offers us help of their own accord. And so we exploit the passive assistance of our citizens. This approach is entirely justified when the interests and objectives of potential helpers coincide with our own. Effectively we – that is the SBU – provide far more help to our helpers than they do to us, but then it's the result that's important, not who helps whom the most! If not for us, no one in UNA-UNSO would ever have known that Shevchenko's secret treasure existed, or that the Russian citizen Sotnikov had already set out to search for it! The important thing is to keep abreast of events and to keep the most capable potential helpers informed. But unfortunately, not once have our helpers been able to help us without our help.

'It's like the unity of the army and the people. If we work together, then inevitable success awaits us. But, as I have already said, first of all we have to learn to trust each other. And so, I beg your pardon, but . . . we must have no secrets from each other . . .'

The colonel sighed heavily, got up and went across to our things.

He began methodically laying everything out on the sand, first of all from Gulya's double bundle, where he found her bright-coloured shirt-dresses and packages containing our reserves of tea and cheese balls. He was clearly dissatisfied with what he found, and so he set about my Chinese rucksack with redoubled energy and zeal. Casually tossing the cans of 'baby food' on to the sand, he pulled out the plastic bag containing the folder with Gershovich's manuscript. He extracted the folder and lifted it up to his eyes. He sneezed and moved it away from his face. He sniffed at it again, cautiously at first, and then as if his mind had been set at ease.

The colonel opened the folder and leafed through the pages, then cast a satisfied glance at me.

'You've carried it a long way. From the Pushche-Voditsa cemetery all the way to Mangyshlak . . .' he drawled in the voice of a man who is saying far less than he knows. 'Now it's my turn.'

'Well, well,' I thought. 'It seems like everyone and his mother was following me around in Kiev! The UNSOvites, and the SBUniks, and the Finnish-baby-food fanciers. It's amazing that I actually managed to get this far alive.'

Once again I recalled the tracks in the sand that I had seen several times since I landed on the shore of the Caspian.

'Colonel,' I asked, 'is it you who's been following me through the desert?'

'How do you mean?'

'Several times in the morning I've seen tracks at the places where I spent the night.'

'Maybe it was them?' he said, with a nod towards Petro and Galya.

'No,' I replied.

Colonel Taranenko frowned. 'Actually, I know it wasn't them – I've been following them myself.' He thought about it, then he

150

shrugged and spread his hands. 'There shouldn't really be anybody else here – all the interested parties are already assembled . . .'

He said nothing for a while. Then he put the folder down on the sand beside the little chair and set about Petro's and Galya's things. He turned out their shopping bag with the long handles, inspected the items that came tumbling out and grunted in satisfaction. He picked up an aluminium *djezva*, a tin of Jacobs ground coffee and a Snickers bar. He cast a cunning glance at Petro and Galya. Galya was lying on her side, looking away from him, and Petro was lying in the same twisted position as me, silently following the colonel's movements.

After going through his prisoners' things and spending about fifteen minutes studying a notebook that apparently belonged to Petro, Colonel Taranenko sat back down on his little folding chair. His face now expressed total self-confidence.

'Right then, we can carry on talking!' he declared decisively. 'Beginning with a presentation by the Rooskies . . .' – he peered shrewdly at me. 'No need to tell me your life story, we've read that already. Let's start with something else – what gave you the idea of interfering in matters that are sacred to every Ukrainian?' He grinned and glanced at Petro.

'What do you mean?'

'Why, your interest in Taras Grigorievich Shevchenko, of course, on such an international scale, so to speak.'

'There's nothing illegal in that, is there?'

'And who said there was? Not me. But I would say that these are rather delicate matters, especially when they extend beyond certain acceptable limits and begin to impinge on the interests of another state . . .'

'You know what,' I said – I had a sharp pain in my neck again and my hands were aching worse than ever. 'It's hard for me to talk in this position –'

'Then turn over into a different one, you don't have to look at me, you could break your neck like that . . .'

I rolled back on to my stomach, with my chin resting on the edge of the bed mat.

'I don't see what boundaries I have crossed, apart from geographical ones . . .' I said, forcing the words out with difficulty, since it was not easy to speak in this position either – I was very short of breath.

'Well, all right, we'll come back to that, but for now, let's have a word with Petro Yurievich Rogulya.' He shifted his gaze to Petro.

'I've got nothing to say to you!' Petro hissed through his teeth. 'Especially in Russian. As a Ukrainian aren't you ashamed to speak a foreign language?'

'And isn't a Ukrainian patriot ashamed of drinking Jacobs coffee and eating Snickers bars?' Taranenko retorted. 'You ought to have brought sweets from Lvov and our own domestic coffee-flavoured beverage!' The colonel sighed heavily. The conversation was going nowhere. He picked the folder with Gershovich's manuscript up off the sand and began turning the pages again, bringing one or another close to his eyes. He found Captain Paleev's denunciatory report, read it carefully and started thinking.

He thought for a long time. I was even starting to nod off – it was the easiest way to distract myself from the aching in my bones.

'Well, what now?' the Adidas colonel's voice said, bringing me back to reality. 'We have to decide what to do next . . . I've already figured that out, so no long discussions are required . . . We have to dig. Only we have to decide how. I don't intend to carry you all the way . . .' The colonel was thinking out loud rather than talking to us.

'So perhaps I'll untie your feet . . . Only not straight away . . . But then . . .' He looked at the can of ground coffee lying among the contents of the empty bags. 'A cup of coffee would be rather nice . . .'

He chewed on his lips.

The sun was rising higher, and the atmospheric warmth of the day was moving down from the sky on to the sand, drying out the pitifully meagre moisture that the night had given to this dead land.

'How do you make coffee here?' the colonel asked, looking at me.

'The women gather kindling and light a fire, then they hang the pot full of water on the tripod,' I replied in a monotone.

'Kindling?' the colonel echoed, looking around. 'Where can you collect that here? I was heating my food with solidified alcohol, but I've run out . . .'

A possible plan of escape took shape in my head, although I still couldn't imagine any way to get rid of the entire group. At least, not just at that moment.

'Gulya knows where to look for kindling, she's from round here.' I indicated my bound wife with a movement of my eyes.

Colonel Taranenko also looked at her and chewed on his lips pensively, ran his hand over his smoothly shaven cheeks and checked with his fingers to make sure that his thick, carefully tended moustache was jutting at the correct angle.

'I tell you what,' he said. 'I'll untie her, she's a foreign national, she can boil the water . . . But you just lie there for now, there'll be plenty of coffee for you too . . .'

The colonel leaned down over Gulya and untied her hands, then her feet.

I thought that as soon as he untied Gulya's hands, she would slap his face. But she rubbed her wrists, sat up and calmly looked around.

'Go and fetch some kindling!' the colonel said to her, and she obediently set off.

'Maybe that's for the best,' I thought about Gulya. 'At least when the moment comes she'll untie me, and then perhaps we can leave the colonel with Petro and Galya. They'll have fun together. And to hell with that diary, they can dig for it themselves – they've got a spade!'

The colonel watched Gulya go with a curious glance, then picked the folder up again and sniffed it. Then he squatted down beside me and sniffed me.

'How come you reek of cinnamon like that? Are you fond of pies with cinnamon?'

'No, it's just that I crossed the Ukrainian-Russian border in a railway truck full of cinnamon, and the smell ate right into my skin.'

'Aha,' the colonel drawled, taking my words seriously.

As the sun rose higher, time started moving as slowly as amber resin. Petro suddenly started coughing drily and asked the colonel for water. The colonel found the canister and gave his bound prisoner a drink. I was amused to observe Taranenko's wheat-coloured moustache and Petro's black moustache move so close together. The colonel seemed to take a special pleasure in raising the canister above the head of the drinking man, as if he were forcing him to take large gulps that almost choked him.

'Hey!' I called out, realising just in time what was happening. 'There won't be enough for coffee! That's all the water!'

The serious expression returned to the colonel's face. He immediately took the canister away from Petro's face and screwed the plastic cap back on.

Soon Gulya came back and started a fire. About twenty minutes later the first steam appeared above the cooking pot.

The colonel took a half-litre mug and an aluminium spoon out of his rucksack. He tipped ground coffee into the mug and sat by the fire, waiting for the water to boil.

Gulya moved away and started packing her things back into the double bundle.

'And what kind of tea do you have?' the colonel suddenly asked her. 'Ceylon?'

'It's all Chinese here,' my wife replied, looking round for a moment. 'There's green, yellow . . .'

The colonel nodded and turned towards the cooking pot. Eventually he poured boiling water into his mug, threw in two lumps of sugar and began stirring it all noisily with his spoon.

'Comrade Colonel,' I said, 'perhaps you'd like some milk?'

'Milk? Where can you get milk here?'

'I've got dried milk, infant formula.'

The colonel glanced carefully at my things, laid out beside the empty rucksack.

'That there?' he asked, pointing one hand at the cans of 'baby food'. I nodded.

'All right then, since you're offering.' He stood up, opened one can and sprinkled two or three spoonfuls of white powder into the mug.

He closed the can tightly and went back to his little chair beside the fire. He blew on the mug and looked at the sky. The coffee was still too hot and he put the mug down on the sand, then rummaged in his own rucksack and took out a beige sun hat with the inscription 'Yalta 86' on it and put it on his head.

'If you'd all stayed at home, I'd have gone on holiday by now,' he declared plaintively. 'Do you think I invented this system? It's all the top brass's idea. All they want is more successful operations for the smallest possible budget! And now my travel voucher to Odessa is down the tubes. It was for the Chkalov sanatorium, too! Now I get to bake in the sun here with you, and there isn't even any sea anywhere near.'

'What about the Caspian?' I asked. The colonel pulled a face and reached one hand down for the mug.

I waited impatiently for the moment when the first gulp would be taken. But the Adidas man Taranenko didn't like his drinks hot. He waited for the coffee to cool down.

He waited for another five minutes and only then did the mug finally approach his lips. I breathed out my tension in a sigh of relief. All I had to do was wait for him to drink enough.

39

As he rose up heavily off the pale-yellow sand of the desert, for some reason Vitold Yukhimovich Taranenko recalled the wattle-and-daub hut of his grandmother, Fedora Kirillovna Karmeliuk, who he thought must have been known to the other villagers all her life, in fact almost since the day she was born, as Granny Fedora. As if she had never had any childhood. The colonel's body ascended unhurriedly, and then he opened his eyes, which he had closed ten minutes earlier, owing to a sudden 'slowing of the circulation'.

He opened his eyes and actually saw the hut far below him,

standing on the edge of the village in the Khmelnitskaya region, in such a remote spot that collective farms hadn't even appeared there until after the war. Yes, the colonel realised that he couldn't be flying over his grandma's hut right now, firstly because he hadn't risen very high yet, and secondly because of the dubious nature of his flight and the mysterious nature of its causes.

'A mirage,' Vitold Yukhimovich thought to himself about the hut, and then immediately looked down again at the solid ground moving away from him.

The air at this height was sweet, and although the sun was hanging above him, he no longer felt the heat. All he could feel was the confusion of his thoughts, which were behaving like new recruits to the army who haven't managed to line up in ranks yet and don't even know how to line up. 'Hey!' the colonel shouted at them in his mind, and they settled down. They became calm and a feeling of bliss filled his soul, allowing him to look around and concentrate on the sensations of flight. The flight continued.

After a few brupt movements with his arms and legs, the colonel acknowledged his own reality and in addition realised that his body's aerodynamic qualities were better with his arms pressed against his sides and his legs held together rather than with his feet apart and arms sticking out. The air was amazingly transparent – he saw a small rock, the size of a tennis ball, flying towards him. It moved closer, and when the ball was only two or three metres away, the colonel saw that it would miss his body by about thirty centimetres. And then Vitold Yukhimovich held out his open hand in the path of the ball and caught it. And this unexpected contact between two objects flying towards other set Colonel Taranenko spinning slowly in the air like a top, clutching in his hand the extra-terrestrial object that was like a tennis ball. Vitold Yukhimovich was spun round several more times and carried off to one side, as if he were dancing a waltz with an invisible partner. And finally the movement stopped and the colonel was left hanging in space. And then he raised the object to his face to see what it was that he had caught and shook his head in amazement – there was a painted egg lying in his hand, decorated with familiar Carpathian designs. Only the colours had already faded and could barely be made out. They must have been bleached by the sun. Without knowing why, Vitold Yukhimovich started turning the egg in his hand and examining the designs carefully – he felt a desire to find a date, he wanted to know how many years this egg had been flying through space. But there wasn't a date anywhere. Nothing but decorative annular designs, in which all the lines – straight, zigzag and dotted – ran together like an infinite thread with no ends.

'Even if it's from last Easter,' the colonel thought, 'that's still a long time ago now . . .'

Then suddenly his attention was caught by something large flying towards him. He turned his head and saw a human figure, not dressed in ordinary clothes, but in a real, genuine cosmonaut's suit, with a helmet on its head. The figure was coming towards him slowly, far more slowly than the egg he had caught. There was something meticulous about the cosmonaut's flight. And when the cosmonaut came close to the colonel, Vitold Yukhimovich could see him clearly – an old man with thin, grey hair, badly shaved, with an embroidered peasant shirt peeping out from under his spacesuit at the neck. While the colonel was examining this old cosmonaut floating independently through space, the cosmonaut suddenly grabbed the painted Easter egg out of the colonel's hand and kicked the colonel. It was a weak blow, of course, there was no pain. But the colonel felt offended.

His fingers clenched into fists. In his mind he was already reaching out for the helmet with his right hand, but then a scientific sort of explanation suddenly came to mind: what if, thought the colonel, he didn't kick me, but merely pushed off in order to carry on moving? After all, there is no gravity here! And as if in confirmation of this idea he saw a smile of gratitude appear on the face of the old cosmonaut slowly drifting away from him. And the old man raised the Easter egg above his helmeted head and waved to him. 'It must be his egg!' the colonel thought. But even so the struggle continued in his mind between resentment at this cosmonaut and the desire to forgive what he had done.

40

While Gulya was untying me, I explained to Petro where the waking spirit of our Adidas man had flown off to and how.

Gulya untied Petro last, and he immediately grabbed his rope and dashed over to Colonel Taranenko, lying beside the small folding chair with a smile on his face.

'I'll teach you to fight against your own people!' he cried.

But just then everything was deep purple to the colonel. His body lay on the warm sand like a dead weight. It was no more than the pledge of his future return to Earth.

'Don't be in such a hurry!' I called, trying to stop Petro, but he had already turned Taranenko's body on to its stomach and was feverishly tying the colonel's limp wrists behind his back.

Petro cooled down after that and calmly tied the ankles together, then sat down on the sand, like a hunter beside a prostrate bear, and lit his pipe.

Galya watched him with anxious agitation, and I read love for this lean, gruff young man in her eyes. Although I didn't even know what their relationship was, who they were: man and wife or simply comrades-in-arms, like Lenin and Krupskaya.

But either way, they suited each other, they were more than merely 'the same blood'. Then I looked at Gulya, busy with something by the fire. She was wearing her dark green shirt-dress and part of her face was concealed behind a semi-transparent screen of dark chestnut hair. Until then I had not really believed that she and I made up the 'we' that is called a family. Yes, she called herself my wife, but we still didn't have the kind of relationship that is like superglue, that makes people inseparable from each other. Our emotions – or at least mine – weren't settled yet, I still wasn't even fully aware of them. I still didn't know what she felt for me. She was still a mystery to me. A mix of concealed steel and outward docility. If I had not met Gulya, I could never have imagined a mixture like that in a single person.

'We need to pack,' Petro said calmly, after saying nothing for five minutes.

He cast one more glance at the colonel's body and got to his feet.

'I'm going to take a look at what he's got there,' he declared as he walked towards Taranenko's things.

The fire was crackling. The pot was hanging over it on the tripod, with Gulya sitting beside it.

I sat on the bed mat, thinking about the colonel who had 'flown away'. I didn't know which way to go now. My goal had suddenly become dangerous. But it seemed impossible to abandon it. The only thing I could do was to achieve that goal and afterwards try to dissolve into the darkness, withdraw from the game. A long life is better than posthumous glory.

'Hey, you, look what I've found in his things!' Petro came over to me and held out a detailed plan of the Novopetrovsk fortifications. It was an old plan, drawn in Indian ink, but not ancient. In the lower right-hand corner I saw the signature of the person who had made it and the date – '1956'.

'Look at this here!' said Petro, jabbing a finger at a little black circle, with the words 'location of old well' written beside it in small black letters.

'So he knew everything, then?' I exclaimed in surprise.

'He didn't know anything,' Petro snapped. 'He had a map, but he didn't know where to search, or else what did he want with us?'

Inside my brain, badly overheated by the Kazakh sun, everything gradually fell into place.

I realised that now we had everything necessary to find the 'treasure' buried in the sand. We even had a spade. And so the joint Ukrainian-Russian-Kazakh journey was moving into its final, concluding stage, after which I would be able to congratulate Petro and Galya, and perhaps Colonel Taranenko, on the discovery of a historical relic and be left alone with Gulya. Yes, the objective of my wanderings had changed. Now there was only one thing I wanted – to be left alone with Gulya and then to decide what we should do, where we should go. My future now appeared to me in a new, unexpected light. It had changed from adventure to romance. 'A romantic journey for two.' I think there's a prize like that in the TV quiz *Love at First Sight*. I had won the prize without even taking part in the show. Now I had to get rid of our companions, whose presence merely hindered the transformation of this journey of adventure into the journey of romance. And all I had to do to achieve that was to find what the great poet had buried in the sand and wave goodbye to those who would carry the item that was found back to my distant black-earth motherland.

Gulya poured tea for everyone and handed out little cheese balls. Galya gave her ball to Petro, and received a Snickers bar and a mocking smile from him.

Petro turned once again to gaze at Taranenko, who was still 'in flight'. Only after a long, weary look at the captive colonel did he take a sip of his green tea and toss a small yellowish ball of cheese into his mouth. He did it so easily and naturally that for an instant he seemed to me like an absolutely genuine Kazakh. 'A little bit longer and all of us here will become Kazakhs,' I thought. 'And any suspicions between nationalities will disappear of their own accord, dissolve in the green tea together with the cheese balls, be rolled out across our tongues and reduced to the consistency of saliva.'

Galya suddenly held out half of her Snickers to Gulya, who took it, put it straight into her mouth and drowned it in tea.

I recalled my recent ruminations on the various ways of achieving harmony between nations. Now I could add Snickers bars to the list of actions and items that eliminate mutual distrust.

'Well then,' said Petro, looking at me, 'time to be going . . . We'll leave this swine here . . .' – he nodded towards the colonel. I shook my head in disagreement.

'We can't – he'll die. He could lie there for another three days, and in three days the sun alone will finish him off! And then in Kiev your friend, SBU Captain Semyonov will ask you: "Where's the leader of your expedition, Colonel Taranenko?" '

Petro scowled and heaved a sigh. 'But what can we do with him?' he asked at last. 'I'm not going to carry him.'

'Perhaps there's no need,' I said. 'Let's roll him into the shade of a rock, cover him with something and untie his hands . . .'

Petro didn't agree and it took me another five minutes to demonstrate to him that my suggestion was not only humane, but also good for us. During the three days he was 'flying', we would have time to sort out the business of the 'treasure' and get away from Fort Shevchenko. I didn't even try to think where we could go. It wasn't all that important just at the moment.

Eventually he gave in. The two of us rolled Taranenko into the pointed inner corner between two spurs and carried his things in there. We covered his head with a T-shirt that we found in his rucksack. We untied his hands. Then Gulya came over and set the aluminium mug, full of water, beside his head and stuck one end of the T-shirt covering his head into the water.

Meanwhile Galya packed our things into the double bundle and the rucksack and her own things into the shopping bag with long handles. Half an hour later we set off.

That evening, after we settled in for a halt, we saw the flickering lights of a town in the distance. The goal was near, and our mood automatically improved. Galya decided to boil some buckwheat and we all waited patiently for our supper, sitting round the little campfire. Suddenly Galya cried out and jumped up. Petro jumped up too, and then we got to our feet. I leaned forward and saw a little chameleon beside Galya's feet. 'Petrovich?' I thought. 'He hasn't been around for ages! I assumed he'd been left behind . . .'

'Don't be afraid,' my wife told Galya. 'He's good. He brings good luck.'

'But isn't it a scorpion?' Galya asked mistrustfully, her voice still shaking.

'No, he's a chameleon. He was travelling with us. He must have fallen asleep and only just woken up,' said Gulya.

'He slept through the most interesting part,' I said, putting in my penny's worth.

We sat down round the fire again, and the cause of all the commotion climbed on to Galya's jeans and froze there with his dragon-head thrust skywards. Galya leaned down and examined him apprehensively.

'Animals like me,' she said thoughtfully. 'Dogs and cats and cows . . .'

'Me too,' Gulya said with a sigh. Petro and I exchanged glances without saying anything.

I thought this was the first time I'd heard the women talking, and I hoped it would continue. It sounded so peaceful that I even tried to breathe more quietly.

And up above, stars suddenly came showering down from the lofty sky. But I was the only one who saw them. No, that's not true, the chameleon did too. The two of us sat there, immersed in the sky. The women made quiet, homely conversation. And Petro smoked his pipe and gazed pensively at the cooking pot in which the buckwheat was boiling.

41

The next day, as evening was approaching, we halted on the edge of what many years earlier had been known by the proud name of the Novopetrovsk Fortress. All that could be seen at this spot now were the remains of walls and isolated blocks of limestone foundations protruding from the sand or the rock face. The transparency of the air was thickening under the pressure of the advancing evening. It was already difficult to make out the boundaries of this fortress and understand whether it was large or small. Even when we took out the 1956 plan that we had borrowed from Colonel Taranenko it was impossible to match up the remains of structures drawn in ink and sharp pencil with the real ruins.

There was nothing we could do except wait for morning. Meanwhile, Gulya started a fire with twigs gathered along our way. And right there beside the fortifications we unexpectedly discovered a dried-out tree trunk. The trunk was as thick as a man's waist, so it wasn't possible to break it across your knee, and Petro and I took turns at smashing it into splinters with the blade of the spade.

Eventually the fire blazed up, with the splinters of the shattered tree trunk lending it unusual brilliance and strength. The water in the canister was running out, and we were being more careful with it than before. We left just enough for the morning tea. We didn't think there was anything to worry about here, since now we were close, not only to the ruins, but also to the people who had settled by these ruins. The town of Fort Shevchenko was somewhere nearby.

I felt more in the mood for strolling through a real town than digging in the sand. The nostalgia of the city dweller was surfacing.

But the evening was rapidly turning into night, and I already knew that we had enough strength only to eat a traveller's supper and spread out the sleeping mats.

42

Vitold Yukhimovich suddenly felt a lack of oxygen. He had lost track of how long he had been flying. Outer space already seemed monotonous to him, especially as nothing interesting had happened since the encounter with the Easter egg and the old cosmonaut. Meteorites of various colours had gone flying past, some of rather large dimensions. And when a meteorite the size of his grandmother's wattle-and-daub hut had come floating by very close, some mysterious force had moved the colonel out of the way, and he had continued to feel the inertia of that movement for about an hour.

But now he was beginning to feel bad. There wasn't enough air, and there was an unpleasant sensation of heat in his head, as if his temperature had risen. At first he thought it must be sunstroke, but when he looked around he realised there wasn't any sun anywhere.

He could see a small yellow planet in the distance, but it was very dim. 'It's not even a moon,' Colonel Taranenko decided, and started thinking about his head again. He slowly reached up to touch his forehead, but it proved to be surprisingly cold. 'Perhaps my hand is very hot and I can't feel the real temperature of my forehead?' Vitold Yukhimovich thought.

Then he noticed internal sensations that put him on his guard – his body was gaining weight, becoming heavier, as if someone invisible was putting bricks in his pockets. He began to be drawn downwards and he made a sharp movement with his arms and looked around fearfully. If he had been in the gondola of a hot-air balloon, he would have gone dashing to throw sacks of sand – the ballast – out of the basket. But he wasn't in the gondola of a balloon. Rather, he himself *was* the balloon . . .

And now he could quite clearly feel the speed and direction of his movement. He wasn't floating, he was falling downwards. As long as he could see below him the bottomless depths of the cosmos, falling wasn't so very frightening, although he had been in a state of nervous tension from the moment the fall began. But then a point suddenly appeared in those bottomless depths and started to grow even as he watched it, gradually expanding into a sphere. It had already grown to the size of a tennis ball, but the colonel realised that this was not a painted egg, it was something far more bulky. After a while the point grew to the size of a planet, and he already knew what planet it was. He still remembered the pictures of this planet in his school textbook. The planet was called Earth. He himself lived on this planet. But the colonel was not cheered by the return to his home planet. The air was burning the skin on his hands and face. 'It's the speed that does that,' Vitold Yukhimovich realised. 'It's the speed of travel through space that makes satellites burn up as they enter the dense layers of the atmosphere . . .' and he imagined with horror the air around him bursting into flame from the friction with his skin and realised that once he entered the dense layers of the atmosphere he would never get back out of them.

And then he saw those dense layers, although to look at they weren't really all that dense. They were more like a semi-transparent, cloudy sphere enveloping his Earth. His speed was increasing. The dense layers were coming closer and in his fear of burning up in these layers Colonel Taranenko closed his eyes. He carried on flying with his eyes closed until suddenly he felt his body break through some kind of shell with a sound like the crack of paper tearing or a plastic bag bursting. The colonel opened his eyes and looked back – now he was flying feet first and the dense layers of the atmosphere had been left behind, with a substantial hole made in them by his body.

Below him lay the Earth.

43

I was the last to wake up in the morning. Petro was standing a little distance away, holding the plan in his hand. Every now and then he swung his head around, evidently searching for some reference point marked on the plan. A fire was crackling beside him, with the last of the water boiling over it.

My spirits rose at the thought that this day could be the decisive one. After all, we had already arrived – without even getting up I could see the ruins of an artillery battery on a low hillock not far away. And although for the time being the undulating surface of the area concealed from my eyes other details of the fortifications that were familiar in theory from the plan, I knew that it was all somewhere close by. As close as a wife can be on the first night of marriage.

Soon we were sitting by the fire with bowls of tea in our hands. I could see businesslike concentration even in Galya's usually melancholy and pensive eyes.

After breakfast Petro laid out the plan of the Novopetrovsk Fortress on the sand and called me over.

'Listen,' he said. 'We'll have to figure out the scale.'

'Well, that's easy, we'll take one distance, measure it on the map in centimetres, pace it out here in metres and divide the centimetres by the metres, and we'll have the scale.'

Petro thought and nodded. 'Only you know what,' he added, 'there are two wells here on the map . . .'

'It's lucky there aren't more.'

'Well, all right, here, you figure out the scale, and I'll take a look around.'

I was left alone with the map. I decided to calculate the distance from the artillery battery to the remains of the foundations of the barracks. While I was sitting on the warm sand leaning over the map, I heard soft, rustling footsteps behind me and turned round. Gulya walked up and sat beside me.

'What do you think, how many centimetres is this?' I asked her, pointing out the distance I had selected on the map.

'Probably thirty-five or forty.'

'And if I walk from the battery to the wall?'

'About three hundred metres . . .'

I nodded. We looked into each other's eyes.

'Do you know what I want more than anything now?' I said.

'To leave all this behind?'

'All of it, except you.'

Gulya smiled. I leaned over and kissed her on the lips.

'Why don't you wear the cap my father gave you?' Gulya asked, glancing up at the sun hanging above our heads.

'I'll put it on, it's in the rucksack . . .'

After pacing out the chosen distance twice, I noted down the result of three hundred and fifty-five metres on the reverse of the map. Then I drew a fine 'centimetre line' between the two reference points on the map. And then I spent a long time dividing the metres into the centimetres, getting things confused and counting all over again. Something always came out wrong. Eventually I worked out that one centimetre on the plan was equal to almost nine metres. Now I had to check this scale against some other distance, and I started studying the map. I decided to take the artillery battery as my starting point again. I drew a mental line from it to the foundation of the soldiers' mess – the distance there was shorter. Then I drew a pencil line divided into approximate centimetres and I went to pace out the real distance.

The result was disheartening – the map seemed to have been drawn by surveyors who were drunk – after several re-counts I was certain that for this distance one centimetre on the map was equal to twenty-two metres.

Still puzzled, I asked Gulya to re-count one more time. Her result was the same.

'What does that mean?' Gulya asked, astonished.

'It means that we'll have to do a lot of digging,' I declared dejectedly.

And just then Petro turned up most opportunely with the spade across his shoulder. He came towards us down a little hill of sand, humming something to himself.

I spoiled his mood straight away and the smile under his black moustache straightened out into the usual line of his mouth.

'Well, all right,' he said after a moment's thought. 'If we know where to look . . .'

'Aha,' I said with a nod. 'From those stones there, probably almost all the way to the sea. And another two or three hundred metres in the opposite direction . . .'

'Here's the spade – get started!' Petro commanded, holding out the instrument of physical labour.

I glanced at the map again, at the two indications of wells that had not existed for a very long time. It would not have been hard to calculate their locations if it had been a normal map. But the only thing here that was almost normal was the spade. Everything and everyone, including me, seemed rather distant from the norm. Except for Gulya and the chameleon, who was nowhere to be seen again – he must have climbed back into the double bundle or he was hiding from the sun under my rucksack.

I took the spade from Petro and started wandering through the not very picturesque ruins.

44

That was the day we started treasure-hunting in earnest, and I must say it proved to be a rather infectious business. The spade 'belonged' only to my hands, and while Gulya was away, having taken the canister to get some water, Petro and Galya walked around after me. I scraped away the sand at several spots calculated approximately from the plan. The sand in this area was remarkably loose and crumbly and I could only dig a hole about sixty centimetres deep before it collapsed.

Working on the check-row system, I left sandy craters behind me every two metres. The first two hours of the search were fruitless, and then I unearthed a large mummified lizard. When they saw me down on my knees, Petro and Galya came running up and also squatted down beside me.

'There really is a lot of work,' Petro said, shaking his head, then glanced round the locality and rested his gaze on the sea that could be seen below us. 'If only we had a regiment of Rooskies with spades!'

I laughed. 'What makes you think the Rooskies would dig for you here?'

'Come on, keep looking!' he snapped, getting to his feet.

I continued with the search, although by this time my arms were tired and my own accommodating attitude was beginning to annoy me. Why should I do what he said? And when would it be his turn to dig?

Soon I noticed that a long thin stick had appeared in Galya's hands and she was using it as a probe as she walked along, occasionally thrusting it deep into the sand.

Gulya was still not back, and that was beginning to worry me a bit. And even without that worry I wasn't excavating all that carefully. I was finding the task of locating some unknown item 'three sazhens from an old well' that didn't exist any more, when I didn't even know where it had been in the first place, not to mention the fact that there used to be two wells around here somewhere, less and less attractive, in fact it seemed quite simply impossible. The sun had given me a headache and I stuck the spade in the ground and went back to my things. I tipped them out of the rucksack on to the sand, found the pointed felt cap and stuck it on my head. I started packing everything else back into the rucksack – the cans of 'baby food', the socks. And suddenly I saw something I'd forgotten about – the Smena camera I had found with the canvas tent at the very beginning of my desert journey.

I was sitting on the sand and all the movements I made were extremely slow. I was simply resting, and as I rested I turned the camera in my hands, after removing it from its leather case. Did it really contain an exposed film? How old was it? If the newspaper that the missing owner of the tent had with him – the one that was now lying at the very bottom of my rucksack – was more or less fresh, then this film had been waiting twenty years to be developed!

'Hey, what are you doing sitting around? Get digging!' I heard Petro shout.

I got up lazily, put the camera in the rucksack and headed for my spade.

And that was how the day passed. As I was on my way back to our campsite, I counted the fruits of my labours – more than forty holes. Forty holes and only one discovery – a mummified lizard! But who knows, perhaps some local history museum might be glad to buy it or at least offer me a mummified jerboa in exchange – there were plenty of those around here too: at least five times that day I had spotted their curious little eyes observing my movements from the low, undulating sand dunes.

As we were drinking our evening tea, the chameleon crept out of the luggage to join us and once again clambered up on to Galya's jeans. This time she stroked him less nervously and smiled.

To everyone's surprise, Gulya told us that she had gone into the town for water and drawn it from a public pump beside a shop selling clothes. Galya's eyes glinted at the mention of a dress shop.

'Is it far?' she asked.

'You're not going there!' Petro shouted at her, surprisingly agitated. 'What did you come here for, to go shopping?' He chewed on his lips and cast a glance of annoyance at Gulya.

'Why don't we see any people round here, if they live close by?'

'They think this place is cursed,' said Gulya. 'A lot of people have been lost here . . .'

'How do you mean, lost?'

'They say that if a weak Kazakh comes here, then straight away he forgets his own language and in a few days he dies from a mysterious melancholy . . . perhaps the lizards here are poisonous?'

Petro looked around him anxiously, although twilight was already thickening the air.

I could understand how Petro felt. The first day of searching had clearly put an end to his illusions about 'easy treasure-hunting', and now there were these local myths . . .

We all fell silent and our silence was rapidly enveloped by the darkness that descended from the sky as the real evening set in. The fire crackled, casting glimmers of light across our faces. A nocturnal freshness appeared in the air, it seemed to wipe down our foreheads, a healing balm after nature's heat. I recalled a student construction brigade from long ago and far away and thought that if I had a guitar in my hands right now, we would sit there until morning, listening to stupid romantic songs.

My mood had improved and I wanted all of us to feel a bit more cheerful. Never mind whatever it was that that was buried here, I wanted to forget the differences that people had invented to divide everyone into 'us' and 'them'. The evening was the same for all of us, and so was nature, and the sand in which we were searching for something or other was all the same colour. And my thoughts and the surprising wishes that I had suddenly felt acquired a clear form and were transformed into a simple request to my Gulya, expressed in a single short word: 'Sing!'

And Gulya started to sing. In the Kazakh language. Her quiet, velvety voice filled the space around the campfire, and it seemed as if even the fire was crackling in time to her song. The song went on and on, and although I couldn't understand the words, in some inexpressible way I felt that I could trust the story that it told. I didn't know what the song was about, who was in it and what happened to them, but the warmth of the song and the warmth of the voice affected me, and I'm sure they affected Petro and Galya too. Once

174

again we were united by a foreign song that neither I nor they could have retold. But I knew that when Gulya finished singing, Galya would ask her what the song was about. And the story that was told would be familiar and comprehensible and exotic all at once. But its exoticism would not be the ethnographical-museum kind. Oh no. Its exoticism would be like a mirror, it would allow us to see that every one of us is distinct from everyone else, exotic for the other person, only not in the way that animals we have never seen before are exotic, but on the inside. Our thoughts and beliefs would be shown to be exotic. And the most important thing would simply be to understand them, and not refuse to understand them out of some acquired habit of disagreement.

The evening lingered on, prolonged by sad Ukrainian songs. At one point I even thought that Petro had begun to sing along with Galya, but when I listened closely, I realised I was mistaken. And once again the songs that rang out created an atmosphere of trust and as I lay down to sleep under the low-hanging sky, we wished each other goodnight for the first time.

But dawn turned the page of a new day, restoring everything to normal, and after a quick drink of tea I picked up the spade and with the sound of Petro's steps at my back, I set off to continue the work begun the day before.

Gulya and Galya stayed with the things and the fire. Petro and I located the boundary of the 'worked' sector of the desert and halted there.

'You're not digging right,' said Petro, surveying the previous day's holes, which had already subsided.

'Well, in the first place, no one ever taught me how to do it and, in the second place – you take the spade and dig, maybe you'll do better!'

Petro stroked his black moustache and gave me a hostile look.

'What did you come here for?' he asked. 'You came to dig, right? So you ought to thank me for giving you a spade!'

I heaved a sigh, adjusted the felt cap on my head, took one step towards the sea from the last hole and thrust the spade into the stand.

The work went tediously again. The closer I got to the sea, the looser the sand was under the surface. At one point the spade struck a rock and I realised that I was simply wasting my time. The well couldn't have been right on the shoreline – it wasn't Caspian water that they used to draw from it!

I walked back to the point I had started from the day before. I glanced round and saw Petro about three hundred metres away. He was standing there, holding a stick in his hand and either gazing at the sand in front of him or lost in thought.

When the sun was suspended at the centre point of the vault of the sky, Galya called us to lunch. We ate insipid unleavened bread cakes that Gulya had brought from the town and washed them down with tea. By that time I had found a brass button from a soldier's uniform in the sand, with the double-headed tsarist eagle. After lunch I held it out to Petro on my palm, without saying anything. He inspected the button curiously, but his curiosity was short-lived, and he started frowning again as he gave it back to me.

The work after lunch failed to produce any surprises. Except, that is, for another mummified lizard, only a lot smaller than the first one. I dug it up out of the hole and immediately covered it with sand again without the slightest feeling of regret as I probed deeper with the spade. By evening, the fatigue was getting too much for me. Not only was I absolutely soaking in sweat, the blisters on my palms had

176

burst and the exposed skin smarted at the slightest contact with the spade. In fact, the spade was gradually becoming my enemy number one.

'That's it,' I decided firmly. 'Tomorrow I'm going on sick leave! I've had enough! Spartacus would have organised a rebellion ages ago!'

That evening passed quietly, without any songs. And we didn't wish each other goodnight.

I sat there beside Gulya, looking up at the starry sky and waiting for a shower of falling stars, so that I could make wishes. But that night the stars were firmly attached to the sky – they couldn't give a damn for me and my painful, smarting palms. And probably for the first time I felt the lofty remoteness of the sky. Feeling out of sorts, I turned on to my side with my face towards Gulya, who was already asleep. I put my right hand on her warm shoulder and froze in that position. And I thought that the chameleon Petrovich also probably froze at those moments when he wanted to halt time, in order not to frighten away a sudden feeling of happiness or simply tranquillity.

45

Another three days went by, but they brought nothing positive. Every day Petro became more irritable and aggressive. And I, exhausted by the heat and the pain in my hands, was in no state to insist on my rights: despite the pain I carried on digging in the sand with the spade.

'I can tie them up in the night if you like!' Gulya whispered to me before we went to sleep.

I shook my head. Previous experience had already demonstrated what tying and untying led to. We simply had to cut ourselves loose from them, but I didn't have either the strength or the willpower. Somewhere up ahead I could still see a vague hope that the search would be successful after all, and I felt as if only that success could free us of their company.

The next morning I started coming across a lot of stones in the sand, both ordinary stones and fragments of limestone blocks that had served as the foundations or walls of some kind of structure. I bent down and examined these stones curiously. Petro was not around – he had obviously wearied of following me. In principle, if the well was outside the fortifications, there couldn't have been any buildings beside it, but then, as I had already seen, a well itself was usually surrounded with stones so that the creeping sand wouldn't fill it in. In any case, I worked more carefully at this spot, and my care was rewarded. I found a gold crucifix for wearing round the neck. Its edges had been badly worn away by the sand, and the small crucifixion itself had been half erased by time. But the discovery lent me new strength, and I continued digging in the sand at that spot with redoubled energy, examining it carefully as I did so. And while I was digging there, the vigour somehow miraculously returned to my body. I glanced around again, this time with lively anxiety, to make sure that Petro was not about.

But there was nobody around, and I carried on with the search. I didn't discover anything else, it's true, but the hope inspired by the crucifix remained as powerful as ever, making me lean my head down even lower to make quite sure that I wouldn't miss any important detail.

There was a surprise in store for me after another half-hour – when I had dug about as far as I could go, I decided to give it just one more shove, and the spade brought up a small yellow key from a depth of almost a metre. I picked it up, rubbed the sand off and inspected it. I was amazed to see that the key was gold – a discovery that naturally brought a smile of ironic mirth to my lips. 'Well, well,' I thought, 'now I'm Buratino . . .'

Focusing on my own ironic thoughts, I sensed something new in myself. I could feel this new thing physically, like an increase in the speed of my blood or the rate of my heartbeat. It was mine, not anyone else's, but at the same time it did not depend on me. For a moment I felt afraid: it was probably like the way people realise in their old age that their sick bodies don't give a damn for the soundness of their minds, their brilliant intellects and their brains that still function perfectly. The body is tired and it wants the soul to clear out . . .

'Maybe I'm ill?' I thought, and started listening attentively to the life of my body again.

I didn't feel any pain and it wasn't like an illness.

'It must be nervous exhaustion,' I decided, and turned my attention back to the little key that I had found. I compared it with the crucifix – the same gold, the same shade of yellow and the same traces of wear from the sand.

I put my finds away and carried on digging, not deepening the hole, but widening it. I was so absorbed in the work that I forgot about the time, and the pain in my palms, and my personal spy Petro, who had gone missing today – which was something I certainly did not regret.

I was flinging the same rocks and sand away from the centre of the hole for the third time when I heard a shout.

'Careful, you idiot! Look under your own feet!' I turned round. Petro was standing not far away. He gestured towards my feet and I saw that there was something black protruding from the sand at a depth of about forty centimetres. We both went down on our knees and started cleaning the sand off the new find with rapid but careful movements of our hands. I noticed that Petro occasionally leaned down and sniffed. I lowered my head too, leaning my palms against the large and so far mysterious object that we had found, and took a sniff. The result was like an electric shock – the smell was so familiar that it was like my own smell.

'Cinnamon!' I exclaimed in instant recognition and immediately pushed myself back up off the black object with my hands.

We were looking at the mummified corpse of a man. Petro also froze and stared. The mummy was lying face down, and so far we had only cleaned off the head, neck and part of the back. The black shrunken skin had the texture of parchment. I remembered the sensation in my palms – the surface they had pressed up against was almost springy. But as well as that I realised that the pain from the burst blisters, which had come to seem almost normal, was gone. When I looked at my palms I was stupefied, the skin was smooth and there was not a trace of any blisters to be seen on it.

Puzzled, I turned my gaze back to the mummy and then looked at Petro. He was cleaning away the sand and stones above the mummy, as if nothing out of the ordinary had happened.

'Well, he can manage here without me,' I decided and simply sat there, watching him work. As I watched, Petro freed the entire black mummy from the sand and called me across.

'Help me turn it over.'

The two of us carefully turned the mummy over on to its back. Now at last we could get a proper look at it. The arms were tied to the body with a faded strip of leather, on which traces of green paint could just be made out. The mummy's legs were tied together with a similar strip. The head was bald, and we both looked below the waist to see if the mummy had been a man or a woman when it was alive. But there was a surprise in store for us. The mummy seemed to have been operated on, either during life or after it. We were obviously looking at what had once been a middle-aged man, with the primary proof of his manhood missing.

'It's a Ukrainian,' Petro said in a quiet, pensive voice.

'How do you make that out?' I asked in amazement.

'You noticed yourself that he smells of cinnamon . . . And that's the smell of the Ukrainian spirit.'

'I smell like that too, and there was the same smell in the late Gershovich's grave when we dug it up. Was he Ukrainian too, then?'

'You don't understand,' Petro said in an unexpectedly gentle voice. 'It's the smell of the spirit, not the nation. It simply means that this spirit entered you and that Jew Gershovich.' And Petro looked up at the sky darkening in anticipation of evening, as if some portent ought to descend from it in confirmation of his words. 'Every nation has fools and wise men, angels and bandits, but the spirit touches with its wing only the very best, and it doesn't look at your passport or check your nationality, it checks your soul.'

As I listened incredulously to what Petro said, I felt the presence of something other-worldly. I wasn't the only one with something new and strange happening inside me, Petro also seemed different and he was talking in an unusually gentle voice. And apart from that, there seemed to be someone else there with us. My gaze fell on the mummy. What if it was alive? I put my fingers to my forehead to check if I had a fever. But my forehead was quite normal.

181

The darkening sky reminded Petro of the time and he stopped talking.

'We have to get back to the girls,' he said. 'How are your hands – not hurting?'

I showed him my palms.

'Look at that!' he exclaimed. 'They've healed up!

At supper, as we sat round the fire, we made conversation concerning exalted matters and worldly problems at the same time. Petro spoke more than anyone else, and from the way that Gulya and Galya looked at him it was clear that this was the first time they had ever seen him like this too. That was understandable enough for Gulya – but for his black-haired girlfriend? Withdrawing a little from the general conversation to immerse myself in my own ruminations over a bowl of green tea, I tried to link my curious internal sensations with the change in Petro's behaviour and almost in his beliefs.

Something had affected us, but what? Solar radiation? The climate? Vapours from the mummy? My internal sensations could have been affected by any of the aforementioned physical factors or any others that I hadn't noticed. But what influence had caused Petro's sudden, surprising eloquence? There was nothing hallucinogenic in the area, and I hadn't offered him any 'baby food' from my cans. What had produced this clear softening of his general attitude?

And the smell of cinnamon? It was real, and it definitely came from the mummy. The same smell that I had picked up from Gershovich's body. Only now it seemed to have left me, as if it had been dried out by the sun and driven away by the desert wind.

'Maybe it's just a smell that's like cinnamon, but really has nothing to do with it,' I thought, clutching at a guess that left at least a tiny hope of some answer in the future.

46

In the morning the three of us left Gulya behind with the things and carried on widening the excavation around the mummy. I didn't show anyone the items I had found the day before – the crucifix and the key. Remembering how rapidly Petro's interest in the soldier's bronze button had evaporated, I didn't think he would pay any attention to them, especially since they didn't smell of cinnamon, which meant the Ukrainian spirit had never come anywhere near them.

The hole had already been widened to five metres in diameter. I was raking away at its crumbling inner edge with my hands. Petro was working with the spade – I didn't understand why he had taken it: perhaps out of pity for my palms that had healed so unexpectedly, or to take the more comfortable work for himself. In any case, whatever the reasons, the outcome suited me. I carefully crumbled away the edge of the hole, peering intently at the sand. So far nothing interesting had turned up, but an incredibly powerful confidence in success held my lips frozen across my face in a smile that was fixed but at the same time bright and absolutely sincere. Several times, looking up from the sand, I caught Petro's gaze on me. He was squinting sideways, but I could see that my smile attracted his eyes like some invisible psychological magnet. At one point I even thought that he smiled too. There was clearly something odd happening to him.

Galya was intently performing the same work as me. But she was even more deeply absorbed in the search for the unknown. For her, as for me the day before, nothing existed apart from the sand in front of her eyes. 'That's the state in which the most remarkable discoveries are made,' I thought, carrying on crumbling the inner edge of the excavation.

My nose caught the smell of cinnamon again – a strong, persistent slightly moist smell. And it was surprising that the sun, which had risen so long ago, had dried out the air and the surface of the sand, but hadn't managed to extract the moisture from the smell of cinnamon.

The smell seemed to be rising from the bottom of the shallow hole, as if it were seeping from below, from somewhere under the mixture of sand and stones that made up the irregular bottom of the excavation.

After a while I found myself enveloped once again by that smell, the same as the first time, when a mixture of surprise and fear had made me take a long soak in a hot bath and scrub myself as hard as I could with a coarse bast wisp after the night at the Pushche-Voditsa cemetery. And then afterwards, when I realised it was pointless to struggle against this smell, a sudden calm had descended on me. And the smell itself had proved to be very refined and gentle, despite its sepulchral origins.

Sepulchral origins! There was a possible explanation for the phenomenon. Yesterday we had found a mummified corpse here. In effect, without knowing it, we had dug up a grave. Dug it up and not filled it in. There was the mummy, lying almost at the centre of the excavation. And it was giving off the smell of the spirit that Petro had talked about at such length yesterday.

I lowered my nose so that it almost touched the sand and sniffed. That same smell of cinnamon . . .

OK, I could go crazy like this!

I took a deep breath, switching my attention to focus on what I could see with my eyes. I started crumbling the sand with the edge of my hand. Suddenly I heard Galya cry out. I looked round. Petro was already squatting down beside her and Galya was holding something up on the joined palms of her hands.

I went over and also squatted down. I looked hard at the long black object that aroused certain vague associations in my mind, trying to link these associations with words. Searching for a name.

'Why, it's . . .' Petro drawled in amazement, touching the object with the index finger of his right hand. 'Why, it's . . .'

I had already realised for myself what it was – the separate mummy of the member that was missing from the large mummy.

'It smells of cinnamon too!' Galya said in a half-whisper, still in the grip of her initial surprise.

Holding the find in front of her face, she kept on sniffing at it, as if to make absolutely certain.

'Put it over there!' said Petro, glancing at the mummy lying behind our backs.

Galya got up slowly, with apparent reluctance, shook off the sand that had stuck to her jeans, carried the small mummy over to the big one and put it down beside it. Then she came back to her place and carried on searching.

Petro smoked a pipe and then went back to the spade. As I approached my edge of the hole, I glanced along the irregular line of the close horizon and saw that the boundary between the visible and the invisible intersected with something that looked like a camel. Yes, there was no doubt about it, a camel had crossed the boundary of our horizon, and beside it I could see the figure of a man. The flux of the hot desert air made it difficult to determine the distance separating it from us, but the distance was getting shorter. I could already tell that the camel was carrying luggage. I looked round to see if Petro had noticed the camel, but he was digging in the sand. Wondering whether to say anything to him or not, I looked at the opposite horizon, beyond which the Caspian Sea lay hidden from our view. At the most distant point of the horizon visible to the eye, to the right of Petro, there was something else moving – eventually I could make out the figure of a man in the distance.

'That's a bit too much for this damned place,' I thought.

But these travellers were still a long way off, so I couldn't be completely certain of the final destination of their journey. After all, there was town close by, they were either on their way to it or from it . . .

Deciding not to distract Petro, I said nothing and went back to my own work post.

An hour later I remembered the two travellers, one of whom had a camel. I got to my feet and looked. And I saw both of them. The man with the camel was getting close, he had no more than half a kilometre to go before he reached us. Approximately the same distance separated us from the solitary traveller, who was evidently walking from the seashore. On looking more closely, I saw that the traveller was carrying a rucksack and wearing a blue tracksuit. And then, as if the air suddenly became more transparent for an instant, I recognised the man. It was Colonel Taranenko approaching. There was no point in keeping silent now.

'The colonel's coming!' I said, and when Petro got to his feet, I also pointed out the man with the camel. Petro was no more interested in the camel than I was. But the approach of Colonel Taranenko set the thoughts in his head moving rapidly.

'I said we ought to tie him up,' he whispered, and then immediately added in a softer voice: 'But then he would have died without water . . .'

Petro spread his hands and shook his head regretfully. Then he turned to me.

'Well, what shall we do?' he asked. I shrugged.

'We can't really apologise for launching him into space!' I replied a minute later.

47

As the two men approached us from opposite sides, one in the company of a loaded camel, my inner tension increased. We stood there without moving. Petro's face was a study in intense resolution. Galya looked bewildered. She didn't seem to know what to do with her hands – she kept lifting them to her face, then lowering them and trying to wipe them on her jeans.

Time slowed down, as if the heavenly projectionist was deliberately stretching out this episode in the movie.

And now I was concerned about the second traveller, the one walking with the camel.

We were at the precise geometrical centre of an imaginary straight line running from the colonel to the stranger with the camel. I suddenly had the thought that all this was simply a coincidence. Our position on the two men's route, that is. And if we moved aside for a while, the colonel and the nomad would meet or, if they weren't intended to meet, they would walk past each other and both continue on their way. However, logic obstinately suggested that the colonel was coming precisely to see us, because he had something to say to us. But the approach of the nomad really was a coincidence, although the consequences of this coincidence were so far unknown. I could guess what to expect from the colonel. Even when considering a colonel in the abstract, it's easy enough to imagine the way he will act. But what could you expect from a nomad, and what made me think he was a nomad anyway? Only the fact that he was walking with a loaded camel?

The sun had already crept a little to one side, abandoning its position at the zenith, and while just recently I had been a man without a shadow, squatting on my haunches and crumbling the sand from inside the rim of the hole, now I had a little shadow anchored to my feet. Time was moving in slow motion, but the sun had not changed its schedule, and the thought came to me that the only clock that would show the right time now was a sundial. Then suddenly I felt like the pointer of a sundial. The pointer has to be the most important thing in a sundial – after all, it stands motionless while time circles around it.

And now the expression on the colonel's face was visible. It was as stony as the face of a statue by Kavaleridze. The teeth were clenched, the jaw muscles were tense. I sensed danger in the very way the colonel moved, and then I saw the pistol in his hand.

'Petro, he's armed!' I said in a low voice.

Petro nodded without looking round.

About twenty metres away from us the colonel stopped, put the rucksack down beside his feet, squared his shoulders and swung his arms, bent at the elbow, through a couple of circles, to loosen up his swollen joints.

'Well!' he shouted. 'Did you think you'd got away?'

We didn't say anything.

'Slipped something in my drink and thought it was all over? That you'd never see me alive again? Yes? Get your hands up!'

He pointed the pistol at me, then transferred his gaze and his aim to Petro. I could see his outstretched hand trembling from the constant effort it cost him to prevent the pistol following its own preference to fall sideways.

I raised my hands above my head, but Petro simply spat good-naturedly on the ground near his feet and smiled entirely without malice as he looked at the colonel, and in this smile, framed by the dangling ends of his black moustache, I saw a benevolence, even sympathy, quite out of character for Petro.

'Vitold Yukhimovich!' Petro said, speaking loudly so that the distance separating him from the colonel couldn't swallow up a single letter of the words he pronounced. 'You ought be resting, not threatening us with your TT! We're all people, aren't we? Surely we can reach an agreement?'

I saw Colonel Taranenko's eyes almost pop out of his head when he heard these unexpected sentiments from Petro's lips. As I watched, he took two unsteady steps forward and an expression of bemusement appeared on his face, exactly like the one that Galya's face had recently worn.

He stopped again, watching us carefully. But there must have been something preventing him from making us out clearly. Possibly fatigue. He rubbed his eyes with his free hand, but still held the pistol up in his right hand, although the barrel of his TT was pointing past us. Petro took out his pipe, lit it and demonstratively released a narrow column of smoke up into the sky.

I lowered my hands. Something strange was happening again. The colonel's belligerence and the determination with which he had pointed the pistol at us were evaporating before my very eyes.

He stopped fiddling with his eyes, rubbed his temple with the fingers of his left hand, looked at the sun and gave us another

189

puzzled look. Then he shook his head in a curious manner, as if he was trying to drive away sleep, and lowered the hand with the pistol.

He took a few more steps and halted about five metres away from us.

'I'm not feeling too good,' he said in a tired voice and sighed. 'If not for you, I'd be in Odessa right now, taking a rest in the Chkalov sanatorium . . . I've been needing a rest for a long time.'

'Come on then, the girls will make you some tea,' Petro suggested in a gentle voice.

Vitold Yukhimovich looked at him suspiciously.

'Your girls made me coffee once already!' he said, but there wasn't a hint of resentment or anger in his tone of voice.

'Do you hear me, eh?' said an unfamiliar voice, suddenly slicing into the calm tranquillity of the conversation.

I looked round, dumbfounded, and saw the Kazakh with the camel at the other side of the hole. The Kazakh was all-over denim – the shirt and, of course, the jeans, and even the belt with the little bag for money and documents attached to it – everything was a worn blue colour. Fastened between the camel's two humps was a bundle with lots of little different-coloured pockets sewn all over it.

'Do you hear me, eh? Do you want to buy food?' the clear-voiced Kazakh continued.

'What kind of food?' the colonel asked the Kazakh over our heads.

'Canned food, chocolate, Iranian macaroni . . .' said the Kazakh, screwing up his eyes to get a clearer look at the colonel. 'I've got bullets for a TT too, really cheap, cheaper than hen's eggs . . .'

'And what can I pay with?' the colonel asked seriously.

'Whatever you like. Dollars, marks, francs, barter . . . You want bullets, right?'

'No,' the colonel replied. 'What have you got in cans?'

'Crabs, very fresh Caspian herring, shrimps . . . all at two dollars a time . . .'

Again my imagination conjured up an imaginary line running from the Kazakh to the colonel, and again it ran straight through us. I wanted to move aside.

But meanwhile the colonel pulled a wallet from the pocket of his Adidas trousers, took out a green note and waved it in the air.

'Give me five cans of herring!' he said to the Kazakh.

'Why give?' the Kazakh asked, suddenly offended. 'You're the customer, I'm the vendor. You come here and buy! The shop doesn't go to the customer!'

'Comrade Colonel,' I said, taking advantage of the pause that followed, 'don't take the Caspian herring.'

'Why not?' Taranenko asked in surprise.

'There's . . . there could be all sorts of things in the can . . .'

'Aha . . .' said the colonel with a knowing smile. 'All sorts of things, you say . . . I get it . . .' And he wagged his thick index finger at me, as if I was a little kid getting up to mischief in kindergarten.

'What's wrong? Don't you believe that I'm a shop?' asked the Kazakh, agitated and upset. 'Here, look, I've got a licence, I've got goods . . . Come and buy . . .'

The colonel smiled, shook his head and then laughed, shook his head again and walked straight by the hole, past us, to the camel-shop, clutching his pistol in one hand and the green banknote in the other, stopping right in front of the camel.

'Five cans of crab,' he said firmly, holding out the ten-dollar bill to the Kazakh.

The Kazakh kicked the inside of the camel's foreleg with his heel and the camel obediently lowered itself on to the sand, folding first the forelegs and then the hind legs. The shopkeeper opened one of the compartments of the large bundle and almost climbed inside it as he took out the cans. He set them out in a row on the sand.

'There, count them,' he said, turning to his customer. 'One, two, three, four, five.' He seemed to be numbering each can separately as his index finger ran along the row.

Then he took a calculator out of the pocket of his denim shirt. Muttering something to himself in Kazakh, he performed the calculation, raised his eyes to look at colonel and declared: 'Ten dollars.'

The colonel laughed. 'And what's this I'm giving you?' he asked, almost sticking the money under the Kazakh's nose.

'Ten,' the Kazakh said with a nod, accepting the note. Taranenko put the cans in a pile and picked them up. He came over to me, put the cans down on the sand and suddenly looked at his right hand, in which he was still holding the pistol.

'Phoo,' he said. 'I was wondering why my hand was hurting . . .'

He unzipped his Adidas tracksuit top and put the pistol in a holster hanging under his left armpit. He closed the zip again and turned to me.

'Tell me, you left Kiev on your own. Where did the Kazakh girl come from?'

'I found her in the desert,' I replied. 'I fell asleep alone, and woke up with her.'

The colonel chuckled and then ran his eye round the edge of the expanded excavation, which had now reached a diameter of ten metres. He saw the mummy.

'What's that?' he asked.

'A mummy,' I replied. 'An old one. It smells of cinnamon . . .'

'Cinnamon?' The colonel took a step towards the mummy. 'Cinnamon . . .' He sighed heavily.

I looked at Petro who was standing there with a laid-back air, watching the colonel.

Galya was squatting to the right of him with her back to us, taking no notice of anyone and still crumbling the edge of the hole.

'Yes,' I thought, 'our colonel doesn't seem to inspire fear in anyone any more.'

Meanwhile, the colonel squatted down beside the mummy, examined it carefully and sniffed at it. Then he noticed the mummified male member. To judge from the fact that he didn't ask any questions, he must have understood everything, or reached some conclusion that he found satisfactory.

'Seems like everything round here smells of cinnamon,' he said thoughtfully as he got up. 'It's a strong smell . . . Very strong . . .'

I sniffed. Either my nose was already so accustomed to this smell that it took it for pure fresh air, or the colonel's sense of smell was a lot keener than my own.

'Strong . . .' he repeated thoughtfully, and I suddenly realised what Colonel Taranenko meant – that the smell of cinnamon possessed some mysterious power, and it was this power that had changed Petro, mellowed his personality and taken away his attitude of aggressive suspicion. The power of the Ukrainian spirit, transmitted by this smell, which had previously held nothing but culinary associations for me – this was the power that the colonel could feel affecting him.

'Petro, look!' Galya called out in a voice of quiet surprise.

Petro squatted down beside her and they both examined

something. The colonel went over to them and stopped. I hurried after him to the site of this latest discovery.

Galya was holding a watch with a leather strap. Petro took it from her, cleaned away the sand clinging to it and looked closely at the dial.

' "Po-be-da," ' he read out, then twirled the watch in his hands, studying it. His face wore an expression of total bewilderment.

I noticed an engraved inscription.

'Petro, there's something on the back of it,' I said.

He raised the watch to his eyes and squinted at it. Its steel back glinted in the sun.

' "To Major Vitalii Ivanovich Naumenko from his colleagues. Kiev, 1968," ' he read.

I glanced at the mummy. I suddenly suspected that there was some kind of connection between it and the watch. Could it possibly be Major Naumenko in person? But who was he and what was he doing here?

The colonel took the watch out of Petro's hands without saying a word and abruptly moved away from us. He stood with his back to us and I thought I saw his shoulders tremble.

Petro looked at the colonel's back too. We exchanged glances. But Galya stayed where she was at the edge of the excavation. Apparently she wasn't interested in men's business.

I heard the sound of a zip fastener opening and saw the colonel's raised right elbow. I was rooted to the spot by tense anticipation – I realised that the colonel was taking the pistol out of its holster. If he swung round now and started shooting, we were done for. At that distance a professional soldier would put us all away in three seconds.

'It's a good thing Gulya's not here,' I thought rapidly, before the silence was shattered by the sound of shots.

I shuddered, but stayed on my feet. Holding the pistol high in his right hand and aiming it at the sky, the colonel fired a few more shots. Then he lowered his hand and his head – I got a good view of his powerful neck.

The silence waited for the echo to fade away and then resumed its rightful place.

We stood there without moving.

Colonel Taranenko turned round slowly. There were tears in his eyes, but his smoothly shaved cheeks were dry. He looked straight through us, as if we weren't even there. He walked across to the mummy and stood over it in silence. Then he went down on one knee.

I thought the funereal silence was never going to be broken. It seemed to have turned to glass. And at the same time the tension mounted. That silence hung over us like the sword of Damocles, rising higher and higher and all the time increasing in size. What would happen when it fell? What would this silence explode into?

Strained to breaking point by the colonel's shots, my nerves refused to settle down. Then suddenly I heard the Kazakh's loud, clear voice again.

'Buy bullets! You've run out, haven't you?'

The colonel turned towards the one-man shop and looked at him sadly with his eyes narrowed.

'How much are your bullets?' he asked in a low voice.

'Three for a dollar . . . ai!' The Kazakh gestured briefly with his hand. 'For you, I'll give four for a dollar!'

The colonel pulled the wallet from the pocket of his tracksuit bottoms, took out another green bill and walked up to the shop, holding it in his hand. The shopkeeper was already rummaging in his bundle to find the required goods.

A jangling sound sliced through the already weakened silence. The iridescent trilling hung in the air, faded away and was then repeated. The Kazakh hurriedly drew his hands out of the bundle, reached into the furthest pocket and took out a mobile phone.

'Yes, yes,' he said in Russian and then immediately switched to Kazakh.

He spoke calmly at first, and then nervously and abruptly. His face turned dark.

Eventually he put the phone away in the appropriate pocket of the bundle, chewed thoughtfully on his lips for a while and went back to selling bullets. He took out a small cardboard box.

'Listen, there's fifty here, take them all!' he told his customer.

'OK, and will you let me make a call? I'll pay.'

'Where do you want to call?'

'Kiev. I'll be quick . . .'

'Twenty dollars then.'

The colonel agreed and when he was given the phone he walked about twenty metres away.

The Kazakh watched him go, and then his face was clouded by thoughts again, no doubt as a result of his phone conversation. He shook his head ruefully.

'Is there something wrong?' I asked. I felt I wanted to be neighbourly with him.

'Ai-ai,' the man-shop said, nodding. 'There are camel races today in Krasnovodsk . . . My camel lost, and I took bets, you understand . . . I'll have to pay . . .'

Petro laughed in surprise when he heard what was wrong.

'Come on then, we'll have lunch together.'

The Kazakh looked at Petro in amazed gratitude.

'Galya,' said Petro, turning to his girlfriend. 'Go back to Gulya and get lunch ready straight away. Say we've got guests!'

As I watched Galya go, I tried to catch at least something of the colonel's telephone conversation. But he was talking quietly and very intently.

48

Soon we set off after Galya. The Kazakh was the only one who decided to stay back for a moment – he said he needed to take an inventory of his stock and bring his records up to date.

There was a surprise waiting for us at lunch – boiled rice. We sat round the fire in a wider circle, so that there would be room for Colonel Taranenko as well. Gulya was not at all surprised to see the colonel. I even thought that when she spooned the rice into the bowls, she gave him more than anyone else.

When the sight of the rice had been transformed into its taste and I was rolling the pleasantly hot, crumbly grains around on my tongue, Petro cautiously asked Vitold Yukhimovich about Major Naumenko.

The colonel halted a spoonful of rice in the air halfway to his mouth, then lowered it back into the bowl squeezed between his legs. He sighed and looked around.

'I knew him well,' he said eventually in a quiet voice, nodding to himself. 'He was a good man. He was carrying out secret research into material manifestations of the national spirit. The organs of state security in every Soviet republic set up departments dealing with that back then. Moscow allocated big money for the research. The ones who got most were the Baltic nationalities, the Tadjiks and us. The Belorussians got the least – apparently they had nothing to investigate . . . I'd just been made a lieutenant and I was assigned to his department . . .'

All of us, even Gulya and I, listened to the colonel attentively and completely forgot about our rice. Noticing this, the colonel paused for a moment.

'Eat, or it will get cold,' he said in a gentle voice. Then he waited until he could see that we had all gone back to eating our rice, which really was getting cold, and continued. 'The department didn't exist for very long. A year, maybe eighteen months. It was very interesting: we studied esoteric Ukrainian folklore, mythology, old manuscripts, even the materials in the archives of the tsarist Okhranka – it turned out that the secret police was interested in this question even at that time. We called in nationalists from the prison camps and interviewed them . . . we kept an eye on groups of harmless nationalists and Gershovich's group.' When he mentioned Gershovich, the colonel looked at me.

'I remember we discovered a number of so-called sacred sites in Ukraine. Usually these sites were located close to an isolated tree – a lime, a willow or an oak. But in the south, in the Kherson region, they were close to the Scythian burial mounds. We established that in the villages close to these sites, the level of crime was several times lower than the average for the Ukraine as a whole, while the general level of intellectual development was higher. There were many other factors that clearly distinguished the people who lived in these villages from those in all the others. Of course, the entire investigation was conducted in the strictest secrecy. All of our records and our analyses were immediately taken away from us and sent to Moscow. And at the time I didn't understand how important this research was.

'All I remember is that Major Naumenko discovered something about material manifestations of the Ukrainian national spirit in Kazakhstan. He put in a request to the Kazakh KGB, which was initially approved. The Kazakhs were willing to cooperate. But then suddenly the order came from Moscow to disband the department and transfer all of its members to different cities, so that the team would not be able to continue working on its own initiative. At that point I wasn't capable of taking any initiative – I was just a dutiful young officer dreaming of a career in the state security services. But I couldn't help admiring Major Naumenko passionately. He was a man of brilliant intellect and pristine honesty . . . After the department was closed, he was posted to the KGB central organisation in Moscow, but when the official car that was supposed to take him to the station arrived at the building where he lived, he had disappeared. His frightened wife showed the driver a note in which he said he was going away for two weeks on a work assignment . . . You can imagine the kind of uproar there was on Vladimirskaya Street! It took the top brass a full day to decide what to tell Moscow.

'The regional state security services combed the forests and villages – all the places he had visited in connection with his research. All his friends and relatives were checked, but he was nowhere to be found. Eventually the top brass had to decide whether to declare him a traitor who had fled abroad or to tell Moscow that he was seriously ill and wouldn't be back for at least two weeks. But in any case it was clear that there was bound to be trouble.'

I suddenly found myself thinking how clearly and concisely the colonel was describing the events of the past. It seemed completely out of keeping with his former shock tactics and clumsy manner of speaking.

My bowl was already empty. I wanted tea, but even more than that I wanted to find out what had happened to Major Naumenko. I heard a camel snorting and looked round – the head of the ship of the desert was emerging over the sandy horizon and with it the shopkeeper.

When he saw the Kazakh and his camel approaching, the colonel stopped talking. He promised to tell us the rest later and turned his attention to his rice.

The Kazakh halted his camel about three metres away from us. He got it to lie on the sand, took something out of his bundle and sat down in our circle. He handed Gulya his bowl, two cans of crab meat and a can-opener. Gulya accepted his contribution without speaking, opened the cans and put some crab meat in everyone's bowl. And she put rice and crab meat in the Kazakh's bowl.

Then she washed out the cooking pot and hung it back on the tripod with water for tea.

'What's your name?' Petro asked the Kazakh, unexpectedly speaking in Russian.

'Murat.'

'Do you live far away?'

'Yes, in Krasnovodsk . . .'

'Do you have a wife, children?'

'Yes, I have a wife. And three sons . . .'

I found this conversation interesting, and I listened attentively. Amazed by Petro's sudden switch to Russian, I tried to detect an accent, but he spoke without one.

The chameleon Petrovich distracted me from the conversation by clambering on to my knee and I plunged back into my own thoughts and feelings. Glancing over the people assembled round the fire, I saw that everyone apart from Petro and Murat was absorbed in their own thoughts. The colonel was sitting motionless, staring at the sand in front of him – no doubt he was recalling what had happened twenty years earlier and was in a sad and pensive mood.

'I wonder if he has a wife and children,' I thought.

I looked at him more closely. I lowered my gaze to his hands, with their thick fingers clenched together. He was sitting cross-legged, with his elbows resting on his thighs. I saw a wedding ring on one finger and a silver ring with a stone on another.

'He's married,' I decided.

The water in the pot was boiling. Gulya had moved close to the tripod and was sitting there on watch. Any moment now she would make the tea. Then what would happen?

'Of course it's hard,' Murat replied to Petro's latest question. 'The tax police here are bandits! If you have a kiosk, they never leave you alone. A camel's the only way out. Serving the needs of nomads . . . My licence says I'm a mobile sales outlet.'

'See how hard it is for people here!' Petro said in Ukrainian, turning to me because he'd noticed I was listening to the Kazakh's story.

I nodded. I wasn't surprised that he spoke Ukrainian to me. He knew that I understood the language.

Gulya was already pouring tea into the bowls.

'Wait!' said Murat. 'I'll be back in a moment!' He ran to his camel and came back with a box of chocolates. He took the cellophane wrapper off it and offered it to everyone in turn.

I took a sweet – the chocolate was melting, and I put it all straight into my mouth, then followed it with a gulp of green tea. The resulting sensation was unfamiliar, but pleasurable. I had always liked contrasting combinations of sweet and salty – sweet tea and a sandwich with pickled herring. This time it was the other way round: the tea was salty and the chocolate was sweet.

'Chinese tea?' Murat asked Gulya. She nodded.

'Wait!' he said, getting to his feet. He ran to his camel again and came back with a large fancy tin of tea.

'Here, it's a present!' he said, handing the tin to Gulya. 'Vietnamese green tea! Pure velvet. Like drinking silk!'

The chameleon climbed down from my leg and set off slowly across the sand, following the precise line of a circle round the fire, as if he were keeping a safe distance. When he reached Galya, he clambered on to her leg. Once he settled in and turned blue to match her jeans, he froze, and nothing moved but his protruding eye, which rotated and occasionally stopped. But it was hard to tell where his motionless gaze was directed.

The Kazakh took a gulp of tea from his bowl, then suddenly seemed to remember something and got to his feet once more. He walked back to his camel and when he returned, he held out a Chinese silk tie in beautiful packaging to Petro.

'Take it, a souvenir of our meeting!' he said. Astonished at his generosity, I suddenly noticed that the colonel was also watching the Kazakh carefully. I could see alarm in the colonel's eyes.

'Murat,' he said in a soft voice, 'it's dangerous for you to stay here too long . . .'

Murat looked at the colonel and smiled, then he jumped to his feet and went to the camel again. He came back with a box of bullets.

'Take them! I can see you're a good man!'

The colonel took his wallet from his pocket and held out ten dollars to Murat.

'What's this, have I offended you?' the Kazakh asked in fright.

'This is a bad place for you,' said Taranenko. 'You must understand! You'll give all your goods to us, and then how will you feed your children and your wife? Eh?'

The Kazakh started thinking. His face gradually turned pale, as if he was beginning to understand something.

'Thank you,' he said in a trembling voice. 'Take them anyway –' He held out the box of bullets to the colonel. 'Thank you very much! I can see something's not right . . . They told me – don't go there, that place is cursed . . . you can end up with nothing . . . Thank you!'

The colonel made the Kazakh take the ten dollars before he would accept the cardboard box of bullets from him.

'You'd better get away from here,' Vitold Yukhimovich repeated. 'Just a moment!' he took out another banknote. 'Sell me two Snickers bars.'

'Why "sell"?' the Kazakh asked, offended. The expression on his face changed, he seemed to be in physical pain, his lips tensed and parted and he brought them back together again.

'Sell them to me!' the colonel insisted. Murat nodded in acquiescence and brought two Snickers bars. He took the money from the colonel.

'Keep the change,' said Vitold Yukhimovich. 'And give the Snickers to Galya.'

Five minutes later, after nodding instead of saying goodbye, Murat ran away from our campfire, dragging behind him the camel that stubbornly refused to move fast.

We watched him go until he finally disappeared behind the crest of a sand dune.

'There,' the colonel said with a sigh, 'that's what Major Naumenko was studying. The material manifestation of the national spirit. The Ukrainian national spirit . . . A weak Kazakh . . .'

'But where does it come from?' Petro asked.

'Where from?' the colonel echoed. 'Where from? Well, basically it's clear enough. Although it still hasn't been proved yet. An analysis of the sand in this area indicates a high level of crystallised sperm. It's fertilised sand, so to speak. Twenty-five years of serving in the tsarist army . . . no women, no joy . . . That's not easy . . . The amount of unused human energy that has gone into this sand . . . You understand me?' The colonel ran a questioning glance around everyone there.

'But surely the soldiers here were not just from the Ukraine?' Petro asked.

'There were soldiers from all sorts of places here, but the victory of a national spirit is determined by its intensity, not its total mass, just like radiation. I think that Taras Shevchenko transmitted his spiritual strength to this place. And when we talk about that strength separately from the man to whom it belongs, it's called the national spirit. It is like the smell of cinnamon in the air. It makes you want to breathe it in . . .'

'But then what happened to Major Naumenko?' I asked.

'I'm afraid all that's left of the major is the mummy. After he left the note for his wife he came here. He set out in secret, in order to verify his conclusions. But by that time this place was carefully guarded – the major wasn't the first one who had wanted to solve this mystery. He didn't come here by the usual route, where he could have been followed, he came via Astrakhan instead. But they were waiting for him here. I'm afraid that first they tortured him, and then just killed him . . .'

'How do you know he was tortured?'

'His severed male member tells me a lot,' the colonel said with a sigh. 'A year earlier Major Naumenko's only child had died of diphtheria. He suffered very badly. He said that life without children was meaningless. He and his wife dreamed of having another child. Whoever was waiting for him here must have known what they could blackmail him with . . .'

'Then,' said Petro, looking the colonel straight in the eye, 'why don't people speak Ukrainian? The national spirit is the expression of the national language!'

'No,' the colonel replied. 'The national spirit is higher than the national language. It changes a man's attitude to his surroundings, to everything around him and to himself as well. The spirit affects a man of any nationality, arousing only the good in him. But language is only the external sign of nationality. The president and a homicidal maniac can both speak it equally well. If you make language the most important aspect of the national spirit, it will become an instrument of segregation and a modern inquisition. A rapist who speaks Ukrainian will suddenly be better than a rapist who speaks Russian. Do you understand?'

Petro listened attentively. He answered the colonel's question with a barely perceptible nod.

'The national spirit teaches us to love the members of all nations, not just our own,' Vitold Yukhimovich added, gazing expectantly at Petro, who was sitting there pensively.

'That's something I still need to understand,' Petro said quietly. He rubbed his right temple with his fingers and started filling his pipe with tobacco.

'You'll have time enough to understand everything,' Colonel

Taranenko said with paternal condescension and turned to look at me. 'There's a lot we still need to understand . . .'

'But what are we going to do with Major Naumenko?' I asked.

'All that we can do . . . He has to be buried with full honours.'

The sound of paper tearing distracted me from my thoughts about Major Naumenko. Out of the corner of my eye I saw Galya rip open the wrapper of a Snickers bar, then divide it in two and hand one half to Gulya.

49

Evening arrived unnoticed. We didn't go back to the excavation site; in fact, we didn't even talk at all after lunch, as if there was no longer any point to our joint undertaking.

Each of us was left to his or her own devices. From time to time Petro fed the fire with the meagre desert brushwood, although the hook on the tripod was bare – the empty cooking pot was lying beside it on the sand. At first I felt like reprimanding Petro for this – the desert had already taught me to be economical with every-thing, especially water and kindling. But Petro's eyes were so thoughtful and sad, that I couldn't bring myself to disturb him. I was also under a gloomy cloud of thoughts and feelings: the colonel's story about the tragic fate of Major Naumenko, and my future, which had retreated even further into the mist – everything made me feel anxious and alarmed. I suddenly felt envious of all the people who lived boring and monotonous lives: the very monotony of their lives, consisting of the five-day working week, parents' meetings and borscht once a week, seemed to me to be a guarantee of a stable and equally monotonous future and a peaceful death. Ah, but come on! What did I want with this monotony? I stopped my snivelling. I had never longed for tranquillity, and I had always been rewarded for its absence. Tranquillity brings nothing but silence and loneliness.

I started thinking about Gulya. Although I had been given to her by her father, she was my most precious reward for not coveting a quiet life.

I glanced round, searching for her. She was sitting on the sand with her back to me, rearranging something in her double bundle. Her emerald-green shirt-dress had a pearly shimmer to it in the warm evening air.

'My future is with her now, and it is no longer mine, but ours,' I thought, gazing at her back. 'We will always be together now, and the very fact that we are so different will save us from the monotonous tranquillity of family life. Where will we live? In Kiev, of course . . . where we have a place to live . . .'

Thinking of Kiev brought back my state of alarm. I wanted to get back there, back home, as soon as possible, but at the same time I felt afraid, more for Gulya than for myself. I was just as defenceless too, but I was far less worried about my own safety. I intended to go back to Kiev with the woman I loved in this strange way. I still wasn't fully aware of how much I loved her – all I knew was that she was the most precious thing I had. In all ages, the one condition required for a calm life has always been the same – don't become necessary to anyone, that is, as they say nowadays, keep your head down. Unfortunately, I had stuck my neck out from the very beginning, and probably too far. If a young fledgling had stuck his head that far out of the nest, he would have fallen and been eaten by a cat long ago.

'Maybe not Kiev. Maybe Astrakhan or any other place where the two of us can settle in at first without much baggage, in some hostel, and then start arranging our lives properly? No,' I realised, 'that's nothing but a fantasy. I can't avoid going home. And there's no point in frightening myself ahead of time – maybe the "baby food" dealers whose plans I spoiled are already lying under the ground at the depth of one and a half metres required by public health legislation. Maybe the people who put them there are already lying there too, and the only difference between them and the first lot is in the dates on the marble tombstones.'

Life is always more interesting than death.

I looked around, Galya was sitting on her bed mat, embroidering something.

In the darkening evening air the only thing my eyes picked out was the ball of red thread on her knees. I found the idyll that had arisen after lunch on that day alarming and moving at the same time. But where was the colonel? I looked around again.

I couldn't see him anywhere. Perhaps he had gone down to the mummy?

Feeling curious, I walked to the edge of the sandy hill and glanced down. The sun's weakened rays no longer reached the site of our search. Down below I could make out the black mummy, but I couldn't see Colonel Taranenko.

Puzzled, but not perturbed, I went back to the fire and sat down beside Petro. I listened to the sound of the fire.

'Petro,' I said five minutes later, 'I want to talk to you . . .'

Petro glanced at me enquiringly. His face was dappled with fire-light, which emphasised the black moustache that drooped down to his chin.

'You know,' I began, 'it seems to me that Gulya and I are

superfluous here . . . This is more your business than mine – yours and Galya's and the colonel's . . . I feel . . . well, how can I put it? I'm Russian. Gulya's a Kazakh. I've only just begun to understand that for you this is a contact with something sacred . . .'

I was speaking absolutely sincerely and the sincerity prevented me from expressing my thoughts more clearly, but Petro suddenly raised one hand to his face, as if he wanted to stop me and I fell silent.

'You're wrong,' he said, speaking in Russian. 'We're not Nazis, and there's no need to be afraid of us. We don't claim that Ukraine is only for Ukrainians. If you love Kiev, then you have to love Ukraine too. But there's no need to put on an embroidered linen shirt and hang an embroidered hand towel over your door . . . All of us together – the Ukrainians, Jews, Russians and Kazakhs – will build a European state . . .'

I was stunned by what Petro had said. It was impossible to believe that this was a member of UNA-UNSO speaking. There was something wrong here. Not only had he started talking to me in Russian, he was expressing thoughts that were more in keeping with the United Nations' declaration of human rights than the ideas of the aforementioned organisation: what I had read in the news-papers about its goals and objectives was the absolute opposite.

'You have to stay with us to the end,' he went on. 'We still have a lot of work to do. When Vitold Yukhimovich comes back later tonight, we'll tell you everything . . .'

'Comes back?' I asked in surprise.

'Yes, he went to the town. He'll bring news. Just be patient for a couple of hours . . .'

I was dumbstruck. Apparently, while I had divided our 'harmonious collective' into three interested parties – Gulya and me, the SBU and UNA-UNSO – the last two had come to terms and formed a single interested party. And now it looked as if they were about to ask Gulya and me to join them.

'I'll go and collect some kindling for tea before it gets completely dark,' Petro said, getting to his feet. His footsteps slithered across the sand behind my back. I was left sitting by the fading fire. I felt a premonition of emotional relief. The explanation for what was happening was somewhere close now. I could feel it. Of course it was very close, down there behind the line of the sandy horizon. It's the sand, I realised. It's the smell of cinnamon, it's the Ukrainian national spirit that has permeated the area around the Novopetrovsk Fortress. That must be the thing that Taras Shevchenko buried in the sand 'three sazhens away from an old well'. It was something invisible, floating in the air, something with an incredible power that was capable of improving people, their thoughts and beliefs. Mysticism? Bioenergy? Karma? Radiation? And what would Colonel Taranenko tell us when he got back from the town in the evening? He was going to tell us something, surely, even if it was only what he had been doing there.

I shook my head to drive away the importunate thoughts and listened to the silence of the desert.

I looked up at the sky, where the distant golden grains of the stars were hatching out.

The approaching night was preparing a starry sky for itself.

50

The colonel came back very late, when a slim oriental moon was already hanging above the ruins of the artillery battery. The fire was giving out a thin stream of smoke, begging for the brushwood lying in a heap beside it, at Petro's feet. Once the colonel had squatted down beside him, Petro set about reviving the flames. Now it was time for tea.

Gulya came over and started dealing with the fire. The colonel nodded, inviting Petro and me to follow him. The three of us walked to the edge of the elevation and sat down on the sand. The colonel looked tired.

'Well then,' he said, 'I've managed to reach agreement on a few things, but we'll still have to monitor everything . . .'

'What is this everything? What have you reached agreement on?' I asked, astounded that I was so poorly informed. 'I don't know anything about this.'

The colonel looked at Petro in surprise.

'What, haven't you explained anything to him?'

Petro shook his head. 'I'm sorry, Mr Colonel, but I can't bring myself to speak on behalf of the SBU.'

'I see . . .' the colonel drawled slowly. 'You still don't understand that we have a common goal – a better future for Ukraine.'

'No, I understand that, but I need time to get used to it.'

'All right then,' the colonel sighed and turned back to face me. 'This is what's going on: first of all we have to take as much of this sand as possible back to Ukraine.'

'What for?' I asked, astonished.

'For the revitalisation of the nation,' the colonel replied. 'You've seen for yourself how it affects people. Not just any sand, of course, but this sand, permeated with the national spirit . . . Anyway, our scientists still have to give their opinion on that question. Our task is to get it to the homeland. And they'll decide what to do with it after that. To be honest, what I'd do is add it to the sandpits at the kindergartens – after all, the children, the new generations, are our future, they have to be quite different, better than us, more decent and honest than us . . . Do you see?'

I nodded.

'So that's why I had a meeting with my Kazakh colleagues today. They promise to help. We'll have to help them in exchange, but that'll come later. The documentation for a Ukrainian-Kazakh joint venture trading in building materials will be ready tomorrow. And then we can export this sand to Ukraine as if it had been quarried. And, of course, we'll have to accompany the consignment.'

'That's all fine, but who's going to decide what to do with the sand after that?' Petro asked. 'The SBU? Won't we be squeezed out?'

The colonel sighed heavily. 'We'll have to discuss all that. In Ukraine they don't know anything about our discovery yet, and I think we'll be able to get the sand through without being noticed. Then we'll store it somewhere and decide what to do according to the circumstances.'

Petro seemed to be satisfied with what he'd heard.

'Major Naumenko's funeral is tomorrow,' the colonel said. 'My Kazakh colleagues will come and help. They promised to be here at twelve.'

I was just about to ask the question that had matured in my mind when Gulya called us to the fire. The tea was ready.

We sat there, drinking tea from bowls, listening to the silence and looking at the stars.

The chameleon Petrovich emerged from somewhere under our luggage that was lying nearby and crept towards the fire. He stopped half a metre away from the flames, then climbed up on to my knee and froze, with his face thrust up into the sky.

When everyone went off to sleep and Gulya took hold of my hand to lead me to our striped bed mat, I realised that I was too agitated. I didn't feel sleepy. I wanted to be alone and I told my wife Gulya so. She nodded understandingly, kissed me and walked away.

Something forced me back from the fading fire. The air seemed cooler than usual, but it wasn't cold. I strolled across the sand to the edge of the elevation.

I looked up at a sky glittering with billions of stars. Then I looked down. The moon's pale yellow light had reached as far as the hollow in which we had dug up the goal of our journey or, to be more precise, the goal of our separate journeys. I raised my left hand to my face and only just managed to stop myself sneezing at the sudden strong smell of cinnamon. Then I sniffed my right hand, with the same result. I looked round at the ruins of the artillery battery in the beautiful light of the moon. A cursed place? What had arisen first – the myth that the place was cursed or the effect of the place, of this sand, on people?

Realising that I couldn't answer that question myself, I tried to distract myself by watching the sky, and I succeeded. I counted five satellites going about their own business, flying between the stars planted so firmly in the heavens. How many years had they been flying like that, fulfilling their cosmic obligations? I remembered the almost daily announcements in the old newspapers: 'Today the sputniks *Soyuz-1554*, *Soyuz-1555* and *Soyuz 1556* were placed in orbit round the Earth . . .' How many thousands of these satellites were there wandering through space now? And was anyone on

Earth keeping track of them? Was there some half-mad scientist somewhere who worried about them, who had adopted all these orphans after the demise of the great space power?

I walked down the hill and strolled across to our excavation. I stopped at the edge of the broad hole with the mummy of Major Naumenko lying almost at its centre. I sat down and lowered my legs into the hole, but they didn't reach the bottom – they were too short by about thirty centimetres.

Immediately I felt a peaceful sensation developing in my chest. My heartbeat seemed to slow down and the blood flowed more calmly through my veins.

'It's so beautiful and peaceful here,' I thought in Ukrainian, and I wasn't even surprised that my thoughts had switched into that language of their own accord. 'It seems so poor, but it's so rich. Did I really have to end up here? But then, if I hadn't ended up here, where would I have been now? Maybe in the next world already? But here I am, alive and happy, and I have a beautiful, intelligent wife ... I just hope it all works out well.'

I sat there until the dawn, thinking in Ukrainian about myself and my life. And when the rising sun had squeezed the thin shaving of the white moon off the sky, the colours I saw took my breath away.

There were only two colours – the yellow of the sand and the blue of the sky.

'Oh, God,' I thought. 'There it is, just like Taras Shevchenko said: yellow and blue! There they are – his favourite colours! The colours that he saw every morning, that reminded him so lyrically of his distant home, the native land that he loved so much and dreamed of returning to!'

The sun rose higher and higher, and I didn't feel any tiredness after the sleepless night. My body was filled with a calm vigour. I could sense a huge amount of secret energy within myself. I didn't know what this energy was waiting for, what it wanted to be spent on. But it was there inside me, it was waiting for its time to come. And it didn't seem to be under my control. It was stronger than me. Perhaps it was a spirit, the same spirit that made people kinder and better despite their own wishes. Or perhaps it was only a small particle of that spirit.

I got up. The sun had not dried out the air yet and it was still carrying a faint smell of the Caspian and a quite distinct smell of cinnamon. As soon as the sun warmed up, both smells would disappear, creep in under the sand, where their moist presence was easier to maintain. And there they would stay until evening, until the heat abated, until the dry air itself wanted to be softened and filled with light moisture, to grow heavier, so that it would not be so easy for the breeze to carry it away from this place further into the desert or the low mountains that framed the desert.

I started climbing the hill, walking towards the thin trickle of smoke rising from the fire that I couldn't see from below. I knew that Gulya was waiting for me by the fire and the water was already boiling in the pot hanging on the hook of the tripod.

51

Shortly after breakfast the silence of the Novopetrovsk Fortress was shattered by the roar of a motor: a powerful, dirty, yellow-green Land Rover stopped beside the fire. It was longer than a usual jeep:

behind the two rows of seats there was an enclosed boot about two metres long. I saw a row of searchlights on the roof of the cab. There were identical searchlights on the steel frame that projected half a metre in front of the bumper. Sitting in the Land Rover were two Kazakhs, both wearing Adidas tracksuits, both about forty years old. The one at the steering wheel got out first. He walked over to the colonel and greeted him. Then the other man got out of the car and joined them in a conversation that I couldn't hear.

Petro and I were sitting by the fire, observing what was going on. Galya was still embroidering something. Gulya had gone to collect brushwood.

When the sportsmen finished whispering, the Kazakhs went back to the car and the colonel came over to us. I could see from his face that he wasn't entirely satisfied with the conversation.

'Get ready,' he said drily. 'We're going in half an hour . . . First we have to dress the major . . .'

'Where are we going?' asked Petro.

The colonel sighed. 'To some holy spot or other. We're going to bury Naumenko there. They've brought a major's uniform.' He nodded in the direction of the two Kazakhs, who were rummaging about inside the Land Rover.

Five minutes later they came over and introduced themselves. One was called Yura and the other was called Aman. Aman was holding a paper bag with a military uniform peeping out of it.

We walked down to the hole in silence. We all worked together, and after about ten minutes the mummy, dressed in a major's uniform, already looked like a man.

Aman went back up, and in a few minutes we heard, and then saw the Land Rover coming down towards us. At the same moment Gulya arrived, carrying an armful of kindling. She exchanged a few words in Kazakh with Yura and nodded sadly. Then he asked her about something.

'What next?' asked the colonel, interrupting them.

'Gulya knows that place too,' Aman told the colonel. 'It's a good place.' The colonel nodded.

'You remember the dervish's grave?' Gulya said to me. 'We spent the night there.'

'That's a long way, isn't it?' I said, trying at the same time to work out how many days it had taken us to walk from there to the fortifications.

'We've got a jeep,' Yura put in. 'It's about five hours' driving round the hills . . .'

When Major Naumenko was put into a black canvas 'sleeping bag' and securely zipped in, tears glinted in the colonel's eyes. We stood beside the bag for a few minutes. Then we loaded it into the back of the Land Rover, in which there were already several limestone blocks, evidently taken from the foundations of the ruins of the Novopetrovsk Fortress

Gulya went back up to the fire. Aman, Yura and I got into the car. The colonel was left alone, standing over the spot where the major had been lying only a few minutes earlier.

'Vitold Yukhimovich!' Aman called to him from the driver's seat. 'Let's go!'

'Do you happen to have a piece of cloth?' the colonel asked, speaking slowly.

While Aman was rummaging in the glove compartment, I got out of the car. It was immediately clear what was bothering the colonel: the major's mummified male member was still lying on the sand.

'Here!' said Aman, holding out a dark green velvet rag through the open window.

217

The colonel took it and squatted down on his haunches. He carefully wrapped the male member in the rag and put it in his pocket. He got into the car.

We drove for an eternity. My backside was aching from the constant jolting and evening was already descending on to the hills. Eventually Aman stopped the Land Rover and I immediately recognised the place, the cleft in the hills with the dervish's grave in the centre.

The vehicle swung round to face the grave and all the searchlights were turned on, lighting the place up more brightly than the afternoon sun.

The load was taken out and the 'sleeping bag' with the mummy of the major in it was laid down, touching the dervish's grave, and limestone blocks were set around it. Then Aman took a strip of green cloth out of his pocket and tied it round the top of the stone column on the dervish's grave, beside the one that was already faded.

Petro watched what was happening with a distrustful air, but he did everything he was asked to do.

Yura took five pistols with silencers out of the Land Rover. He kept one and handed out the others, so now we were armed.

The colonel hefted the pistol in his hand, as if he were assessing its weight. His face took on a harsh, steely expression. He raised his hand, pointed the pistol upwards and looked at us. We followed his example. I just had time to glance up at the sky, and I spotted a satellite drifting slowly past above our heads.

The colonel pulled his trigger. There was a gentle click and a shot. We all fired too. Three times each.

'Keep the pistols,' the colonel told me and Petro.

Then we all drank a hundred grams of vodka, sitting there on the hard salt crust beside the dervish's grave. In memory of the major. In all my life I couldn't remember a silence that had been so funereally solemn.

When I walked away a bit to take a leak, I spotted the small hollows of tracks in the sand. Someone had come out of the desert, very recently, on to this strip of salt crust that served as the foundation of the hills. I immediately remembered the tracks I had seen at the places where I spent the night. I looked around, feeling tense. Suddenly I was afraid. I felt as if someone invisible was following me. I gripped the pistol with the silencer in my hand and felt how useless it was.

I went back to the grave, brightly lit by the searchlights of the Land Rover, and called Aman aside. I showed him the tracks.

'That's Azra,' he said calmly. 'The good angel of death.'

'The angel of death?' I echoed, trying to remember which of us had drunk more.

'Yes,' said Aman, 'the angel of death. The angel that accompanies solitary travellers and sometimes appears to them in the form of a scorpion or a chameleon.'

'Is this some kind of legend?'

'Yes. But when there's no other possible explanation, legends come to mind.'

I pondered that.

'Then does this angel bring death?' I asked after about a minute.

'This angel is a woman. She follows the traveller and protects him on his journey. She follows him and decides whether to help or hinder him. If she doesn't like him, she sends a scorpion, and the traveller dies. If she likes him, she sends a chameleon, and the traveller lives. A chameleon brings good luck . . .'

'And what's she like, this Azra?'

'Do you think I've actually seen her?' Aman said with a shrug. 'They say that the spirit of a woman who loves the traveller settles in her temporarily. Sometimes she can come to him in the form of this woman . . .'

'Interesting,' I said in a quiet voice and glanced at the tracks.

The tracks were becoming less and less distinct even as I watched. The sand was smoothing out its surface.

When it was almost morning, after Aman had brought us to the fortifications and driven away, taking the sleeping Yura with him, I asked the colonel why the major had been buried there, beside the dervish.

The puffy-faced colonel looked me keenly in the eye, as if he was checking whether I would be able to understand him.

'They said a grave like that would make a reliable link in the chain of Ukrainian-Kazakh friendship . . .' he sighed, and then added. 'And apart from that, our embassy hasn't got the money to send the body home . . . I'll take a part of the body to Kiev.'

I nodded. I could see how bad the colonel was feeling. I didn't want to bother him any more, and I followed Petro's example – as soon as we got back he had fallen on to his bed mat beside Galya and was already snoring away with all his might.

'Goodnight,' I said to the colonel.

He grinned wearily and gestured to direct my attention towards the summits of the hills, with the light of the advancing day already percolating through from behind them.

I fell asleep with my arm round Gulya, thinking about Azra, the good angel of death who took the form of a woman in love with you.

52

I woke up when it was close to midday, clutching the pistol with the silencer.

I glanced round. Gulya and Galya were busy with something by the fire, Petro was still asleep. There was no sign of the colonel. It was a few minutes before I was fully awake and recalled the events of the previous day.

I put the pistol away in my rucksack and did two minutes' worth of exercise – a couple of squats and a bit of arm-waving to pep myself up a bit.

The sun was hanging directly above us, driving the shadows straight into the sand.

I walked across to the women and out of the goodness of their hearts, they gave me a bowl of tea that was already growing cool – they had obviously just drunk tea themselves, delighting in the absence of men. Galya was wearing her eternal jeans, and the dark red T-shirt above them elegantly emphasised her small breasts. Gulya was wearing her lettuce-green shirt-dress today.

'I wonder,' I thought, 'how she will dress in Kiev. After all, in an outfit like that she won't even be able to walk down a deserted street in peace!'

'Did the colonel say where he was going?' I asked the women when I had finished my tea.

'He set off a long time ago, about three hours,' Galya replied. 'Maybe to the town.'

'And he didn't say anything?'

'He said he'd be back for lunch.'

I nodded. Galya and Gulya were just starting to prepare lunch, so it looked as if it wouldn't be too long before the colonel came back. Driven by curiosity and a feeling of hunger, I stood beside the fire and watched our cooks closely for a while. Galya rolled out a thin sheet of dough and cut it into little rhomboids, while Gulya cut dried meat into strips on the other end of the same board. There was a pile of purple onions cut into rings lying in a tea bowl beside them. My nostrils were tickled by a pleasant, salty smell. It looked as if lunch was intended to be a special celebration. I gulped.

'What are we having today?' I asked.

'Aman left a little bit of mutton, we're going to have Kazakh soup,' Gulya replied without turning round.

I heard a cough behind me. Petro was awake. He propped himself up on his elbows and moved his head left and right. Then he lay back down and gazed with sleepy eyes at the white sky, flooded with the bright midday sunlight.

The colonel really did get back in time for lunch. It was as if his nose had warned him of the possible consequences of being late. The thick mutton soup in the pot was almost ready, and its smell created an atmosphere of anticipation around the campfire. Yesterday's hundred grams of vodka taken *in memoriam* was still waiting for the food that should have followed.

After lunch the colonel called me and Petro aside.

'You need to get some sleep before the evening,' he said in a kind, fatherly tone of voice. 'There'll be a lot of work to do tonight.'

We obediently made for our bed mats. After the delicious and filling lunch, drowsiness fogged my mind as soon as I lay down on my back and covered my face with the Kazakh felt hat that Gulya's father had given me as a present.

I was woken by the roaring of engines. I raised my head. The noise was coming from behind the close horizon of sand, beyond which lay the slope down to our excavations. I walked to the edge of the high ground and, looking down, I saw an excavator and two large KrAZ dump trucks. One of the trucks was standing a little distance away from the pit and the driver was sitting on the step of his cabin smoking. The other truck was in position for loading, and its driver was wearing a respirator.

The excavator was scooping sand up out of our pit and tipping it into the back of the dump truck, which was already half full. When I looked closer, I saw that the Kazakh in the excavator was also breathing through a respirator. Colonel Taranenko was standing at one side and watching the loading.

I walked slowly down to the pit and approached the colonel.

'Things are moving,' he said to me. 'It's time you were packing your things.'

'What?' I asked in surprise. 'Are we leaving?'

The colonel nodded. 'Aman will be here in an hour. We're going to travel with the load. It's a long journey to Krasnovodsk, more than six hundred kilometres.'

I sighed. In the desert I had grown unused to sudden movements, so I found the idea that I had to pack my things in a hurry extremely disagreeable.

I walked back up to our camp in a very irritable frame of mind.

I tried to take wide steps, but the sand seemed to be laughing at me, crumbling away under my feet and slowing me down. In the end the sand won – by the time I reached the top I was already calm and a little bit tired.

I told Gulya that we had to pack, and she obediently set off towards our things. She folded up the striped bed mat and put it in her double bundle. Then she went to the fire to collect the tripod, cooking pot and other kitchen accessories.

I looked all around. The mechanical din of the excavator conflicted with the dead beauty of these ruins. I tried to count how many days we had spent here, but the noise distracted me. All right, I thought, we have a journey of six hundred kilometres ahead of us – there'll be plenty of time to count the days, and to think about lots of other things . . .

53

We set out as evening was coming on. The two trucks with the sand drove in front. The Kazakh Yura, whom we had already met, was riding beside the driver in the first truck, Vitold Yukhimovich was in the second. The remaining four of us followed on behind in Aman's Land Rover. Aman switched on all the headlights, and the two dump trucks driving ahead of us seemed unreal, as if we were watching a movie. It was a winding road and every now and then the leading dump truck slipped out of the corridor of light. But soon we were lined up again in a more or less straight column and drove on, slowly making our way up into the Karatau Mountains. Of course, it was purely a matter of convention to call these hills mountains. Compared with the Caucasus, they could easily have been called a plain. But even so, they looked incredibly beautiful in the moonlight, which lent them the unnatural bluish colour of a landscape that was more lunar than earthly.

Sometimes we were jolted quite hard, and I turned anxiously to the rear window to see if our things had been thrown out of the back. But the rucksacks, bags and bundles packed against each other seemed to be less affected by the bumps in the road than we were.

The sky was lit up by more and more stars, but we could see them only through the back window of the Land Rover – the bright light from the double row of headlights rendered everything ahead of us invisible, apart from a section of road and two dump trucks.

We reached the port of Krasnovodsk at about one in the afternoon. There were some twenty vehicles waiting on the ferry dock, mostly cars. The ferry, *Oilman*, with its sides covered in rust, did not inspire great confidence. Even the rust on its sides was of two colours: the lower metre and a half had a dirty greenish-brown sheen, but the rust above the waterline, which was now high out of the water, was the traditional brown colour. Aman had already told me that there were only two ferries operating on the Krasnovodsk–Baku routes: the *Oilman* and the *Friendship*, so the chances that this ferry would sink on this particular run, taking us with it, were minimal.

The dump trucks joined the queues for embarkation, but the way on to the ferry was still closed off with a red-painted chain.

The ferry was like an ordinary dry-cargo vessel. It was several times smaller than the floating fish-processing plant on which I had sailed from Astrakhan to Komsomolets Bay. In fact, the only thing that really allowed this vessel to be called a ferry was the bow, which could be lowered to make a bridge for vehicles during loading and unloading.

While I was looking around, studying the half-abandoned port, with its dock cranes frozen in a variety of poses, with its rusty structures protruding here and there out of the reddish earth that also seemed to be covered in rust, Colonel Taranenko came over to the Land Rover.

He asked me and Petro to step away from the vehicle.

'The ferry will leave in about two hours,' the colonel said. 'Listen to me carefully. From now on, you are working for the company "Karakum Ltd". Here are the documents for the sand.' He handed me a large, thick envelope. 'There's money in there too. I'll catch up with you along the way, I've still got business to finish here. You and the drivers will disembark in Baku, they'll transfer the load and show you which road to take out of the port to carry on. At the Azerbaijan–Dagestan border they'll take a fifty-dollar transit charge off you, and there will probably be other problems as well. There are three thousand dollars in the envelope, that should be enough to get you to Rostov-on-Don. If it isn't, then you have guns. But use them carefully.' The colonel paused briefly to give Petro and me a chance to absorb what he had just said. Then he continued. 'You'll have to wait a few days in Rostov. My advice is to send the women on from there on a passenger train. There's no point in doing that from Baku, it's too dangerous. Right then, all the best until we met again! Good luck!'

The colonel shook our hands and walked back to Aman, who was standing beside the Land Rover and smoking.

Petro and I stood there, absolutely dumbfounded. I was holding the large envelope in my hands.

I could still hear the colonel's voice ringing in my ears and I had stopped thinking about the decrepit appearance of the ferry on which we were about to sail across the Caspian. The journey to come was causing me more serious concern now. Not only for myself, but also for Gulya. Above all for Gulya. It would be stupid to expect that we could travel across the Caucasus without any problems, especially in these times, when there was still shooting going on in Dagestan and Chechnya.

I looked at Petro. To judge from his glum expression, he wasn't particularly happy about the journey ahead either.

'Well, what are we going to do?' I asked.

'What can we do?' he replied fatalistically. 'We have to carry everything through to the end.'

He took out his pipe and lit it.

I nodded, and thought to myself: If you were a Palestinian, you'd probably be delighted at every opportunity to die for your homeland and Allah.

I looked round at the Land Rover. Galya was sitting on the metal side step, but Gulya was nowhere to be seen, and that made me feel worried. I went over to Galya and asked where Gulya was.

'She went in there,' said Galya, pointing to a large shed with its rusty doors standing half open.

'What for?'

'To get changed.'

I set off towards the shed, but before I was even halfway there, Gulya come out towards me, wearing jeans and a grey T-shirt. She was carrying her folded dark red shirt-dress.

'Do you know where we're going?' I asked her in a whisper.

'Yes,' she answered and smiled.

'Maybe it would be better if you stayed here? And then you can fly to Kiev, when everything's been sorted out. I'll meet you there.'

Gulya shook her head.

'You and I are one now: husband and wife,' she said. 'I might get lost without you, you'll get lost without me. I don't want to be left alone . . .'

I hugged Gulya, pressing her tightly against myself, and I felt her hugging me back with her strong, beautiful arms.

'Which of us is going to protect the other?' I wondered with a hint of irony.

'Everything will be all right,' Gulya whispered in my ear, and sealed her words with a kiss.

54

As soon as the two Azerbaijanis in dirty blue overalls appeared beside the red-painted chain cutting off the entrance to the ferry, a sizeable crowd of people who wanted to be passengers gathered at the mooring. The queue of vehicles stretched for about two hundred metres, as far as the rusty shed, and its tail was hidden behind it. The word 'TURKMENBASHI' was written on the roof of the shed in white letters a metre high, and this surprised me for moment, until I realised that this was the new name for Krasnovodsk.

Both of the dump trucks were now in the front ten vehicles. I looked round sadly at the Land Rover. It inspired more confidence in me than the KrAZ trucks did. And although I had no particular reason to trust either Aman or Yura, I would have felt far easier in my mind if they were setting out with us. It was entirely logical for them to stop here, though – they were simply staying on their home territory. But why was Colonel Taranenko staying behind with them? What business was it that was keeping him here in Turkmenistan, if the most important task of all was to deliver the sand to the Ukraine?

The red-painted chain clattered to the ground. One of the Azerbaijanis lazily hauled it away, shoving it against the side of the ship with his feet. The other stood in the middle of the opening and waved for the first vehicle to move forward. A red Zhiguli drove up to him and stopped. The driver – a short, skinny Caucasian – got out of the car, counted out the right number of banknotes to the guy in overalls, went back to his car and drove on to the deck.

The supervisor watched carefully to see where the Zhiguli went and where it stopped, then turned back and waved for the next vehicle to move up.

The sun was scorching. I took the pointed felt cap out of my pocket, opened it out and put it on my head. Then I went back to Gulya.

'Hasn't Aman told you anything?' I asked.

'About what?'

'About our journey . . .'

'No,' said Gulya. 'He just wished me good luck. Three times.'

'Three times?' I asked.

She nodded.

I looked round and glanced at Aman, Yura and the colonel, who were standing between the jeep and the shed, calmly discussing something or other. I looked at Petro and Galya, who were sitting silently on the steel step of the Land Rover. Despite my own inner tension, there was an incredibly calm atmosphere that enveloped everything in the port. I couldn't help noticing the cool, calm expressions on the faces of Petro and Galya, and the carefree air of the colonel and his colleagues. Even the loading of the ferry was somehow proceeding too calmly, with no hurry, no fuss or shouting. The pedestrian passengers were waiting patiently as the vehicles drove on to the deck one after another.

The second Azerbaijani in blue overalls started helping the first: he walked on to the deck and watched to make sure that the drivers parked their vehicles closer to the centre of the tightly packed rows, without leaving any space unused.

The tail of the queue of vehicles moved into view from behind the shed, and soon this snake on wheels had crept all the way on to the ferry's deck, filling up all the space.

Half an hour later, after boarding the ferry and piling our things together on the upper deck, the four of us watched the port of Krasnovodsk moving away, and the brown Land Rover gradually being transformed into a dark blob.

The sea was calm. The dirty, dark green water, covered with a mother-of-pearl film of crude oil, swayed gently as the ferry sailed unhurriedly on its way.

The seagulls called loudly as they alternately overtook the ferry and flew back to its stern.

But no one threw them any food. The passengers, most of whom were Kazakhs and Caucasians, sat on their bags and suitcases without speaking.

'Let's take a stroll,' I suggested to Gulya.

Leaving Petro and Galya to keep an eye on the things, we walked across the deck and round the sides of the ferry, studying the horizon on all sides.

The damp air smelled of salt and iodine. And the sun, which was hanging between us and the shore, didn't feel hot.

We stood at the stern with our arms round each other, watching the low waves creep away from behind the ferry towards the shore that was retreating into the past. From that distance we could make out the part of the town that had been hidden behind low yellow hills to the right of the port. Ordinary five-storey blocks of flats.

'Have you ever been to Krasnovodsk?' I asked Gulya.

'No.'

'Neither have I,' I laughed.

There was a Kazakh family beside us, sitting on a camel-hair blanket spread out at the edge of the deck – a husband, a wife and three little girls, the youngest of whom was about three and the oldest about eight. They were dressed in city clothes, without any bright colours. Dull dresses. And the parents, who were about thirty years old, were dressed modestly, as if they deliberately wished to avoid attracting attention.

Suddenly another girl of about ten sat down beside them and I realised that she was also a member of this family. She had brought a two-litre can – the same kind that I used to take to collect the milk in my childhood. There was steam rising out of it.

'There's hot water here,' I said to Gulya and nodded at the can.

I set out, carrying the cooking pot in my hands. When I finally found the place where you could get hot water, it turned out that on this ferry you had to pay for everything. The cooking pot held two litres.

'One dollar,' said the Azerbaijani in control of the tap of the water tank. 'Maybe you'd like some instant soup? Or grain to boil? We have everything, all at good prices . . .'

I looked in the large envelope that Colonel Taranenko had given me, found the wad of dollars and took out the smallest note – a ten – then went back to the water tank.

The Azerbaijani didn't have any change, so I had to take three packets of instant soup made in some Arab country or other.

After lunch, we settled down in a double row at the edge of the boat and dozed.

Time passed slowly. I opened my eyes every now and then to see if the sun was still high in the sky. Eventually I looked and the sun was already on its way down.

I got to my feet and leaned my chest against the side. The sea was still as calm as ever, but it was a bit cleaner. The horizon had moved closer. Between us and the horizon there was a cargo ship sailing in the opposite direction, going about its own business.

I watched it for a while, glad to have something to fasten my gaze on at least.

The others were asleep. Petro was snoring gently. Looking round, I saw several more groups of sleeping passengers. Almost everybody on this ferry seemed to be travelling in families. And almost everybody around me was sleeping on blankets spread out on the deck.

The wind grew stronger and the swaying gelatine surface of the calm sea was broken up into rows of low waves. The ferry started rocking – the sea seemed to be trying to lull it to sleep, like a child in a pram. I immediately recalled the floating fish-processing plant: in fact, it didn't actually surface out of my memory – it was my body that remembered the way the huge monster swayed on the waves. My hands remembered the trembling metal of the side that I clung to during that swaying. And that storm, the only sea storm of my entire life, was played out in front of my eyes like a movie newsreel. The crashing of the waves in the night, the creaking of the metal under the pressure of the wild water and me, clasped tight in Dasha's embrace to stop me falling, while she, who was well used to storms, slept calmly through the wild raging of the Caspian elements. How much time had passed since then? How many days and weeks?

Not so very many, it seemed, but now all that was part of the distant past, a past to which I could never return.

I looked down at Gulya. She was sleeping on her side, with her head resting on Galya's bag. The jeans suited her better than the shirt-dresses. She had immediately become one of us, as if she had simply changed her clothes after performing in a folk-dance ensemble. But even so, remembering her father and sister and those days spent in their *kibitka*, I realised that her view of life could never be the same as mine.

Now, at least, there was no external difference between her and us – me, Petro and Galya, that is. 'But in reality,' I thought, 'it must take a great effort to conceal her excitement and everything she thinks about our journey and our future together in general.' I didn't really believe all that strongly in her eastern spirit of resignation. And yet at the same time I trusted her completely, I trusted her more than Petro or Galya or – especially – the colonel. She was from another world, but she was my wife. Although our marriage was more of a mystical event, thrust upon us by the heavens above, than a reality behind which there lay concealed – as there must be behind every reality – the document that substantiates it.

I suddenly heard a quiet clanking sound behind me and instinctively swung round. Standing about ten metres away from us behind a capstan engine was a short, swarthy man about forty years old. As soon as our eyes met, he turned his head abruptly and strode away rapidly. After he'd gone about ten metres, he disappeared behind an iron staircase that led to the covered lifeboats hanging above both sides of the ferry.

He disappeared, but for several seconds I could still see his swarthy face in front of my eyes. He didn't look like a Kazakh or an Azerbaijani. More like a well-tanned Slav. But then I forgot his face and my thoughts focused on Gulya again: I imagined her on the streets of Kiev, sitting at a table in a cafe or in my flat beside St Sophia's Cathedral, on the square that was filled with the chiming of bells every Sunday.

As darkness advanced, the horizons came to life, and here and there in the distance I could see the lights of invisible ships and fishing schooners. On the deck the ship's lamps glowed dully behind their oval grille-work covers. A bright yellow light poured down from the captain's bridge, but it was blocked off by the lifeboats hanging above the deck and the iron gangways and stairways, so that the only drops of it that reached us fell as patches on the inner deck.

After catching up on our sleep, we felt wide awake, despite the darkness and the waves that were rocking the ferry like a cradle.

Petro was twirling the pistol with the silencer in his hands.

'Put that away,' I told him, leaning closer.

'It's an awkward weapon,' he said, stowing the pistol in the bag. 'The silencer's very heavy. Do you know when we'll get to Baku?'

I shrugged. That was something I'd like to know myself.

'I wish we were already on that train,' Petro sighed. Then he turned to his girlfriend and said, 'Galya, make some coffee.' Galya took out her coffee apparatus. She tipped coffee into the *djezva*, added some water from the canister that had been refilled in the port of Krasnovodsk, lit a tablet of solidified alcohol and set the *djezva* on the blue flame.

55

A few more hours went by. The sea calmed down again, and the waves eased off. The ferry sailed close by an oil-drilling platform with the bright flame of a flare dancing above it like a beacon.

Gulya and I were standing at the side again. My hand was resting on her shoulder. We silently watched the blazing flare until it was left far behind.

Petro was sitting on a bed mat, smoking his pipe and generously sharing the light tobacco smoke with us. Galya was sleeping. The only sound in the silence of the dawn was the droning of the ship's engine. But we had rapidly grown accustomed to this mechanical sound and no longer noticed it, as if it didn't even exist. For us it was simply a part of the silence.

'Hey,' I whispered to Gulya, 'where's our little chameleon?'

'In my bundle,' she whispered back in my ear.

'Isn't it stuffy for him in there?'

Gulya laughed. 'Of course not. He likes it much better than the desert.'

I heard the hollow echo of rapid footsteps somewhere behind me and turned to look. The shadow of a man slipped up the lower steps of the iron staircase leading to the lifeboats.

'Someone isn't sleeping,' I said.

'It will soon be morning,' Gulya whispered. 'Look, there's the waterfront!'

I turned to follow her gaze, looking straight ahead in the direction of the ferry's movement. In the distance I could see constellations of little lights rising up into the air.

'Petro!' I called in a gentle voice. 'Baku!'

He got to his feet and came over to me, still with the pipe in his mouth. He looked hard at the distant lights. Then he tapped it against the side, knocking out the smoked tobacco. He sighed.

'In three or four days we'll be home,' he said in a fatalistic voice, as if he didn't want to go home at all.

'Provided there are no adventures on the way,' I said. He turned towards me with a sad look and nodded.

'It would be good if there were no ad-ven-tures . . .' he said.

About forty minutes later the ferry came to life. The passengers woke up and started gathering their things together and folding up the blankets and sleeping mats laid out on the deck.

Petro went over to the KrAZes – he wanted to check the plan of action with the drivers. Galya woke up, splashed a handful of water from the canister into her face and got to her feet. She looked curiously at the lights of the city that our ferry was approaching – they were closer now. Then she offered to brew coffee for Gulya and me and we eagerly accepted.

'Everything's good,' Petro said when he got back. 'They'll load everything themselves, and we'll travel in the guards' carriage, accompanying our cargo.'

Galya made coffee for Petro too. When he finished his favourite beverage, he lit up his pipe again.

'You could try not smoking for one day at least, your tobacco's almost run out already,' Galya reproached him.

'We'll find tobacco and coffee in Baku,' Petro replied calmly.

The halo of the rising sun appeared above the horizon behind the ferry. The darkness was rapidly dispersing almost before our very eyes, making way for the new day, for new light. The passengers lined the entire edge of the deck, contemplating the smooth surface of the water and the approaching city. We could already see the port, with the jibs of the cranes rising up above it.

We sailed past tankers, cargo ships and trawlers standing at anchor in the roadstead and our mood improved. The energy bubbled up inside us, even though we had been awake most of the night.

'Everything will be just fine,' Petro declared with firm, even slightly aggressive confidence to no one in particular. And after this declaration he raised his pipe to his mouth once again and drew on it. 'Everything will be really fine!'

'A spirited attack is already half a victory,' I thought, feeling glad for Petro and envying him slightly.

At least another two hours went by before the ferry finally docked and allowed the thirty-something vehicles, including our two trucks, to drive off its deck. Now they were all standing in line on the long, broad quayside, waiting for the group of Azerbaijani customs men who had surrounded the first car – a grey Volga that had not seen a bucket of soapy water and a rag in a very long time.

We were also standing on the quayside with our things, waiting for the trucks with our cargo to approach the customs service barrier. On all sides the port stretched out as far as the eye could see.

The piers bit into the Caspian Sea one after another, like long fangs. Some had a single ship standing at them, while others had several small vessels. There were different-coloured flags waving above the ships – the new flags of new states. I glanced round curiously at the radio antenna of the ferry *Oilman* and saw the new flag of Azerbaijan fluttering on it.

Suddenly an alarming thought interrupted my study of the port. The main thing they did at customs, I thought, was to check baggage! I recalled my rare crossings of the Soviet-Polish border, with the stony-faced customs men in green uniforms who had made me open my suitcases and tip out the contents of my bags straight on to the lower bunk of the compartment.

'Petro!' I said in alarm. 'We have guns . . . And this is the customs! We could get caught.'

'Have you read the newspapers at home?' Petro asked me calmly.

'In Azerbaijan the average monthly income is twelve dollars. Take a look at the notes we have in the envelope!'

I pulled the envelope out of my rucksack, glanced inside it and rustled through the notes without taking them out – the wad of dollars was mostly twenties and tens.

'There are twenties and tens,' I said, turning back to Petro.

'You see,' he said with a smile. 'Let's say it's ten for each of them, we'll give them forty.'

My moustachioed partner's optimism calmed my nerves. I set aside forty dollars in my pocket and stuffed the envelope back deep into the rucksack, almost down at the very bottom, close to the Smena camera, the cans of 'baby food' and the pistol with the silencer, so that it wouldn't be too obvious if the customs men decided they wanted to take a look inside anyway.

And then I watched the customs men at work. They worked at a leisurely pace.

As far as I could see, their job consisted of talking to the driver and receiving a certain amount of money from him, but from the quayside it was impossible to see exactly what sum and in what currency. I finally calmed down and began glancing round at the sea, the ships and the port buildings again.

'Kolya,' Gulya said in a warm whisper that tickled my ear. 'I think we're being followed . . .'

She gestured towards the ferry, and I saw a man I had noticed before – the suntanned Slav type dressed in canvas trousers and a blue sweater. He was standing sideways-on to us, examining something on the waterfront.

There was a half-empty kitbag dangling behind his shoulder. Even from where I was standing I could see his snub-nosed profile. His light brown hair stuck up in an untidy grown-out crew cut.

'He was looking at us and our things for a long time,' Gulya whispered.

I nodded.

Looking at someone for a long time didn't necessarily mean that you were following them, I thought, but in my heart I felt that Gulya's suspicions were correct.

The first of the KrAZes drove up to the customs barrier. Petro and I were watching the customs men closely now. Both drivers got out and talked calmly to the customs men about something. Then one of them showed the customs officers some documents and papers that were obviously to do with the cargo. One customs man studied them carefully and gave them back to the driver, but that was obviously not the end of the conversation. About two minutes later the driver with the papers walked over to us, leaving his partner and the trucks at the customs barrier.

'The documents aren't in order,' the Kazakh driver said as he reached us. 'They say we're not registered for transit!'

'And are we?' I asked

'See for yourself!' said the driver, handing me the papers. I ran my eye over them, but basically all I understood was that the Ukrainian-Kazakh joint venture 'Karakum Ltd' had dispatched twelve tonnes of building sand to Kiev via Baku, Makhachkala, Rostov-on-Don and Kharkov.

'What do we do?' Petro asked the driver.

'Pay,' he said with a shrug.

'How much?'

'Two hundred will do it,' the Kazakh suggested.

Petro gave me a thoughtful glance. I understood without having to be told. I opened the rucksack, took out the sum required and handed it to the driver.

Five minutes later the truck had passed the customs barrier and stopped beside a block of containers stacked four high. One of the drivers got out and waved to us.

Galya helped Gulya to throw the double bundle over her shoulder and then grasped the black shopping bag in her arms. We walked slowly up to the customs post. When we got there the final vehicle had just left.

'Pa-ass-ports!' a customs man with a short grey moustache commanded. 'Where are we going?'

'To Kiev,' I replied for all of us.

'Transit?'

I nodded.

He studied our passports and compared the photographs with our faces, and then kept hold of the documents.

'What are we carrying?'

'Personal items,' Petro said in Ukrainian.

'What?' asked the customs man, pricking up his ears.

'Personal items,' Petro said more quietly in Russian.

'You can talk your own lingo at home, but here you answer in Russian!'

Realising that the situation had to be saved, I drew the customs man's attention to myself.

'How much do we have to pay for transit? We're on our way back from my wedding,' I said, and nodded at Gulya.

'Wedding?' the customs man asked, suddenly smiling. He looked at my wife, still a smile on his face, and wagged his head in approval. 'How much did you pay?'

'A lot!' I said, making it up as I went along.

'A Kazakh girl?'

This time Gulya nodded.

'Ai, good for you,' said the customs man, looking at me again. 'Better travel to a long way than just pick up what's lying in front of you! Give me twenty dollars each and be on your way!'

I only had forty dollars in my pocket and I didn't want to get anything out of the rucksack while he was watching me. I cast a quick glance at Petro. He understood.

'What's the best way to get to Kiev from here?' he asked the customs man.

The customs man thought about that, looking down at his feet. While he was thinking, I managed to open the rucksack and reach straight into the envelope.

'You know,' said the customs man, raising his eyes to look at Petro, 'there's a goods train from here to Rostov every day. There are wagons for Rostov and for Kiev. Go and have a word with the dispatchers, it'll be safer than going on the passenger train . . .'

I smiled as I clicked the spring catches on the rucksack shut. The customs man had advised us to do just what we were intending to do. Which meant the colonel really had worked the route out thoroughly before he briefed us.

We paid the fee for transit and set out towards the truck. Only one of the drivers met us, the other had already gone into the Baku Port cargo depot to make arrangements for a goods wagon.

'Listen, can you get me some coffee and something to smoke?' Petro asked the driver in Russian.

'What kind of coffee?'

'Ground, of course.'

The driver nodded.

At Petro's request I handed the driver a twenty-dollar greenback and he disappeared behind the huge four-storey block of containers, leaving us to guard the trucks. About fifteen minutes later he came back with a cellophane pack of ground coffee and a similar, smaller pack of tobacco.

'What, is there a shop here then?' I asked the driver, thinking about what I would like to buy for the journey.

'A shop?' the driver laughed. 'This whole place is a shop,' he said, gesturing round at the port. 'They've got everything here! Vodka, cars, tinned goods . . .'

'I get it,' I sighed, suppressing my mounting consumerist hankerings. 'We'll wait for the lights of the big city.'

'Everything's more expensive in the city,' the driver responded.

I didn't say anything to that.

Soon his partner came back.

'We have a wagon,' he said. 'Only it's not very good . . .'

'What does "not very good" mean?' Petro asked him.

'It hasn't got any cover. It's an ordinary bulk wagon, and they've made a compartment inside for people accompanying the cargo, but there's no roof . . . We could take another one with a roof over the compartment and buy a tarpaulin from them to cover the sand . . .'

'How much does it cost?' Petro asked in his fatalistic voice.

'Two hundred and fifty . . .'

Petro looked at me and I suddenly realised that I was finding the responsibilities of treasurer rather burdensome. Why had I kept the envelope in my hands? Now, when the dollars ran out, Petro would look at me as if I was an embezzler, not a treasurer.

'You know what, why don't you pay for everything?' I said, reaching into the rucksack.

I handed him the envelope in full view of the driver. Petro was clearly annoyed. He counted out two hundred and fifty dollars and handed the envelope to Galya.

'Look, you be our bookkeeper, just to make sure everything's all right!'

Galya nodded docilely, but I spotted perplexity and concern in her eyes. She put the envelope in her shopping bag, then spent a long time shoving it down deeper between the other things. Eventually she pulled the bag's zip fastener closed with an effort and looked enquiringly at Petro. He merely nodded his head.

The second driver was already walking along the massive bulk of the containers towards those sounds so familiar from my childhood – the metallic clanging, scraping and banging of railway wagons being coupled together.

Looking around, I spotted the swarthy Slav peeping out from behind the base of the nearest port crane about a hundred metres away.

I nudged Petro with my elbow and directed his gaze towards the stranger.

Petro whistled thoughtfully and turned back.

'We're either being escorted or set up . . .' he whispered towards me.

When I looked in the direction of the nearest crane again, there was no one there.

56

Evening brought an unaccustomed coolness, as if Baku and Krasnovodsk/Turkmenbashi lay on different lines of latitude. Maybe Turkmenistan was closer to the sun than Azerbaijan, or maybe there was already a breath of autumn in the Caspian breeze.

We sat on our bags, which were set out in a circle on the ground. Once again, just like in Mangyshlak, there was a fire burning at the centre of our circle and water boiling in the cooking pot. Only the fire was a bit stronger – here the broken wooden crates that were lying around in such great numbers served us for firewood. Life in the port had already come to a standstill – the cranes were motionless, with their jibs thrust up into the sky. There were several other fires burning on the quayside, and the passengers who were warming themselves round them would be setting off in a few hours with the ferry *Oilman* on its return journey. There were about fifteen cars dozing in a queue at the entrance to the quay.

'Kolya,' Galya said to me, with an unusually serious expression on her face, 'how many dollars are left in the envelope?'

'We paid eighty for transit, two hundred and fifty for the wagon, another two hundred for the transit of the cargo . . . that makes five hundred and thirty, plus minor outlays, thirty or forty dollars. Three thousand minus five hundred and sixty.'

'Two thousand four hundred and forty,' Galya said with a nod and wrote the figure down in a little notebook. 'And was there exactly three thousand to start with?'

'I didn't count it.'

'You ought to have counted it,' she said with a sigh. 'All right, we'll check it later . . .'

The relative silence of a port in the evening was broken by the roar of engines as the two KrAZ trucks joined the back of the queue. The doors of the trucks slammed as the drivers got out. They lit up and sat down on the step of first truck, and then one of them came towards us.

'Everything's in order,' he said. 'How about some tea?' He nodded towards the pot full of boiling water.

Gulya started, took a pack of tea from her bundle and tipped a handful straight into the water. Then she brought out the drinking bowls.

'Sit down,' Petro said to the driver. The Kazakh settled between Galya and Petro.

Gulya wrapped a towel round her hand, lifted the cooking pot off its hook and deftly poured out the tea.

Then she gave everyone a little salty ball of cheese.

'The last ones,' she said with a sigh. We held the tea bowls in our hands. The tea was still too hot. I had already popped the ball of cheese into my mouth, and its salty flavour spread across the roof of my mouth, making me feel thirsty. I wanted to wash the saltiness down as quickly as possible, but I forced myself to wait patiently until the tea had cooled a bit.

'Here are the documents,' the Kazakh said, handing the papers to Petro. He took a gulp of tea, and only then popped the ball of cheese into his mouth. 'We're going back now. When we finish our tea, I'll show you to the wagon . . .'

I took a small sip – no, it was still too soon to drink it. The Kazakhs' throats were obviously more resistant to heat, I thought, looking at our driver. We hadn't even asked him his name. Now he and his partner would go away and remain in our memories simply as two Kazakh drivers who had transported our sand from Mangyshlak to Baku. And maybe that was right, after all, the only conversations we'd had with them had been brief ones about the job. We had nothing else in common. And anyway, if you asked every chance acquaintance that destiny brought your way what his name was, you couldn't possibly remember all the names . . .

The wind off the Caspian was blowing more strongly now, and I started feeling cold. My hands held the bowl and absorbed its warmth, but the warmth didn't move beyond my wrists. It would make sense to get my windcheater out of my rucksack, I thought. But the thought remained a mere thought. I found a more rational way to get warm – I simply got up and moved the rucksack I was sitting on closer to the fire.

Now, although the wind was blowing on my back, the heat from the fire was stronger. I was already drinking my tea, and the ball of cheese was losing weight, getting smaller and smaller as it rolled around on my tongue and transmitting its saltiness to the bitter green tea.

'I'll just be a moment,' the Kazakh said, putting his empty bowl down on the ground in front of him.

He walked over to the trucks and came back with a paper bag in his hands.

'Here,' he said, holding out the bag to Gulya. She looked inside it and smiled.

She said something to the driver in Kazakh. Probably thanking him. He answered her in Kazakh too. Then he turned to us.

'Let's go, or they'll move the wagon – then it'll be hard to find.'

Petro scattered the fire with his foot and then stamped out the burning boards. Gulya gathered up the tea bowls and the tripod and put them away in her bundle. The Kazakh easily tossed her double bundle over his shoulder and strolled off along the wall of transport containers. We followed him.

About two minutes later we stopped in front of two wagons coupled together.

'That one's yours,' said the Kazakh, pointing to the wagon on the left. It looked like an ordinary goods wagon. But when I tried to slide its door open, the Kazakh stopped me.

'The compartment has its own entrance,' he said, pointing to the left side, where I saw a rather strange little door that looked as if it had been carved bodily out of the wooden wall of the wagon. 'If you roll this one back' – he pointed to the centre of the wagon – 'the sand will fall out.'

I walked up to the side door. Two small steel steps had been welded in place underneath it, with the lower one a good fifty centimetres off the ground. I opened the door and glanced inside, but I couldn't see anything except intense darkness.

'Here, take the torch,' the Kazakh said.

I ran the torch beam over the interior of the compartment for accompanying personnel. The door led into a little hallway. I could see two doors at the end of it – one leading into the toilet, that is, into a small square space with a round hole in the wooden floor and an old door handle nailed to the floor on the left of the hole. On the right of the hole there was a ten-centimetre nail protruding from the wall, evidently for spiking newspapers that had already been read. I remembered the solitary newspaper that was lying somewhere on the bottom of the rucksack, the one I had found together with the Smena camera in the tent that had almost become my grave.

The second door led into a compartment with four bunks and a small table.

The lower bunks were made of wood, covered with imitation leatherette. But the upper ones were clearly imported items. They had been torn out of written-off German wagons and nailed to the wooden walls of this compartment. Somehow it seemed clear to me that Petro and I would be inhabiting the hard lower bunks. 'All the best for women and children,' I thought and laughed to myself at the old Soviet slogan.

'Hey, Kolya, where are you in there?' I heard Petro's voice call from outside.

I went back to the open door and was immediately handed the shopping bag by Petro.

When I'd loaded all the things inside, I went back to the Kazakh standing by the wagon.

'Listen, sell me the torch, will you?' I asked him.

'Better take my matches, my torch won't be much good to you. It's Chinese, you won't find any batteries for it.'

'Is there any door between the compartment and the sand?' I asked, stuffing two boxes of matches into my pocket.

'Of course, from the toilet.'

I shook the Kazakh driver's hand in farewell and went back into the wagon, closing the door behind me. I walked through into our compartment with a lighted match – Galya, Gulya and Petro were already sitting on the lower bunks. I sat down beside Gulya and blew out the match. The darkness was immediately unbearable. I put my arm round Gulya and pulled her against me. Then I found her warm, smooth face with my hands and kissed her. These embraces calmed me and made the darkness surrounding us less ominous.

'They could at least have made a window,' Petro's voice said in the darkness.

We heard a ship's whistle in the distance. Then silence fell again and lasted for twenty or thirty minutes, until it was replaced by a dull hissing sound that grew louder and louder. As the noise approached, it acquired rhythm. The blow, which could not have been called unexpected, almost threw Gulya and me off the bunk. The wagon jerked and began creeping slowly along the rails. The iron wheels counted off the first joint and then stopped. There was another blow, and this time Gulya and I were thrown back against the wooden wall of the compartment. The railwaymen had obviously set to work sorting out our train. There were indistinct shouts, punctuated by blows and jerks that felt less palpable now. We were somewhere in the middle of the future train.

A match flared and lit up Petro's face. In that light the long sides of his black moustache looked even longer. He took from the bag his pipe and the pack of tobacco bought in the port. The match went out, but he didn't need light any more. I heard him open the pack and fill his pipe. The air was infused with an unfamiliar acrid smell.

Another match flared up. He was already gripping the pipe in his teeth.

'Petro, go and smoke in the toilet, please,' Galya said to him. Petro got up without a word and left the compartment, lighting his way with the same match, which was still burning. The three of us were left there. We heard more shouting outside and someone ran past our wagon with a stamping of feet that seemed unnaturally loud to me. The hollow, rhythmic tapping of a hammer on axle boxes approached our wagon and moved past it.

'Are we going to leave now?' Galya asked.

'Probably,' I replied.

My mood had really improved. I felt like a little pick-me-up, and I asked Galya to brew us some coffee. I held the box of matches out to her and our hands sought each other 'by voice guidance'. Eventually she struck a match and the small flame illuminated our faces and the table made of tightly packed wooden boards.

Galya took out a block of solidified alcohol, set it in the centre of the table and lit it.

When the match went out, we were still illuminated by the blue flame of the alcohol, only it was not as bright. Galya set a wire stand over it and put a *djezva* on the stand. Gulya took the bowls out of her bundle.

My God, I thought, when was the last time I sat at a normal table? My heart was warmed by a feeling of domestic comfort.

Petro came back into the compartment just as Galya was pouring the coffee into the bowls. The compartment was filled with the aroma of coffee, but there was more of that aroma in the air than there was coffee in my bowl. I took very small sips, trying to make the pleasure last.

The alcohol tablet carried on burning, performing the function of a candle.

Petro coughed and picked up his bowl.

'It's the wrong tobacco,' he announced sadly and sighed. He took a sip of coffee and started coughing again. I heard Galya give him several thumps on the back.

'Not so hard, not so hard!' Petro exclaimed and stopped her. 'Why don't you make more coffee instead?'

Galya obediently started rustling the packet of ground coffee.

'A little glass would go down well now,' Petro declared cheerfully.

'You're not allowed,' Galya replied.

'We don't have anything with us anyway . . .' I said.

The railwaymen started shouting again on the other side of the blank wall and we fell silent and listened. They were shouting at each other in Azerbaijani, so we couldn't understand them anyway. Soon everything went quiet and the only sound in our ears was the rhythmic clattering of a train in motion.

We were moving. The port must have been left behind now. The compartment was filled with a strong smell of coffee – Galya was pouring the second *djezva* into the bowls. My eyes had adjusted to the darkness and the diffuse light from the blue flame of the alcohol tablet, so that I could make out Galya, Petro and Gulya's faces and even the expressions on them.

This time Petro drank his coffee without hurrying, keeping the bowl in his hands for a long time.

Not even the gloom in the compartment could conceal the confident joy in his eyes. Galya was pensive and Gulya, when I turned to look at her, moved her face close to mine – her beautiful slanting eyes looked deep inside me with an expression of love and devotion. Unable to resist, I leaned forward and touched my lips to hers.

Petro smacked his lips noisily, which stopped me short.

'You're a fine grown man,' he said, smiling. 'But you behave just like a teenager! Can't you understand that we're dealing with matters of state importance here?' He raised one arm in a gesture that lent additional weight to his words.

'Listen, she's my wife and I have the right to kiss her whenever I want. You might be dealing with state business, but I'm on my way home.'

'We are also going home, to our fatherland,' Petro said, nodding. 'But never mind, kiss as much as you like, or as much as she likes!' He waved one hand through the air. 'For indeed, you have already done a great deal for Ukraine, you may kiss . . .'

Petro spoke these final words without the slight trace of mockery and my momentary annoyance evaporated. Just as my desire to kiss had evaporated. What was left was a certain puzzlement. Those resounding words spoken by Petro – 'we're dealing with matters of state importance', 'we are going home to our fatherland', 'you have already done a great deal for Ukraine' . . . All these common-place newspaper and street-banner clichés had suddenly given my thoughts an untypical emotional colouring. I started thinking about the immediate future, about Kiev. The job we were doing would soon be done, and when we arrived and delivered this sand to the right place, we would be heartily thanked by the state.

Maybe they would give us some kind of reward too? Well, at least they would do the one little thing that I would ask them to do: free me of the threat that might not even exist any longer. What would it cost them to give a guarantee of my safety? The SBU had its hooks into everybody; even those who were still free. If the SBU told them: 'Don't touch him!' then no one would lay another finger on me! And Gulya and I could have a happy, peaceful life. A joyful life.

'We'll have to take a little bag of that sand for ourselves,' Petro said in a low voice, turning towards Galya. She nodded.

'We'll take a bag of sand, and when we have a son, we'll put a little bit of sand in the pram, so he'll grow up a real Ukrainian. It's not so important for you,' Petro said, looking from Galya to me, 'you're Russian; no matter how much you might want it, you'll never be Ukrainian . . .' And Petro sighed, as if he found it unbearably sad that I would never be Ukrainian.

'But why would I want to be Ukrainian, if I was born Russian?'

'Do you live in Ukraine?' Petro said, answering a question with a question.

'What of it? I have a Ukrainian passport too.'

'A passport's one thing, the soul's another. The soul inside you is Russian, a wide, massive soul . . .' Petro said and laughed.

I looked carefully at his face and his eyes. His eyes seemed hazy and unfocused to me. There was something wrong with him. Even Galya was looking at him in alarm.

Petro laughed again and fell silent.

'I need a smoke,' he said after a couple of minutes. He took his pipe off the table, stuffed it with tobacco from the bag again, lit it directly from the alcohol tablet and went out into the hallway.

'We should sit him on the sand,' I joked, looking at Galya. 'The Ukrainian spirit will teach him to love foreigners!'

Galya was just about to reply when we heard Petro laughing in the small hallway. He laughed for several minutes without stopping, choking on his own laughter, while we sat there, stupefied.

The sound of the train's wheels and Petro's laughter were so discordant that I was visited by thoughts of a lunatic asylum. Then suddenly these two sounds were joined by a third – several blows on the wooden roof of the compartment. Winding my acoustic memory backwards, I counted the blows – there had been four or five of them. Heavy and hollow, like footsteps amplified by the enclosed acoustics of our compartment.

But Petro was still laughing, and Galya was already running out into the hallway.

'What's wrong with him?' I asked.

'Maybe he's smoking something he shouldn't?' Gulya suggested.

I thought about that. Then, reaching across to the lower bunk opposite me in the dim light of the alcohol tablet, I found the pack of tobacco that Petro had bought in the port. I took a pinch of the tobacco, sniffed it and chewed it. As a non-smoker I couldn't really tell how good or bad the tobacco was. I shrugged.

'Give it to me!' Gulya said. I handed her the bag.

'That's not tobacco,' Gulya declared definitely. 'But he didn't ask for tobacco.'

'Then what did he ask for?' I said in surprise.

253

'He wanted to buy "something to smoke", and for us, "to smoke" means something quite different.'

I understood everything now. And I regretted my part in the conversation on the national theme. It turned out that I hadn't been arguing with Petro, but with the weed that he had inadvertently got stoned on. And immediately another conclusion sprang to mind – narcotics expel the national spirit from the body. Forever or only temporarily? I didn't know yet, but I would be able to find the answer to that question the next morning.

I tied the pack shut and dropped it under the table in the hope that it wouldn't be required any more.

Galya brought Petro back about fifteen minutes later. He could barely set one foot in front of the other. Gulya and I helped to lay him out on the bunk. We covered him with sleeping mats taken out of Galya's bag.

'I feel cold,' Petro whispered as he fell asleep.

When he was sleeping, Galya took a sleeping mat in her hand and climbed up on to the upper bunk without saying a word, then lay down quietly to sleep.

Gulya and I took the camel-hair blanket out of her bundle and settled down together on the other lower bunk. I lay on the outside and Gulya lay against the wall. The bunk was pretty narrow: the two of us could lie pressed up against each other on our backs or our sides, but every time Gulya turned over from one side to the other, I was left hanging over the floor, with one arm stretched out in front of me.

Realising that if I fell asleep, I would stay asleep only until I fell off, I tried to distract myself with various thoughts and memories. And the first thing I remembered was the stormy night in the cabin on the floating fish-processing plant when the gently snoring

Dasha had anchored me down with her strong arm. Had that berth been wider than this one? Probably it had, but not by much. But then, Dasha had been several times wider than Gulya.

Gulya was already asleep, lying on her stomach with her face turned towards me. The alcohol tablet was burning out on the table – its flame was reduced to the size of a match's flame now and was about to go out at any moment.

I got up quietly, trying not to wake Gulya, then climbed on to the upper bunk and lay down on my back. Gazing into the darkness of the wooden ceiling, I suddenly noticed a narrow crack, through which a distant star was trying to peep into our compartment. I attempted to get a better look at this star, but when I raised my head I lost it. The ceiling looked completely solid to me now. I lowered my head back down and fell asleep, lulled by the rhythm of the train.

57

When I woke up, I realised that it was morning only from the razor blade of sunlight slanting in through the crack in the ceiling. There were thousands of specks of dust swarming about inside the bright blade.

I glanced down from the height of my bunk. Petro was still sleeping, with his face tucked into the corner of his bunk. Gulya was sitting at the table – all I could see were her arms. I looked across the compartment – Galya was lying on her back with the sleeping mat pulled up under her chin. Her eyes were open. She was staring at the ceiling.

'Good morning then, is it?' I said, lifting myself up on one elbow.

'Good morning,' said Galya, turning towards me and then immediately looking under her bunk. 'Petro, get up!'

I jumped down and my gaze fell on the place where there is usually a window. In the dull, diffused light I could make out a kind of square on the wooden wall above the table. I stepped towards it, leaned across and snorted loudly in delight at my discovery. I was looking at a window or, at least, a window opening that had been boarded up from the inside. I could even see the heads of the two nails used to secure the screen in place. The energy that had accumulated inside me while I was sleeping required an outlet, so I asked Gulya to move back towards the wall of the compartment, climbed on to the lower bunk and kicked the wooden screen with my right foot. The boards cracked, but the screen didn't yield.

'What are you doing?' Petro asked, raising his head in alarm. I kicked the shield again with all my might, and immediately a shaft of light broke into the interior of the compartment. It was a broad, horizontal shaft that intersected with the knife blade of light falling from above. After the third blow, the shield gave a loud crack and went flying out of the wagon, to be left somewhere behind us, and the sun shone in through the window opening so brightly that we all screwed up our eyes, and Petro even put his hands over his.

To me the combination of the hammering of the wheels and direct sunlight was like music. I played with the sunlight, not turning my head away or putting my hand over my eyes. My eyes were closed, but the power of the sun pierced through my eyelids, giving birth to fantastical spots of colour. And the new air that had burst in through the window swept away all the odours in the compartment, replacing them with the fresh, damp smell of the sea.

Five minutes later, we saw that we were travelling along the shoreline, along the Caspian, sometimes rising a little above it, sometimes almost approaching right to the water's edge. The beauty of what we saw left us speechless.

The window was not the only discovery we made that morning. By the light of the sun we discovered a box of tableware, spoons and forks under the lower bunk, as well as a Primus stove with a bottle of kerosene and four old camel-hair blankets with faded oriental patterns. And later I noticed that someone had glued a portrait of Pushkin – probably cut out of an old number of *Ogonyok* magazine – on the wall that was also the door into the cargo section of the wagon.

We were clearly not the first inhabitants of this wagon, and we were filled with gratitude to our predecessors. Everything had been carefully cleaned and stowed away. Even the copper of the Primus stove gleamed as if it had never been used.

'Well, we paid for a first-class carriage,' I thought, remembering the dollars we had given to obtain the wagon. Now it felt worth it.

Petro deftly filled the Primus stove with kerosene and lit it.

'I'm sorry about yesterday evening,' he said to me in Russian, which made me realise that he really was feeling guilty. 'It was the tobacco . . . it's not the right kind . . .'

'It's not tobacco at all!' Galya said in an angry voice that was louder than usual. 'You were high on drugs!'

Petro looked round the compartment. Realising what he was searching for, I took the bag out from under the table. He scooped the 'tobacco' into the palm of his hand and lifted it up to his eyes.

'Yuck!' he said with a shake of his head. Then he held his hand out of the window and the 'tobacco' was whirled away by the wind.

'The things that happen!' he said to himself. Then he looked at me again. 'I'm sorry anyway, Kolya. I don't remember what I said . . .'

'It's nothing,' I said, with a wave of my hand.

Galya had already set the cooking pot, full of water, on the stove. It didn't stand very firmly on the flat grille, but fortunately the grille had a round opening in the middle, and the rounded bottom of the cooking pot sank two or three centimetres into the opening, making the overall structure relatively stable.

Gulya sliced a strip of dried meat into small pieces on the table. I leaned down curiously over the meat.

'The driver gave me it, it's mutton,' Gulya said, nodding towards the paper bag lying beside her on the bunk. 'We'll have soup.'

The atmosphere of domestic comfort continued. I looked out of the window at the sea with the sun rising higher above it. At the vineyards that had suddenly insinuated themselves into the narrow space between the wagon and the sea. The train was moving unhurriedly, allowing me to examine carefully everything that we rode past. I watched as two women in black sprayed the grapevines and then as two young boys sailed their boat out from the shore to go fishing. Their oars dipped into the water in a regular rhythm.

'What do you think, Kolya, what are we going to do with this sand?' Petro asked behind my back.

I shrugged, thinking that the question sounded simpler than it was.

'To be honest, I don't know,' I admitted. 'It obviously has to be used in some rational way . . . But it's a big country, and there's not much sand . . .'

'Not much,' Petro said, nodding. 'Not much at all.'

I looked round and saw that he was deep in thought now.

'How about sprinkling a little bit it into children's sandpits, like the colonel said?' he suggested, then scratched the back of his head and ran his fingers down the sides of his moustache, as if he were smoothing them out. 'We can't spread it right across Ukraine in any case . . . Maybe the colonel will think of something? They've got plenty of clever people working in the SBU. And since they've been dealing with this business before, maybe they know what to use it for . . .'

'Yes, the colonel has probably thought of something,' I said, agreeing with Petro in words, although I didn't really believe that Vitold Yukhimovich had any specific plans for the sand.

After lunch we all lay down on the bunks, intending to take a 'quiet hour', like in a kindergarten.

It was several hours since the sun had peeped into our window. It was hanging somewhere high up in the sky above the train. But the warmth that its morning rays had left inside the compartment was still present in the air that we were breathing.

Gulya was lying on the upper bunk now, and I was below her, on the hard boards covered with imitation leatherette. I didn't feel like sleeping, but it was pleasant just to lie there, swaying in time to the rhythm of the moving train. I closed my eyes as I lay on my back and I imagined I was a hero returning home from a war. In some strange fashion this hero acquired the appearance of one of the Zaporozhian Cossacks engaged in the collective composition of a letter to the Turkish Sultan in the well-known painting by Repin. I had a long topknot on my head.

My steed, weary of the boundless steppes, could barely move its feet. Of course he was struggling, for there was a beautiful Turkish girl with slanting almond-shaped eyes sitting behind me – an exotic reward, won in battle with the janissaries.

Actually, I had found her after the battle, when all the janissaries were lying dead beneath the walls of the small Turkish settlement. We had walked through the village, collecting all the gold and silver that we could find in the houses and the courtyards, and I spotted her hiding behind a trunk in one of the houses. At first my brother Cossacks had laughed at me – after all, each of them was carrying home a kilogram or more of jewels – but gradually the note of envy in their mocking comments became clearer and louder, especially in the evenings, when we sat round our campfires, after the large communal mug of vodka had already been passed round the circle and was about to go round again.

Then I had realised that it would be safer to continue my journey alone than with all the others. And, waking at dawn, I had woken my captive, whom I never allowed to leave my side for a moment. And my steed had carried us on towards Kiev, away from Secha and its laws. 'My days as a Cossack are over,' I thought gladly, holding the reins with my left hand and patting my Turkish girl on the thigh with my right.

As I dozed, I got so carried way with this fantasy that I didn't notice when the sound of the train disappeared.

'Kolya,' Petro's voice said somewhere above my head.

'What?' I said, half sitting up and immediately sensing that something was missing.

It wasn't just the sound that was missing. The train wasn't moving. Outside the window there was a frozen square of sky, sea and dirty-yellow seashore.

'It must be the border,' I suggested as I got to my feet.

'What border?'

'Between Azerbaijan and Dagestan.'

Petro looked bewildered. He stuck his head out of the little window.

'There's nothing here!'

Suddenly someone sneezed close to the wagon. Petro stuck his head out again, then looked back at me in astonishment.

'There's no one there,' he whispered.

We froze and listened. We could hear the sparse calls of gulls from the sea. Some insect or other trilled outside the window. Then once again there was the sound of a dull thud from somewhere close by.

Petro's tension was transmitted to me. Beginning to feel nervous, I opened the rucksack, found the pistol on the bottom, took it out and laid it on top of the other things. I glanced out of the window myself, but I couldn't see a single living soul.

'We ought to check the sand,' Petro said, nodding towards the wall separating us from the cargo section of the wagon.

'Let's go,' I said in a whisper.

In the toilet we stopped in front of the low door locked with a bolt – the way through into the cargo section. After opening the door and bending over double to squeeze through, we found ourselves directly below a blazing sun, facing a hill of sand covered with a single piece of tarpaulin and moulded into a rectangular shape by the walls of the wagon. The summit of the hill was precisely at the centre of the wagon. The tarpaulin crackled under our feet and I felt the sand moving beneath it.

Petro gave a sigh of relief, then climbed to the top of the mound and stopped. His head was now higher than the sides of the wagon. He glanced around, then suddenly froze and raised his hands in the air.

I didn't understand a thing. Petro stood there motionless, with his back towards me, holding his hands up. His head was inclined slightly downwards. I immediately squatted on my haunches, trying to make sense of what was going on. But so far there was nothing else happening. Trying to move as quietly as possible, I crept a little higher up the tarpaulin hill and stopped about a metre and a half away from Petro.

'Get up!' said an unfamiliar, harsh voice. I froze.

'You get up, or your buddy will fall down!'

I realised that these words were addressed to me. I paused for a few more seconds, but then got to my feet anyway. Standing down in the far corner of the wagon was the same swarthy Slav with the short, uneven haircut whom I had seen on the ferry and at the port. He had a pistol in his right hand and a half-eaten sandwich in his left – we had obviously interrupted his lunch.

'Hands!' he shouted at me, and I raised my hands, inspecting his lair as I did so.

We had clearly been travelling together from the very beginning. He had stamped flat an area in the corner that was about the same size as a bunk in our compartment and laid out a large fluffy blue towel on top of the tarpaulin. Lying right in the corner was his kit-bag, a plastic bag with tins of food and a pitta bread broken in half.

'When the train starts to move,' the swarthy guy said sombrely, 'you' – he jabbed one finger towards Petro – 'will help your friend here to jump over there!' He nodded towards the side wall of the wagon. 'And then I'll help you myself.'

Keeping his eyes fixed on us, the swarthy guy raised the sandwich to his mouth and took a bite.

As he chewed, his jaw muscles moved in a regular rhythm, like some well-tuned mechanism. The upper part of his face remained as motionless as his gaze.

I don't know how much time passed before the train suddenly jerked and started slowly gathering speed.

I lowered my hands and the swarthy guy immediately shouted at me, still chewing.

'Come on!' he yelled, pointing his pistol at Petro. 'Stand with your back to the wall and give your comrade your hands.'

Petro looked at me, perplexed.

I wouldn't have liked to be in his place at that moment. But, to be quite honest, I didn't like my place all that much either.

After the next yell, Petro leaned his back against the inside wall of the wagon and locked his hands together in front of himself.

I glanced at Petro. I didn't want to fall outside the wagon, but I resented the swathy bastard disturbing our cosy domestic arrangement. Resentment transformed my fear into fury at the Slav. Resentment for the way he had spoiled the holiday that our journey home was just about to become.

Petro seemed to understand what I wanted to do and he gave an almost imperceptible nod.

I squinted at the man. He had finished his sandwich and was glancing at the plastic bag of tins. The barrel of his pistol was pointed at Petro. It seemed like the right moment to me and I raised my foot, set it in my partner's locked hands and took hold of his shoulders. I squinted sideways at the swarthy guy again – he was squatting down beside the bag, but his eyes were still fixed on us.

'OK,' I thought. 'Now lose your concentration for just a moment!'

But he didn't – he did something else. He transferred the pistol from his right hand to his left. I noticed that the handle of the pistol was wrapped in blue electrical insulating tape. And then I gathered myself and straightened up, pushing off from Petro's hands. The swarthy guy was about two metres away. I saw him open his eyes wide and take the pistol back into his right hand, I saw his forefinger reach for the trigger. The barrel was pointed at me.

Suddenly there was a loud shot. I fell straight on top of him, pinning him against the wall of the wagon. And I heard a scream. At first I thought it was me who had screamed because of pain that I wasn't yet aware of. I lay on top of the Slav, with my head pressed against the wall of the wagon. There was a sharp pinching pain in the top of my head. 'Surely he didn't shoot me in the head?' I thought, feeling alarmed. There was a roaring inside my head too. And my hands were shaking. I raised my head with an effort and saw Petro standing there. He grabbed hold of my hand and pulled me off the swarthy guy.

I slowly got to my feet, but found it hard to stand. The trembling in my hands was still as bad as ever. I wanted simply to sit down on the tarpaulin and stay there, to gather my wits. I'd already realised that I'd escaped with a bump and a bruise on the top of my head.

I glanced round and saw Gulya standing by the opposite wall of the wagon with a pistol in her hand. It was the pistol with a silencer that I had left on top of my rucksack.

Gulya was looking straight at me and her unwavering gaze was filled with strength and love. I walked over to her on legs that I could barely control and we put our arms round each other.

We stood there, embracing like that, for several minutes and then collapsed on to the tarpaulin. Lying there, I noticed that Galya was there too – I saw her back beside Petro's. They were fiddling with something beside the swarthy guy.

'We have to tie him up,' Petro said in a quiet voice. Galya went into the compartment and came back with a ball of string.

'Is he alive?' I asked, lifting up my head.

'He's alive, the rotten dog!' Petro answered without turning round. I lay there for another ten minutes or so and then got to my feet. Gulya supported me and we walked across to Petro and Galya.

The Slav was lying on his side, unconscious. His hands were tied behind his back. His feet were tied together too. I saw a red furrow across his right temple, with blood oozing out of it. Galya took a handkerchief out of the pocket of her jeans and pressed it against the wound.

'Concussion,' she said.

In his kitbag we found three clips of bullets, a battered Russian passport with the photograph removed, a notebook, a wad of roubles and a hundred-dollar bill.

'We ought to get rid of him.' Petro said pensively. 'He might have escaped from prison – look.' And he pulled up the man's dirty blue sweater to reveal a blue tattoo of church domes.

The tattoo reassured me somewhat. What interest could a criminal have in our sand? It would take an incredible amount of imagination to find an answer to that question, I thought, and then suddenly the answer came of its own accord, from a different angle. The swarthy guy must simply have wanted to rob us. He had figured out, or guessed, that we had money. He had been following us since the ferry, after all. He was probably going to do it at night, when we would be asleep . . . And then I asked myself why I found it reassuring that the sand had nothing to do with this business. I asked the question, but I couldn't answer it. There was something not right here. Or had the bang against the wooden wall of the wagon knocked all the logic out of my thoughts?

'Give me a hand!' said Petro, touching me on the shoulder, and I came back to reality.

Reality looked as follows: Petro had already taken hold of the swarthy guy's bound legs and waited for me to grab the arms.

Galya helped us to drag him to the little door that led to the hallway via the toilet.

There we took a breather and then made another spurt, following which the swarthy guy was left lying in the hallway in front of the open outer door. Outside the door the Caspian landscape drifted past, but now the sea had moved a little bit further away and once again there were rows of vineyards extending between its blueness and us.

I stuck my head out through the opening of the door and looked down at the embankment of dirty-brown stones that seemed to be sunk into the frozen lava of the clay.

Galya came out into the hallway. She had a bandage in her hand.

'What are you doing?' Petro asked in amazement. 'What if he' – he nodded towards me – 'needs the bandage, or I do?'

Galya hesitated, but even so she bent down over the Slav guy and bandaged up his head.

'A very fine com-mis-sar!' Petro drawled, looking at the bound man. 'Come on, let's toss the damn swine out!'

The two of us took hold of the swarthy guy behind the shoulders and pushed him out of the wagon.

He went crashing into the bushes growing between the embankment and the vineyards.

Petro closed the door without saying a word and walked back into the compartment. I walked in after him.

'I'm feeling a bit hungry all of a sudden,' Gulya said with a faint glint in her eyes.

Petro started, dashed out of the compartment and came back a minute later, carrying a plastic bag. It was the swarthy guy's stock of food supplies. Three cans of pink salmon, fish mince and a can of 'Caspian Herring'. I immediately took this last can in my hand and lifted it up to my eyes. 'The Communard Fish Processing Plant. Astrakhan.' I flung the can out through the square opening of the window.

'What's wrong with you?' Petro asked me suspiciously. 'Lie down, it must be your nerves. No, wait. Galya, take a look at his head!'

Galya's medical inspection left me wearing a bandage too.

'Another commissar!' Petro laughed. I obediently clambered on to the upper bunk and lay down, listening to Galya and Gulya discussing supper in quiet voices.

58

During the night the train jerked to a sudden halt. I was sleeping on my side with my head thrown back.

The hammering of wheels outside was replaced by brisk shouts in an unfamiliar language and the rumble of cargo wagon doors being rolled back.

I glanced out through our ever-open window. The train was standing at a platform illuminated by double lamps on pillars. In addition to the lamps, we were also illuminated by eight search-lights coupled together on a tall mast, the kind you usually see round the edges of a sports stadium. Some distance away from us, men in military uniforms were swarming round the last two wagons in the train.

The light was so bright that I couldn't see anything beyond the edges of the platform. It was as if we were stuck in a kind of canal lock, with walls of light on all sides.

At least an hour went by before the soldiers reached our wagon. By that time we had already realised that the train was standing on the border – beyond two lines of rails at one side of our wagon there was a large board with the words: 'Welcome to Azerbaijan'.

'Hey, come out!' shouted a soldier who had approached the wagon. 'Customs!'

Petro and I got out. Petro brought the documents for the sand with him.

The customs officer held out his hand and was immediately given the relevant papers. He glanced at them briefly, returned his scrutinising glance to our faces and paused. Then he smiled. The smile seemed to turn the expression on his face inside out, immediately making it clear that he would be hard to talk to – he had looked far more affable before the smile.

'Well then, "Karakum Ltd",' the Azerbaijani said acidly, maintaining his forced smile. 'What duty are we going to pay? With an inspection or without?'

Petro and I exchanged glances.

'What's the difference?' Petro asked.

'With an inspection is cheaper – three hundred dollars. But, you understand, we'll have to turn everything upside down, unpack everything . . . And without an inspection is five hundred dollars.'

'But all we've got is sand . . .' I said, and immediately regretted having opened my mouth.

'Sand? From Kazakhstan to Ukraine?' The Azerbaijani's smile stretched right out to his ears. 'Tell me, have you run out of sand in Ukraine, then? What kind of fairy story are you giving me? We'll examine your sand one grain at a time – you'll be standing here for a year!'

'It's all right, it's all right . . .' said Petro, holding up his open hand to stop the customs officer. 'We'll pay the duty for no inspection.'

It seemed to me that the Azerbaijani was actually disappointed, as if he had just been preparing himself to have a good shout at us and put us in our place, but we had already raised our hands up and surrendered, willing to do whatever he wanted.

'All right,' he said to Petro after a long pause, during which he wiped the smile off his own face. 'Bring the payment.'

While Petro was gone the customs officer inspected the bandage on my head curiously.

'Fell off the bunk, did you?' he asked, smiling again.

'Yes.'

'You have to be careful in these wagons. It's not a sleeper carriage.'

I nodded, afraid that if I said anything else, the customs duty might suddenly increase.

Finally, after giving the customs officer five hundred dollars and staying for a few minutes longer while he counted the money three times, we went back into the compartment.

We sat there in silence, waiting for the train to move off. There were another twenty wagons ahead of us, and we heard snatches of conversation in Russian. We were clearly by no means the only people accompanying loads on this train.

'He didn't even check our passports!' Petro exclaimed in amazement.

'Well, we paid for no inspection,' I said. 'He didn't come into the compartment and he didn't meet our beautiful ladies.'

'And thank God for that,' Petro sighed.

'It would never even enter that customs officer's head that there were women travelling with us,' I thought.

59

The train was moving slowly. Outside the window that couldn't be closed, the night continued.

Azerbaijan was behind us now, and once again we were lying on our bunks, waiting for morning to come.

I didn't feel like sleeping, and from time to time I hung down from my upper bunk and glanced out through the window. Sometimes my gaze picked the distant light of a ship or a schooner out of the darkness. The little lights seemed to lend my thoughts a certain romantic energy, but it was the energy of sleep, not of wakefulness. Eventually I fell asleep with a smile of relief on my face. I could feel that smile. And again I had a strange dream, in which I was a Ukrainian, only this time not a hero, but a ragamuffin fleeing from Turkish captivity. I was walking along the seashore in Bulgaria, picking bunches of wild grapes as I went. Then I joined a band of gypsies and went as far as Bukovina with them, helping the gypsies to steal horses and burn out their owners' brands with a hot iron. It was a strange dream, but the strangest thing of all was that everyone in the dream – the Bulgarians, the gypsies and me – spoke in beautiful literary Ukrainian, as if we were characters in some novel.

After I woke up I lay on my back for half an hour, wondering if it was the close proximity of the sand that gave rise to such dreams.

Outside the window the sun was already rising and once again there were vineyards slowly slipping past between us and the sea.

'Wonderful,' Petro said with a sigh. 'We travel on and on, but we don't know what's there, on the other side of the wagon. There could be mountains there, and we can't see them . . .'

In the morning we ate the stale pitta bread, washing it down with tea. Everyone was in good spirits, as if the worst was already behind us.

After breakfast, Galya took the bandage off my head. She looked at the bruise and said that everything was all right. The used bandage went flying out of the window.

'You know,' said Petro, leaning down closer to me. 'I had a wonderful dream about Shevchenko, only he was speaking Russian. He'd lost some little key or other and he'd been searching for it, searching for a long time . . .'

The expression on my face must clearly have seemed very odd to Petro. I bit my lip and narrowed my eyes as I drew the parallel between the Ukrainian language that had crept into my dream and Shevchenko starting to speak Russian in Petro's dream. And I also recalled the little gold key that had been found in the sand and was now lying in the pocket of the rucksack.

Petro opened his mouth and leaned forward even closer, as if he were about to say something. After pausing for about a minute with his narrowed eyes fixed on me, he asked: 'What are you looking so surprised about?'

I smiled. 'My latest dreams have been in Ukrainian, and I spoke Ukrainian in them.'

Petro shrugged. 'Well, so what?' he said, straightening his back

271

and casting a quick glance at Galya, who was sitting beside him. 'When I was a child I dreamed that I was singing in English with the Beatles and talking to them in English. But I was studying German at school . . . It's only dreams.'

'Only dreams,' I agreed.

'I had dreams in Russian too when I was little,' Gulya put in.

'That's because you have too many Russians in Kazakhstan,' Petro said.

'Petro!' Galya looked reproachfully at him.

'Well, there are lots of them everywhere,' Petro said, assuming that by adding that he would somehow soften the meaning of what he had said.

I was suddenly overcome by an irresistible urge to laugh. Petro looked at me in surprise. For no particular reason, I had suddenly remembered a joke about a New Russian going to an old Jew and saying: 'Pops, give me some money!'

'What's wrong with you?' Petro asked me in Russian.

'Oh nothing,' I said, struggling to stop myself laughing. 'I just remembered a joke . . .'

'Which one?'

And then I thought that if I told him the actual joke that I'd remembered, he would think I'd lost my marbles.

'This Georgian traffic cop stops a Russian driving a Zhiguli in Tbilisi,' I began, telling the first joke that came into my head. ' "You", he says, "exceeded the speed limit. Write an explanation in Georgian." "In Georgian?" the Russian exclaims in amazement. "I don't know Georgian." But the traffic cop just stands there without saying anything, waiting. The Russian thinks and puts fifty bucks into his driving licence, then hands it to the Georgian, who takes it and puts the money in his pocket. Then he says: "There, you see,

272

and you said you didn't know Georgian! But you've written half the explanation already!" '

To my surprise the joke didn't raise a smile from my listeners. Petro looked at me expectantly. I could see either pity or unease in his eyes.

'I don't like jokes about nationalities,' he said in Russian after a few minutes. Then he switched back to Ukrainian and said: 'Probably when we get to Kiev, I'll have a laugh over a glass of vodka. But it's too soon to laugh yet . . .'

That made me feel sad. It's never too soon to laugh, I thought, disagreeing with Petro. I could have imagined a situation in which it was too late to laugh. But even when it's too late to laugh, laughter can simply change its meaning, transforming itself from the laughter of merriment to the laughter of despair, the laughter of a madman.

I glanced out of the window and saw that little holiday homes, gardens and grape-green courtyards had appeared between us and the sea. And everything was such a bright green that it was hard to imagine that the calendar autumn was already near. It was hard to imagine that this mass of green could turn yellow and red, or even completely colourless once the leaves had dropped to the ground.

Something soft struck me on the face and dropped on to the table. I shied back from the window.

There was a fig lying on the table. Then several more came flying into the compartment.

'Kids having fun,' said Petro, glancing out.

I glanced out too and saw some grubby boys standing along the embankment, waving to us.

Gulya took a fig from the table and put it in her mouth.

The attack put us in a good mood again. We picked the figs up and rinsed them in the cooking pot and threw the water out of the window.

'Not very many,' said Petro, staring at the underripe fruit lying in two rows on the table.

Then he took one and popped it into his mouth too. He chewed on it with relish.

'We need a drink of coffee,' he declared in a loud voice full of life and looked at Galya.

60

Another two hours went by and the train stopped again. Looking out, we saw another goods train between us and the sea. But between us and that train there was a space of about fifteen metres covered with rails and more rails. The place resembled a marshalling yard.

A panting locomotive went by between the other goods train and us.

'I wonder where we are?' I said. Gazing out of the window again I saw a fat little railwayman moving towards us from the tail end of the train, carrying a long-handled hammer and tapping on the axle boxes with it.

'What station is this?' I asked him, when he got close to our wagon.

'Derbent goods station,' he replied, jerking his head up and looking at me curiously.

Petro immediately squeezed in beside me.

'Hey,' he shouted, 'is there a shop near here?'

'Yes, just outside the fence,' the Dagestani replied.

'And how long are we going to be waiting here?'

The Dagestani checked his watch and thought for a moment. 'An hour, probably. What is it you want to buy?'

'Tobacco.'

'I can sell you mine,' the Dagestani suggested. 'For a good price. I grow it at my dacha . . .'

'No thanks,' said Petro, shaking his head. 'I think I'll go to the shop . . .'

'Why take the risk?' the Derbent railwayman said.

'What risk?' Petro asked in surprise.

'You see,' said the Dagestani, twisting his lips into an ambiguous smile. 'You are an individual of Slavonic nationality, and there aren't any individuals like that here any more. They all left. Do you understand? They'll take you for a tourist or a deserter from Chechnya. And that would be bad!'

Petro heaved a sigh.

'Don't get the wrong idea, they're good people here,' the Dagestani went on. 'It's the times that are bad now. Come back in ten years and you'll be an honoured guest! Ask where Musa Gadjiev lives, anyone will show you. Come and stay here, swim in the sea. Only later, in about ten years' time! Would you like me to go to the shop myself, so you won't too think badly of me?'

The fat man looked in through the window at Petro with a glance that was almost ingratiating.

Petro sighed again, took ten dollars from Galya and handed them to the railwayman.

'Not our money,' he said, shaking his head. 'Never mind, I'll buy you some with my own. Will Prima suit? It's good here, from Makhachkala . . .'

Petro nodded.

The fat man asked us to keep an eye on the hammer he left under the wagon and walked away.

Twenty minutes later he came back and handed Petro a block of Prima – twenty packs glued together with paper tape. Then he gave him back the ten dollars.

Bemused, Petro put the Prima on the table and shouted 'thank you' after the railwayman.

I felt the urge to break into laughter again, but this time I refrained. I looked at Gulya and we smiled at each other. Galya was sitting there with a smile on her face too. Only Petro, still bemused by what had happened, maintained a serious air. He found an empty cellophane bag and started tipping the tobacco from the *papyrosas* into it.

The train had already started moving, and he was still twisting the tobacco out of the *papyrosas*, although it was clear that he was fed up of doing it. Finally he swore, took out his pipe, stuffed it with Prima tobacco and went into the hallway, leaving behind on the table three packs of *papyrosas* that had not yet been gutted and a cellophane bag three-quarters full of tobacco.

A few hours later, when the sun had stretched the shadow of our wagon to its maximum limit, the train began gradually moving away from the sea. Or perhaps it was the sea that was moving away to one side, and we were travelling straight on? Sitting in the wagon, it was hard to tell, but the landscape outside the window was changing, becoming less romantic. The place of the vineyards was taken by endless rows of garages, then there were more holiday houses, only these dachas looked a lot poorer than the ones we had passed before Derbent.

A city drifted slowly past our window, a city of Khrushchev-period five-storey apartment blocks, private houses and pipes that were laid directly on the surface of the earth – they crossed the roads at a height of three or four metres, and then sank back to ground level again. It was as if all of the city's intestines, normally prudishly concealed under the ground and occasionally peeping from behind iron manhole covers – had burst out into the open and stayed there. Perhaps it was to make life easier for the repair services, or perhaps there was another reason. Pipes of various diameters also crossed the railway, all following the same line. I watched them go by in amazement: as twilight came they gave the city a look like some faraway world or something from an old children's book.

When the train slowed down, I saw two young lads sitting by a campfire on the railway embankment.

'Hey,' I shouted, 'what city is this?'

'Makhachkala!' one of them shouted, and the other one waved,

I waved back and sat back down beside Gulya.

'Makhachkala,' I repeated, focusing my attention on the lighted Primus stove.

It was almost time for supper. Petro was opening one of the cans of food that we had won in battle. Gulya was mixing up soup in the cooking pot. The compartment smelled of mutton fat.

'How good it would be to go straight to Rostov with no stops,' I thought hopefully.

61

Three hours later the train braked sharply in total darkness. The Primus stove and the cooking pot with the leftover soup went flying off the table. We jumped to our feet. Petro struck a match and looked out of the window, as if the match burning in his fingers could cast any light on anything.

Gulya felt around on the floor, found the Primus stove and the cooking pot, and picked them up.

We heard the roar of an engine outside.

I stuck my head out of the window, squeezing in beside Petro. There was a vehicle moving towards us from the tail of the train, lighting it up with its full-beam headlights. It was driving slowly and we must have watched it for about three minutes before Petro whispered: 'A truck!'

I looked more carefully and saw that there were men standing in the back of the truck.

Two beams of light from pocket torches ran across the goods wagons as the truck crept past them.

'Further, further!' someone shouted. Petro and I exchanged glances, then Petro climbed down on to the lower bunk, got his shopping bag and took the pistol with the silencer out of it. Then he struck a match and lit a tablet of solidified alcohol.

'Get under the bunk,' he said to Galya. She obediently did so. Then Petro looked into my eyes, as if he was expecting me to tell Gulya to hide there too.

I thought for a while, then took out my pistol and put it under the sleeping mat on my right.

'Maybe I should make coffee?' Gulya asked unexpectedly.

I turned round. She was looking at Petro.

'No thank you,' Petro said and sighed. The truck was approaching our wagon. Petro took his pistol off the table.

'Stop, it's here. That wagon there!' said a hoarse voice outside.

We heard the truck come to a halt. The driver switched off the engine.

The beam of a torch suddenly broke in through the opening of the window and I started.

'Hey, lads, is there anyone there?' asked the voice that we had already heard.

Petro got up, froze and then looked around anyway. I stuck my head out and immediately shut my eyes, blinded by the light of the torch.

'Come out,' someone invisible said in calm, affable voice.

'What do they want?' Petro said, when we had left the compartment and were standing in the hallway.

I shrugged.

Jumping down from the welded iron steps, we found ourselves by the side of the truck. The man with the torch immediately came across to us.

'Roll back the gates,' he said, without any particular threat or insistence in his voice. He spoke faultless Russian, without any trace of an accent, and that reassured me a little – I had been prepared for an encounter with Chechens.

'Are you going to check it?' Petro asked cautiously, approaching the centre of the wagon.

'What for?' the man with the husky voice asked in surprise. 'We've got everything well under control anyway. Unload this and load that, and everyone goes his own way! Come on, get a move on! Where's the Moldovan?'

'What Moldovan?' Petro said, stopping in front of the sliding door and glancing in bewilderment at me.

'That bastard!' the man hissed. 'I'll break his ribs for him, that lousy damned courier.'

He spat down in front of his feet and then looked around. He fixed his gaze on me and forced a smile.

'Never mind, never mind, come on, lads!' he said, nodding to reassure either us or himself.

But I still couldn't understand what was going on. One thing was clear: these guys who had come out of the night were behaving as if we knew all about their business. Perhaps our tattooed travelling companion, who had left our wagon involuntarily, was the Moldovan who was supposed to have enlightened us. All we could do was make guesses and wait for everything to become clear.

I walked over to Petro, tore the lead seal off the wire wound round the handle of the wagon door and pulled the door towards me. The door opened with difficulty, and only half a metre. Two men came across and helped me slide it all the way.

'Come on, back it in here!' the husky-voiced man yelled into the darkness.

The engine started up again and the truck swung round and set its back end against the open wagon.

Petro and I moved aside and watched as several men clambered into the wagon and rolled up the tarpaulin. To our amazement, by the light of the torches we saw ordinary sacks piled up into a hill underneath it.

The night crew began dismantling the hill, carefully stacking the sacks they removed against the inside wall opposite the opening. A pyramid of green wooden crates was revealed under the sacks.

'Stop, lads!' we heard someone in the wagon say. 'Right, shine a light over here!'

They left the pyramid of crates and moved over the right-hand corner. We couldn't see what was going on, but we remembered what had happened there recently, only the day before. And we looked at each other.

'They're not armed,' I whispered to Petro. A man with a torch appeared at the opening of the wagon. The beam of the torch slid across our faces.

'Come here!' he said in a husky voice. We went towards him and climbed into the wagon.

'Why are you so laid-back?' the man asked, raising the torch so that it was shining into Petro's face, almost touching him. Petro put his hand over his eyes. The man moved his hand away.

'Don't cover them up!' he said, peering into Petro's pupils. 'What happened here?' he asked.

'Nothing,' Petro answered and pushed the hand with the torch away from his face.

'Nothing?' he echoed suspiciously. 'And what's this?'

He shone the beam into his left hand, on which a pistol with its handle bound in blue insulating tape was lying. We didn't say anything.

'Ivan!' the man called, turning round. 'Check the crates!'

To me they were all Ivans. It was impossible to make out their faces in the darkness. A taciturn group of men, all about the same height and quite certainly of the same profession, which was not yet clear to us. I felt a sudden suspicion that we simply wouldn't have enough time to understand anything.

Ivan's dark figure went back to the pyramid of crates. Two torches illuminated them for him from the right-hand corner.

Ivan muttered something to himself as he moved a few boxes. He leaned down.

'Looks like all of it,' he said in a tired voice.

'Looks like, or *is* all of it?' asked the man with the husky voice, who was clearly the leader of this team.

'Is all of it.'

The beam of the torch slid across our faces again, as if demanding our attention.

'So what happened here?' the man with the husky voice asked again, more gently this time.

'We travelled in the compartment, not the wagon,' Petro said quietly.

A chilly shiver ran down my spine. I was frightened that now these men would want to go into our compartment – and then what?

'Now, why treat us like idiots?' the head man asked in a pained voice. 'Didn't your mummy ever teach you to tell the truth? It doesn't hurt to tell the truth.'

In the silence that followed these words I mentally took my leave of Gulya and my own life. I felt guilty, as if I'd let almost everyone down, especially my Kazakh wife, for whom I had proved to be such a fatal present.

Ivan walked up to the head man, who took hold of the pistol and turned it in his hand.

'It's the Moldovan's,' he said. 'He's got an allergy to iron, and he wraps everything in insulating tape: knives, and forks . . . the stupid jerk.'

'So what did you do?' The beam of the torch shone into my face again. 'Did you fall out with him?'

'Aha,' Petro answered for me, and the beam of light immediately jumped to him. 'I pushed him off . . .'

282

'Yes?' the head man exclaimed almost in delight and chortled loudly. 'Well, all right, that's your business! You can slit each other's throats for all I care. Just as long as the load's always intact!'

We stood there, turned to stone, and he tossed the pistol he had taken from Ivan out through the open door of the wagon, into the night.

'Hey!' he called to his men. 'Work!'

We moved away to the side wall of the wagon and stopped there, covering the little door that led into our compartment via the toilet. Nobody took any more notice of us.

The men transferred the wooden crates to the truck. The upper crates of the pyramid were smaller and shorter that the lower ones. One of the men, who was carrying a crate on his own, stumbled and fell, bridging the gap, with his feet in the wagon and his torso in the truck. As the crate hit the wooden platform of the truck, it gave out a metallic clanking sound.

'Guns,' Petro whispered to me.

'Hey, stop lying down on the job!' the head man shouted hoarsely at the fallen man.

Each of the lower, longer crates was carried by two men. I squatted down, pulled one of the sacks towards me, untied it and stuck my hand inside.

The sack was full of sand.

'What's in it?' Petro asked, squatting down beside me. Instead of answering, I held out the open neck of the sack and he put his hand in too. He looked at me in surprise, then pulled out a handful of sand, raised it to his nose and sniffed. He smiled, opened his hand and held it out to me. My nose caught a strong smell of cinnamon.

Petro tied the sack shut and got to his feet.

'Let's go,' he said, nodding towards the open door of the wagon, with the yellow moon hanging in its upper left corner. 'They've unloaded everything . . .'

No sooner had we taken a couple of steps than the men appeared in the opening again.

They started carrying small white sacks into the wagon and tossing them on to the spot where the crates had been. One of them – I thought it was Ivan – stayed there and levelled out the sacks tossed on to the floor of the wagon with his feet. Then he stamped down the second layer.

We stood there, holding our breath.

After several layers of these sacks had been laid in the place of the pyramid, the men started packing sacks of sand around them and on top of them.

'You can get out – we'll fix everything up here just the way it was before!' one of them shouted to us.

We jumped down out of the wagon.

The sky was covered with stars. I threw my head back, trying not to think about anything.

When my neck got tired, I looked at Petro. He was standing beside me, thinking about something and gazing down at his feet.

There was a loud rustling of tarpaulin from the wagon.

'Move away a bit!' someone shouted.

The door of the truck slammed, the engine started up, and it moved a couple of metres away from the wagon, then stopped.

The men closed the door of the wagon and the head man came up to us.

'Have you got anything to smoke?' he asked wearily.

'Yes, Prima,' Petro said with a nod, and was just about to move towards the steps of the compartment, but I grabbed hold of his arm.

He stopped, and I quickly set off for the wagon. I went into the compartment, rummaged about under the table and found the pack with the contents that had given Petro a laughing fit. I brought it out and handed it to the head man.

He took out a pinch of the 'tobacco' and sniffed it. His face broke into a broad smile.

'Thanks, guys!' he said. 'You've got heavier stuff than this under the tarpaulin. Safe delivery! See you next time.' The head man turned and walked to the truck.

'Where are the others?' I asked Petro, noticing that we had been left alone.

The truck's engine roared and it set off, feeling out the way ahead with its headlights. Another pair of headlights flashed on not far from us and moved off after the truck. It was a Niva. Either the truck or the Niva sounded its horn and literally a few seconds later the wagons of the train gave a rumble and a jerk. We jumped into our own wagon and closed the outside door of the hallway. When we walked into the compartment, Gulya wasn't on the lower bunk. I raised my head in fright and saw her lying on the upper one.

Galya was sitting at the table. As soon as the train picked up speed, she lit an alcohol tablet and started brewing coffee.

Petro stuffed his pipe, lit it from the blue flame and went into the hallway.

I followed him. We stood there for a while, facing each other in the narrow hallway and not saying anything.

Petro opened the outer door and the hammering of the wheels became louder. We were riding past occasional lights, both close up and in the distance. And up above the stars were shining. The sky was cut off by a smooth black line – the train was climbing into mountains.

Petro breathed out tobacco smoke and the hazy cloud flew away through the open door.

'What are we carrying?' he asked quietly, lowering his head.

'Narcotics,' I replied just as quietly. Petro sighed heavily.

'And I thought it was sand,' he said in a weary voice.

'We're carrying sand too . . . only it seems to me that there isn't very much of it . . . we had two dump trucks full . . .'

Petro nodded without raising his head. He put his pipe to his mouth again.

I remembered that in the documentation for the load it said twelve tonnes of sand. Twelve tonnes was probably a full wagon, or at least half a wagon. But how much did we have here? I started thinking, trying to figure out the number of sacks of sand.

'No, no, that's a stupid waste of time,' I decided and glanced out of the open door.

The sky was rising higher and higher above the mountains that thrust up from below.

'Back in a moment,' Petro said and went into the compartment. He came back without his pipe, but with two bowls of coffee in his hands.

'What are we going to do?' I asked, warming my palms on the hot bowl. 'Wait for the first station and go to the militia? Eh?'

'Then what will happen? They'll arrest us, throw the sand away, and the narcotics . . . who knows what they'll do with them . . . He sighed again and took a sip of coffee. 'We have to get the sand to Ukraine, and then we can go to the militia, it's our militia there . . .'

'Yes, the Ukrainian militia would be more likely to believe that we were transporting sand from Kazakhstan, and not guns or narcotics . . . especially if we asked Colonel Taranenko to confirm that our story was true.'

'We can't turn back,' Petro declared coolly, but there was no note of despair or particular concern in his voice. He seemed to have calmed down now that he had realised there was no easy way we could get out of this situation. 'We have to keep going, otherwise we'll never know anything. God willing, we'll get the sand home, and then we'll see what we have to do.'

I squatted down and leaned back against the wall. I drank the strong, bitter coffee in small sips and watched the sky trembling to the hammering of the wheels.

I remembered the beginning of my flight-cum-voyage. It had begun with three cans of narcotics taken from the 'baby food' store and it was ending in a goods wagon carrying 'heavy stuff' from the Caucasus in white sacks hidden under sacks filled with our sand. All that cinnamon-flavoured mysticism seemed like a fairy tale for children right now.

'The material manifestations of the national spirit . . .' I thought, remembering the colonel, and nodded bitterly. A fine colonel, I thought, a brilliant mind, to turn two completely different idealistic idiots into couriers accompanying deliveries of guns and narcotics!

My thoughts went back to our excavations beside the ruins. There had been a smell of cinnamon there, and a body that smelled of cinnamon. The little gold cross and the gold key that I'd found in the sand there were still in the pocket of the rucksack. Those discoveries were real. And so was the watch that Galya had found. All that was normal, none of it transgressed the bounds of reality. Even Major Naumenko's funeral had been relatively normal. But the things that had happened after that? Digging out the sand, loading it into dump trucks, the ferry *Oilman*? And the colonel promising to catch up with us along the way and staying behind in Krasnovodsk on some important business?

287

'It seems to me that Taranenko set all this up in advance,' I said to Petro. 'The sand is a myth! They'll just stick us in a nuthouse if we start telling anyone about sand that can change a man's psychology . . . we've got involved in criminal dealings . . .'

'You're wrong,' said Petro, speaking Russian. 'Don't you remember how the Kazakh trader almost gave us all his goods? And do you think I would ever have spoken Russian to you before? Just because we can't explain the mystery of this sand in scientific terms doesn't mean that it isn't real. We don't have the knowledge!'

'That's certainly true,' I said with a bitter laugh. 'And it looks like it's too late for us to be taught.'

'You're wrong to be cynical – cynicism is probably the greatest tragedy of our generation, and if faith in the sand at least rids us of that misfortune, then there will be some hope for a better future for the entire country.'

'Faith in the sand?'

'Oh, it's not the sand,' Petro said, raising his voice nervously. 'It's the spirit dissolved in the sand.'

'Well, let's wait and see, maybe the colonel will turn up after all and tell us the full story in detail. About the sacks of sand, and the other sacks too,' I said, getting slowly to my feet.

My coffee was all drunk. I didn't feel like sleeping, but I had no desire to stay there beside Petro in the hallway either. My nocturnal cynicism had clearly offended his faith and there was no point in continuing with our conversation.

I went back into the compartment and lay down on my bunk.

The alcohol tablet was still burning on the table. The women were sleeping.

When I turned over on to my side, my ribs encountered

something that shouldn't be there. I pulled the pistol out from under the sleeping mat and stuck it into the rucksack.

62

In the morning I awoke to a long-forgotten sound – the whispering of rain. Against the background of this whispering the drops of water seeping through the wooden roof of the compartment fell with distinct, regular blows. Gusts of wind were tossing rain in through the opening of the window and fine drops were falling on my face, but I noticed them only after I woke up. I ran a hand over my cheeks and felt as if I had just washed my face.

I was the last to wake up – all the others were wide awake. Gulya was sitting beside me on my bunk. Petro and Galya were sitting opposite us. Everything was normal, except for the damp wind that every now and then tried to put out the hot Primus stove, on which the cooking pot was standing.

Everyone was drinking tea. I sat up and Gulya took hold of the pot with a towel and poured me some too.

'We passed Grozny during the night,' Petro informed me.

As I drank my tea I apologised to him for my cynicism of the night before.

'That's OK, it happens,' he said amiably. The wet foliage of trees, the roofs of houses and small country roads flashed by outside the window. One of the roads happened to run right alongside the embankment. The grey sky reminded me of autumn.

The train hurtled along as if it was trying to outrun the rain. A wet platform with a squat one-storey station building went flashing past. 'Labinsk Station.' There was a bright yellow, warm light in two windows of the little building.

I realised that we were out of the Caucasus. We were still descending from its foothills, slithering down on to a plain, the name of which we did not know as yet. But the Russian names of the railway stations flying past gladdened my heart. I glanced at Petro – his face was regally calm, the firmness and self-confidence had returned to his eyes. Perhaps he had been calm and sure of himself last night in the hallway too. I was the one who had lost my cool, trying to find an instant way out of the situation that had suddenly seemed clear to me. I was the one who had felt betrayed by everything and everyone – by Colonel Taranenko, and this sand, and my own former idealism – and I had tried to force Petro to share my disillusionment and lack of faith. But he had brought me coffee and lectured me on the harmfulness of cynicism. Yes, cynicism was harmful, especially mass cynicism. But there wasn't any cynicism in what I had said the night before. At least, it didn't seem to me that there was. I could probably say the same thing again right now – several hours of sleep had not changed my opinion.

My condition had not changed. But probably our spiritual condition was far more important at the moment. If a substantial error helped Petro to maintain his composure, there was nothing wrong with that! Let him continue in his error! I would have been glad to be deluded myself, to ascribe a wonderworking power to this sand and rely completely on that power for the future revival of Ukraine.

'Kolya!' Petro said, distracting me from my thoughts. 'What if we throw all of these narcotics off while we're moving?'

'What are you saying?' Galya exclaimed, giving him a stern glance. 'What if children find them?'

Petro took no notice of Galya's response and kept looking at me, waiting to hear my opinion.

I ran a hand through my damp hair and thought, trying to find an answer to his question.

'You realise they'll check at the border,' Petro continued. 'First the Russian customs and then ours. If any of them look under the tarpaulin, we're done for.'

'Somebody will look,' I agreed. 'Maybe we really ought to throw them off the train.'

'If we could throw them into a river,' Gulya suggested.

Petro laughed. 'That is, ask them to let the wagon stop on a bridge and wait there for an hour!' He shook his head.

Fifteen minutes later Petro and I crept through into the cargo section of the wagon.

We walked across the slippery tarpaulin in the rain.

'Right then, shall we try it?' asked Petro, stopping by the wagon's sliding door.

We tried to open the door, but it was jammed tight. It didn't have any handles on the inside, and we were bracing our hands against wet wood and our feet against slippery tarpaulin. Our feet just slithered away and the door stayed where it was.

'It's not going to work,' I sighed, taking a step back in the rain that had suddenly become stronger. I pulled a few splinters out of my hand and looked round at Petro.

'You know, when we push the door, we stand on the sacks, and our weight makes them hold the door even more tightly shut!'

Petro found the edge of the tarpaulin and lifted it back, exposing the sacks of sand that were bracing the door shut.

'Maybe we could move them?'

'I don't think that is such a good idea after all,' I said, stopping my partner. 'We don't know who's meeting the other sacks, and where.'

Petro looked at me, bemused.

'Maybe in half an hour the train will stop and a truck will drive up to our wagon. What are we going to do then? They're not likely to leave us alive.'

Petro sighed. There was water dripping from the ends of his black moustache. We were both soaked right through.

'All right, let's go back to the compartment,' he said eventually. 'We need to think a bit more . . .'

Once inside we wrung out our clothes, leaving a sizeable puddle on the floor. Gulya rubbed me down with her sleeping mat and Galya rummaged in the black shopping bag and set a half-litre bottle of Stolichnaya vodka on the table.

Petro was drying his hair with a towel. He froze and gaped wide-eyed at the bottle.

'You said you hadn't brought any!' he said in an angry voice.

'It's for medicinal purposes, for emergencies . . . It was taped to the bottom of the bag with –'

'Why, you . . .' Petro said, and his eyes glittered, but then he glanced sideways at me and forced a smile. 'See how . . . economical she is.'

Petro ripped off the thick metal foil cap and poured vodka into two bowls, trying to estimate how much went into each one. There was about three hundred grams left in the bottle.

'Come on, warm yourself up,' he said, nodding at my bowl. We drank briskly with no toasts.

'More?' Petro asked, lifting the bottle up off the table.

I nodded.

Soon the empty bottle went flying out of the window.

Another station with a Russian name went rushing past. The large drops of rain drummed on the roof of the compartment.

Petro leaned back against the wall. We sat there, saying nothing and listening to the rain.

The vodka induced in me a joyful indifference to the immediate future.

It was obviously good vodka, the kind that our people had drunk both before the revolution and after.

The train was lulling me to sleep. The hammering of the wheels fused with the drumming of the raindrops on the roof. I lay down on the lower bunk with my legs pulled up under me in order not to get in Gulya's way.

As I was falling asleep, I felt Gulya's caring hands covering me with a blanket.

The cosy warmth hastened the arrival of sleep.

63

I was woken in the night by an extraneous noise. The train's wheels were hammering out a monotonous rhythm on the joints of the rails, but my ears were already accustomed to that rhythm: something else had insinuated itself into the sound of the moving train. And there were spots of yellow light drifting through the darkness of the night outside the window.

I lowered my feet on to the floor and moved closer to the window.

Running alongside the railway line was a broad highway, with an endless column of covered trucks driving along it. Their headlights diluted the darkness, lending it a hint of yellow. Each truck's headlights shone straight on to the back of the one moving in front. I saw soldiers dozing inside one of the trucks, sitting on the benches along the sides.

The train began slowly overhauling the military transport column. A blue signboard flickered past in the light of the headlights: 'Tikhoretsk 50 km, Kushchevskaya 120 km, Rostov-on-Don 225 km'.

The column halted and we left it behind. Now the highway was an uninterrupted belt of black running alongside the railway. There were no more vehicles and the extraneous noise had disappeared.

I looked at the sky, at the motionless stars. We really had outrun the rain – all the stars were hanging in their right places, with not a single one hidden behind a cloud. There was a fine sunny day waiting for us up ahead, and I wanted to believe that the weather would not be the only good thing about it.

Before the dawn came I managed to fall asleep again, sitting at the table with my head resting on my arms.

When I woke up I took my time opening my eyes.

The sun was rising from behind the train, and not a single ray of its light entered the window of the compartment, but outside the window everything was radiant. And the highway was still running on in the bright sunlight, was once again filled with its own automotive life. An Icarus bus with a sign saying 'Rostov–Kropotkin' went streaking by and a heavy refrigerator truck lumbered heavily past our wagon.

I poured some water from the canister into a drinking bowl, went out into the hallway and had a wash. Setting the bowl down on the wooden floor, I opened the outer door, and noise and fresh air burst into the hallway together. The wind dried my wet face in a moment.

We were already eating our meagre breakfast in silence when the train slowed down and began pulling left. The highway moved away from us, and so did the rails of the main line, glinting in the sun. Now there were broad fields of maize beside us. Petro and I looked at each other.

Galya put her bowl of tea down on the table and turned to Petro.

'Did you dump the narcotics?' she asked with an anxious expression on her face.

Petro shook his head.

'Well, you say something to your man at least!' Galya said, looking at Gulya.

'Women shouldn't interfere in men's business,' Gulya said in a quiet voice.

Galya merely shook her head at that.

The train swung even more to the left. Petro put his head out of the window and looked ahead, along the line of the train.

'What can you see there?' I asked impatiently, infected by Galya's nervousness.

'A depot.'

I looked out of the window too and saw that we were approaching a goods train halt. I could count dozens of trains on our right. We couldn't see how many there were on the left. Every few metres a new line branched off to the right, taking us further and further away from the fields of maize.

The train slowed down as if the driver was afraid of missing the side branch that he needed. It stopped. It set off again. We were pulling into the lines of trains. There was one more branch line still unoccupied between us and the nearest one.

I looked at the next goods train as we slowly crept past it. It was a complete assortment – refrigerator wagons alternating with dirty tank wagons and ordinary goods wagons like the one that we were riding in.

'If we're lucky, we'll go on from here without any excess cargo,' I said, hoping to reassure Galya. After all, it was during the last halt like this that the night crew had turned up and let us know what we were carrying.

But that time, of course, the train had stopped in a deserted spot and it had happened at night, whereas now the joyful sun was rising higher and higher above the newly awoken earth. So it was illogical, to say the least, to be thinking about deliverance from our unwanted cargo just at that moment.

The train stopped and Petro and I watched the locomotive leave. It was strangely quiet on all sides.

Petro filled his pipe and got out of the wagon. He stopped under the window.

'It's really warm!' he said.

We got out too. There was a warm wind roaming through the open corridors between the rows of goods trains. There was rubbish crunching under our feet. There was that familiar railway-station smell of burned rubber. There were birds singing in the sky above us. And somewhere nearby there was a grasshopper fiddling away. This mixture of wild civilisation and wild nature, in which sound contradicted smell, gave me a chilly feeling in my soul. I looked round at Gulya.

She was standing with her eyes closed and her face turned towards the sun.

'Can you hear anything?' Petro asked me. I listened. Somewhere in the distance I could hear the rhythmical sound of a train. When the sound stopped, I heard voices. The breeze died down for a moment and the voices sounded a little bit louder, but still too quiet for me to be able to make out anything.

We left the women by the wagon and set off along the next train, listening. Somewhere nearby there was a clinking of glass and we stopped. I dropped to the ground and looked under the wagon. My eyes encountered the frightened gaze of a thin black cat, who immediately leapt back and ran away, leaving an empty beer bottle behind. I was about to stand up again, but my attention was caught by a movement within the limited field of view from under the wagon. Three rows of iron wheels away I saw two crates and two pairs of legs in the gap between trains. There were two men sitting there, talking about something calmly, although I could only judge that from the calm inflections of their voices.

'There's someone there,' I said to Petro.

He squatted down too and glanced under the wagon.

'Go and take a look!' he said.

I crawled under one wagon and then another, then stopped.

'Vasya's been gone a long time,' I heard a man's voice say. 'That's not right . . . That's the way to get a smack across the head!'

When I crawled out from under the wagon, the two ragged tramps sitting on the empty crates stared at me in amazement. An old man and one who was fairly young. The ground beside them was littered with numerous cigarette ends, two empty beer bottles and one wine bottle.

There was a dirty sleeping bag lying behind the crate on which the old man was sitting.

'Hey!' said the young man, getting up off his crate. 'We've only been here since yesterday. We haven't stolen anything or broken anything . . . Don't throw us out!'

Realising immediately that I was hardly likely to learn anything from these two, I crawled back under the wagon.

'Tramps,' I told Petro. He nodded without taking the pipe out of his mouth. Looking round, I saw Gulya and Galya shaking out a blanket by all four corners. Every flap sent a cloud of dust rising up above us.

Petro and I watched our women for about ten minutes, until they had shaken out all the blankets and sleeping mats. Then they went back into the compartment but, to judge from the rubbish that came flying out of the window every now and then, the clean-up was continuing.

'Kolya,' Gulya called to me.

When I walked over I was handed the empty five-litre canister. With the tramps' help I located a tank of drinking water at the edge of the fields of maize.

Galya wanted to boil up the remains of our buckwheat, but her plans had to be postponed. The shaggy-haired tramp Vasya turned up at our wagon, wearing a grubby raincoat and carrying a bucket.

'The lads sent me,' he said after introducing himself. 'I went to get some crayfish – take fifteen for yourselves.'

Petro brightened up when he heard the word 'crayfish'. He squatted down beside the bucket that was standing on the ground and looked at the green creatures swarming in it.

'Take them, take them,' grubby Vasya encouraged him. The tramp looked about forty years old. 'It's a pity there's no beer. We finished the beer yesterday. They go down a real treat with beer!'

Petro collected some crayfish into a bag and thanked Vasya, then went into the compartment. The crayfish were tipped straight from the bag into the boiling water. They slowly turned red, and the way they looked started giving me an appetite.

But not even crayfish could completely distract me from the uncertainty of our immediate future. While we were still travelling and I could see that we were going to Rostov, my heart had felt easy. A journey is already action in itself. But this dead end?

But then, the more I thought about the situation and how deserted and strange this place was, the more likely it seemed to me that this was where the event that would simplify the remainder of our journey would take place.

And that was what happened. We heard the sound of an engine as we were lying on our bunks, resting after lunch.

I glanced out of the window and saw a military ZIL. It drove past and stopped immediately after our wagon. All this seemed perfectly logical to me. What didn't seem logical was that a major and two warrant officers with automatic rifles jumped out of the cab.

'Don't leave the compartment!' the major shouted, stopping under our window.

Another three soldiers in camouflage suits jumped down to the ground. We heard the door of the wagon rolling back with a creak and the tarpaulin rustling.

The soldiers worked as a team and without a pause. It took them ten minutes to unload the white sacks.

'Is that the lot?' the major's voice asked.

'Yes,' someone barked back. Petro and I were sitting opposite each other at the window. He could see more of what was happening.

When the ZIL left, Petro heaved a sigh of relief.

'They left something in the wagon,' he said.

'Let's go and take a look!' I said.

We clambered through the little door from the toilet to the cargo section of the wagon. The crumpled tarpaulin was lying in the far corner, the sacks of sand were scattered around in disorder, and there was a large bundle wrapped in an oilcloth lying by the closed door.

We went over to it. The bundle was closed with a zip fastener. When Petro opened the zip we froze and drew in our breath. All we could see through the parted zip was that the body was dressed in military uniform.

Petro sat down on a sack of sand. The zip whooshed shut again.

He looked at me in confusion, as if he was asking what we should do.

I shrugged and spread my arms. It looked as if one unwanted cargo in our wagon had been replaced by another that was even less wanted.

'We have to think of something,' I whispered. 'Only don't say anything to them.' And I nodded towards the compartment.

'Let's put him under the tarpaulin for now,' Petro suggested. 'And then maybe we'll throw him out on the way.'

We stretched out the tarpaulin and tucked its edges into the cracks between the sacks and the walls of the wagon.

64

As evening started to come on, we lit a fire beside the wagon and sat around it on empty crates that we had found nearby. The uncertainty of our immediate future was beginning to get on my nerves.

Petro sat there without speaking, his head in his hands. Galya and Gulya were talking about something, but I was absorbed in my own thoughts, and didn't listen to their quiet conversation.

Analysing the events of the last few days, I became more and more convinced that we had already outlived our usefulness. There was only one question remaining: Who had been toying with us, who had directed this entire epic adventure with the sand, under cover of which we had carried guns to the border between Dagestan and Chechnya, and then taken on a load of narcotics to Russia? We were obviously stuck in a dead end now, and not just on the railway. No one needed us any longer, just as no one needed the body that the soldiers had left us as a souvenir. It was stupid to hope that our wagon would set off down the rails again. Except perhaps on a return journey . . . but even that would probably happen without us.

I thought it best not to share my thoughts with Petro. Let him come to the same conclusion himself, and then we could think about what to do next. But how long would I have to wait?

I imagined Petro and me as tramps sitting on these same crates round this same fire. Whichever way you looked at things, that was certainly one of the possible outcomes.

But Galya and Gulya didn't fit into that outcome.

Meanwhile, they continued their quiet conversation. Galya was talking about her childhood in a village near Lvov and her parents' little farm. She spoke Russian with a noticeable accent.

We suddenly heard several voices laughing drunkenly behind the wagons. 'More tramps have arrived,' I thought.

The stars appeared on the dark sky, the brightest ones first. The fire crackled, diluting the railway-station smell with its smoke. Its flames reminded me of autumn, of the ritual burning of autumn leaves at my parents' dacha, of my childhood.

That evening brought more than just nostalgic memories. The

sound of an approaching train caught our attention. The women stopped talking. We turned our heads in the direction of the main line to Rostov. The powerful beam of the approaching locomotive's searchlight reached us, pushing the twilight aside, out of its corridor of light. The train started slowing down about three hundred metres away. The searchlight was so bright that my eyes watered and I turned away and saw our shadows on the dirty ground.

The train was already crawling on to the only free branch line, between us and the 'assorted' train. It went by slowly, followed by a string of covered goods wagons with letters and numbers stencilled all over their sides.

About five minutes after the train's arrival we came back to life. Petro put more wood on the fire and went across to the wagon opposite us.

' "Property of Bataisk Goods Station," ' he said, reading out the stencilled words.

My eyes had recovered from the aggressive searchlight and were reaccustoming themselves to the gentle light of the fire.

'Do you know where this Bataisk is?' Petro asked me.

'No.'

'A bit further on, about five kilometres from here,' a familiar male voice said somewhere close by.

I looked round. I couldn't see anyone within range of the fire's ability to illuminate our section of the corridor between the two trains.

'Who's that? Is that you, Colonel?' Petro said.

A bottle of beer came rolling out from under the wagon belonging to the Bataisk Goods Station. And then another one. The glass of the bottles jingled as it went over the stones.

When the bottles had stopped at our feet and the renewed silence was beginning to seem alarming, another bottle came rolling out from under the wagon.

'Have you got anything to open them with?' asked the familiar voice.

'Well, you bastard, Colonel!' said Petro with a sigh.

'What's wrong?' said Vitold Yukhimovich, scrambling out between the wheels of the Bataisk wagon. 'Got a fright, did you?'

Petro didn't answer. He just sighed again.

'Do you have anything to open them with?' the colonel asked again, looking at me.

I picked up one of the bottles, hooked the edge of its top on to the iron step of our wagon and slammed my fist down on it from above.

'Welcome!' I said, holding the open bottle out to the colonel.

The colonel accepted the bottle, took a gulp of beer and wiped off his short moustache with his free hand.

'Why welcome?' he said, as if nothing out of the ordinary had happened. 'I got here before you did!'

I just shrugged at that. A sudden surge of tiredness had erased any desire to ask the colonel all the questions that had accumulated in my mind.

'He won't stay long,' I thought.

'Well,' said the colonel, surveying us cheerfully after his second gulp of beer, 'had a rest? Now it's time to do some work!'

We all gaped at him confusion.

'Get ready to go,' he said.

'Where to?' I asked.

The colonel looked at his watch, turning the face towards the fire.

'We're leaving in forty minutes,' he declared.

'On what?'

'On a train. Only not that one!' he said, nodding towards our wagon. 'I'll explain everything later.'

This promise from the colonel sounded very apposite to me. Petro got up off his crate and glanced expectantly at the women. Gulya and Galya got up too.

'Well, come on, come on,' the colonel said to them.

Vitold Yukhimovich stood close beside the wagon while we collected our things together. When I looked at him through the gaping window of the compartment I noticed the sadness in his face. The flickering patches of light from the fire created a dramatic, theatrical atmosphere. In this illumination the bags under his eyes looked like bruises, and his face was deathly pale. The colonel's moustache, usually so neatly trimmed, had lost its fine shape.

'He obviously didn't have an easy journey either,' I thought. No, I didn't feel sorry for the colonel, I didn't feel any sympathy for him. If I felt sorry for anyone just at that moment, it was our women and the idealist Petro. And I felt sorry for myself, of course. Colonels are never idealists. Our colonel was no exception, which meant that all his problems were merely the concomitant burdens of military service. Or secret service, rather. 'Perhaps he's a romantic and an adventurer,' I suddenly thought. 'After all, if his age is anything to go by, perhaps he joined the KGB when intelligence officers were the only ones who could travel freely round the world . . . I'll have to ask him if he's done a lot of travelling.'

Our things had been gathered together. Galya and Gulya had tidied up our compartment and carefully put the camel-hair blankets and the tableware away. They had cleaned the Primus stove with a rag.

'Get a move on!' the colonel's voice shouted in through the window. At the door of the wagon he took Gulya's double bundle and flung it over his shoulder. He picked up Gulya's bag and set off towards the back of the train.

'Vitold Yukhimovich!' Petro called to him. 'What about the sacks of sand?'

'That's not the right sand,' the colonel said, looking back.

'How do you mean?' Petro exclaimed. 'It smells of cinnamon!'

'Of course it does,' Colonel Taranenko agreed calmly. 'Five kilograms of cinnamon went into those sacks! Let's go, I'll explain everything later.' And the colonel strode on.

'And then there's the body!' Petro said thoughtfully as he set off after the colonel. The colonel stopped.

'What body?' he asked in surprise. 'Where from?'

'A sol-dier's body,' Petro replied as he walked along. 'It's all right, I'll explain everything later!'

When we reached the last wagon of our train, we stumbled across a lot of railway tracks and walked past several other goods trains standing as close together as cows in cattle pens.

'That one's ours!' the colonel said. He waited for us all to catch up, then ducked into the gap between the trains.

We obediently followed him. Someone waved a hand up ahead and the colonel, who was walking in front of me, waved in reply.

We stopped beside an ordinary goods wagon. I was surprised to see that the man waving to the colonel and waiting for us was none other than the tramp Vasya, who had regaled us with crayfish. Vasya helped to carry our things into the cargo supervisor's compartment of the wagon. When I gave him a enquiring look he just smiled and said nothing.

'Vasya,' the colonel said a minute later, 'are there any wagons for Moscow here?'

'Yes,' said Vasya, nodding.

'Some soldier's body has been left behind in our young friends' wagon,' the colonel said with a smile. 'You and your colleagues load it on to the next Moscow train . . .' He suddenly lost the thread of his thought and turned to Petro. 'Petya, how was the body packed? Or was it simply . . .?'

'In a bag with a zip,' Petro replied.

The colonel thought about that for a minute.

'Vasya,' he said, 'hold the train – say there's a fifteen-minute delay. Then get straight back here!'

Vasya ran to the locomotive and the colonel clambered back under the wagon without saying a word to us.

'He's gone to visit the corpse,' I thought. We looked around the new compartment – there was already a whiff of European civilisation here. The compartment was specially made, with a genuine glazed window, and a toilet with a mirror and a washbasin, and the hallway had a small boiler for water and a box of coal briquettes.

Petro and I put down our things and left the wagon, leaving the women in the compartment. This wagon was the property of the Baku Depot.

'So our sand's here,' said Petro, nodding at the sealed sliding doors.

'Yes, probably,' I agreed.

Petro went out into the hallway and tried to open the door into the cargo section of the wagon, but it was locked with a key. We had to return to the compartment.

A few minutes later Vasya and the colonel came back at almost exactly the same time. There was a radiant smile on the colonel's face.

'We have an opportunity to leave a good impression behind us!' he said gleefully, looking at Vasya. 'Move the body to the nearest

Moscow train and have one of the tramps write a note: "Greetings from General Voskoboinikov". Put the note into the sack. Let them clean out their own ranks!'

'All right,' Vasya replied with an eager glance.

'Well, that's all. Take care!' said the colonel, offering Vasya his hand. 'God willing, we'll meet again!'

Two minutes later we were sitting on the lower bunks. I was sitting with Gulya, and Petro, Galya and the colonel were sitting on the opposite side of the table. The colonel had taken off his watch and put it on the table, and now he was calmly watching the second hand. He carried on doing that until the train gave a jerk. The wagons of the next goods train crept slowly past our window.

I suddenly thought that there were only four bunks in this compartment, but there were five of us. I looked around carefully and noticed that the colonel's rucksack was not there. Out of curiosity I leaned down and glanced under the lower bunks.

'Lost something?' Vitold Yukhimovich asked me.

'Yes,' I replied, 'your things.'

'Aah!' he laughed. 'What an observant lad! They're not in here, I'm going to sleep in the wagon. But if you invite me to breakfast, I won't take offence.'

'And are the sacks in the wagon?' Petro asked gloomily.

'No, the sacks aren't in this wagon. They're in the next one,' the colonel said without turning round. 'And there's no need for you to worry about them.'

Petro reached under the table and took his pipe and the bundle of Prima tobacco out of the shopping bag.

He filled his pipe in silence, shook a box of matches in his hand, got up and went out into the hallway.

'Sometimes even I have to do what has to be done, not what I

307

want to do,' the colonel said as he watched Petro leave. 'But that's all right. That's life . . .'

65

An hour and a half later, when the train had already passed Rostov-on-Don, the hot water from the boiler melted the ice of mistrust. The colonel was in charge of the boiler, and he carried five glasses of boiling water into the compartment and dropped an identical tea bag into each one.

'I even have sugar,' he said, extracting several small packets of 'railway sugar' from the pocket of his denim jacket. 'Help yourselves!'

'And what's in this wagon?' Petro asked him after we had drunk our tea.

'Chinese toys and Vietnamese balsam,' the colonel replied with an amicable smile.

'Toys?' Petro echoed incredulously and chortled.

'Come on!' said the colonel, getting up from the table. He stopped at the door of the compartment and looked back. Petro and I followed him out into the hallway. He unlocked the door into the cargo section with a key and let us through ahead of him.

The wagon was stacked up to the top of its walls with cardboard boxes and plywood crates. A narrow passage between the boxes and crates led to a small area free of cargo next to the sliding doors. By the dim light entering from the small ventilation window we saw two pallets lying there, with a blue sleeping bag spread out on top of them. Beside them were a plywood crate that obviously served as a table and the colonel's rucksack.

We stopped in front of this sanctuary.

'I didn't bring you here to show you round,' Vitold Yukhimovich said behind us, and his voice sounded unusually dry and severe.

He took a seat on his improvised mattress and narrowed his eyes as he looked up at us.

'I have no intention of explaining myself or apologising to you,' he declared in rather sombre tones. 'You got involved in this business of your own free will, so don't go playing the victim! If it wasn't for me you'd be sitting somewhere with the Kazakh secret service and answering their questions all night long. Concerning illegal excavations and narcotics in baby-food cans. When I came round in the desert with a splitting headache and my feet tied together, I didn't take offence. I simply wanted to catch up with you and give you a good beating, and that's what would have happened, if not for that sand. Or perhaps it was just fatigue, and not the sand at all? I give you two minutes to decide how we're going to talk to each other from now on: on equal terms, with total mutual trust, or like a colonel talking to a couple of privates who have ended up in the guardhouse?'

The colonel took a watch on a leather strap out of the pocket of his denim jacket and wound it. He pulled up the jacket's rather long sleeve and glanced at his own watch.

'So which watch shall we set our time from?' he asked. 'The idealist's?' He lifted up the watch with the leather strap on his open palm. 'As you can see, the idealist left the world of the living a long time ago, but his watch is still ticking! Or the pragmatist's?' He glanced down at his left hand.

We said nothing. I don't know what Petro was thinking about

309

at that moment, but my own thoughts were circling somewhere far away, over Kiev. And I wanted to join them there. 'Everything will work out just fine,' I told myself firmly. 'I just have to wait a while.'

'One more minute, and I'll make the decision!' the colonel said in a chilly voice.

'All right,' Petro said with a heavy sigh, 'we'll talk on equal terms.'

'Look at that,' I thought in relief. 'Crude force has conquered . . . or, as they used to say: "Friendship has triumphed!" '

I chuckled and the colonel, noticing my chuckle, gave a smile too.

He reached into his plywood crate and took out a fancy green bottle. He got to his feet.

'I have not deceived you in any way,' he said, speaking calmly now, and unscrewed the cap of the bottle. 'Your health!' He took a sip from the mouth of the bottle and held it out to me.

I looked at the label – it really was Vietnamese balsam.

A sticky warmth spread through my mouth after the first sip, and I took another. Then I handed the bottle on to Petro.

Half an hour later we were still the colonel's guests. We were sitting on plywood crates at the plywood 'table' drinking more Vietnamese balsam by the light of a burning candle, but by this time we were drinking out of disposable plastic cups that Vitold Yukhimovich had hoarded. The conversation really was being held on equal terms, with the colonel joking and trying to create a relaxed atmosphere. Petro strove stalwartly to keep a serious expression on his face, but the Vietnames balsam proved to be a rather potent beverage.

Later I realised that the colonel had been joking more for himself, that he had needed to relax. But even so, from time to time the tiredness wiped the smile off his face.

Once or twice Petro tried to ask the colonel serious questions, but Vitold Yukhimovich just laughed them off.

'We'll talk tomorrow,' he promised Petro as he poured the remains of the balsam into his own cup. 'But now it's time for bed!'

We left the colonel and went back to the compartment.

'Well?' Gulya asked me. 'Are you going to have supper?'

'Tomorrow,' I replied, clambering up on to the top bunk.

66

The next day started unexpectedly early. I was woken by the silence – that often happens when someone has been used to falling asleep with noise. And it was unnaturally bright outside – there was a yellowish-red light pouring in through the window.

Looking out I saw the bright 'suns' of the spotlights and other lamps that were lighting up the train and immediately realised why we had stopped – THE BORDER!

I heard voices approaching outside.

I got up quietly and walked out of the compartment. I opened the outside door and glanced into the space that was flooded with powerful artificial light.

Vitold Yukhimovich was approaching the wagon, accompanied by a young customs officer in a green uniform.

'These two here are mine!' said the colonel, pointing at our wagon and the one behind it.

Then he looked at me. The customs officer looked at me too.

'This is our man escorting the load,' the colonel told the customs officer, at the same time gesturing for me to disappear.

I yawned demonstratively and closed the door to the hallway. Then I listened.

The two men's voices began slowly moving away.

I went back into the compartment and glanced out of the window. Now they were standing beside the wagon which the colonel had said was carrying the sand. I could see that they were talking calmly, as if all the questions had already been settled a long time ago, if not in advance.

I observed them for about five minutes. Then I saw a customs officer with a briefcase approach them. He took some papers and seals out of the briefcase and started explaining something to the colonel in detail, jabbing his finger at the papers. It all ended with the papers being transferred to the colonel's hands and his shaking the customs officers by theirs, before he walked back towards our wagon. I moved away from the window and froze, listening.

The outer door into the hallway clicked. I thought that now the colonel would look into the compartment and explain something. But he went straight through to his lair. The lock of the door into the cargo section rasped twice. So he had shut himself in.

The train started to move and slowly pulled out into relative darkness. I lay down again.

'Almost home,' I thought, realising that any moment now we would be on Ukrainian territory.

The renewed hammering of the wheels began lulling me to sleep. I closed my eyes.

In my dreams I saw a sea, probably the Caspian. I was being rocked to and fro, side to side.

Then a warm hand was laid on my lips and the touch of another woke me.

'Quiet, Kolya, quiet!' whispered Gulya, who was sitting beside me. She kept her hand over my mouth.

'What is it?'

'Were you having a nightmare?' she asked.

The train jerked again, stopped and moved backwards.

'I was dreaming of the sea,' I replied, pulling up my legs and sitting cross-legged. 'Where are we now?'

I glanced out of the window, but I couldn't see anything. My dream must clearly have been a short one, if it was still night outside.

'We've been here for twenty minutes already,' Gulya whispered. 'Going backwards and forwards.'

But now we were travelling straight ahead, not backwards and forwards. The rhythm of the iron wheels speeded up. Artemovsk Station drifted by, brightly illuminated.

'It's Ukraine already,' I whispered to Gulya when we had left the station behind us. 'Have you been awake for a long time?'

'Two hours,' she answered.

'Listen, have we passed the Ukrainian customs?'

'Yes,' Gulya said, nodding. 'Men in uniforms with a dog walked along past the wagons.'

I found such a brief and clear description of the Ukrainian customs both amusing and reassuring. The sleep had already been blown clear out of my head.

'By evening we'll be in Kiev,' I whispered to Gulya. 'We'll leave the things at my place . . . at our place . . . and go out to a cafe. I'll just have to ask my "bookkeeper" Galya for half the bucks I've saved . . .'

'And then what?' she asked.

313

'And then we're going to live. Like normal people,' I said, and Gulya smiled.

'Let's lie down for a bit longer,' she suggested. We settled down comfortably on the lower bunk. I lay against the wall and she was on the edge. But we lay facing each other. I put my right arm round her and she put her left arm round me. The train swayed us to and fro, and we kissed as if we were playing a game.

'I have my diploma with me,' Gulya suddenly whispered. 'I can work as a doctor . . . All right?'

I looked at her in amazement.

'You want to work?' I asked, and then realised that my question sounded rather stupid.

'Yes,' Gulya replied. 'Until we have children . . . Stroke me!'

I stroked her hair. She lay there with her eyes closed and the corners of her mouth twitching gently.

I thought I was happy. 'Thought' because it was an odd kind of happiness. There was an admixture of quiet fear, the fear of responsibility. 'Our future will begin this evening,' I thought, and tried to picture that future. But no image would come. Of course, it wouldn't be all that easy to see. And my imagination was tired too, it had stopped believing in miracles. Scepticism, or perhaps even cynicism – that was what I had acquired in the course of this journey. Now I needed to be cured of it. My hands, feelings, head and mouth had to recover their taste for life. I needed to drink 'a different coffee'. I needed to freshen up my soul. After a rest my body would recover from its tiredness.

I suddenly realised that there was a multi-stranded thread linking the soul with the body – the nerves. They made your hands shake, they gave a dream the intensity of a nightmare. The different coffee that I had just invented for myself would hardly be capable of

314

enlivening my soul without affecting my body at the same time, without transmitting some kind of charge along the irregular threads of my nerves – unless perhaps it was milky coffee, with milk from a can of 'infant formula'.

I pulled Gulya close and nuzzled her hair.

67

Next morning we were woken by the colonel. After first knocking on the door of the compartment, he waited for two minutes, thinking that would be long enough for us to get up and greet him with a vivacious smile. But when he came in, we were all still lying down. Although we did have our eyes open.

The colonel was smoothly shaved and his moustache had recovered its former tidy, distinguished appearance.

'The water has boiled already,' he announced and glanced at his watch. 'We have one hour left for drinking tea. I give you three minutes to get up!'

He smiled and went out. When he came back we were already sitting at the table.

'Right then, shall we cross the t's and dot the i's?' he asked, half serious and half joking, as he stirred the almost insoluble 'railway sugar' into his tea with a spoon.

The train started taking a bend, and I automatically looked out the window. The horizon resembled a palisade of immensely tall factory chimneys. The chimneys were silent, and the sky above them was blue and clear.

'We'll be in Kharkov in an hour,' Colonel Taranenko began. 'That's why I woke you up. Our last chance to talk. Only to begin with I'm going to do the talking.'

He smiled and gave us all a rather tense glance.

'I'll listen to what you have to say afterwards,' the colonel continued, 'but first you have to listen to me. Listen closely, without interrupting. Agreed?'

Silence signified consent. The colonel gazed round at us all again and maintained a two-minute pause.

'I'm staying in Kharkov, you'll go on . . .'

'What about the sand?' Petro asked, staring stubbornly at Vitold Yukhimovich.

'We agreed that you would listen carefully and not interrupt me! You can ask questions afterwards, if there are any.'

The colonel chewed on his lips for a moment.

'All right, about the sand . . . The sand is no longer with us. The wagon carrying the sand stayed behind in Artemovsk. Neither I, nor you, nor all of us together have the right to decide what to do with it. But together we have achieved the most important goal – we have delivered the sand to Ukraine. And that will stand to our credit . . . I can promise you only one thing – that I will try to let you know any news about that sand. But it's in your interest not to talk to anyone about it. In the first place, they won't believe you. In the second place, if you do start talking about it, you'll never hear any more news. But you might learn that you are wanted by the Moscow FSB on suspicion of trading arms and narcotics in the northern Caucasus. By the way, that situation was forced on us. There was no other way we could have got the sand through. Unfortunately, to achieve a lofty goal you have to get your hands dirty!' The colonel sighed heavily. 'And now for something else.

'You, Kolya,' he said, turning to me, 'cannot go back to Kiev. I don't care where you manage to hide for the time being, but hide you must. I think you trust Petro more than me, so leave your contact details with him and we'll let you know through him when you can go back to Kiev. I think the SBU will manage to clear a landing strip for you somehow. Only you'll have to wait for a month or two. But you two,' he said, turning his attention to Petro and Galya, 'can simply go home. Let me repeat once again, it is in your own interest not to say anything about the sand. You didn't go for sand! You went in search of treasure – let's say spiritual treasure. You went and you came back. You didn't find anything. But you are richer in experience of life, and one of you' – the colonel cast a cunning glance in my direction – 'actually did find his treasure.' He looked at Gulya. 'In short – life goes on. The future ahead is bright. Let us remember only the good things from the past and forget our mutual grudges. That's all!'

Having concluded his monologue on a note of exalted sentiment, the colonel sighed in relief and took a sip of tea.

I thought about where Gulya and I could go now. I didn't have any relatives in Ukraine. There were people I knew, but I didn't want to descend on them out of the blue with Gulya in tow. It was one thing to turn up for a couple of days, but we were talking about at least a month here . . .

I looked at Gulya.

She snuggled against me.

'Everything will be fine,' I whispered in her ear.

Petro sat there in silence, with his lips twisted out of shape. The dejected droop of his black moustache reflected his condition perfectly.

'Well, all right,' he said eventually, peering at the colonel through narrowed eyes. 'You have outwitted us, Mr State Security Officer. But there's one thing I don't understand: what are you doing playing games with Vietnamese balsam?'

'It's my hobby,' the colonel said with a smile. 'Small-scale legal import and export . . . And it's good for the family budget – like having an allotment for growing vegetables. Puts a bit of food on the table . . .'

Petro simply shook his head.

'I'm going to get ready,' said the colonel. 'Do you have any money left?'

Petro looked enquiringly at Galya. She nodded.

'That's good. Who knows, maybe we'll meet again soon!'

Vitold Yukhimovich carefully closed the door behind him. We sat in silence for another five minutes, with the tea turning cold on the table. The outskirts of Kharkov flitted past through the window.

'Let's go to Kolomya,' Petro said unexpectedly, looking at me. 'You can live with my parents for the time being. And we'll go on to Kiev . . .'

I was genuinely shocked. I found it hard to believe that at that moment Petro was thinking about me and Gulya.

68

Vitold Yukhimovich obligingly bought us the tickets to Kolomya. Unfortunately, the tickets were not all in the same compartment, but in two neighbouring ones. When the train started, we persuaded a forty-year-old couple to swap places with Gulya and me, and so we carried on travelling all together, as we had done from the very beginning of our railway adventure. It was getting dark outside, the twilight was thickening and the little yellow lights of stations too small and insignificant for our train drifted past outside the window.

The female conductor brought us tea and biscuits and we drank our tea in an atmosphere of welcome tranquillity.

Soon after that the same conductor brought us clean bedclothes. And when we had finished taking tea, we settled down for the night, allocating the places on the upper bunks to our women.

When the light was turned out, I clicked the latch shut on the door so that our sleep would not be disturbed by any nocturnal visitors. But even so, our sleep was disturbed very early in the morning. We heard noises and shouting from the next compartment, the one in which Gulya and I could easily have been travelling. We turned on the light and listened in silence.

'Someone came in here during the night!' a man's voice shouted. 'It's not ours! You ask them!'

But the train continued to clatter rhythmically over the tracks, completely unconcerned about what might be happening in one of its carriages.

Meanwhile, another man's voice told someone to get dressed and collect his things. It was just starting to get light outside.

The train slowed down as it approached the narrow platform of a small station. Pressing my face to the window, I saw a police Gazelle and a white Zhiguli beside the single-storey station building.

There were several men in militia uniforms and civilian clothes standing between the cars and smoking. They glanced at the braking train, dropped their unfinished cigarettes and hurried towards the train. I thought I saw their eyes follow our carriage as it moved slowly past them.

The noise from the next compartment emerged into the corridor. Then it stopped. I tried looking out of the window, but I couldn't see anything or anyone beside the carriage,

'What's happening out there?' Petro asked.

'I can't tell. They've taken someone off the train . . .'

Meanwhile, the train jerked and set off again, as if it had pushed off from that narrow platform.

In the morning a different conductor, a younger woman, brought us our tea.

'They arrested some drug dealers,' she said in answer to my question. 'They pretended to be so respectable – a married couple, they said they were – but they found an entire bag full of those drugs in their case! He was shouting that he didn't have any bag . . . Someone planted it, he said. But they arrested them anyway!'

The conductor seemed genuinely pleased by this latest victory of the valiant militia over the criminal world. But I was seriously alarmed. Of course, I had heard that the trains in Ukraine were crawling with narcotics couriers, but I couldn't help feeling concerned at the thought that I could have been in that compartment the night before.

'It's all right, don't get so worried,' Petro reassured me.

It was raining in Kolomya.

In the fifteen minutes it took us to walk from the little station to Petro's parents' house we got absolutely soaked through. The rain had been following us ever since Ivanovo-Frankovsk, but as long as we were still in the train, I had kept hoping that it would carry us out from under the low, heavy clouds. It hadn't.

So there we were, standing on the porch of an ordinary two-storey house. Petro knocked.

As soon as the door opened, Petro's fat old mother wiped her hands on her apron and hugged him. Then his father – tall and thin – came out.

'Daughter, a dress like that's for going to church in, not washing the dishes!'

'Let me switch the television on for you,' the old man said to Gulya, and without waiting for an answer, he went across to the locker standing in the corner, took the cover embroidered with red cockerels off the television, turned a switch, waited for the image to appear and started adjusting the twin-horned internal aerial.

Gulya obediently sat on a chair in front of the television and I was left standing by the door.

Hearing the sound of wooden steps squeaking behind me, I looked round and saw Petro coming down with his pipe in his hand.

He gestured for me to follow him out on to the porch. I stood under the overhang, watching the monotonous rain while he filled his pipe.

'Galya and I are going to Kiev tomorrow,' he said eventually. 'You can stay here with the old folks, no problems. When I find out something, I'll call you!'

'All right,' I said with a nod.

After that we stood there in silence for about ten minutes. I listened to the rain and breathed in the light tobacco smoke from his pipe. 'Do we really have nothing to talk about?' I wondered. Whatever way you looked at it, we had spent more than a month together.

'We might not have become friends, but then tying someone up hand and foot isn't a good start for friendship,' I thought. 'What *is* a good start?' I asked myself, and instead of an answer for some reason I remembered a song I had known since my childhood: 'Where Does the Homeland Begin?' Nevertheless, he had brought us here to his parents' house. Of course, that wasn't necessarily friendship. It was simply being humane. But it still wasn't clear to me what was really more important in this life: being friends or treating each other humanely.

There was a big surprise waiting for me that evening. As if in mockery of my sweet memories of the only night that Gulya and I had spent together, old Olga Mykolaivna announced that she had made up beds for Petro and me in the sitting room, and for Gulya and Galya upstairs.

Perplexed, I went up to Petro and asked him in a whisper what this meant. After all, it would surely have made more sense for him to spend the night with Galya too.

He just smiled into his black moustache.

'It's their house,' he said, nodding towards his parents. 'What they say is the way things will be!'

I slept badly that night. I woke several times and listened to the rain rustling in the leaves of the trees. Once I got up and went over to the window. I spotted a dark-coloured Zhiguli on the opposite side of the street. The light was on inside the car and the man in it was reading a book that was resting on the steering wheel. I only realised the strangeness of it all in the morning. But in the middle of the night I was haunted by a cold feeling of unnatural loneliness. My hands longed for another's warmth, I yearned to embrace Gulya and press her tightly to me. That first night seemed so close and at the same time so far way. Then once again the rustling of the rain and Petro's snoring stilled my thoughts and I lay there as if turned to stone.

69

In the morning after breakfast Gulya and I went to see Petro and Gulya off at the station.

It wasn't raining, but the sun wasn't shining either. The leaden sky was creeping along under the pressure of a wind that we couldn't feel at all down below. Gulya had put on her jeans and T-shirt, although they weren't completely dry yet. As we walked along she kept looking upwards anxiously every now and then.

Several times I recalled the car that I had seen through the window in the middle of the night.

The train stops for ten minutes at Kolomya, but when we reached the station, it turned out that it was half an hour late. We had time to drink a coffee and eat a salami sandwich each at a little table in the station cafeteria – and we all did this in silence. But just before we got up from the table Petro looked intently into my eyes and said: 'There's an envelope with money in it on the table in my room. It's for you.'

As we were walking up to the right carriage on the platform, I thought that we were being followed – the two men in brown leather jackets who were standing by the next carriage were watching us really closely. Watching us and talking, without turning towards each other.

As he was getting into the carriage, Petro said one phrase to me:

'You're not such a bad guy!' Gulya and Galya said goodbye more warmly – they kissed.

Squinting sideways, I noticed the two men in jackets get into the next carriage.

I didn't like the look of that and I felt concerned for Petro and Galya. But some other part of my mind laughed at me and my almost certifiable paranoia.

We hurried all the way back to Petro's parents' house. The sky seemed to be waking up, ready to shower down more rain at any moment. There were already isolated drops falling to the ground.

We just managed to walk up on to the porch and stop under the overhang in front of the door before the rain started.

It's autumn, I thought. Now the season would keep us under house arrest in a strange house. In our minds we would cross off the days of the month and the weeks. I would wait for a telephone call after which we would be able to move to house arrest in Kiev. No, in Kiev everything would be simpler. In the first place, I had an umbrella at my flat. We would buy another and go walking in the rain. Or perhaps the rain would have stopped by then? Then we would be able to listen to the golden autumn rustling under our feet . . .

The old man switched the television on again. He himself sat there with the newspaper in his hands, and old Olga Mykolaivna busied herself with something in the kitchen. The endless rain outside the window created the illusion of evening.

When the evening finally came and we ate supper, I asked the old woman if I could move into Gulya's room now that Galya had gone.

Olga Mykolaivna looked at me severely.

'Are you married or registered?' she asked. 'No. So how is it possible? It's not right. What would Gulya's father say?'

I heaved a sigh, realising that I could continue this conversation as long as I liked, but the result would still be the same.

'Don't be miserable,' the old woman said with a sigh. 'You love Gulya and she loves you, so you can wait a bit!'

When I shared the sad news with Gulya, she laughed.

'What's wrong with you?' I asked.

'It's just like back at home.'

'Why, do people get married there?'

'No, nowadays they get registered . . . at the registry office . . . Getting married is more beautiful. When I was studying in Alma-Ata I saw this television programme . . .'

I realised that I couldn't live in the same house as Gulya and not be with her at night. All my nights would turn into one endless nightmare. I would embrace the pillow, listen to the rain and feel a lonely chill that not even a pile of fluffy blankets could warm. No, I'd simply go crazy!

'What's to stop you getting married here, in Kolomya?' I asked myself. 'There's nothing to stop you . . . What do you need to do it? Just a church and the mutual desire.'

'Let's get married,' I suggested to Gulya.

She didn't answer. She just gave a broad smile and closed her slanting eyes.

She was obviously imagining our wedding. Then she leaned forward and kissed me.

'All right,' I thought that evening, as I lay down on the divan in the sitting room, 'I'll put up with one more night and then tomorrow morning I'll start taking measures.'

In the middle of the night I was woken by some kind of noise. Looking out of the window, I once again saw a car on the street, with a man sitting in it, only this time he was holding a newspaper instead of a book.

I woke up when the clock said half past six. I got up, got dressed and glanced into the kitchen. Olga Mykolaivna was screwing the top on to a three-litre jar of cucumbers.

'Oh, you're up already!' she said happily. 'Good morning!'

'Good morning,' I replied. 'Olga Mykolaivna, Gulya and I would like to get married . . . Here in Kolomya.'

'And why not?' The old woman's eyes lit up. 'We have such a lovely church here! You just have to talk to the priest, he's the one who decides things! We can go together, after lunch.'

Like a portent of good things, the sun came out for a short while after lunch. Gulya, Olga Mykolaivna and I set out. The air still smelled of rain and the street was wet. We walked along past the private houses with their different-coloured fences.

'It's quite close, not far at all,' the old woman said. 'About five minutes from here.'

Soon we saw a blue dome ahead of us. We followed the road, houses and vegetable gardens up the slope of a hill until a small brick church appeared. It had a golden cross gleaming on the top of its blue dome.

The road came to an end at the gates leading into the small churchyard. There was a wooden bench on each side of the church gates.

On the left I could see a well with a separate brick-paved pathway leading to it.

Further on, beyond the well, there was single-storey house with a red-tiled roof.

'That way, that's where we need to go,' said Olga Mykolaivna, pointing at the house. 'That's where our Father Oleksa lives.'

The priest was thirty-something years old. Skinny, with long hair tied back with a rubber band and a high receding hairline. He received us cordially.

He sat us on an old sofa in the drawing room and sat down himself on a chair, making it quite clear that he was ready to listen to us.

'These two are friends of my son,' the old woman told him. 'They want to get married . . .'

'Are you baptised?' Father Oleksa asked, looking at me.

'I was baptised as a child,' I replied.

He looked at Gulya. 'And what faith are you?' he asked in Russian.

'None . . .' she answered. 'I'm a Kazakh . . .'

The priest laughed. 'Would you like some tea?' he asked, and without waiting for an answer, he left the room.

'He's a good man, everyone here loves him,' the old woman said.

Ten minutes later we were all sitting at the table drinking tea. The sun was shining again outside and it looked as if it was set to shine until the evening.

'She has to be baptised,' Father Oleksa said, nodding at Gulya as he sipped his tea.

'All right,' Gulya said willingly.

'You have to choose the godparents,' the priest went on. 'Then we'll name the day . . .'

The mention of godparents gave me pause for thought. Choose godparents in a town where we knew only one old couple? That wouldn't be so easy.

I cast an anxious glance at the old woman. She nodded reassuringly to me, as if she had guessed what I was thinking.

At supper that evening Olga Mykolaivna declared that she wanted to be Gulya's godmother.

'And the old man can be the godfather,' she said, looking at Yury Ivanych. 'He doesn't have a daughter of his own, so let him have a goddaughter, and such a lovely one, such a beauty.'

I was glad that what was happening meant I would become Petro's relative. But did he want that? What would he say when he found out? I let these questions go unanswered. I wanted Gulya. Every 'I want' has to be paid for, and the payment I would have to make was not so very great. Although it was a bit unusual, this price. The Asian bride-price would have seemed more natural to me just then. But like the result of my journey which, contrary to all my partly material expectations, had proved to be exclusively spiritual, the price of the chance to be united as soon as possible with the one I loved could not be measured in money or valuables.

I had to accept two new relatives and call on God to witness the purity of my intentions. I think I would have paid more to achieve my goal.

'Grand,' said Yury Ivanych, and I abandoned my thoughts to look at him.

Either he had taken a long time to think about it, or the thoughts had moved through my head with the speed of light, but I didn't immediately realise what he meant.

'All right,' he repeated, 'I'll be the godfather . . .'

70

That night I didn't sleep soundly, but at least I did sleep.

I dreamed of the she-camel Khatema, to whom I owed my life. In my dream I seemed to see the entire story of my rescue from the outside. I saw myself being dragged out from under the sand in the tent, and then the order of events became confused, and although I had been saved, somehow I had been abandoned in the desert and I was walking barefoot over the hot sand, all on my own. As I walked along I saw a piece of faded canvas sticking out of a low sand dune. I pulled on it, then went down on my knees, worked away with my hands until I pulled out the same tent in which I had settled down to spend the previous night. Once again I found the old newspaper and the Smena camera in it. After that I dreamed of heat, endless heat, the sun from which it was impossible to hide and the hot T-shirt I had used to cover my head. The heat was becoming unbearable and I even woke up covered in sweat.

It was dark. I got up off the divan and went across to the alarm clock on the sideboard, feeling the chill of the wooden floor on my feet. Four o'clock in the morning. I went to the window and saw a car again. This time it was a Volga standing in front of the house and there were two men sitting in it with the dim light turned on. I had no doubt at all that their presence was connected with us in some way. But in what way exactly?

Were they protecting us? Or spying on us? I decided not to say anything to Gulya about them just yet: with our wedding so close, their regular presence seemed an unimportant detail.

A couple of hours later I greeted the dawn. Olga Mykolaivna came downstairs and went straight into the kitchen. As the morning began, it acquired sounds. Outside, birds started singing; in the kitchen, Olga Mykolaivna clattered dishes.

I didn't want to distract her, and so I sat on a chair by the window. I looked at the leaves touched by the sunlight but not yet touched by autumn. I thought about Gulya.

The next day Father Oleksa baptised Gulya and hung round her neck the little gold cross with the half-effaced crucifixion that I had found in the sand beside the Novopetrovsk Fortress. The silver chain was a gift to Gulya from her godmother, Olga Mykolaivna.

I bought myself a silver chain and cross in the church. But when I got home, I replaced the cross with the little golden key found at Mangyshlak and hung the little key on my neck. 'Pinocchio probably wasn't baptised,' I thought to myself with a smile. I remembered our little chameleon, who had disappeared somewhere, and felt sad. If I allowed myself to be superstitious, then his disappearance meant the end of all my good luck.

Two days later we got married. Gulya put on her emerald-green shirt-dress for the church, but the old woman persuaded her to put a raincoat over it, so that curious neighbours wouldn't trail after us to the church. She knew that we wanted to get married without any strangers present, and in that little town everybody except Petro's parents and Father Oleksa was a stranger to us.

Father Oleksa locked the doors of the church from the inside and married us. He read the service in Ukrainian, but afterwards, when we were already husband and wife and had exchanged rings, he congratulated us in Russian and invited us to drink tea.

That was how we celebrated our wedding – by drinking tea in Father Oleksa's house and eating supper with the old couple. I bought a bottle of champagne in a shop for supper, and after the champagne, at Yury Ivanych's insistence, we each took a hundred grams of vodka.

I thought that Yury Ivanych would have been glad to carry on sitting at the table for a while, but at half past six Olga Mykolaivna began clearing the plates off the table.

'The young people want to make love,' she told her old man, and her eyes glinted as she said it.

That night the old one-and-a-half-size bed in Petro's room didn't seem narrow to us. Gulya went down to the bathroom and doused herself with water several times. She came back wet, and I dried her with my own skin again. The sheet was warm and wet, and the light blanket lay on the floor until eventually, when I got up off the bed yet again, I kicked it under the writing desk. Several times when our passion abated we lay on our backs with our shoulders pressing against each other, listening to the night. When I was tired, I even started to doze. But the sound of her footsteps, the squeak of the door and the distant creaking of the stairs roused me before her wet hands touched my chest. Gulya lay down on top of me, kissing me with her moist lips, rubbing her wet cheeks against my face. The cool moisture invigorated me. I pressed Gulya against myself and stroked her back, her arms, her thighs.

'Stroke me again!' she begged me in a whisper, and I stroked her, stroked her endlessly, until we both exploded with love, which dried us better than any towel and then made us wet again. The alternation of water and heat seemed to go on forever.

After the sleepless night we felt more hungry than tired. I went downstairs and found Olga Mykolaivna in the kitchen.

'Oh, good morning. Why have you young people got up?' she asked with a smile as she tossed a thick pancake on to a pile that was already quite high. 'I'm cooking breakfast for you . . . And there's a present for you over by the door.'

'Oh, you shouldn't have bought anything for us,' I said, smiling.

'It's not from us. Some young lad brought it earlier.'

I went to the front door and picked up a cloth shopping bag from the floor. Looking inside, I saw two cans of infant formula like the

331

ones I used to guard at the store not so long ago, and a large box of sweets. I took the box out. The sweets were called 'Evening Kiev' and on the lid there was a picture of Kreshschatik Street, with its bright lights.

I took the present to our room. I opened one of the cans and realised that the powder inside had nothing at all in common with dried milk. I opened the box of sweets, expecting a similar piece of deception. But the sweets proved to be genuine. I left them on the table and hid the cans under the writing desk.

I looked round at Gulya – she was sleeping sweetly on her side with her beautiful face turned towards me. I only had to look at her for all my anxiety to fade away and be replaced by an unquestioning belief in happiness.

Outside the sun was shining and the green leaves were rustling. The alarm clock said ten o'clock.

Five minutes later the house was as silent and still as in the deadest, darkest night. I went back to bed and we slept pressed close against each other, and once again the old one-and-a-half-size bed didn't seem narrow.

71

The next day Olga Mykolaivna freed part of the sideboard and half of a wardrobe for our things. Gulya hung her clothes up on hangers and arranged our things on the shelves. I took over the upper drawer of Petro's writing desk and put the trophies from our expedition into it – the Smena camera and the old issue of the

Evening Kiev newspaper: God only knew why I hadn't thrown it out.

One evening several days later, when, for lack of anything else to do, I was inspecting the camera I had found in that tent yet again, I was overcome by curiosity. I closed the curtains tightly, opened the back of the 'Smena' and felt for the film.

'What could there be on it?' I wondered. 'If all this belonged to Major Naumenko, then why did he take such a cheap children's camera with him? Why did he leave it in the tent? Why was the tent buried under the sand?' Of course, I knew myself what a sandstorm in the desert was like. It could easily have been that he barely managed to scramble out of his half-buried tent and wouldn't have had time to worry about his belongings. But then all of his things would have been under the sand. And how far could he have got without any food and water?

The more I thought about it, the more obvious it seemed that there was no connection between Major Naumenko and the tent that I had given to Gulya's father. But that did nothing to reduce my curiosity. Even if the camera belonged to a simple tourist from Kiev (to judge from the newspaper, he must have been simple), the intervening twenty years had lent my discovery more than mere historical interest. If that man had disappeared, his family or some of his friends must still be alive, and they should know where he had intended to go. And surely there was an old tourist club somewhere, with its old-timers and veterans, for whom my discovery would be a genuine gift, an occasion for remembering the past and even, perhaps, solving some mystery – after all, a man's disappearance is always a mystery. Of course, I might just happen to find the actual owner of the camera, the man who had abandoned everything as he fled from the sandstorm.

My thoughts led me back to the events preceding my own journey. I remembered how I had looked for Lvovich and Klim. I remembered how curiosity and the desire to solve a mystery that I still didn't understand had led me to the Pushche-Voditsa cemetery.

Basically, my presence in Kolomya was also the result of that curiosity.

I took the yellowed newspaper out of the drawer, opened it up and switched on the table lamp. I looked through the headlines, which mostly reflected the everyday working life of Kiev and the achievements of the hero-city, and was disappointed not to discover anything interesting. I picked up the camera again. There were still two frames that had not been exposed yet.

'I have to finish the film and have it developed,' I decided. When Gulya came upstairs to our room, I switched on the light and sat her down on a chair.

'Smile,' I said, winding the film on with one finger.

I took two snaps of Gulya and put the Smena away in its case.

'Where did you get the camera from?' she asked in surprise. I told her and reminded her about the tent.

'And you think something will come out?' she asked.

'Maybe it will.'

She smiled.

The next morning we took the camera and went for a walk round the town. The weather was delightful – the sun was shining and there was a light, gentle breeze blowing into our faces.

We walked to a new housing estate where there were a few nine-storey buildings. On the ground floor of these ugly structures there were shops. We walked past a furniture shop and an auto-spares shop. We drank a cup of coffee in a delicatessen and asked the saleswoman where the nearest photo studio was. It turned out to be very close.

The photographer – a man of about fifty, wearing a blue overall coat, tracksuit bottoms and old trainers on sockless feet – was more of an enthusiast than a businessman. When I asked him how much it would cost to develop the film, he chuckled and said: 'You can give me a bottle of vodka if anything comes out.'

Then he went into his darkroom, which was closed off by a heavy black curtain as well as a door. When he came back out he handed me the camera and wrote his telephone number on an envelope for prints.

'Here,' he said. 'Give me a call in a couple of days. If a woman answers, ask for Vitya.'

I phoned two days later.

'Come and take a look,' said Vitya. There was no emotion in his voice, but it had a note of ambiguity that I found intriguing.

I went to the photo studio on my own. Gulya stayed behind to help the old woman bottle tomatoes.

On my way there, I noticed that the same white Zhiguli overtook me twice. I looked round before entering the photo studio, but didn't see anything suspicious.

'Come through here,' said the photographer, peeping out of the darkroom when he heard the ring of the little bell attached to the door. He reinforced his invitation by beckoning to me.

I went in and closed the door behind me. The red photo lamp standing on a shelf at the level of my head filled the room with a rather mysterious illumination.

There was a pile of empty developing trays of various sizes on a table. Large prints were drying on strings hanging just below the ceiling, like washing hung out to dry. I looked closely at one of them, thinking that they were the prints from my film.

'Just a moment, just a moment,' said Vitya, standing with his back to me. He opened a drawer, and took some photographs from a small envelope made of photographic paper.

'I think that twenty years ago someone would have killed for these photographs,' he said, stepping away from the table to make room for me. 'The quality's lousy, of course. Very grainy.'

I took a few photographs and laid them out. Then I leaned down and looked at them. On one I saw a schooner, photographed from the highest point of the shore, then I saw the same schooner from a different angle, simply a shot of the line of the seashore that I knew so well from my recent journey, and then two group photographs of five men, with four standing and one sitting in the centre.

'What is there here to kill for?' I asked, looking round at the photographer.

'Take a look at these ones. A close look.'

I took the prints. The one on top was already familiar: four men standing, one sitting. I looked more closely. It seemed to me that the man in the centre was sitting on the sand in a rather odd position, but nothing else caught my eye.

'Take this,' said Vitya, handing me a magnifying glass.

Through the magnifying glass the meaning of the photo changed abruptly. I saw that the man sitting on the sand was tied up. His ankles were bound together and his arms, tied at the wrist, seemed to be pulled down over his raised knees. The four standing men were gazing into the camera lens with confident smiles. The seated prisoner was looking off to one side, his head was inclined slightly and his mouth was slightly open.

'Is he alive here?' I asked.

'He might be there. But in the shots that follow – I don't think so.'

I looked at the next photo: two men in boots and long black jackets with hoods were carrying the prisoner along by his arms and legs. His head was dangling limply. In the third photograph I saw the four men standing by a small hillock of sand. There was a sapper's spade stuck in the sand next to one of them. A stick was thrust into the top of the hillock and a pair of field glasses were tied to it by their strap. The structure seemed like a parody of a cross on a grave.

'Well then, you owe me a bottle,' Vitya said pensively. 'We can consume the contents at my place – I live close by.'

I put the photographs down on the table. The photographer slipped them back into the envelope of photographic paper and handed the envelope to me. Then he gave me a little box with the exposed film.

'Wait in there,' he said, nodding towards the studio's reception area. 'I'll get changed.'

We stopped at the wine counter in the delicatessen.

'What shall I get?' I asked.

'Port, red,' said Vitya. 'Up on the shelf over there. Where it says "Massandra".'

We took the bottle to his place. He lived in a small private house with chickens strolling around in the yard.

'I'd rather drink vodka,' he said, sitting down at a table with a tablecloth covered with dirty blotches, 'but I can't.'

'The liver?'

'A wedding,' the photographer sighed. 'I have to photograph a wedding tomorrow, and you can't do that when your hands are trembling . . .'

He moved to open a tin of something, sliced some bread, took out plates, forks and basic wine glasses.

While we were drinking and eating, he didn't mention my film and the photographs once. He told me about himself. About how he used to live in Uzhgorod, how he used to be a high-class photographer, but he drank too much and eventually his wife had thrown him out of the house. At first he had lived with a friend, and between them they drank away the proceeds from the sale of his two best cameras, a Pentax and a Nikon. Then his mother had died in Kolomya and left him this little house. At first he was going to sell it, but feared the money would have been spent on vodka, so he had decided not to.

He had given up drinking and moved here. He found a job straight away in the photo studio and sometimes he earned a bit on the side with the militia – they picked him up from home in a car and took him to photograph crime scenes.

When the port was finished, Vitya pulled himself together and got up from the table.

'So now I have to catch up on my sleep before the wedding. And your wife's probably waiting for you. Who is she, a Tatar girl?'

'Kazakh,' I replied.

'Well done,' said Vitya, with a brisk shake of his head.

I didn't understand what the precise object of his approval was.

As he saw me to the gate, he said: 'Mine was Hungarian. May God preserve you from that nationality . . .'

72

It took me about twenty-five minutes to walk home. It was still light, although the sun was already sinking towards sunset. On the way I checked the envelope of photographs and the box with the film in it several times.

The door was opened by Olga Mykolaivna, who caught the smell of drink immediately and her face took on a severe expression. She glanced round to make sure there was no one nearby and whispered to me strictly: 'You shouldn't go drinking with our menfolk. They'll lead you into bad ways, and you're young and have a beautiful wife!'

'I won't do it again,' I whispered jocularly and glanced into the kitchen, then into the sitting room.

'Gulya's in your room,' said the old woman, nodding towards the staircase. 'She's reading. There's *Santa Barbara* in half an hour – come down!'

The next morning it was raining again. I woke up feeling hungry, with a heavy head. Gulya was already pulling on her jeans.

'Where were you yesterday?' she asked, turning towards me. 'You came back merry and untalkative, and went straight to sleep.'

'I'm sorry, I was at the photographer's place. Let's have a bite to eat, then I'll show you something!'

After breakfast we went back up to our room. I took out the photographs and laid them out on the table, then I sat down comfortably and switched on the lamp.

'Where are my photos?' Gulya asked. I ran my eyes over the rows of prints, but I didn't see Gulya's portraits. I counted the photos – there were only thirty-four.

'They probably didn't come out,' I said. We looked at the

photographs together. I found the three that Vitya had pointed out, gave them to Gulya and looked through the rest. I was quite sure now that all the photographs had been taken on the shore of the Caspian, not far from the place where I had found the tent. There was the fishing schooner, at first far away from the shore, then getting closer and closer. Then a boat with men in it between the shore and the schooner. Men on the shore, dragging something out of the boat. It was like frames from an old movie, and if not for those three photographs, my interest in the film would have evaporated completely.

'Yes,' Gulya sighed. 'Did they kill him?'

She gave me back the photos and hugged me from behind.

'Probably. Or he died after they beat him . . .' I said, looking at a photo in which four men were dragging the boat on to the shore. There were sacks of something lying in the boat.

'You know,' I said, looking up at Gulya, 'something's not right here . . . All the photos except those three are perfectly objective. They're taken from the outside – nobody is posing. But here everyone is looking into the lens. Everybody except the prisoner.'

'Maybe they were taken by different people?' Gulya suggested.

I thought about that. There were six men in the photographs, including the bound man. But in any one photograph there were no more than five.

In the 'grave' photograph there were four men standing, and the fifth must have taken it. That meant the sixth man really was buried under the sand, below that improvised, almost comical cross. So it seemed that the photos of the schooner and the men in the boat and the five men on the shore had been taken by the prisoner. Evidently before he became the prisoner.

I shared my thoughts with Gulya.

'So he was following them?' she asked. 'What for?'

I shrugged.

'Kolya, let's lay the photographs out in the order in which they were taken.'

I liked Gulya's suggestion. I took out the film and the two of us stretched it out in front of the table lamp, searching for the frame that corresponded to each print and laying the prints out in order on the table. When we reached the last two frames, we looked at each other. Instead of portraits of Gulya, they were blank.

'Never mind, we'll get ourselves photographed at the studio,' I promised.

Laid out in order, the photographs confirmed our conclusions. The man with the camera had been waiting for the schooner to arrive, then he had shot the boat, in which five men had brought something on shore. Then they had spotted him, taken away his camera, tied him up and photographed themselves with him. But obviously not as a memento, otherwise they would have taken the camera with them.

'It's strange that the Smena was lying in the tent,' I said. 'In their place I would have kept it, or thrown it into the sea . . .'

'The desert's as good as the sea,' Gulya said. 'Anything you drop on the sand is buried in an hour or two. There are no people there, nobody lives anywhere nearby . . .'

'I wonder if they're still alive?' I said, looking closely at the faces of the men in the photographs. They were thirty or forty years old. 'Probably they are.'

'Then we ought to hand the photos over to the militia.'

'Are you crazy?' I said, turning to Gulya. 'What will the militia do with them? We don't even know where it happened. Obviously it's somewhere abroad. Who's interested in delving into events that happened twenty years ago, and in a different country?'

I slipped the prints back into the envelope and placed it in the drawer of the desk.

'It was only a suggestion,' Gulya said in an apologetic tone. 'Perhaps that prisoner has relatives and they don't know what happened to him . . .'

'Perhaps,' I agreed.

That was the end of the conversation, and we went downstairs.

We ate lunch with the old couple. Potatoes, salad, meat rissoles. Compote for dessert. I felt as if we'd been living there for several years, that we were Olga Mykolaivna's and Yury Ivanych's natural children. That we were going to carry on living in this house in Kolomya until we died . . .

I shook my head sharply and looked at the tears of rain running down the window.

Yury Ivanych got up from the table and put on his jacket.

'I'll go to the post office, maybe they're paying the pensions,' he said as he went out into the corridor.

The rain that had put us under house arrest again reminded me of Kiev. The three of us sat at the table in silence.

'Maybe I should start keeping chickens?' the old woman asked thoughtfully and then shrugged in answer to her own question.

Rain prompts different thoughts and questions in everyone. I looked at Gulya.

'Let's go for a walk,' she suggested in a quiet voice. 'There are two umbrellas hanging on the hallstand.'

'Yes, go for a walk, why don't you?' Olga Mykolaivna said to me. 'I'll stay at home. Sitting at home is good for the health too!'

When we got back from our walk we were staggered by news that Yury Ivanych had brought back from the post office. The night before a photographer who worked in Kolomya's only photo studio had been murdered. They had found him dead this morning. And all his cameras and equipment had been stolen.

I was struck dumb by the news. That night I got up carefully, so as not to wake Gulya, and went over to the window. I saw a car on watch in our street again.

It wouldn't have been logical to link the presence of the car with the murder of the photographer. It was clearly just the times that we lived in. Tense times, with lots of murders.

73

Two days later the postman brought me an appointment slip for a long-distance telephone call. It was from Kiev, so my mood improved immediately. 'Petro must have found out something, or the colonel has made good on his promise,' I thought on the way to the post office.

The post office was a long way from the house, so I went out half an hour before the time indicated for the call. Gulya stayed at home.

I walked along the asphalt surface of the road, avoiding the puddles that reminded me of the previous week's rain. Those long-lasting puddles demonstrated the powerlessness of the autumn sunshine. 'October is already here,' I thought, recalling the line from Pushkin. There was a time when that line used to make me laugh out loud, because it was the answer to the question: 'Where in *Eugene Onegin* does Pushkin mention the Great October Revolution?' But now as I thought about the arrival of October, the only thing I felt was the tenacious chill in the air, which ignored the sun's presence as completely as the puddles did.

I gave the telephone operator my slip of paper and sat down on a bench facing the row of empty telephone booths. The round clock on the wall said eleven o'clock.

Half an hour later I went back to the operator and asked her to check the appointment for the call. She looked up from reading a women's magazine, took my piece of paper and called the exchange. 'Irochka, check number thirty-seven. Kiev.'

Then she glanced at me indifferently, said 'Wait!' and stuck her head back in her magazine.

I returned to my seat.

I heard the sound of a car stopping on the street and when I turned round to look out of the window, I saw a brown Zhiguli No. 6. A respectably dressed man wearing spectacles got out of it and came inside. He cast a calm glance at me, went over to the telephone operator and asked her something in a quiet voice. Then he glanced at me again and came over.

'Nikolai Ivanovich Sotnikov?' he asked, stopping in front of me. His intelligent eyes were narrowed in a smile behind the lenses in his slim metal spectacle frames.

'Yes,' I said, puzzled.

'Let's go, there's something we have to talk about,' said the man.

'I'm waiting for a call . . .'

'Don't bother, I'm the one who sent you the appointment,' he said. 'Let's go.'

'Are you from Vitold Yukhimovich?' I asked.

'Who?'

'From Colonel Taranenko . . .'

'Close,' the man said with a nod.

We walked out of the post office and got into the brown 'No. 6'.

'You can call me Alik, or Alexei Alexeevich,' the man said as he started the engine. 'This is a beautiful area – are you fond of unspoiled nature? Of course you are, otherwise what would you have been doing in the desert?' he said and turned towards me with a calm smile.

Then he polished the drop-shaped lenses of his spectacles with a handkerchief and put the spectacles back on his slightly snub nose.

We drove past the railway station and turned on to a street that I didn't know.

'Where are we going?' I asked, seeing that we were driving out of Kolomya.

'I want to show you a very good sanatorium,' said Alik. 'For future reference . . . It's a place where you can rest and recover your strength . . .'

The No. 6 swung out on to the main highway and started driving behind a trailer with Polish number plates.

Alexei Alexeevich stuck his nose out to the left a couple of times, thinking of overtaking the trailer, but decided not to risk it. We drove along the edge of a pine forest at a speed of no more than sixty kilometres an hour, which was probably why my driver's face turned so sour.

His appearance and his way of speaking, pronouncing every word and every letter clearly, expressed a remarkable self-confidence. The basic expresson of his face was affable, even without a smile. A man with a face like that couldn't help but inspire trust.

'I'm sorry we're moving so slowly,' he said, casting a quick glance at me. 'The highway's not usually this busy . . .'

About fifteen minutes later we turned into the forest and started driving along a deserted asphalt road that was as smooth as glass and just wide enough for one car. We drove in through a pair of open gates, turned to the right and stopped in front of a wooden cottage with a porch and a broad glazed veranda. Before we got out of the car, Alexei Alexeevich reached over to the back seat and took hold of an elegant leather suitcase.

He walked up on to the porch, opened the door with a key and looked round at me.

We walked on to the veranda, then opened another door and found ourselves inside a comfortable, spacious room with an open fireplace.

'Have a seat, Nikolai Ivanovich,' said Alexei Alexeevich, sitting down on a polished table and moving a chair up beside him. 'This place isn't being heated yet. I think it's warmer outside,' he said, rubbing his hands together.

I sat down. I was burning with curiosity, desperate to discover why he had needed to bring me to this sanatorium. Obviously not in order to say hello from Colonel Taranenko and tell me I could now go back to Kiev. Especially since his response to the colonel's name had been rather uncertain.

Meanwhile, Alexei Alexeevich opened his leather briefcase, took out a big envelope, laid it on the table and looked at me expectantly.

'I think you can guess what state agency I work for,' he said with a gentle smile. 'My colleagues in Kiev asked me to have a word with you. About your journey. Before we talk, let me tell you that like the rest of the country, we work according to different rules now, and that means we no longer rely on the assistance of unpaid enthusiasts. If they decide in Kiev that your information is valuable – you'll be paid.'

He opened the envelope, took out several large photographs and laid them on the table in front of me.

I was surprised to see Petro in one of the photographs, sitting at a table in a cafe with two men I didn't know. I was even more surprised when I saw myself in another photo, following a chess battle in University Square.

When I looked up at Alexei Alexeevich my face must have expressed extreme bewilderment.

'I'm sorry,' he said. 'I've only just received the instructions from my colleagues in Kiev. I'm not interested in who you know in these photographs. They are just to refresh your memory. I'm going to give you some other photographs now. Look through them very carefully, while I make some coffee.'

Alexei Alexeevich took another large envelope out of his briefcase, placed it on the table, and then he left the room.

There were about twenty prints in the envelope. I ran through them quickly first: groups of people in the street, at a table set for a celebration, at a funeral.

'The photos in my desk drawer are far more interesting than these,' I thought and starting looking through the prints more attentively.

In the first photo I counted twenty-two faces and I didn't recognise a single one of them. My curiosity waned with every minute that passed. They had brought me to this sanatorium only to let me know that they knew all about me and to show me some photos with dozens of faces that I didn't know.

The next few photographs only reinforced my disappointment, but then came the turn of the funeral photographs. In the first one my eye was caught by a thin young guy walking in the middle of the funeral procession. He was looking round, as if someone had just called his name, and his face seemed vaguely familiar to me. In the next photo from the same funeral I noticed two men a bit older. I stared hard at the print, trying to remember where I could have seen them.

Alexei Alexeevich came back into the room and set down a tray with a coffee pot and two little cups.

'Well?' he said. I shrugged uncertainly.

'There are a couple of faces, but I can't remember where I saw them.'

'The coffee's ready. Take a seat and we'll look at them together.'

Alexei Alexeevich poured the coffee into the cups and a powerful aroma permeated the air in the room. 'Colombian,' he said in the satisfied voice of a lover of life. 'I didn't offer you sugar. Shall I bring some?'

'No thank you.'

'So, who have you recognised here?'

I showed him the young guy and the two men. He took those two photographs and I started looking through the rest of the funeral ones. The thin young guy showed up again. And beside the grave, which was already covered with wreaths, another face caught my eye. It was a military man in the uniform of a major. He looked as if he really wanted to smile and was having difficulty restraining himself. His lips were tense, and his eyes were very wide open. He was looking away from the grave.

'That man too,' I said, pointing at the major. Alexei Alexeevich thought for a moment and took another sip of coffee.

'I tell you what, Nikolai Ivanovich, let's run through your journey together.'

'From the very beginning?'

'Oh no, I'll tell you where to start . . . There are some things we already know. Start from Krasnovodsk.'

I began telling my story, recalling some of the details as I went along.

'The people,' said Alexei Alexeevich, interrupting me. 'List the people you saw, and then look at these photographs. It will be easier that way.'

I told him about the Kazakhs – the drivers and Colonel Taranenko's two colleagues.

Then I told him about the ferry, the *Oilman*. When I remembered the ferry, I suddenly recognised the guy from the funeral photographs – he was the swarthy Slav who had followed us, the one we had had to deal with on the train.

I told Alexei Alexeevich about the swarthy guy, how he had tried to get rid of us and how we had thrown him off afterwards.

'Did you kill him?' Alexei Alexeevich asked, eager to make certain.

'I don't know,' I told him. 'He was concussed, unconscious. We threw him off in that condition. We found out about him afterwards. His nickname's the Moldovan.'

Alexei Alexeevich seemed pleased with that. He circled the guy's face with his pen on the photograph and wrote something on the back of it.

We talked for about half an hour. I remembered another three men – they were all from the same chain of events. Two had taken part in unloading the guns and loading the narcotics into our wagon, and the major had unloaded the narcotics on the railway siding near Bataisk.

'All right,' Alexei Alexeevich said eventually. 'That was a useful session. By the way, a cottage like this costs only twenty dollars a day. Including meals. It's an official departmental sanatorium . . . And those lads' – he nodded towards the photographs –

'are former colleagues of ours. Trying to make a bit of money . . .'

He stopped and chewed on his lower lip. His face took on a sad expression.

'Did they ask you to pass anything on to me?' I asked.

'How do you mean? Money? Or what?'

'No, what I'm interested in is if I can go back to Kiev or not.'

'I don't know,' said Alexei Alexeevich. 'They didn't tell me anything about that. But I can ask. I'll be reporting on our conversation tomorrow anyway.'

'By the way, I have some interesting photographs too,' I said in the most mysterious voice I could manage.

'What kind of photographs?'

'It's not easy to describe in a couple of words. It looks like the murder of a man who was following someone . . .'

'Did you take them yourself?'

'No, it's an old film, from 1974. It was in a camera that I found in the desert.'

'That's interesting,' he said with a nod. 'Will you let me have a look at the photos? Perhaps our archive department will buy the film from you.'

We agreed that Alexei Alexeevich would drive me home from the sanatorium and wait outside for me to bring him the old photographs.

As we drove along, I tried to understand why he hadn't mentioned the colonel even once and why, if he knew so much about my journey, he didn't know anything about why I was in Kolomya. I realised that his colleagues in Kiev had enlightened him about my journey. But they couldn't have known about that without Colonel Taranenko's help! So why hadn't there been a single word about him?

'All right,' I thought, 'when I give him the photos, I'll ask him to find out from his colleagues if I can go back to Kiev. It will be good if they take an interest in my old film. The film in exchange for a "landing strip" and a promise of safety.' I wondered if maybe the guys I had prevented from grabbing the contents of the storeroom had already gone on to the next world, and it was pointless to get the jitters about them.

But no, as long as I didn't know for certain, it made good sense to stay worried. Only dead men never worry! We reached Kolomya very quickly – there were no cars on the highway.

After I'd given Alexei Alexeevich the envelope with the photographs, I told Gulya about the trip to the sanatorium with him and our conversation. We were sitting in our own room and Gulya chewed on her nails as she listened to me. She was obviously very nervous.

'Everything will be fine,' I said, trying to reassure her. 'If we don't hear from them in a week, I'll go to Kiev anyway. After all, they found us through Petro. Maybe he knows something?'

74

I didn't have to go to Kiev. Four days later, in the morning, the familiar brown No. 6 stopped outside the gate. Alexei Alexeevich, once again dressed in a respectable suit and tie, invited me out 'for a ride'. He asked me to bring the film and the camera with me.

'Back to the sanatorium?' I wondered as we walked to the garden gate. In addition to Alexei Alexeevich there was a heavyset man sitting in the car. He had a double chin that must have made him look older than his real age.

'This is Oleg Borisovich, from Kiev,' Alexei Alexeevich said, introducing him. 'So, where shall we go?'

'Do you have a decent restaurant with separate compartments?' Oleg Borisovich asked.

Alexei Alexeevich laughed. 'There is one establishment where we can sit on our own . . .'

About ten minutes later the No. 6 braked to a halt beside a small pavilion. I read the name on it – 'Honeydew Cafe'.

Oleg Borisovich glanced at this establishment and knitted his brow in a frown.

'This isn't the capital,' Alexei Alexeevich said in an apologetic voice, 'but in this place we can get food and drink and I can ask them not to let anyone else in . . .'

Oleg Borisovich clambered out of the car with some reluctance and some difficulty.

The cafe had only just opened. We were the first customers of the day. The young-looking waiter or manager with short-cropped hair greeted us with a smile.

Alexei Alexeevich whispered something to him and he got out the 'Health Inspection Day' sign from behind the counter, hung it on the outside of the door and locked the door from the inside.

We sat down at a rickety table which was, nonetheless, covered with a clean white tablecloth. The youthful gentleman proved to be the waiter, or at least to be combining that duty with his others. He brought us a carafe of vodka, halves of boiled eggs decorated with red caviar and a small sliver of butter and a vegetable salad.

'An ashtray,' Oleg Borisovich said in a hoarse voice, taking a pack of Marlboros out of his pocket.

Oleg Borisovich lit up and then produced an envelope. I realised that it contained my photographs. 'They've taken the bait,' I thought, although that had been clear enough from the very beginning – after all, they had asked me to bring along the film and the camera.

'Have you told anyone about this?' Oleg Borisovich asked, with a nod at the envelope.

'My wife. She's seen them.'

'You're not married.'

'Not registered,' I corrected him. 'But we got married here.'

'Who else knows about the camera and the film?'

'The photographer in the photo studio, he developed them.'

Oleg Borisovich nodded. He inhaled and then slowly let the smoke escape from his mouth.

'And what about the friends you shared these adventures with? This Petro from UNSO? His girlfriend?'

'No, they don't know.'

Oleg Borisovich smiled and his smile seemed to shift the excess weight of his cheeks to his double chin.

'Why didn't you tell your friends about your discovery?' he asked.

Meanwhile Alexei Alexeevich had filled the glasses from the carafe and put some salad on his own plate. He added two half-eggs with caviar to the salad.

'I thought it was just a camera, I didn't know what was in it . . .'

'But how did you know that the film was from 1974?'

'There was a newspaper in the tent – the *Evening Kiev* for 15 April 1974, so I thought the man must have bought it on his way there and simply not bothered to throw it away . . .'

'Do you have the newspaper?'

'Yes.'

353

'And the tent?'

'I gave it to my wife's father.'

'A fine little story,' Oleg Borisovich drawled in a sing-song voice and picked up his glass in both hands. 'Well, Mr Sotnikov, you have no idea just how much you have earned! Your good health!'

We clinked glasses and drank, then started on the hors d'oeuvres.

I spread half an egg with butter and caviar on to a piece of bread.

'What have I earned?' I thought. This Oleg Borisovich was obviously a big wheel. And if he had flown in from Kiev just for the sake of this meeting, then my discovery might turn out to be worth too much. And too much was not always good. If a man built up too large a debt with someone, it was cheaper for him to kill his creditor than to pay back the money.

I squinted sideways at Oleg Borisovich. He spotted my glance and stropped chewing.

He extinguished the cigarette that was smoking in the ashtray.

'Show me the camera!' he said.

I took out the Smena and handed it to him.

He took it out of its case and inspected it carefully from all sides. He raised the lens to his eyes. Then he moved his plate aside, put the camera on the table and took a Swiss army knife out of his pocket. Opening out the little screwdriver, he prised up a small lever of some sort beside the lens, which came away from the body of the camera, together with part of the front panel.

Oleg Borisovich smiled. 'It's almost an antique now,' he said sadly. 'See, this is where the micro-cassette for parallel or independent shots was inserted . . .' he pointed to a little niche. 'Someone removed it . . . Someone who knew where to look for it . . .' Oleg Borisovich stared at me. He was about to say something, but the appearance of the waiter with a tray prevented him.

The waiter set down plates of chops and rice in front of us. He wished us *bon appétit* and withdrew with decorum, as if he was deliberately moving slowly.

'And this . . . Colonel Taranenko, does he know about the camera?' Oleg Borisovich asked.

'No.'

'Oleg Borisovich grunted contentedly, picked up his knife and fork and attacked his piece of meat.

'Should I ask him about Kiev or not?' I thought feverishly. 'Should I wait until he tells me himself? But he might not say . . . How can I tell?'

'Does your wife like to gossip?' Oleg Borisovich asked, holding a piece of meat in front of his mouth.

'No, she's a Kazakh,' I said, and immediately thought that perhaps not all Kazakh women were as laconic as Gulya.

'A Kazakh,' Oleg Borisovich repeated pensively and dispatched the piece of meat into his mouth.

He chewed slowly and abstractedly, as if it was some secondary kind of activity. The main activity was taking place in his head – he was thinking.

Alexei Alexeevich filled the small glasses again.

'What's her name?' Oleg Borisovich asked.

'Gulya.'

'To Gulya!' he said, raising his glass.

We drank. Silence descended on the table again. The pork was well cooked and generously peppered. One thing that definitely united us all was the enjoyment of the delicious meat.

I suddenly thought that they must be saying so little about the colonel, and even pretending that they didn't know him, because he really was connected with some secret department. After all, they hadn't mentioned the sand or asked me about it. I hadn't said anything about it either. Even when I was telling them about the journey from Krasnovodsk to Bataisk, I had mentioned the crates of guns and the narcotics several times, but I hadn't said a word about the sand.

Oleg Borisovich reached into the inside pocket of his jacket again. He took out an ordinary envelope and handed it to me.

'These are you tickets to Kiev. For tomorrow,' he said. 'Where's the film?'

I handed him the little box with the film in it.

'In the morning of the day after tomorrow you'll be in Kiev. I wouldn't advise you to go home just yet. Stay with friends. Call me at eleven o'clock. We'll meet and I'll settle up with you for your discoveries.'

I was astounded. My face obviously expressed such an odd mixture of emotions that Oleg Borisovich couldn't help chuckling. He probably liked surprising people.

I took the tickets out of the envelope and looked at the number of the train and the type of carriage. Two tickets for a sleeper carriage!

'They're genuine!' said Oleg Borisovich. When the waiter brought the bill, he and Alexei Alexeevich argued politely for several minutes over who was going to pay for lunch. As I expected, Oleg Borisovich won. And he carefully tucked the bill away in his wallet.

Outside the cafe there was a surprise waiting for us. All four wheels of the No. 6 had been deflated. Alexei Alexeevich swore, adjusted his spectacles and looked around. Oleg Borisovich heaved a sigh.

Oleg Borisovich took me right back to the gate in a taxi. I was still in a highly agitated, slightly perplexed state. When Gulya asked me 'Well?', I showed her the tickets. And for the first time I saw a smile of happiness on her face and tears in her eyes at the same time.

'We have to buy some suitcases,' she said. 'It won't feel right with the bundle . . .'

I nodded.

75

The train arrived in Kiev half an hour late. The autumn sun was shining above the station. There was a crowd of porters and people meeting passengers beside the carriages. One of the porters dashed forward to help when he saw me climbing down on to the platform with two suitcases in my hands and a rucksack on my back.

After haggling to agree a price, we loaded our things on to his trolley and Gulya and I followed him to the taxi rank. The trolley squeaked.

The bustle of the previous day seemed to be continuing. The cabbage pie hastily baked by Olga Mykolaivna was lying in my rucksack. 'When you get to Petro's place it will be empty, there'll be nothing to eat . . .' she had said, standing over us with the pie in her hands as we were stuffing our things into the suitcases we had bought that morning. And she had come back again several times, always with something else. She had given Gulya an embroidered Ukrainian blouse. Then she had brought a jar of jam. And then she had written Petro's addresss and telephone number in Kiev on a piece of paper yet again. 'Put this in your pocket, if they steal the other note, you'll find him from this one. Say hello from us, tell him to come!'

The taxi driver ripped us off, taking five dollars for a five-minute ride, but I didn't have the strength or the desire to argue with him.

Petro and Galya gave us a warm welcome, like members of the family. And for a minute I also felt an invisible bond of kinship between us.

They gave us their bedroom and we took our things in there and got changed.

After that I left Gulya in Petro's flat and went out into the street. I bought a telephone card and called Oleg Borisovich.

'Welcome home, Nikolai Ivanovich!' Oleg Borisovich said happily. 'Let's make it half past twelve by the patriarch's grave, under the clock tower of St Sophia's Cathedral.'

'All right.'

'See you there,' Oleg Borisovich said and hung up.

I went back to Petro's place.

The sun was shining outside. There were twenty minutes to go until my meeting with Oleg Borisovich. I left Gulya with Galya again – Petro had gone out somewhere on business of his own – and set off to the meeting.

Oleg Borisovich arrived at the meeting place in a black BMW. He climbed out of the car with some difficulty, leaned down to the open door and said something to the driver, then came towards me.

He was wearing an elegant grey suit which, while not concealing his ponderous figure, in some mysterious way managed to draw all your attention to itself and its fine cut. In his left hand he was carrying a leather briefcase.

'Well, how was your journey?' he asked after nodding in greeting.

'Fine, thanks.'

'Let's go and sit down in the sunshine,' he said, gesturing towards the open door into the monastery park.

We sat down on a bench that was free. He put the briefcase on his knees and crossed his arms.

I looked round. There were several young mothers pushing their babies in prams. There was a pair of pensioners sitting two benches away from us. There was a photographer, draped with equipment, waiting for work at the entrance to the cathedral. Beside him on a tripod there was a stand showing examples of his photographs.

'Do you have some kind of bag with you?' Oleg Borisovich asked, turning towards me.

'No.'

'Really?' he said in surprise. 'Are you going to carry the money in your pockets then? Although, of course, you don't have very far to go.'

'Money?' I said.

'Why, yes, I told you in Kolomya,' said Oleg Borisovich, looking at me and smiling, seeming to enjoy my bewilderment.

'Tell me,' he went on. 'Apart from the tent, the newspaper and the camera, did you find anything else there?'

'No.'

'Well, all right,' he said, slapping the briefcase lying on his knees. 'In here there are ten thousand dollars . . . Five thousand for the camera and the film, three thousand for making sure that no one but you and you wife will ever know about the film.'

'And two thousand?' I asked, perplexed.

'The two thousand – that's part of a different payment, an advance, so to speak . . .' Oleg Borisovich opened the briefcase slightly, lowered his head, glanced inside and slammed the lid shut again.

'You're probably wondering why you're getting such a lot of money.'

I nodded.

Oleg Borisovich took an envelope out of the inside pocket of his jacket. It contained only the same three prints from the old film that the deceased photographer Vitya had pointed out to me.

'This man here is Ivan Rogovoi,' said Oleg Borisovich, pressing his index finger down on the first man from the left in the photograph with the prisoner sitting on the sand. 'He's now a deputy in the Russian Duma. This one' – he moved his finger to the second standing man – 'is the vice president of Sakha Diamond Export Ltd. The third man is now in the leadership of the Belorussian KGB . . . The one on the right was a director of the Construction Investment Bank in Moscow. He disappeared without trace two years ago.'

'There was another one,' I said. 'In the other photos.'

'Yes, yes,' Oleg Borisovich said, nodding. 'So far we don't know anything about him.'

'And who is this?' I asked, pointing to the bound man.

'That's my brother, Major Naumenko.' Oleg Borisovich said in a trembling voice. 'I'll tell you more about that sometime, but I have to go now.'

'Major Naumenko?' I said. 'But he was buried beside the dervish's grave! That is, this means someone else was buried . . . is he here?' I asked, indicating the photograph of the sandy grave with my eyes.

'No, he's in the other place. There's no one here,' said Oleg Borisovich, looking at the photograph. 'They piled the sand up like a grave for a joke. A bit of fun . . . But they took my brother to Mangyshlak on the schooner. We still don't know what happened there.'

I suddenly realised that the story Colonel Taranenko had told us didn't match the story told by these photographs.

'Wait,' I said to Oleg Borisovich. 'If he went there to find out about the material manifestations of the national spirit, why was he observing the schooner?'

Oleg Borisovich answered my queston with a glance of mute dejection.

'You should never combine a spiritual quest with operational work,' he said after a pause. 'Either one or the other. Or death . . .'

He opened the briefcase, took out a brown paper bag and handed it to me.

'Don't lose it,' he said, trying to smile. We walked towards the exit of the park. Any moment now he would get into the dark blue BMW and drive away. And I wanted so badly to ask him another couple of questions. And, of course, to hear the answers.

I gave him a sidelong glance. He noticed it. We were already gettting close to his car.

'And where's Colonel Taranenko now?' I asked in a low voice.

Oleg Borisovich raised his eyebrows in surprise at the question.

'I think he's in Odessa, in the Chkalov sanatorium. Taking a rest . . . Well, all the best! Here's my card. Give me a call if anything comes up!'

'But when can I move back home?' I enquired.

'Tomorrow after lunch,' he replied.

I watched the car leave, then looked at the neat little rectangle of cardboard and read: '*Oleg Borisovich Naumenko, Director, Ukrainian-Kazakh Joint Enterprise Karakum Ltd.*'

Feeling puzzled, I walked straight across the square to my house, swinging the brown paper bag in time to my steps. I stood outside the front entrance for a couple of minutes. In just one more day I would be living at home again.

76

The next day we gathered up our things, declined Petro's kind offer of help, flagged down a private car and drove to St Sophia's Square for three hryvnas.

Everything inside me was seething in joyful anticipation. And for some reason I thought that Gulya must be feeling genuinely proud of me at that moment.

We walked up to the third floor and put our things down. I took the key out of the pocket of the rucksack and set it in the keyhole, and only then spotted a little brass plaque that had been hung on the wall to the left of the door. I took a step to the left and read the plaque. My jaw dropped.

The sign informed me that the space behind this metal door was the 'Baby Food Store of the Corsair Charitable Foundation'.

After several seconds of total stupor, my hand automatically reached for the doorbell. I pressed the button several times. There was no sound on the other side of the door. Nobody came hurrying to open up the storeroom that used to be my flat.

My eyes slid down to the key sticking out of the keyhole. I hadn't even tried to open the door. It would be stupid to suppose that the owners of this 'store' had not changed the lock . . .

To my surprise, the lock was still the same one and it yielded easily to my key. I opened the door apprehensively, peeping in first, then stepping inside and asking Gulya to wait on the landing.

The flat looked the same as ever. I couldn't spot any obvious changes. Eveything was just covered in dust.

I calmed down, deciding that the plaque was an attempt to frighten me by those people I had kept out of the genuine storeroom. Quite a lot of time had gone by. They must have put up the sign, thinking that I was here, in Kiev. And then they'd probably forgotten about it. I called Gulya in and carried our things through to the hallway, then went back into the room. This time my gaze lighted on something incomprehensible. A standard, two-metre door that looked as if it led through to the neighbours had appeared in my little flat's only room.

Puzzled, I walked over and halted in front of it. I remembered that the person living on the other side of the wall was a retired lawyer, whom I used to run into occasionally on the landing, but had never had any kind of conversation with.

I pulled on the door and it opened. Behind it there was a room just like mine, except that it had a modern desk with a fax-phone standing by the only window, and along the wall were rows of cardboard boxes with the familiar Finnish baby-food labels.

I went in, closed the door behind me and walked over quickly to the desk. The first thing I noticed was a little semi-transparent plastic box containing a pile of business cards. I opened the box, took out a card and raised it to my eyes.

'Nikolai Ivanovich Sotnikov, Director, Corsair Charitable Foundation.

'Kolya,' Gulya called to me.

I went back into my own room, still clutching the business card

363

with my name on it. Everything was jumbled up inside my head.

Half an hour later the flat had been put in order. The kettle was boiling on the cooker and the contents of the suitcases were lying on the floor. The bright-coloured shirt-dresses were in a separate pile of their own.

My rucksack had also been half emptied.

'We need to put everything away somewhere,' Gulya said, sounding rather bewildered. 'And this too –' she lifted up the mat that we had slept on in the desert. Lying underneath it was the pistol with the silencer, which I had already forgotten about.

'There should be enough room in the wardrobe,' I said, glancing at the massive ancient wardrobe that took up half the space in the hallway. 'But first we'll have some tea.'

She suddenly spotted the bag of money sticking out of my pocket.

'Did you buy something yesterday?'

'No, I sold something, more like,' I answered, going over to the table and spilling several thick wads of green bills on to it.

Gulya stared at the dollars in amazement.

'It's for the film and the camera,' I explained. 'Only they asked me very seriously not to say anything to anyone. All right?'

Gulya nodded.

'And that's not all,' I went on. 'It seems like I have a new job . . .'

I handed Gulya the business card that I had taken from the desk in the room that had been attached to my flat.

While Gulya was studying the card, I went over to the phone and called Oleg Borisovich.

'What's this storeroom doing here in my flat?' I asked in a rather sullen voice.

'It's your storeroom,' Oleg Borisovich replied calmly. 'You used to work in it. You've already been paid for your enforced period of absence from work. And now you've been promoted . . .'

His calm, 'Olympian' tone of voice left my thoughts totally dead-ended.

'So what am I supposed to do?' I asked him.

'Nothing. Work, work and more work, as the great Lenin instructed us . . .'

There was a hint of irony in Oleg Borisovich's voice now.

'Don't worry!' he reassured me after a pause. 'If the plaque annoys you, you can take it down. But no one's going to relieve you of your position as director. Call me if there are any problems!'

And he hung up. I turned to Gulya. She was watching me tenderly and the expression in her eyes needed no explanations.

'My God, how lucky I was to find her,' I thought.

We had a drink of tea and ate a piece of cabbage pie, then went out for a walk. The sun was still shining. Gulya kept pausing all the time and looking around wide-eyed at the buildings.

'It's more beautiful than Almaty!' she said. I had never been to Almaty, not even when it was still Alma-Ata, so it was hard for me to make the comparison. But I was quite willing to believe her. I found it hard to imagine a city more beautiful than Kiev.

The sun shone into my eyes without blinding me. 'Hi!' someone said as they walked past. I looked round, but I didn't recognise the person from behind.

It was my city, but while I'd been away it seemed to have become more independent, it had gone running on ahead, and I would have to catch up with it, come to terms with it again, become a little part of it, dissolve into its air. I was already familiar from the past with this sensation of temporary rejection. After a few days, everything would be the way it used to be. The invisible flows of current between the city and me would be restored.

And normal life would be restored too, only now everything would be different. Everthing would be good in a different way. Good enough for two.

77

The next day we received our first guests – Petro and Galya. I had phoned Petro the previous evening and he had seemed pleased to get my call.

He had told me he had something to show me.

I can't say that I felt very intrigued just at that moment. I was more concerned with the idea of removing the Corsair Charitable Foundation sign from the wall on the left of my door. And in any case, my curiosity had been satiated for a year ahead. Not to mention the fact that during our first supper at home that evening – vermicelli from my old food reserves – I had been assailed by thoughts that I simply couldn't ignore. I had suddenly realised that all knowledge is an obligation, that any satisfied impulse of curiosity obliges you not only to whoever satisfied it, but also to your newly acquired knowledge or information. I already felt that I owed a debt to Oleg Borisovich. Not for the ten thousand dollars, of which two thousand were either part of some mysterious future payment or, as Oleg Borisovich had said, compensation for enforced absence from work. Or maybe they really were some sort of advance?

For what? I didn't know that yet. Was it something to do with his obvious trust in me? After all, he had told me about the men in the photographs. He hadn't told me a lot, but enough for me to understand that three men who were now in the top echelon of Russian business and politics had been involved in a murder twenty years earlier. Oleg Borisovich probably knew a lot more about those men. He must know what they had been doing back then. Now I thought that it would have been better for me not to know anything about the men in the photographs. But it was too late already.

It was drizzling outside. Petro and Galya left their open umbrellas to dry in the hallway.

We sat down at the table and poured wine for the women and vodka for the men. The hors d'oeuvres were modest, but if we had had hors d'oeuvres like that in the desert or later on, in the goods wagon, we would have been absolutely delighted. Lightly salted cucumbers, Borodinsky black bread, ham and Dutch cheese. Even when I was buying all these things in the nearest delicatessen, my heart had sung. This was also a part of coming back home – the return to the old gastronomic values, to the everyday ritual of snacks with drinks. The excision of this ritual from a man's life is a heavy punishment. Indeed, the punishment of prison, properly conceived, is precisely the separation of a man from his customary rituals.

We all drank for the occasion. Then we told Petro and Galya how Gulya had been baptised and we had got married.

'Well, now you'll have to learn Ukrainian!' Petro said to Gulya. She and I exchanged glances.

'All right,' she said, 'if Galya will help me . . .'

We sat there making half-jocular, half-serious conversation like that for about another two hours. Then, while Gulya was making tea, Petro brought his bag in from the hallway.

'You know,' he said, 'we found something there, near the

367

fortress, but we didn't show you it . . . Take a look . . . Better late than never.'

He took something wrapped in newspaper out of his bag. Then he unwrapped it. It was a silver casket about half the size of a brick.

I picked up the casket, feeling the pleasant coolness and heft of silver. On the smooth upper surface there was an engraving in beautiful handwriting: 'To my dear Taras from A.E.' I tried to open the lid, but the casket was locked.

Petro smiled at my enquiring glance and took the casket out of my hands. He shook it and I heard something light shifting about inside it – most probably papers.

'It's locked. We decided the honest thing to do would be to open it together . . . Do you have any tools?'

I took the casket back from Petro and looked at the small keyhole.

'Maybe we don't need to force it,' I suggested, looking into Petro's eyes.

'We don't want to force it, just unfasten the screws so that it will open.'

I took the golden key from round my neck, then put the key in the keyhole and handed the casket back to Petro.

'I'm sorry, I didn't show you everything I found either,' I said to him. 'Open it!'

He looked at me in amazement, then looked at the casket. He turned the key, and we heard the quiet click of the lock.

Lying inside the casket were small pieces of paper covered with writing and folded in half.

'Letters?' I asked.

Petro nodded. He took out the top one, ran his eyes over it and glanced into the casket again. I was surprised not to see any joy in his face.

' "Dear Taras Grigorievich," ' he read out in Russian. ' "You do not need to fear my husband. He is well disposed towards you and will be glad if you agree to dine with us occasionally. A.E." '

He took another sheet of paper out of the casket.

' "I am expecting you at midday," ' Petro read. ' "You promised to show me something interesting in the Turkish cemetery. You will be amused to know that Dr Nikolsy tells everyone you are a cashiered major. He also says that you are teaching him to speak Ukrainian." '

I took a sheet of paper out of the casket too and unfolded it.

' "My dear Agafya Emelyanovna," ' I read to myself – it seemed to me that Petro was only reading the notes aloud because of his mood of disappointment. ' "I do not know what has caused the cooling in relations between us and why you have begun to avoid me. For all my love of solitude, my walks with you brought me genuine pleasure. I only hope that Iraklii Alexandrovich has not been induced by some hostile instigation to prevent you from associating with me. Although in his place, I would abandon my ingenuous attitude for jealousy. With my most sincere regards, Private Taras Shevchenko." '

When I raised my eyes from this note, which had evidently never been sent, Galya was already reading the others, with her lips moving soundlessly. The casket on the table was empty.

I handed the note I had just read to Gulya. The room was unusually quiet. I poured two glasses of vodka for Petro and me.

'Do you know how much this is worth?' I asked, nodding at the casket.

'Maybe it's worth plenty, but it doesn't do anything for Ukrainian culture . . .' he said and shrugged, with an expresson of profound disappointment on his face. 'The great Ukrainian poet writes his love letters in Russian . . .'

'The great Ukrainian poet also wrote several novellas in Russian,' I said. 'That didn't make him any less great. It simply shows that he belongs to two cultures.'

'What belongs to two cultures doesn't belong to anyone,' said Petro, suddenly switching into Russian himself. 'You know, two Ukrainian writers bought a house together at Konch-Ozero. Now they're not writing any longer, they're too busy suing each other in order to work out who the house actually belongs to . . . If no one has even thought of translating his novellas into Russian yet, then no one is going to be interested in these letters.'

'Then what do you propose doing with them?'

'I don't know.'

'Let's have some tea,' Gulya said, in an attempt to distract us from our disagreeable conversation. She succeeded.

We sat there drinking rather cool tea and eating custard pastries from a little baker's shop that had opened up two blocks down the road while I was away.

'You could sell it all at auction,' I suggested to Petro when his mood had improved. 'You probably need money, don't you?'

'Well . . . yes,' he drawled thoughtfully. 'We need money. They're putting me forward for election to the Rada.'

'Really?' I said in surprise. 'Why didn't you tell us straight away? It's a good excuse for a drink!'

We poured wine for the women and more vodka for ourselves.

'To victory!' I said, toasting Petro.

'Maybe we really could auction it,' he said, switching back to his native Ukrainian. 'Only I can't make myself that obvious, some people might not like it . . .' He looked enquiringly at me. 'Maybe you could sell it? . . . I'd give you a commission.'

'I'll try,' I promised.

I had no idea even where to start looking for that kind of auction. But as they say, nobody had pulled my tongue – not the first time, when I suggested the idea to Petro, or the second time, when I promised to try to make something of it.

'Listen, someone gave us something else for you too,' said Petro, reaching into the bag again.

He drew out the folder with Gershovich's papers, and then a shoebox.

'From the colonel. A man in civilian clothes came. He said Taranenko had sent him.'

I put Gershovich's folder on the edge of the table, took the lid off the shoebox and saw a little chameleon inside. He lifted his ugly face and looked at me.

'Gulya,' I called.

She came over to me and we gazed at the chameleon in amazement.

'How on earth did he get hold of him?' I asked.

'How should I know?' Petro said and shrugged.

When they were leaving we all hugged and kissed and agreed to phone each other regularly. No one had mentioned the sand while we were sitting at the table. It occurred to me only when Gulya and I were left alone in the flat. Maybe Petro had been asked not to bring the subject up with me. If so, we both had something to hide from each other, and yet we could still quite sincerely feel that we were friends.

That night I was woken by the phone starting to ring and suddenly stopping again. I walked across to the table in the darkness, listening to the silence of the flat, and I heard a rustling behind the door leading into the communicating room. I walked through, and in the moonlight that was falling on the desk I saw a long white tongue of paper slipping out of the fax.

When it had slipped right out, I turned on the light and leaned down over the desk. The fax, addressed to Nikolai Ivanovich Sotnikov, director of the Corsair Charitable Foundation, was a request to issue three cases of Finnish formula to the Makarov Infants' Home. It informed me that a certain Pyotr Borisovich Luminescu would collect them tomorrow with a properly executed requisition order. It looked as if my work as a director had already begun. But the one thing I didn't want was to know the contents of those cases. I couldn't care less whether the infant formula was past its sell-by date or still good for sale, or wasn't even infant formula at all! I really couldn't give a damn. Let it simply drift past me, let them come and collect it, let them take it . . . Just as long as my main life, my life with Gulya, was calm and happy.

78

Two months later, closer to the time when the snow first lingered for a little while, I remembered these thoughts of mine and realised that I had been wrong. By then Taras Grigorievich's casket and letters had already travelled the long and winding road to an auction in St Petersburg and back to Kiev as a gift from a rich Ukrainian in Tyumen to his historical homeland. The newspapers had even written about the gift.

I gave all the six thousand dollars in proceeds to Petro – his opponent in the election was some businessman with unlimited financial resources. Petro won. When he paid a brief visit to us with a bottle of good cognac after his victory, I noticed that he had trimmed his moustache a bit shorter. That was when he told me about his recent meeting with Colonel Taranenko. According to the colonel, part of the sand had been sent to the Crimea for testing. We could only guess at what the nature of this experiment might be.

Winter was setting in. Gulya and I looked out of the window and watched the white snowflakes slowly floating down to the ground. The chameleon stood motionless on the windowsill, staring fixedly at the glass as if he were stuffed.

'Azra,' I said, looking at him and remembering our second night beside the dervish's grave, when we buried Major Naumenko.

'What?' Gulya said.

'Azra, the good angel of death . . . Aman told me the legend . . .'

'Azra,' Gulya repeated thoughtfully. 'That was what my mother wanted to call me. My father was against it. He liked the name Gulya.'

I started thinking, and remembered those tracks in the sand.

Gulya told me again that she wanted to work. And I nodded without saying anything.

But I thought to myself that it would be better for us to remain inseparable, to be together day and night until spring came. To go out into the streets sometimes, to listen to the snow crunching under our feet, and then come back to our cosy home. To talk at night when we were tired after making love. And to dream out loud. To dream about anything at all.

I was alarmd by the presentiment that someone or something would interrupt the tranquillity of our winter. That circumstances would prove stronger than love. That I would have reason to curse my curiosity and pay the bills presented to me by life over and over and over again.

I put my arms round Gulya and squeezed her tight. I tried to make myself not think about anything, just watch the snow.

I succeeded.

Epilogue

A few days later I was leafing through Gershovich's manuscript. Outside the window the snow was still falling.

Gulya was in the kitchen, making Kazakh soup.

The little chameleon, who had become attached to his window-sill, was lying there on a tiny cushion that Gulya had sewn especially for him out of an old flannel shirt of mine.

My gaze came to rest on a page with a diary entry. The date at the top of it was: '21 June 1969'.

' "Seek the spiritual, and you find the material," ' I read. ' "Seek the material, and you find either death or nothing." I was telling Naum about that today. We were drinking coffee in the "aquarium". He only laughed. He's in good spirits – he's been made a captain in the State Security Service. Now how will he manage to split himself between his old passion for philosophy and his new operational reality?'

'The circle is closed,' I thought, glancing at the motionless chameleon. 'Gershovich was friends with Captain Naumenko, and I met the deceased Major Naumenko . . . also thanks to Gershovich. One dead man introduced me to another . . .'

Outside the window the snow was falling and I was in a profoundly wintry mood. I recalled the part of the major's body that Colonel Taranenko had taken with him. He had brought it back to the homeland. I wondered if that body part had already been buried.

Or cremated. Had there been a guard of honour and shots fired up into the sky, as there ought to be at an officer's funeral? Had the deceased man's brother, Oleg Borisovich, been present? Had there been a smell of cinnamon at the funeral?

I suddenly realised that I was indebted to Gershovich for more than just my acquaintance with other dead men. I was also indebted to him for having met Gulya, Petro and his parents, Galya and many others. The late Gershovich had managed to introduce me to lots of people. Although he himself had apparently been an extremely solitary individual. The rusty cross on his grave, which I had disturbed, betrayed an acute lack of near and dear ones.

My rational gratitude to Gershovich gradually transmuted into a feeling of pity for him and remorse for his death. I remembered the dervish's grave in Mangyshlak, the small white stone column with the strip of green cloth tied to its top. And I remembered the second strip of green, tied there by Aman in memory of the major who was buried close by.

It seemed to me now that the major had also been a dervish in some ways. And so had Slava Gershovich. They had both sought something and both, apparently, failed to find it. Had I found what I was seeking? No, I had found something quite different. I had found Gulya, and I was glad of it. I was happy.

A couple of days later Gulya and I took a trip to the Pushche-Voditsa cemetery. We laid a bouquet of carnations on Gershovich's snow-covered grave and I tied a strip of dark green velvet to the top of the rusty crooked cross.

We stood in silence by the grave for a few minutes and walked back through the deserted cemetery towards the exit. Towards the tram stop.